Dedication

This novel is dedicated to all the wonderful people and fans who have helped me, in ways big or small, to make my Artesans series so successful. I'm sure I've missed someone out, and if I have, I apologize.

Here goes: To my husband, Dave, and to my parents, Barbara and Dennis Snell. To my brother, David Snell, and to David Shepherd. To Mikey Brooks, and to Diane Dalton. To Rhett and Emmaline Hoffmeister. To Janet Morris, and to Katy Sozaeva. To Rachel Summerhill, and to Dan Gamble. To Gordon Long, and to Lynette Bicknell. To Bob Watson, and to everyone at Loving the Book Launch Promotions. To Sara Stephens, and to Jennie Harborth. To Astrid Haigh-Smith, and to Andy Angel. To Diccon and Teresa Dadey.

Many thanks to you all!

Praise for the Artesans of Albia series:

"Cas Peace's *Artesans of Albia* trilogy immediately sweeps you away. The series propels you into a world so deftly written that you see, feel, touch, and even smell each twist and turn. These nesting novels are evocative, hauntingly real. Smart. Powerful. Compelling. The trilogy teems with finely drawn characters, heroes and villains and societies worth knowing; with stories so organic and yet iconic you know you've found another home—in Albia. So start reading now. I, for one, can't wait to find out what will happen next.

~Janet E. Morris, author of *The Sacred Band of Stepsons* series; the *Dream Dancer* series; *I, the Sun*.

✦ ✦ ✦ ✦ ✦

"I have just loved this entire series. Cas Peace is a master storyteller, providing a depth and breadth of information about her worlds and their people that is just staggering. Her characters are complex and multi-dimensional, and I have very much enjoyed reading this series. I am also looking forward with great anticipation to her next novel in this series. I heartily recommend this series to anyone who enjoys epic fantasy, strong world-building, and beautiful storytelling. Highly recommended!"

~ K Sozaeva, *Amazon Vine Voice and Top 1000 Reviewer*

✦ ✦ ✦ ✦ ✦

"As a fan of the late great David Gemmel I think I have finally found an author who is similarly inspiring. It's how fantasy should be written. Less about the world building and more about the characters. I didn't want to stop reading."

~ML. H, *Amazon reviewer*.

✦ ✦ ✦ ✦ ✦

"A superb read. Non-stop intrigue and action. I literally could not put it down. Anyone needing a good series to read should take up Book 1 and get started. Cas Peace has created an unforgettable hero(ine) in Sullyan, and a world that ranks alongside Middle Earth and Westeros."

~David C Snell, *Amazon reviewer*.

Published by Albia Publishing 2017

First American Paperback Edition

This is a work of fiction. Names, characters, places, and incidents either are the product of the author's imagination or are used fictitiously. Any resemblance to actual events, locales, or persons, living or dead, is entirely coincidental. The publisher does not have any control and does not assume responsibility for author or third party websites or their content.

Copyright©2017 by Caroline Peace
Editing by Diane Dalton
Cover art by Mikey Brooks: www.insidemikeysworld.com
Author Photo by Sandy Kitching: www.theearlybirddesign.com

Visit Cas Peace at her author website: www.caspeace.com

ISBN-10: 1-939993-72-5
ISBN-13: 978-1-939993-72-4

Other titles in the Artesans of Albia series:

Trilogy One: Artesans of Albia

Book One: King's Envoy

Book Two: King's Champion

Book Three: King's Artesan

Trilogy Two: Circle of Conspiracy

Book One: The Challenge

Book Two: The Circle

Book Three: Full Circle

Trilogy Three: Master of Malice

Book One: The Scarecrow

Book Two: The Captives

Book Three: The Gateway

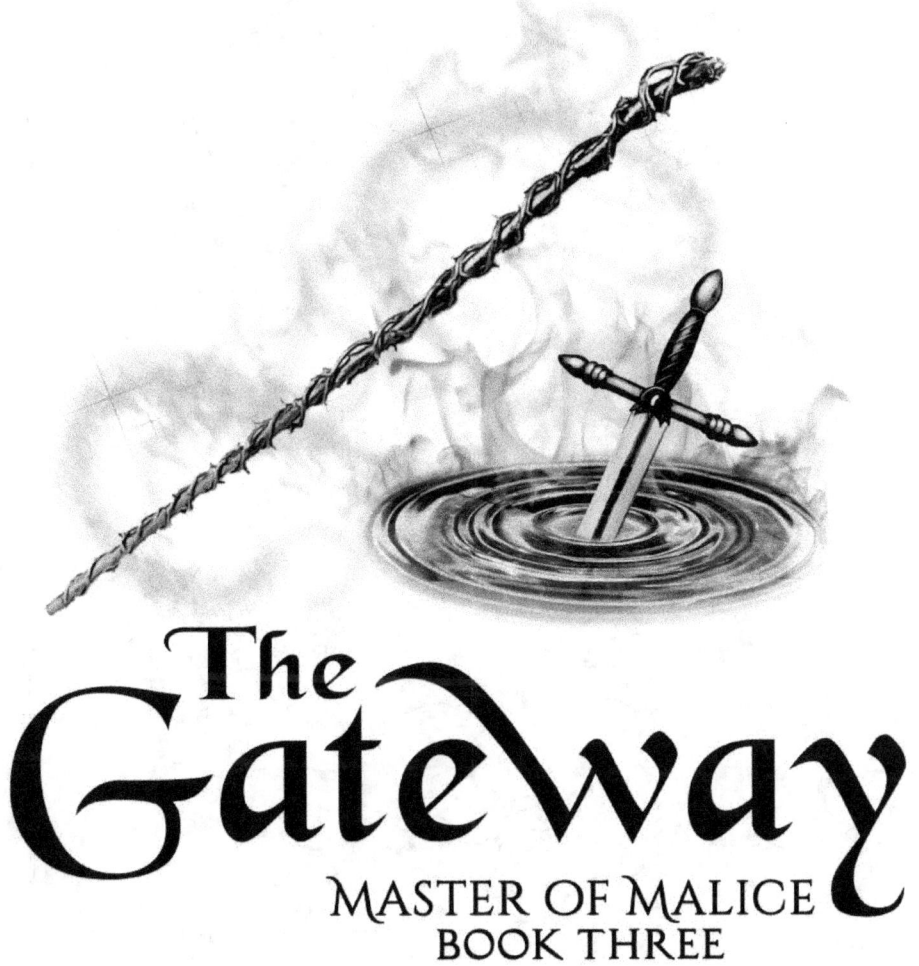

The Gateway

MASTER OF MALICE
BOOK THREE

Cas Peace

Albia Publishing

The Kingdom of Albia in the Realm of Albia, (not to scale)

Realm of Andaryon. (not to scale.)

Chapter One

Timar Pharikian looked down on his son's bowed head and smiled in genuine pleasure. The marriage contract had been approved and all was in readiness to fetch his son's beloved for her official state visit to Caer Vellet. Now Aeyron knelt before him, formally asking his blessing to wed Princess Lirina of Dalkia. This was what he had longed for: the fulfillment of Aeyron's desires in the form of a young woman who could share his vision for the future and who would help free Andaryan women from the yoke of subservience that had hung around their necks from time immemorial.

He looked forward to the reactions of the nobles when they realized what Aeyron had in mind. The court at Caer Vellet led society's fashions; lords all over Andaryon would find it hard preventing their ladies from claiming the same privileges Lirina would enjoy. The lord who kept his women from sharing the duties of her province would incur Prince Aeyron's wrath. Reluctant nobles would soon fall into line when faced with trade restrictions and withdrawals of privilege.

Pharikian's smile widened. He would take great pleasure from the discomfiture of not a few noble lords.

Stretching out his hand, he laid it on his son's head. "Arise, my son. Gladly do I grant my blessing. Bring your beloved here that she may see her future home and learn the courtly duties she will be expected to perform. The Princess may stay as long as you both wish. Quarter her within our private apartments and assign guards to her person. Her father will expect us to treat her as one of our own—she must have an escort of Velletian Guard, both for herself and her ladies."

Aeyron rose, his face flushed with pleasure. He had waited long for this moment and could scarcely contain his excitement. Not only would he see his love again and bring her to her new home, but today was the first day of the late winter Trade Fair, and the Citadel exuded a holiday atmosphere. The Fair traditionally heralded the approach of spring, even though there was still a month to go before winter loosed its grip, and Caer Vellett used it as an excuse to forget winter's hardships and revel in the season's turning.

Aeyron was unable to hide his chagrin. In his eagerness he had forgotten to make even these most necessary arrangements. "Very well, Father. I will speak with Barrin before I go. I am sure he already has it in hand."

"Barrin will go with you," the Hierarch added, fixing his son with a stern eye. "Anjer has already instructed him to lead your honor guard."

Aeyron's face paled as he inclined his head. Pharikian knew he had buried their knowledge of Baron Reen's unquantified threat, and the day's excitement would have pushed it further from his thoughts. He regretted the necessity of mentioning it, but they could not ignore the threat. Sullyan's warnings and the chaos in Albia were too fresh to be forgotten.

Pharikian took his son's maimed right hand. "Take good care, my son. Be vigilant and wary. Do not let the anticipation of future happiness and the love in your heart distract you from your duty. You must convey the Princess safely, and you must protect yourself as well. Once you are here, you can relax. Until then, keep your shields up and remain on guard at all times."

"I will, Father."

Aeyron held his father's gaze, answering the deep fear he read there. Having so nearly lost his only son, first to the Baron's malice and then to the resulting depression, Aeyron's life was doubly precious to him. Now that his son had found someone to fulfill his life's purpose, Pharikian feared even more for his safety. If anything were to happen to further blight his life, he would not survive it. Not even with the loving support of his father and his adoptive sister combined.

Putting aside these thoughts with an effort, the Hierarch smiled. "Go, Aeyron. Go to your Princess. I can see how you yearn to be gone. I will arrange for her quarters, and there will be a full royal guard awaiting you on the Plain. Go and bring your intended home."

He handed Aeyron a parchment. "Take this for her father. It is my seal of approval and my pledge for the match. Give him my regards and tell him I look forward to seeing him here for the wedding. Now go, with my love."

✢ ✢ ✢ ✢ ✢

Aeyron strode down the corridors of the Palace, collecting his squire, Rigel, on the way. Rigel bore a gift for the Princess and also a package for her sister, Kyrie—a letter from her suitor, Jay'el. The squire nodded to his master and fell in beside the Prince as he made for the courtyard. When they emerged into the pale-washed chill of the morning, Barrin had their honor guard ready. Twenty swordsmen, mounted and armed, dressed in their parade best, their swords and buckles gleaming, saluted their sovereign lord.

Two grooms held riderless horses. One was Aeyron's mettlesome chestnut, which raised its head and snorted, recognizing its master. The other was a sleek, finely bred dappled mare, a present for the Princess Lirina. Both beasts shone, manes flowing and tails gleaming, their harness polished and supple. Aeyron grinned at the sight his guard presented, satisfied they would make a suitable impression on the insular Dalkians. He strode across to Barrin, leaving Rigel to fix his saddle packs and mount in anticipation of their departure. The squire took the dappled mare's lead rein.

The Commander of the Velletian Guard saluted his monarch, and Aeyron saw the gleam of pleasure in the man's pale eyes. Barrin was as glad as anyone at Aeyron's good fortune. The marriage of the Heir and the getting of children was a guarantee of the succession, and every Andaryan felt more settled when the Hierarchy was assured. The inevitable and often bloody scuffle for power following the death of a monarch could be averted by a strong Heir. Aeyron was already co-ruler and he was long past the age when most sons were married. His bachelor status had been cause for uncertainty, at least among the nobles. It was no secret that some of them would challenge for the Hierarchy should Aeyron fail to wed and produce an Heir.

Aeyron returned Barrin's homage and took the reins of his warhorse. Tirado, whose name meant "courage" in the old High Language, nuzzled his master's hand, hoping for a tidbit. Aeyron stroked his nose and the stallion ceased his questing.

"Barrin, I trust you have detailed men to be the Princess's honor guard while she guests with us?"

Barrin grinned. Aeyron approved of the way in which Sullyan managed her command and tried to emulate her practice of encouraging discussion and free comment among the men of the Hierarch's forces. It had taken some time, but the Andaryan troops responded. Aeyron's reforms were supported by Lord General Anjer, so there was none of the bowing and scraping that would formerly have attended a Prince's commands. Barrin had no fear of rebuke as he replied, "I have it already in hand, my Prince. Did you think I would allow your intended to go about the Citadel unescorted? She shall have an honor guard of six handpicked, trustworthy men."

Aeyron clapped him on the back. "Good man, I knew I could trust you. Well, then, if we are ready, shall we go fetch my bride?"

The company let loose a rousing cheer as Aeyron sprang into his saddle. Tirado curveted beneath him, tossing his fine head. Aeyron swept his hand into the air and brought it down with a flourish, and the men on the gates opened them wide. Making a fine show, the band cantered in orderly formation out of the courtyard and down the Processional Way, heralded and acclaimed by the townspeople they met. The entire Citadel knew of his errand that morning and many turned out to speed him on his way.

Nearing the southern gates, they found the streets thronged with people lining their route to the Plain. Cries of goodwill and wishes for safety sounded on all sides. At the end of the street, General Ephan stood by the gates in full battle dress, his personal company around him. He saluted as Aeyron drew rein.

"We wish you good speed and a swift and safe return, Highness. We will await you on the Plains to welcome your Princess home."

Aeyron gave a wave and a smile of thanks, too full of impatience to reply. He urged his men onward and they passed below the Citadel walls, cantering easily out onto the Plain and away from the constant stream of merchants thronging the roads. The Citadel would be crowded when he returned later that day. The long-awaited Fair and the added attraction of seeing the Prince's intended bride had brought them flocking to Caer Vellet. Many traders who came for the Fair would bless their Prince's timing.

Turning his thoughts to the pleasurable duty ahead, Aeyron gathered his will and prepared to open the Veils.

✢ ✢ ✢ ✢ ✢

Cal and Tad waited for Sullyan outside the College, having been summoned by Bull. Both young men were red-eyed and strained, pale-faced and angry. When Sullyan arrived, both were surprise at the presence of Elias at her side. Bull had not told them the King would also be going on this sudden, urgent mission.

Cal had left Jay'el and two other swordsmen to guard the children. The young Andaryan seaman had wanted to come with them, but acknowledged the necessity of staying on guard. Bull would share the task of watching over Elias's Heir in Sullyan's absence. What happened when she returned would depend on the outcome of her raid. Tad and Cal fell into step behind Sullyan and Elias as they made their way to the barracks.

Dexter and the rest of Sullyan's company awaited them, the muted sounds of anxious conversation and the bitter smell of fellan pervading the long building. Some fifty men came to attention as the small party entered, saluting their senior officer and their King. There was surprise on some faces when Sullyan returned their homage but Elias did not. Glances of concern were exchanged.

"Be at ease, gentlemen." Sullyan's voice was harsh, devoid of its usual lilt, and the atmosphere changed, becoming expectant. Wil passed her some fellan; Bull served the King.

Sullyan took a seat on the edge of the central table, cradling the steaming cup, gaze roving around the men.

"Gentlemen, I have come to ask for your help. Captain Dexter has already pledged your commitment and I am grateful. But I wish you to know what we face before I accept your support.

"It is now confirmed that our enemy is indeed Baron Reen, exiled three years ago for High Treason. Some of you are aware that it became apparent at his trial that the man possessed latent Artesan powers. I now know that he has since learned to use them.

A terrible accident befell him on the island of his exile, which forced his dormant powers to emerge. This accident left Reen brutally scarred and pushed his unstable sanity too far. When he discovered that the lad who had been his lover and who had selflessly spent himself to save him was an Artesan, the Baron savagely destroyed him, taking possession of his soul."

There were murmurs of disgust and disbelief. Sullyan ignored them.

"Reen escaped the island, using the lad's stolen strength to sustain him, and found a refuge, a place of safety in which to recover. From there, he plotted and carried out cruel and relentless vengeance on those who had betrayed him, and his crimes so far have been vicious. His lover, Serrin, was only the first. I believe he was also responsible for the murders of Lord Neremiah, Princess Seline's nursemaid, Major Denny and his entire company, and at least two others. He is also responsible for the attempted murder of First Minister Levant, and probably for the abduction, if not murder, of his niece, the Baroness Jinella. We know that he took Major Tamsen, and I believe that he also has Taran Elijah. He has killed Major Tamsen"—her voice faltered, but she forged on, quieting the shocked and angry exclamations of the men—"and it is likely Taran has suffered the same fate. For all these crimes, and for the original charge of treason, Reen's life is forfeit.

"I will not mislead you; he has done all these things for a greater reason than mere personal vengeance, and this morning he made that reason clear. He is now in a position of power and is a very dangerous foe—probably the greatest we have ever faced. He forced Taran to contact me to plead for rescue, in order to bring me to him. I do not have to tell you what duress Taran must have endured. He would have sold his own life rather than lure me into a trap. I believe the Baron intends to destroy us, to destroy everyone who is an Artesan, and absorb the powers we possess. Once in a position of unassailable strength, he will turn his attention to the realm. With every Artesan dead, the King's forces in disarray, and Elias vulnerable, he will attack the King, bringing civil war once more upon the land. He intends to impose a new regime on Albia, a xenophobic regime of intolerance, and I do not intend to let that happen. However, I cannot stop him alone."

The men voiced their approval and support, voices angry and muted. Many of the swordsmen looked to Elias, wondering why he stood so silently behind her, why he had not addressed them personally, and why the General was absent. Dexter asked one of the questions uppermost in their minds.

"Colonel, were you able to discover the Baron's place of refuge?"

She turned her gaze on him, unable to conceal the use of metaforce that was allowing her to function under the terrible scourge of her pain. Gasps rose as she answered bleakly, "Bordenn. The monster is laired in the palace."

Dexter stared in horror, comprehension and dismay flooding his features. His voice sounded strained as he said, "Then we have already failed, and the Major and Taran's deaths can be laid at our door. How can you want us with you?"

Many of the men turned pale. One was heard to groan, as if in deepest pain. Sullyan glanced sharply at him.

"Pengar, take your hands from your face. I will not permit you to despair. I need you to guide me, I need your wits and intelligence, and I need your experience. All of you, I need you, every one! Whatever you feel for what went before, put it aside and do not fail me now. This is our chance to avenge Major Tamsen, Owyn Denny, and all the others the monster has killed. This is our chance to exact retribution for their pain and their deaths."

Pengar raised his head, his eyes red and bleak, but he faced her with courage and nodded, drawing a brief but genuine smile from Sullyan.

Dexter's discomfort was acute, but he was willing to put it aside for the chance of redeeming his failure. "When do we leave, Colonel?"

Her gaze swung over them once more, approval overshadowing the pain. "Do I take it you are all willing?"

Their immediate response filled the room. She accepted their pledge, turning back to the Captain. "Once we have planned our strategy. I want to know all you can tell me of the palace, of the area, of the strength of Lerric's guard. I want to be swift and I want to be sure. Oh, gentlemen, there is one thing more."

She had their full attention; they were avid for action.

"There will be one other among our company, another sword to strengthen our arms. Gentlemen, this is Swordsman Elias, and he will be under my command until we return. You will treat him as any other of our number. Anyone who feels unable to do so will remain behind. Speak now."

Stunned silence reigned as they digested this alarming piece of news. Glances were exchanged, both puzzled and concerned. Then Dexter took up the challenge and excelled himself by stepping forward and holding out his hand, speaking clearly so that all could hear him. "Welcome to our company, Swordsman Elias. We are glad to have you among us."

Elias reacted well, taking the Captain's hand and nodding at the men. Dexter's easy acceptance broke an uncomfortable moment, averting a potential crisis. Sullyan drew them close and began to discuss her plans.

Chapter Two

eyron and his company arrived on Dalkian soil, having traveled through the First Realm of Endormir. The Prince had decided against going through Albia, knowing the problems that beset his adoptive sister. Protocol demanded he contact either her or General Blaine for permission to cross into Elias's lands, and in the light of recent events he decided not to trouble them. Endormir was largely deserted while in the grip of its infamous winter tempests. Most of its inhabitants either roamed through Albia or his own realm, or else sheltered in their hide-covered winter retreats; no one would object to their passage.

It was unpleasant indeed when they emerged into Endormir's ferociously icy climate, but it took only moments to pass safely back onto Andaryan soil. Shaking the snow from their cloaks and blinking ice from sore eyes, the royal band rode toward the harbor town of Perinath, where Lord Seyakin had his palace.

Aeyron had sent a messenger two days before to warn the lord of his arrival, and he fully expected to be met along the way. Dalkia was a flat province, bordered by the hills of Cheos to the north and rising only at the gentle cliffs to the east of Perinath's harbor. They had a good view across the land as they rode, and were able to spot Seyakin's welcoming force long before the two groups met. Barrin ordered his men to draw rein when the Dalkian force came in sight, easily identifiable by the warship crest on their banner. He deployed the band in formation around their Prince as the southerners approached.

Aeyron sat the restive Tirado easily. The stallion, picking up his rider's anticipation, tossed his head, sending his chestnut mane flying and displaying the sheen of his burnished copper coat. It was all Aeyron could do to hide his mounting impatience as they waited for the southern lord's men to draw near.

The Prince's eyes widened in surprise as the leader of the small force came close enough to be identified. Seyakin himself had come to meet him. Flattered by the honor, Aeyron nudged Tirado forward, extending a hand in greeting to the bearded Lord of Dalkia. In his turn, Seyakin smiled a welcome, clasping Aeyron's maimed right hand with only the merest hint of reaction. The two men had met before, and Seyakin was aware of the Prince's disfigurement. Aeyron knew the lord would broach the painful subject and was not looking forward it. Any prospective father-in-law would address it, even with the lowliest of suitors. The Crown Prince of Andaryon should not expect to be treated differently.

The older lord nodded gravely. "Greetings, Highness, we are humbled by your wish to visit us again. I am pleased to see you safely arrived. I trust your journey was uneventful?"

Aeyron smiled. "It was if you discount nearly freezing our eyeballs as we passed through Endormir." He hoped his casual tone would prove a cue for Seyakin. Aeyron wanted this meeting to proceed as easily as possible. He was here not as co-ruler of the realm, but as a prospective husband, and he wished Seyakin to follow his lead. The pomp and ceremony attending a formal royal visit was not the atmosphere Aeyron wished to foster.

Fortunately, the sixty-three-year-old Seyakin was a shrewd man who recognized the urgency of a heart strong in love. He had lived with his daughter's constant questions ever since the Prince's first visit, and if Aeyron's feelings for Lirina were even half as intense as hers for him, Seyakin saw little point in standing on ceremony. He could hardly ask for a better match—the Hierarchy of the realm coming into his family was an unlooked-for advancement. If his daughter did her duty and produced a male heir, his line would rule the realm and Dalkia's prosperity would be assured.

He shook his head and nudged his mount closer. His men fell in behind. "How those poor nomads endure such conditions, I'll never know. I've never been there myself, not being blessed with the Artesan gift, but I have heard about their terrible winters. We are more fortunate here on the coast; we rarely experience more than a degree or so of frost."

Barrin's men parted for the Dalkian swordsmen and allowed them to surround their lord and the Prince. As they rode toward the city, Aeyron kept his eyes open, mindful of the Hierarch's warning, and saw Barrin doing the same. Yet the journey passed peacefully and the company soon came in sight of the harbor, its sparkling blue waters and air of activity unfamiliar to the landlocked Velletians.

Many ships rode at anchor, or swayed and dipped their bowsprits beside the wharves, their bare masts reaching for the washed blue sky. Men swarmed all over them, unloading and repairing, cleaning and caulking, carrying cargo and yelling incomprehensible orders. The wharves were crowded and no one seemed to take much notice of the cavalcade riding through them, despite the presence of their lord and the Prince of the Realm. Aeyron raised his brows at this lack of respect, but Seyakin didn't seem to mind, riding his tall dusty black through the throng, watching his people going about their business and missing nothing of the activity that flowed around their group.

Aeyron found Barrin at his shoulder, his stern face a mask of disapproval. "I don't think I like these southerners much. They don't acknowledge their lord or give proper welcome to their

Prince. I hope this isn't an indication of their character."

The Prince could see his point, yet he was unwilling to judge. The commander fell silent, glaring at the crowds, his hand on the hilt of his sword. Barrin's discomfiture had an effect on Seyakin's guard; their leader eyed Barrin suspiciously, not liking the way his hand stayed on his sword hilt. Casting the commander a warning glance, Aeyron spoke casually to his host.

"The people of your city are more relaxed than mine, my Lord. I cannot imagine the citizens of Caer Vellet simply going about their business should their nobles ride through the town, least of all their ruling lord."

Seyakin turned pale-green eyes on his daughter's suitor and a look of understanding crossed his features. "Ah, my Prince, are you feeling slighted? I see by their eyes that your escort disapproves of my people. Were you expecting acclaim and the cheers of the populace? I can arrange such a welcome, if that is what you wish."

Barrin flushed at what he saw as Seyakin's disrespectful attitude, and his hand tightened on his sword hilt. Aeyron's curiosity was piqued, however, and he wondered if the older lord was testing him. They had not spent much time together yet, and neither knew the other's character. Seyakin would have heard the rumors spread by Aeyron's nobles concerning his friendship with Albians and his intended reforms. Perhaps the man had decided to try the mettle of this maimed Prince. Aeyron smiled inwardly. If he had, he would receive a surprise.

He turned to Barrin and gestured. The commander reluctantly released his weapon, but his eyes remained firmly fixed on the older lord.

Aeyron smiled easily at Seyakin. "No criticism intended, my Lord. You know why I am here. I have not come to review the rule of your House. It was an observation only. I am not able to go about my own city in such dispassionate circumstances, and I find it refreshing."

Seyakin regarded him silently before replying, his voice flat and devoid of inflection. "I do not foster ostentatious shows of respect among my people, Prince Aeyron. This is a working port and a busy town, and I am a working lord. Both my daughters aid me in the business of the city and I know you approve of this. If we were accosted by cheering crowds whenever I or my family came among the populace, we should never get anything done. We save the banner-waving for special occasions. Be assured, if your suit for my daughter's hand is approved, you will see a spectacle to rival anything your Citadel may host. Now tell your men to relax, you are all safe here. Despite their appearance of absorbed employment, my people are watchful and loyal. If anyone were to offer you harm, Prince Aeyron, you would see how ferocious they can be."

Seyakin continued the ride in silence. Aeyron, put in his place and quietly amused, shook his head at Barrin's scandalized expression. Seyakin was indeed testing him, and also testing his control over his men. The Prince had already spotted guards among the crowd—Seyakin would take no chances with the safety of a Prince of the Realm. Despite the lord's words implying doubt as to his daughter's eventual fate, Aeyron was confident of Seyakin's acceptance. After all, what lord wouldn't covet a link to the Hierarchy, and especially the overworked lord of a bustling harbor city?

Smiling to himself and settling into the role, Aeyron relaxed as he looked about him, taking in the delightful, unfamiliar sights of the city.

They passed out of the harbor and rode through market streets and residential areas. Perinath was a medium-sized city that had grown up piecemeal, but the districts looked prosperous and tidy. Perhaps he was guided along the most favorable routes, but Aeyron saw nothing that hinted at a poor quarter. The houses were small but well kept. The streets were free of rubbish and the cobbles in good repair. The smell of brine pervaded everything, but it was not unpleasant. Seabirds called raucously from rooftops. The citizens went about their business, and although many clearly recognized their lord and Aeyron, too, no one reacted with more than a stare. They rode unmolested as they approached Seyakin's palace.

The palace was like much of the city, designed to be functional rather than decorative. It was surrounded by a stout defensive wall enclosing a space of grassy park. The building itself appeared at the end of a short ride, its white-faced stone gleaming in the morning sun. It was smaller by far than the Imperial Palace, but Seyakin maintained a much smaller retinue.

Once again, Aeyron gained the impression of a thrifty man who made the most of his wealth rather than squandering it. Seyakin's assertion that he was a working lord was borne out by what could be seen around the palace.

There were guards on the gates and smart salutes were exchanged. Even Barrin could find no fault with the deference of the swordsmen. It was understated yet respectful, and Aeyron approved. He followed his host into the courtyard, dismounting onto gravel raked and swept clean. Grooms waited to take the horses, and Aeyron gave special instructions to the man who took the dappled mare. Barrin's men formed into an honor guard and Rigel walked at Aeyron's back as Seyakin waved them into the palace.

Inside, stewards came to convey the Prince to a suite of rooms where he could rest and refresh himself. He was eager to see the

Princess, but protocol dictated Seyakin be permitted to speak to his daughter alone before she met the Prince. Aeyron and Rigel entered the suite, thanking the steward, who left them alone.

Aeyron strode to the window and stared out at a winter garden. His squire laid their packs on the floor and poured a measure of dark ruby wine for the Prince from a crystal decanter on a polished marble table.

Aeyron took it gratefully. "So, Rigel, what did you make of that?"

"I think his Lordship is not quite what he seems."

Aeyron regarded his squire. Rigel was twenty-six years old and had been Pharikian's page before Norkis, entering Aeyron's personal service once he was old enough to do so. Aeyron valued him for his frank and plain speech, and he often made observations Aeyron might have missed. "What do you mean?"

"My Lord Seyakin would have you believe his province is well governed but essentially poor." Rigel took a sip from the glass he poured for himself. Many nobles would have raised their brows at a mere squire partaking of wine meant for a Prince, and some would have flogged him for his impudence. Aeyron, however, permitted his close servants freedoms not commonly enjoyed, and Rigel knew how to behave. Anyone entering the Prince's rooms unannounced would have found the squire attending his Lord most assiduously with nothing out of place.

"He wishes to be seen as hardworking," Rigel continued, "someone who has little time for leisure and no thought for his own importance. But it is a carefully staged charade. Take this wine, for example, and even the decanter. This is Cheosian red, my Lord, and a very fine vintage, if I'm not mistaken—"

"Which you never are!"

"—and this decanter is Falleran crystal. And you know how expensive *that* is."

"Yes, I do. But I fail to see your point. Wouldn't you put out your best wine and crystal if you were receiving a Prince of the Realm? Especially one who comes courting your daughter."

Rigel grinned. "That's exactly my point, my Lord. With the greatest respect, you see what you expect to see. You find nothing odd because it is what you or your father would do, and neither of you have reason to resort to such tactics. But consider, my Prince. If you wish to appear less wealthy than you are, if you wish to create the impression of a hardworking noble who has earned what he has, would you parade such luxuries? Would you not rather offer your second best wine, and serve it in goblets of silver?"

Aeyron shook his head, amazed as always at Rigel's devious mind. "All right, then, squire, I accept what you say. So what is the meaning of this? A slip by some servant? And what has Seyakin to gain by such deception?"

Rigel's grin widened. "Definitely a slip, and one that will be paid for. I saw the steward's face as we entered, and he was not a happy man. I would bet on some page being starved of his supper tonight. As for what the Lord hopes to gain, that is obvious. He took great pains to tell you his daughters help him manage his lands. So how will he cope when you take the eldest away? How high will he set her bride price as compensation for her loss?"

Aeyron snorted. "Oh, come, Rigel, that's going too far! You are suggesting her father will sell her like cargo from one of his ships. And you infer all this from the look on a steward's face? You have been drinking too much Cheosian red, my friend! I obviously allow you far too many privileges. Maybe I ought to starve *you* of supper once in a while."

Rigel swept an obsequious bow. "Whatever my Lord commands. But I should, perhaps, tell you that I am currently bedding one of the kitchen maids, and she will do anything for me ..."

17

Aeyron threw a cushion, which the squire dodged. "Impudent youth! Shouldn't you be polishing my sword or something?"

Rigel sobered, for although it was a joke, the Crown Prince was right. They probably didn't have much longer before Seyakin would be ready to receive them. He waved Aeyron toward the washroom and began laying out fresh clothes for his Prince.

"You just wait and see," he called as Aeyron disappeared into the washroom. "See how hard he pushes you on the subject of her bride price. I will be happy to accept your apology for doubting my shrewdness later."

✥ ✥ ✥ ✥ ✥

It took Sullyan the rest of the morning and most of the afternoon to formulate her plans. Her men gathered round her, answering her questions as to the layout of the palace, the barracks, the position of the palace relative to the town, its defenses, and the strength and discipline of Lerric's guard. Maps and room layouts were sketched on parchment and possible traps identified. Cal and Tad listened intently, having no experience of Lerric's palace, and Elias sat well to the back of the group, speaking only when he was asked to give what detail he could of its interior and the private rooms.

He also gave his opinion of Lerric's probable stance over the Baron's intentions, given what he had seen of the elderly man's demeanor. However, he cautioned them against looking to Lerric for last-minute support; Sofira was likely to overrule her father if she was indeed loyal to Reen. Elias's contribution to the discussions, accompanied by none of the usual deference due his status, gradually eased the tension his presence caused. The men began to accept him among them in the light of Sullyan and Dexter's unchallenged authority.

Food arrived at midday. Blaine had sent word to Goran's kitchens and his serving lads brought steaming stew, fresh bread, and fruit. Sullyan managed to eat some stew, although she mainly existed on fellan, provided by Wil. In the middle of the afternoon, just as they were finalizing the distribution of their strength under the three commanders, the General himself walked into the building followed by Bull.

The men rose and saluted their leader. Elias rose with them and it was a tribute to their increasing acceptance of him that he found it hard to stop himself saluting his own General. Sullyan glanced across at him as she guessed the General's intentions. She called Bull over.

"Bull, take Elias to Quartermaster Adyn and have him issued combat leathers and cloak. Those court velvets will be no use where we are going. And check his horse's harness. I want no trappings of royalty visible when we leave. Dismissed."

Bull threw her a salute and beckoned to the King. Sullyan spared Elias not one glance and he followed Bull meekly, accepting he would truly be treated as any other swordsman.

Once they had left, Sullyan set the rest of the men to checking weapons and harness in preparation for departure. Dexter sent one of them to oversee the horses. Sullyan caught the General's eye and the pair of them moved farther down the long building until they were out of immediate earshot. Blaine watched her as cautiously as a hunter watches a wounded boar. Sullyan frowned, irritated by his manner.

"Speak your mind, Mathias," she said, trying to keep the edge from her voice.

Blaine winced. "Must you go?"

She stared at him, incredulous. "I will not even grace that with an answer."

Blaine sighed and rephrased his query. "Are you sure it's wise for you to lead this raid? It's you the Baron wants, we all know that. You'll be walking into a trap, and one he's had time to perfect. You may be forewarned, but you can't know what awaits you. You're taking a huge risk. If we lost you ..." Blaine swallowed. "If he succeeds in taking your power, the realm will be lost. He has the Major's powers and Taran's too—add yours to the tally and no one in the Five Realms will be able to stand against him. Not even Pharikian."

Sullyan gazed into his hard blue eyes. It was not the realm Blaine feared for, but her. He was unable, as usual, to speak plainly of his emotion for fear of it taking him over, of losing control. He had never learned that in order to control emotions it was necessary first to accept them, to experience them, to give them free rein, to acknowledge and submit to the forces that gave a body life. A soul without emotion was a fire with no warmth, and to deny one's true feelings was to deny one's own spirit. But Mathias Blaine had never found the courage to explore his soul's roots, and this was what had held him back from his full Artesan potential.

She could not tell him this now. She had tried before, when she was younger, and had not understood his reluctance. Comprehension came with maturity, with experience, and she had been able to see the stoked fire of his love that he strove so hard to subdue. It was useless to advise him now. He was the way he was and would never change.

She spoke as gently as her wounded heart allowed. "I will be careful, Mathias." The pain swelled and roared inside her; she would never be free of it until death reunited her with the mate of her soul. "Do not forget—although Reen may now have power, he is unskilled in its use. Knowledge is no substitute for experience; training and instinct will win over usurpation every time. That is why I will wait no longer. Every hour we delay gives him time to learn. I do not go into this blind."

Blaine's expression hardened. "Have you thought he might have raised the province? He might have forced Lerric to call on his levies even before we arrived at the palace. Just because we saw no sign of them doesn't mean they're not there."

It was highly unlikely and he knew it. He was talking for the sake of it, trying to dissuade her, even though he knew she was committed.

"I am going at night for that very reason, although I doubt he has. The nobles would kick against turning out in the depths of winter. Wil Gerion saw no men massing as he rode through the countryside. I wager the escort would have heard rumors of such plans in the tavern you slept in, if not the one they visited in Daret. It would be impossible to prevent the townsfolk from speaking of it. No, Mathias, I do not anticipate having to fight Lerric's nobles. You are right, I am the one Reen wants—it was an entirely personal message he sent me, one guaranteed to inflame me. He believes himself safe, unassailable, and I intend to show him the error of his pride."

Blaine would have said more, but the man Dexter had sent to see to the horses returned with the news that Solet had them ready. The Captain glanced at her and she gave him a faint nod. She gazed up at Blaine, wishing he would let her go, wishing he would speak his heart, if only this once. It might afford him the release she could not grant him.

He saw the look and flushed. She thought then that he might speak. She sensed he was closer to admitting his feelings than he had ever been in the past. Yet he remained silent and she lowered her eyes, drawing a breath of frustration. Then he amazed her, and all of the men, when he suddenly stepped closer and embraced her openly, the most public sign of his regard he had ever shown. She was stunned but quickly recovered, briefly returning his embrace. The moment was too awkward and too many eyes watched them for it to be easy, but she did her best, smiling up at him, her eyes dry. She swiftly stepped away.

"We will return as soon as we may, and I will keep you informed."

"Stay safe, Brynne," he told her gravely, and she was not the only one to hear the catch in his voice.

Chapter Three

Prince Aeyron stood as the light knock sounded on his chamber door. He nodded to Rigel, who opened it. The steward who had shown them in appeared, his eyes flicking to the empty crystal decanter. Aeyron caught his squire's smirk but did not allow himself to react. They would discuss their findings later, once this meeting was over.

Aeyron was nervous, although he tried to hide it. This unprecedented situation was of his own making and he must handle it with serenity and calm. He was Prince of the Realm and co-ruler of Andaryon; he could have taken any woman he chose without putting himself through this ritual of seeking permission. There were even laws permitting him a number of concubines should he feel so inclined, and previous Hierarchs had kept slave girls for dalliance, using their brides only for the begetting of heirs.

It was such casual dismissals of a woman's worth that Aeyron wished to abolish. Once he had sole control of the throne, he intended to rescind those ancient, barbaric laws. He had Gaslek working on the procedure already, knowing how the nobles would buck against the change. His nervousness was unnecessary, but it troubled him all the same. He wanted Lirina to love him for the man he was, not the power and position he represented. It was hardly possible, he knew, and unfair of him to expect it of her, but he hoped she could see past his titles and would allow herself to treat him as a suitor for her heart. Squaring his shoulders and composing himself, he gestured for Rigel to precede him from the chamber.

The young squire took up the packages they had brought, taking care to include the two parchments he had been given. One was for Seyakin, and one was for Kyrie, although both would be read by the lord. As yet, Jay'el had not proved his worth. Whatever the younger Princess felt for the youth, he would have to direct his correspondence through her father until accepted as her betrothed. Casting a glance over his shoulder at Aeyron's set face, Rigel followed the steward from the room.

Barrin and the Prince's honor guard fell into step beside Aeyron. His men flanked both Prince and squire as they walked the hallways, swords at their hips, eyes watchful. The steward led them to Seyakin's audience hall. The doors stood open, and heralds blew a rousing fanfare when Aeyron's escort came into sight. Seyakin stood beside a marble table flanked by luxuriously upholstered chairs, and there were more decanters on the table, along with goblets which looked to be gold.

Seyakin was dressed in the colors of his House. His symbol was the warship and his colors were those of the sea; aquamarine, jade-green, deep ocean-blue. The colors were muted, not garish, and his mantle was subtly trimmed with purple, to show his allegiance to the Crown. As Aeyron approached him, Seyakin swept the most respectful of bows, belying his earlier, somewhat disparaging attitude.

"Be welcome, my Prince, to the House of Seyakin."

Aeyron stretched out his hand and the older man took it, kissed the Imperial ring, and led Aeyron toward the top chair. Aeyron bowed his head and sat, the lord seating himself on his right. Aeyron's honor guard withdrew, ranging themselves around the walls. Seyakin's steward stepped forward and offered the Prince wine, and as he poured the ruby vintage Aeyron caught

Rigel's pointed look and raised brow. Forcing down an inappropriate smile, Aeyron took up the gold-chased goblet and raised it to his host. Seyakin did the same and the atmosphere relaxed.

Aeyron avoided Rigel's eye as he spoke. "This is a very fine Cheosian red, my Lord. Easily one of the best vintages, I would say."

"I am pleased to offer it, my Prince. It is not often we enjoy such luxuries, but we were fortunate enough to offer safe harbor to a Cheos ship a month or so ago. Her captain parted with some of her cargo in gratitude."

Aeyron accepted the lord's explanation but caught the slight movement Rigel made. He tried not to let the squire's amusement distract him.

Seyakin placed his goblet on the table. "So, my Prince, I am intrigued by the manner of your proposal. May I enquire as to your reasons for this radical departure from tradition?"

In reply, Aeyron waved his squire forward. Rigel knelt before the lord, holding out the first parchment, the one signed by the Hierarch's hand. Seyakin accepted the letter, unfolded it and read, while Aeyron sipped at his wine, covertly watching the lord's reactions.

Seyakin laid the letter down and turned an evaluating look on Aeyron. "I never doubted you had the wholehearted support of your royal father, my Prince. His assurances for the safety of my daughter while in your care are unnecessary, although I appreciate his gesture. What I am most curious to hear are your reasons for these reforms. I would be interested to know how you came to consider them. Forgive me, Prince Aeyron, but I am bound to ask—does it have anything to do with the injury you suffered?"

Aeyron felt his face flush, although he was ready for the question. Seyakin was within his rights, and Aeyron was constrained to answer. Besides, he desired Seyakin's understanding and support. If his plans were to work, this first step was vital. Other lords, once they heard of it, would question Seyakin, and his responses could well affect the success of Aeyron's reforms.

The Prince faced the older man and related his reasons, telling the tale of his capture by the Baron, Sullyan's rescue, and her part in his subsequent recovery. Seyakin listened in silence, his face giving nothing away.

When the Prince fell silent, taking refuge in his goblet, Seyakin folded his arms. There was respect in his eyes. "I thank you for your openness, and also for your trust. Some might have shrunk from telling that unpleasant tale, and I can see how hard it was for you. You obviously suffered greatly at the hands of that man. I believe it is a measure of your quality that you overcame such a blight to your life, and I accept with no reservations your assurances as to your fitness to rule. The confidence of your father in appointing you co-ruler says much for his faith in your abilities. It only remains for me to say that I have no valid objections to your suit for my daughter. I will be delighted to place her in your care. It will come as no surprise to you that an alliance between our Houses is not something I would refuse, but I want you to know that my acceptance of your proposal is not entirely dependent on your position or wealth. I love and value my daughter, and I truly believe you will cherish her as I do and make her the husband I know she deserves."

Aeyron let out a breath. Although the outcome of his proposal had hardly been in doubt, the lord's final words were the ones Aeyron most wanted to hear, and he accepted them in the spirit they were offered. "I thank you for your sentiments. I give you my word that my love and protection will surround her always."

Seyakin bowed his head and raised his goblet; the two men drank to the acceptance of the betrothal.

Seyakin put his goblet down and cleared his throat. "I will send for her shortly, Highness, for I know she is waiting. She has been eagerly anticipating your arrival and is ready to accompany you. I am sure you wish to return with all speed to the Citadel, as you must have duties awaiting your attention. But if you will forgive me, there is one thing we have yet to discuss."

Aeyron heard Rigel's slight shift in position, but ignored it. He decided to let Seyakin make the running. He wanted to see if Rigel's assessment was correct. He was becoming increasingly impressed with the younger man's perceptiveness and wondered if he wasn't wasted as a squire.

Aeyron raised his brows as if he had forgotten the vital matter of the bride price. "And what is that, my Lord?"

Seyakin glanced down at his hands and Aeyron stifled a smile. "My Prince, I have told you how I rely on my daughters. Their involvement in the government of my lands and business interests are of inestimable worth to me. And while I would never wish to belittle Lirina's undoubted beauty, I do believe her acumen has been a factor in your proposal."

"Indeed."

There was the merest pause before Seyakin continued, as if he hoped Aeyron might save him the embarrassment. "Then you will not be surprised to learn that I will be hard pressed to cope without my eldest daughter. I will miss her aid and experience greatly. Kyrie does her best, but she is not as level-headed as Lirina and does not wholly share her interests. My investments are bound to suffer without her. I do not wish to sound mercenary, Highness, and I fear to offer you insult, but in our dealings to date we have never yet mentioned bride price."

Rigel coughed and Aeyron turned to him. "Are you quite well,

Squire? Did you want to ask leave? I am sure my Lord will not be offended if you need to retire."

Rigel stared at his Prince for a fraction of a second before inclining his head. "Your Highness is most kind, but I assure you, I am well. A slight tickle of the throat, my Prince, nothing more. Pray do not concern yourself."

Aeyron turned back to Seyakin, trying not to laugh. It would not do to insult the lord by appearing flippant. Despite Aeyron's departure from tradition, Lirina's bride price must be agreed.

"As her father, my Lord, it is for you to set the bride price." He noted the flush of discomfort that touched Seyakin's cheek. "If it is your business interests that most concern you, I urge you not to fear. There are many in my court skilled in the matter of investments. I would be happy to assign one of them to you until you can train one of your own to take the Princess's place."

Seyakin paled then hurriedly composed himself. Aeyron struggled with his amusement. An Imperial clerk going through his affairs was the last thing Seyakin wanted. It would be bad enough losing a daughter who knew the intimate details of his accounts; having a stranger advising him and reporting to the Prince was clearly not a situation he could countenance.

"That will not be necessary, Highness, although I thank you for your most generous offer. I merely ask that you uphold my daughter's honor and show her the depth of your regard. You know the store these ladies put on attracting a significant price."

Aeyron allowed his smile free rein. Seyakin's ploy was a neat one. Not only was his honor guard ranged around the room, but the lord's steward still hovered by his elbow, drinking in every word. Whatever price Aeyron agreed would be all around the city by the morrow. He raised his eyes to Seyakin's and boldly named a figure, one he and his father had already decided on, and one that caused the lord to gasp. It was with great satisfaction that Aeyron heard Rigel's gulp.

"I trust this sum pleases you, my Lord? Does it fully convey my regard for your daughter? Will it suffice to bolster your coffers and compensate you for her loss?"

Seyakin closed his mouth and rose to his feet. He took Aeyron's hand and brought it to his lips. "Oh, indeed, Highness. Forgive me if I seemed venal—such matters are awkward to discuss. I meant no offense, nor did I mean to imply any slight on your affections. I know my daughter will do well in your care, and to be grandsire to the future Hierarch is more than I deserve."

Aeyron's grin widened and he waved Seyakin away. "Sit, sir, I beg you. We are nearly related, after all. You are to be my father-by-marriage and I do not insist on such formalities from those who are close to me."

Seyakin released Aeyron's hand and returned to his seat. The Prince regarded him with a serious look. "You will find, my Lord, that I have more reforms in mind than the value of women. I expect those about me to give me advice and offer their thoughts. Once we are wed, your daughter and I will expect you at court whenever your duties can spare you. But now, if you please, I can wait no longer. I have offered my suit and you have accepted. I desire to see my bride, and to take up her hand. I have gifts to offer her, and a letter for your youngest. Will you not send for your daughter?"

Seyakin smiled at the wistfulness in Aeyron's tone and waved a hand at his steward. The man hurried to the door and spoke to the heralds, who blew a peal of silver notes that echoed through the halls. Aeyron waited, holding his breath, more eager than even he had realized to see once more the woman he had chosen.

The wait was brief. Almost before the peal had died away, he heard footsteps approaching. A small party made its way down the hall; four pages in the lead, four ladies behind them. The first two were ladies-in-waiting, and behind them walked Lirina and her sister, eyes demurely downcast, faces serene. Yet as they entered the room and came closer, Aeyron could see the gleam of his intended's frost-pale eyes, and the slight upward quirk to her pink lips. He stood at once to greet her.

The four pages bowed and retired to the side. The ladies-in-waiting gave dainty curtseys, eyes lowered, faces flushed at the presence of the Prince. They also stood aside, and then Kyrie came forward, casting Aeyron a glance from her darker green eyes. She dropped a deep obeisance and Aeyron stepped closer, taking her hand to raise her.

"Princess Kyrie, I greet you. I trust I find you well?"

"I am well, Highness, I thank you for your courtesy." Kyrie gave him a shy smile, never glancing at his injury. She did not have the poise of her elder sister, although Aeyron believed it would come with time. She was very young and unused to such occasions. He returned her smile, trying to put her at ease.

He released her hand and she retired to her father's side, clearing the way for her sister. Lirina came forward, and for the first time in weeks Aeyron looked upon his intended. Lirina was taller than her sister; almost as tall as Aeyron. She was slim, even willowy, and the long tresses of her dark auburn hair trailed down her back over the glossy green of her gown, a translucent shade reminiscent of the sea and echoing the pale green of her eyes. Her skin was creamy, and she carried her height with easy grace. She held her betrothed's gaze a moment too long, the flush in her cheeks plain to see. To hide her emotion, she sank to the floor, according obeisance to her sovereign and Prince.

Hardly more composed than she, and surprised at himself, Aeyron stepped forward. He stretched out his hand, hoping she would not see the tremble he could not quite hide. She took it in both of hers and kissed his Imperial ring, letting her lips linger longer than was strictly necessary. She remained in a curtsey and Aeyron was captivated.

"My Lady," he murmured huskily, and she turned up her face. It took a discreet cough from Seyakin to remind them they were not alone, and they both flushed. Aeyron raised his Princess and led her to the table, seating her in his chair and taking the one to her right. Seyakin waved his younger daughter to the table and took a seat himself, accepting more wine from his steward. Rigel came forward and poured for the Princess, offering the goblet to her most gallantly. She smiled at him as she accepted, sipping daintily to hide the depths of her feelings.

Aeyron gestured to his squire and Rigel handed him a package. It was a slender square box wrapped in purple velvet, and Aeyron laid it on the table in front of his betrothed.

"My Lady, you know why I came here today, and I am pleased to tell you your father has accepted my suit for your hand. From this moment we are betrothed, and it would give me great pleasure if you would accept this small token of my deep affections."

Lirina smiled shyly and reached for the box. She unwrapped the purple velvet and revealed a slim golden casket, delicately chased and finely wrought. Her eyes misted as she traced the patterns on the lid. Lightly, she eased back the lid, giving a gasp of wonder. Nestled within the box on a bed if gold tissue was the most delicate fillet of gold and jade-pearls. Coming from a sea-faring province and trading in marine goods, Lirina knew the value of the priceless jade-pearls, and what she held in her hands could have purchased her father's palace. She stared up at Aeyron with awe.

"Oh, Highness, I hardly know what to say! I have never seen anything more beautiful."

"I have," murmured Aeyron, and she blushed and dropped her eyes. "Do you like it, my Princess?"

Her head came up. "How can you ask such a thing? I have never owned anything as rare as this."

"I had it made especially for you, and I want you to wear it when you meet my father at the banquet tonight. But, Liri, we are betrothed now, will you not use my name? I would like to hear you say it."

She gave him another shy smile, and stretched out her hand. "Aeyron," she whispered.

He took her hand and held it, gazing into her eyes. Seyakin watched, his pleasure in his daughter's happiness plain on his face, but was forced to remind them once again they were not alone.

"Highness, did you not tell me you also brought something for Kyrie?"

Aeyron came back to himself, tearing his gaze from his Princess's brimming eyes. "Oh, I nearly forgot! Princess Kyrie, please forgive me. Jay would have my hide if I left here without giving you his letter."

Aeyron gestured to Rigel and the squire approached Kyrie, passing her Jay'el's letter, which she then offered to her father. The lord shook his head and she opened it herself, flushing with pleasure as she read her intended's words.

"Is he working hard, your young seaman?" her father enquired, glancing from Kyrie to Aeyron. The girl held out the opened parchment and this time her father took it, skating over the endearments until he reached the meat of the news. He cast her a glance and returned the letter, which she folded and held tightly in her hands, pleasure in her eyes and a flush on her cheeks.

"Time will tell," Seyakin said, grinning at Aeyron.

The Prince nodded. "I believe that young man may yet surprise you, sir. You might find him more than a replacement for the skills of your eldest daughter. Especially when he is working for his own gain as well as yours. He is heir to his father's extensive shipping concerns, which bring us much revenue. He will not let you down, you can be sure of that."

Kyrie shot Aeyron a grateful look, and he grinned back at her like a brother. But Aeyron had other things on his mind, and now that the formalities were over, he was eager to convey his bride home. He stood.

"My Lord, I really think we should prepare to leave. It is not far off midday and I am needed at home. I have horses waiting in the courtyard and my guard will see to the baggage. Liri, I have another surprise for you. I have brought you a mount, one I chose myself. I trust you will like her. She has been well trained and comes from impeccable breeding."

Liri smiled with pleasure. "I am sure I will love her, Aeyron. I thank you."

Seyakin stood, drawing his daughters with him, and both he and Kyrie embraced Lirina. The younger sister had tears in her eyes, but Liri's were shining; she was more than eager to go with her Prince. Rigel led the way to the hallway, where Barrin had his men fall in around the Prince and Princess, escorting them through the palace and out into the late morning light. As Aeyron had said, all the horses were waiting, and while Barrin's men saw to the arranging of the Princess's belongings and the carriage provided for her ladies, Aeyron showed her the sleek dappled mare.

"Her name is Hakira, which means 'faithful heart' in the old High Language. I thought it an appropriate name. Do you like her?"

The Princess stroked Hakira's soft velvet nose and the mare nuzzled her fingers. Lirina looked up at Aeyron with eyes full of happy tears. "Oh, she is lovely! But I hope she's quiet, for I am not much of a rider. I know boats best. I could sail you out to Tallig, and even round the cape of Selkiar in a storm, but riding a horse is not something I have done often."

"I assure you, my love, she is a gentle ride. I hope we will enjoy many outings together. You will have to talk to Brynne about sailing. I have little experience of boats. Perhaps we can learn from each other."

Liri eyed him. "Brynne is your adoptive sister, is she not? The Albian Artesan? I have heard much about her and I would be interested to meet her. Will she be at the Palace tonight?"

Aeyron shook his head as Rigel signaled all was ready for departure. "I think not tonight, Liri, but you will meet her soon. She has expressed the same wish, and she visits us frequently. You will like her, I hope—she is very dear to my heart and precious to my father."

Lord Seyakin embraced his oldest child once more and lifted her into the saddle. Aeyron swung up onto Tirado, feeling Liri's admiring eyes on his body like the caress of her hand. He accepted the dappled mare's lead rein from Seyakin. "Take good care of her, Highness. I am trusting you with her safety. If any harm should befall her, you will answer to me, Crown Prince or no!"

"Have no fear, my Lord. This woman is as precious to me as my own life. No harm will come to her, I give you my pledge."

Barrin gave the signal and his men surrounded the party. Rigel drove the carriage containing Liri's ladies. Already in conversation with them, and with his eye on one beauty in particular, the squire drew in behind the royal pair as they rode out of the courtyard, followed by Seyakin's men. They would escort the Prince's party to the north of the city, where open country would provide a site for their crossing.

Lirina turned in her saddle and waved to her father and sister until the palace was out of sight. Then she turned her eyes northward and sat Hakira quietly, allowing Aeyron to lead her toward her new home.

Chapter Four

Sullyan's company emerged into the wintry afternoon light to find their horses waiting, the last few arriving from the horse lines led by Solet's small army of stable lads. Drum blew out his lips when he saw Sullyan and danced on his feathered hooves, eager to be gone. Cal's mount, a tall iron-gray with dark mane and tail, stood next to the black stallion, and Elias's young warhorse, Darius, shook snow from his mahogany mane.

The King strode toward them from the quartermaster's hut, dressed in dark leather like an ordinary swordsman, his thick, fleece-lined cloak swirling around his heels. Bull followed him, his expression stern.

Catching Sullyan's nod, Dexter called, "Mount up!" The company settled into saddles and gathered up reins. Bull stood at Sullyan's stirrup once she was settled on Drum and she glanced down at him, her sword rearing high at her back, her eyes huge and full of pain.

"Take care of Morgan for me," she whispered, her voice too hoarse to carry.

The big man stared up at her. "You just be sure you come back to him. That little boy needs you. Don't leave him an orphan. You know what *that's* like."

She glared at him and opened her mouth to spit a retort. Yet the tears in his eyes brought up her short. She could feel the love he emitted, his familiar, soothing touch on her mind, and she understood. He was not being willfully cruel; he was reminding her of her responsibilities, of what she stood to lose, and he was telling her that, despite what she had lost, she was not alone. She could hardly berate him for that, even though it stabbed a sharp pain through the bleeding wound in her heart. She closed her eyes against it.

"I will not throw my life away, Hal, I promise you that. But I must avenge him. I could never forgive myself otherwise. Wish me luck, dear friend, and pray for me. Pray for Robin."

She wheeled Drum away, the stallion tossing his head, laying back his ears at the other horses in his path. They parted for him with no direction from their riders; he was herd-leader, obeyed without question. She nudged him to the front of the company and turned to ensure they were all ready.

Elias was the last to mount, having exchanged a final word with the General. He clasped Blaine's hand, their earlier argument forgotten, and swung up onto Darius. The mahogany-bay mouthed his bit, sensing his rider's excitement. Sullyan sensed it too and frowned. This was what Elias had craved for so long in the depths of his heart—to join her in battle and fight at her side. Only once had it happened before, on a journey from Loxton when a raiding party of demons directed by the Baron ambushed them under the cover of a rainstorm. Sullyan had fought to defend him, along with the rest of his escort, and he had drawn his sword alongside her in his own defense. He was skilled, she knew, but this was different. Now he was part of her company, under her orders, and she was responsible for him. He would join with her men, lend his strength to theirs in the raid, each defending the other. He would play his part or he would die—as a swordsman, not a king.

She studied him as he heeled Darius into place behind Dexter, as he had been told to do, and set his face to the wind. There was no time now to question her decision to take him. She turned, gave the order to move out, and the whole unit stepped forward as one, following her out into the snow.

Despite her conviction and concentration, she felt the weight of eyes on her back. Blaine and Bull watched from the lee of the barracks, grim-faced and hard-eyed. From a window in the Manor, alone and tearful, Rienne stared into the distance long after her man had vanished from sight.

✤ ✤ ✤ ✤ ✤

The company moved into the extent of the Manor lands, riding in pairs down the track leading toward the ridge. Hoods were raised against the cold, but the wind still flayed their cheeks. Elias kept station to the right of Wil, who had been paired with him and instructed to keep an eye on the King. Before him rode Dexter and Sullyan, behind him streamed the rest of the men. At the head of his section, Cal rode with Pengar, the younger man still unsure of himself, still dwelling on his failure in Daret and the disappearance of his close friend, Col. He intended to use this raid as an opportunity to erase the stain of failure for the both of them and win back their tarnished honor. Cal could see the light of fanatical determination in his eyes. He had offered to partner Pen on this raid in order to watch over the young man in case he should sell himself short. Death was often too easy an option when living might serve the greater purpose.

In an orderly line they rode up the ridge, bunching closer together when the space permitted. Down the incline, they made for the river, Sullyan's favored location for a trans-Veil tunnel. She reined Drum to a halt on the snow-covered banks, the big black snuffling at the ice that crusted the edges. She waited until they were closely gathered before reaching within for the General's pattern. Elias watched and waited, his excitement growing. She could only hope he would contain it. This was a serious business and he must concentrate on the wider issue of bringing to justice an escaped murderer and traitor. Pushing him from her mind, she communed with the General, requesting knowledge of her destination before she opened the Veils.

Just above the ice-rimed water, a shimmer grew in the freezing air, glittering in the failing light, eerie in its opalescent beauty. Some of the men caught their breath. No matter how many times they traveled it, the substance between the realms never failed to fascinate and humble them. It still had the same effect on Sullyan, even after twenty-seven years of life.

Yet she was not thinking of such things right now. She had her directions from the General. Casting out her power, she took hold of the substrate and forged a way through, anchoring her structure in the fields of Bordenn. Lerric's province was mainly flat pastureland with only a few gentle hills swelling to the north as it met the border with Garon. Daret was in the southwest of the province, not many miles from the sea, and its surroundings were flat and featureless. Sullyan intended for them to emerge in open countryside, well away from the town, and trust to the falling darkness to cover their strange arrival. Holding the tunnel, she gestured for Dexter to lead the men through.

Once the last man had passed her, she nudged Drum with her heels. The big black moved forward, unfazed by the gray shimmer around him. Drum was one of only a few horses who could travel the Veils by himself at need. His full brother, Mandias, now thirty years old and retired, had the skill, as did Robin's horse, Tobias. Sullyan had hoped that Darius, another of Mandias's colts, might also show the trait, but so far he had not. She collapsed the structure behind her mount's black tail and emerged into a snowstorm beside her shivering men.

"Where are we, Wil?" she shouted against the wind.

The corporal scanned what he could see of his surroundings, narrowing his eyes against the stinging snow. "I reckon we're about three miles from Daret, Colonel," he yelled back. "I think this is the road I followed. If we carry on, we should see the town on our left. The barns we're aiming for will be alongside the road."

Pulling their cloaks tightly about them and watching as best they could, they forged on into the evening. The snow packed in behind the horses' hooves, and within a few minutes of their passing, no traces remained. Sullyan kept Wil beside her and set the fastest pace the horses could manage, warming their muscles and keeping them from freezing. She had decided to aim for the barns where Col and Pengar had been found, for despite Pen's reluctance to see them again, it was their best option for keeping the horses safe.

Whether they should take them to the palace or not had been the subject of long debate between Sullyan and her men. She did not intend to ride up to the gates of the palace. For one thing, it would announce their presence when she favored stealth, and for another, their mounts would be vulnerable when the fighting moved inside the walls. All the Manor stallions were battle-trained. They could be left unattended and would defend themselves against strangers. If a swift escape became necessary, Sullyan could summon Drum through her link with the horse and he would lead the others toward them, sparing them the necessity of carrying their wounded through the snow.

After a couple of miles, Wil gave a shout, pointing ahead. "Those are the lights from the town, Colonel. The barns should be just up here on the left."

Sure enough, the solid shape of snow-covered barns soon loomed out of the darkness. They slowed the horses and Sullyan sent Ralf and Tad on ahead to scout for occupants, although she was sure there would be none. The barns were for fodder storage, not livestock, and at this hour of the day and in this weather, any livestock would have been tended hours ago. Nevertheless, she did not intend to take any chances. She breathed a sigh of relief when Tad touched her mind, giving the all-clear. She signaled the men and rode up to the barns.

Once safely inside, they dismounted, brushing snow from the horses' coats so they would not get chilled as they waited. The dark barn was rickety but relatively draft-free. There was plenty of stored hay and some of the men pulled sheaves of it down, spreading it out for the beasts.

"Leave them harnessed." Sullyan gave Drum a final pat, telling him, "Be sure to come when I call you!" The stud ignored her and lipped up a mouthful of hay. She turned to regard the men gathered before her. Eyes gleamed in the darkness and breath plumed white. Every little sound from their movement and chime from their steel rang too loudly in the calm of the barn. But there was no one to hear them as she spoke her final words before beginning their move on the palace.

"Remember your sections and watch your captains. Tad, Cal, we will have to shield as we approach the palace. The Baron may be expecting us and I would not give him advance warning. Once we are in and separated, keep me apprised of your movements, especially if you find Taran. Sofira and Lerric are to be taken alive and unharmed at all costs, but the Baron is to be left to me. If anyone engages him without my express instruction, he will forfeit his place in this company. Do you understand me?"

Her gaze swept them all and came to rest on Elias. The King had the grace to flush. He nodded his acceptance, but she held his gaze briefly, just to be sure he had heard her. The steady return of his stare despite the heat in his face satisfied her, and she slid her sword to her hip. They belted their cloaks tightly and the men moved behind their captains. Sullyan led the first section, Dexter the second, and Cal led the third. Swiftly and silently, they left the barn, emerging into the stinging, howling wind of the snowstorm.

"This is getting worse." Elias's comment barely reached Sullyan's ear, although he strode close to her side. She tossed him a look, but didn't trouble to reply. It was hard enough slogging through the snow without finding the breath to speak. The King's expression turned grim and he fell silent, trudging at her side.

It was just over a mile to the palace from the outskirts of the town, and the way was deserted. Due to the darkness and the heavy snow, it was impossible to tell whether anyone had come this way earlier, but Sullyan's opinion was that the Baron would not permit forays to the local tavern tonight. After his provocative message to her that morning, he would be anticipating her attack. She fully expected to find Lerric's entire guard on high alert and sentries patrolling the walls. When they finally made out the black spires of the palace against the slightly lighter skyline, she halted the men and had them use their eyes, scanning for any flicker of firelight on weapons to pinpoint wary sentries. Disturbingly, there was nothing.

She called Dexter forward. "I know you formed a low opinion of Lerric's men while you were here, but surely he set night watches?"

Dexter's eyes never left the palace walls. "He did, Colonel, although they were never what I'd call alert. I got the impression no one had ever assaulted the palace. It was more for show than defense."

While this might be true of an old and complacent king, she knew it would be folly to assume the Baron felt as secure. The only unknown was whether Reen had sufficient control over Lerric to force the king to change his attitude toward the palace defenses. Sullyan was not prepared to gamble that he did not. Sofira would see the sense of increased vigilance, even if her father proved unwilling. Sullyan gestured to Dexter. "Send scouts. Until we know where the watchers are, I will not approach too closely."

Dexter nodded and moved away, issuing orders over the blast of the wind. The rest of them huddled together while the four scouts, one of them young Tad, ran swiftly and separately toward the palace walls. She did not have long to wait before one of them came racing back.

"We can see no sentries on the walls, Colonel. We approached unchallenged and listened very carefully. No one heard anything beyond the walls, and neither could we see any reflections from braziers. The courtyard's deserted."

Sullyan cast a puzzled gaze at Dexter and Elias. "How can that be? Surely he cannot be foolish enough to believe himself so secure? Why make such a challenge as he did this morning if not to provoke an attack?"

Elias snorted. "I wouldn't put anything past that bastard. If he was here during my visit, laughing at us right beneath our feet, he probably thinks himself invincible. He's hardly sane or rational, after all. Besides, would he expect you to respond so quickly? As you said, he's not skilled with his powers. He probably doesn't know how fast you can move a body of men."

Dexter shook his head. "It's more likely he's laid some kind of trap, Colonel. This is just something to confuse us. He's probably got men hiding, waiting to circle and surround us."

That was Sullyan's thinking, also. Elias was wrong. Reen did know how swiftly men could move between the Veils. Both Robin and Taran were experienced in conveying forces through the substrate. She had to assume the Baron knew what they knew. So, then: a trap. Yet one she was forced to spring, or they would get nowhere.

She gestured the men forward. They approached the dark palace cautiously, finding the scout's report accurate. The three men who had remained by the walls had seen and heard nothing while waiting for their comrades. Sullyan signaled Dexter to put the men into action.

The palace walls were not overly high, only the height of two tall men. With lookouts posted to watch for the enemy, Tad, Okin, and Gart scrambled onto the shoulders of their tallest comrades and were boosted to the top of the wall, ready to drop back down at the first sign of resistance. All three men disappeared into the compound and Sullyan held her breath, waiting for the noise of alarm—an alarm that was never raised. She shivered with foreboding as the bolts of the main gates slid back. This was ominously easy so far.

Tad met her at the gate and he pulled the heavy wooden leaves aside as the company entered the dark courtyard. It was completely deserted, with virgin snow covering the cobbles, showing only the tracks made by Tad, Okin, and Gart. Sullyan shook her head at Elias's puzzled glance. She did not like this eerie silence and lack of resistance either. The men gathered around her as she took in the derelict appearance of Lerric's palace, silent in the strange surroundings.

She beckoned Dexter and murmured to him. He passed her order on and a man sprinted for the stables off to their left. Sullyan turned to Elias, who was staring at the palace with a strange expression. "What is it?"

"It's *all* boarded up. When we were here before, it was only the lower floor. Sofira told us it had become unsafe and needed repair. But now *all* the windows are covered. You can't see a chink of light or a flicker of candle. Do you suppose it's been abandoned? If they discovered the foundations were unsound, they'd have to leave, wouldn't they? It would explain why there are no guards. I know he has grown lax, but surely not even Lerric would allow his men to shirk night duty."

She frowned. "Dexter?"

"It's a possibility, Colonel. All the men we spoke to were wary of the lower floor. They had been told to avoid it because it was so unsafe. Not even the servants went near it, apparently."

Sullyan mused on their words, although she had her own ideas as to why the lower floor was off-limits to servants and soldiers. She could also think of a very good reason why the Baron would block out the daylight. His terrible ordeal at the silver pool had left him scarred in many ways.

The man who had gone to the stables returned before she could offer an opinion and confirmed her hope. "He's there, Colonel. He's thirsty, but well enough. I found some water for him. There are a few other horses, too."

Sullyan sighed with relief. That was one weight off her mind. "I thank you, Rhyn." To Elias's quizzical look, she said, "The Major's mount, Tobias. I wanted to make sure he was safe. I do not intend to leave him here. Robin would not w—" She swallowed, continuing quickly, "His presence here confirms that the palace has not been deserted. The lower floor was only unsafe due to the Baron's presence. The other story was concocted to keep prying eyes away while he formulated his plans and gained his strength. Now he sits within, awaiting our attack and brooding on his revenge."

Elias stared at her. "And you're going to walk right in? Don't you think we need a new strategy now we've seen the place? It's going to be as black as Perdition in there with no light! We need more men, Colonel. Who knows how many he has waiting for us? It's suicide to go in there now."

She gazed at the palace, avid hunger making her sharp. "If you wish to back out, Elias, I can easily send you home. You are forgetting your oath. You swore to follow me and obey me as a member of my company. Do you now retract it?"

The men watched their King, fearing an outburst. Yet Sullyan's strength, determination, and the deep hurt behind her eyes silenced Elias's protests. He backed down, amazing the men by affording her a salute.

She glanced at him briefly, wasting no more breath upon the matter. "Dexter, Cal. We will enter by the east tower as we planned. It will be dark, as Elias pointed out; find brands to light your way if you can. If not, go slowly and silently. Dex, you take the lower floor and be extremely careful. Cal, you will take the upper floor and be sure, both of you, to check *every* room and cupboard, no matter how small. Any resistance you encounter is to be neutralized, but stop short of killing if you can. Lerric's men may have been forced into this. Given the opportunity, they may well surrender. If you can imprison them rather than kill them, do so. And if you find … anyone, then contact me. Just remember, leave the Baron to me."

She turned her gaze on the King. "Elias, stay close. I do not want the Baron's men taking you captive. It will be bad enough if they use Taran against us. With you as well, they would have all the power necessary to force me to yield. Now, swords at the ready and stay alert. Let us hunt this traitor down."

Elias drew his sword and followed her up the slick tower steps. The stiffness of her back and waves of furious purpose that flowed from her as she prepared to meet her bitterest enemy were palpable. She could not imagine what they would find within the sinister, darkened palace. She opened the outer door, which gave easily, and slipped silently into the eerie darkness.

Chapter Five

Once inside the palace, Sullyan's company separated into their prearranged groups. Dexter had Tad in his band to enable him to contact Sullyan at need. Cal led the other for the same reason. The men gathered behind their leaders and prepared to search through the darkness.

No fires burned in the hearths lining the hallway that faced them, but there were unlit torches in sconces and Sullyan had the groups take one apiece. She risked a small amount of power to call Fire to the torches. If the deserted nature of the palace was designed to lure her in, then the Baron already knew of their presence. The slight comfort afforded by the torches and the advantages of clearer sight outweighed the disadvantage of alerting an enemy. She gave a final nod to Dexter and Cal, and the three sections split to make their own advance.

Dexter and his group soon found the hidden doorway that led to the lower floor. It was covered by a heavy black drape, and it was also locked. The other two groups had already disappeared into the gloom by the time one of the men hacked away the lock, and Dexter led his men down into the stygian depths of the narrow stair. Sixteen men crowded at his back, Tad protected in their midst. The youth was a talented swordsman, despite being the youngest of the group; it was his Artesan abilities that led the men to cluster around him. An instant link to their Colonel should not be unnecessarily risked.

Reaching the bottom stair, Ralf held the torch aloft so the light spread as far as possible, his ginger hair reflecting the dancing fire. There were other unused torches on the walls and some of the men took them down, lighting them from Ralf's brand. They searched the darkness silently, alert for any sound, scanning the closed doorways and taking in the freezing and abandoned air of the place.

Surrounded by cold stone and ragged, fading tapestries, Dexter wrinkled his nose in disgust. A nauseating odor pervaded and stung his nostrils. Judging by the reactions of the other men, and especially young Tad, they could smell it, too.

"Gods, what *is* that stench?" he muttered, giving the signal to move forward. He remembered the outbreak of sores he had seen on some of Lerric's guard, and suddenly wondered if they had all succumbed to some dreadful winter plague. It would explain the apparent abandonment of the palace, and also the terrible reek that clogged their throats. He gestured to the man on his right and sent a small party toward the first door they could see, while he and the rest of his group approached the one to their left.

Dexter's doorway gave onto a suite of rooms, all pitch-dark except for the light from the wavering torches. With Tad at his shoulder, he set them to searching the suite, which showed signs of recent occupation. They opened cupboards and prodded behind drapes, finding nothing of interest. He was about to collect them and return to the hallway when a shout and the sudden clash of steel from outside made him jump.

"Quickly!" he yelled, as the sounds of fighting grew louder. They all sprinted for the door, but it suddenly slammed shut on them, trapping them inside. They wasted valuable minutes wrestling with whoever held the door shut. As it opened inward, and all the bolts were on their side, they eventually won the contest and spilled furiously into the hallway, finding themselves facing an indeterminate number of guardsmen, shadowy in the flickering light.

Their comrades were still inside the first room they had entered and were under attack, while the swordsmen facing Dexter's group filled the hallway, preventing them reaching their friends. Dexter yelled orders at his men and sent them to attack, the cries of their fellows in the right-hand room galvanizing their efforts.

The swordsmen facing them were not highly skilled, or maybe their stamina was low. They were also not as numerous as Dexter feared. They gave way before his force like corn before the reaper, and soon the Kingsmen forged a way through, coming to the defense of their beleaguered comrades. The enemies in the hallway, those still alive, were quickly cowed, and Dexter ordered Tad and Gart to guard them while he dealt with those attacking the rest of his men.

Caught between two forces, Lerric's men either succumbed or surrendered, throwing their weapons to the ground and standing sullenly before their captors. Dexter leaned on his sword once the fighting was over, wiping the blood from a shallow cut on his sword arm. He counted heads. Only ten men had faced his sixteen. The shadows and narrow confines had made it seem like more. Six of the ten were still alive, although one was fading fast. Of the Kingsmen, none had been killed, but Charrin would be lucky to walk again. He had taken a nasty slash to the leg and Dexter thought his hamstring had probably gone. Swearing in anger, he kicked the nearest downed foeman as he crossed to Charrin, bending down to see to the wounded man.

"I'll be all right, Captain." Charrin clutched his leg, his face white, his voice hoarse.

"Yeah, sure." Dexter ripped cloth from one of the dead guards' cloaks to bind the wound. The thin cloth tore easily and it soon stemmed the bleeding. "You'll have to wait here while we search the rest of this floor. You can watch over this lot for me."

Dexter had his men disarm and truss the living guardsmen, then he sat Charrin next to the door with his sword across his knees. He left the man with a torch and instructions to sing out should he have need of them. Charrin grinned up at him, his face drained and his eyes full of pain, yet glad to be left with a task to perform. Dexter clapped him gently on the shoulder and drew the rest away.

They continued down the cold, dark hallway, shoving doors open and exploring empty rooms. They stayed together in case of other attacks, but were not disturbed again. Soon, they arrived at a door that was different from all the rest in that it had bolts on the outside, and even through the wood it exuded a smell of stale urine and fear-induced sweat. Tad swayed suddenly on his feet. The Captain placed a hand on his shoulder to steady him, registering the anguish behind Tad's eyes.

"What is it, lad?"

Tad turned to look at him, his face faintly green. He shook his head slightly. "I can't say, Captain," he whispered, horror lacing his tone, "but you wouldn't want to have experienced whatever happened behind that door."

Dexter's mouth formed a grim line and he looked meaningfully at his men. They nodded their understanding. Dexter pushed Tad behind him and reached out a hand to draw back the bolts.

The room that lay revealed to Ralf's torch was unremarkable in its plainness, yet Tad gasped in shock and reeled as if a gale had suddenly blasted him. Gart had to catch him from behind or he might have fallen. His face was drawn as if in pain. Dexter waited until he was steadier before entering the room.

He gazed around at the cool embers of a recently-dead fire, the unnamable stains on the floor, the lengths of chain hanging from rings sunk into the far wall, and the stark and empty bed, also adorned with chains and manacles. He walked slowly forward, a strangled moan from Tad stopping him before he reached the bed.

He swung to face the boy. "What, Tad? What do you feel?"

The youth, white and shaking, took two trembling steps into the room. His eyes were full of horror, fixed on the grubby mattress of the bed as if mesmerized. Blindly, he stretched out a hand. "Robin!" His voice was strangled, pleading, and he seemed unaware he had spoken.

Dexter grasped his arm, shaking him urgently. "Are you saying the Major was here, lad?" He interposed his body between Tad's eyes and the bed. "Can you tell us what happened?"

With visible effort, Tad dragged his gaze to Dexter's, and the Captain received the full force of the boy's anguish. A swell of grief-stricken tears threatened to unman him and he had to turn away. Tad's violent trembling and the sweat beading his face told its own story, and suddenly Dexter didn't want to know any more. He let Tad go and moved away, struggling to find his voice in a throat suddenly tight and painful. He sent the men out of the terrible room and closed the door firmly, cutting off some of Tad's distress. The boy began to breathe more easily, although he was still white and sweating.

Another door sat to their right and, when opened, it revealed a small, plain room with a stout wooden door opposite the first. This one was secured by bolts and an iron latch with a ring handle. Dexter had seen it before, only from the other side, and knew even before he opened it that it led into the deserted courtyard. A swift glance outside confirmed that no enemies lurked to cut off their retreat. He fastened the door once more and turned to his men.

"Right, lads, we've seen where the Baron kept his captives, and you know what probably happened to them. Distressing as it is, we still have work to do. Let's make very sure we've examined every inch of this floor and left no hiding places unexplored. Charrin will let us know if company arrives. It's time to start searching for hidden doors, cellars, that sort of thing. Get yourselves torches, and get on with it. Tad, you're with me."

They did as he told them and it was some consolation to Tad, although admittedly not much, that he was the one to find the hidden door that led to a dank and musty downward stair. He wasn't surprised when Dexter refused his request to be the first man down it.

✣ ✣ ✣ ✣ ✣

Cal led his fifteen men toward the large sweeping stair to the left of the main hallway. His men also found themselves torches and these lit the backs of Sullyan's group as they vanished into the distance, searching methodically through the many rooms on the main floor of the darkened palace. Cal sucked in a breath, trying not to inhale the foul miasma that drifted occasionally on the stale air, and led his men up the stairs.

They emerged into a broad, carpeted hallway studded with many doors on the right-hand side. These all turned out to be storerooms, mostly small, for fresh linen and pillows, bedding and drapery. At the far end of that hallway, they discovered the narrow service stairs leading back down to the lower floors. He had his men thoroughly examine all the storerooms, even to the extent of driving swords into various piles of luxurious bedding. Then they retraced their steps and crossed a short transverse passageway on the left, which led to yet another broad hall.

This one was more sumptuous than the first. The shadows cast by the torches flickered over gold leaf, polished brass, and silver door handles. The carpet was as rich as the one in the other hall, and fabulous tapestries adorned the stone walls. Although all the windows had been boarded over, their rich red drapes still hung in graceful folds right to the floor. Firelight winked in the silver of lamps affixed to the walls, and the whole place smelled more wholesome and lived in. Despite its obvious comforts, this hall was as silent and eerie as the rest.

Pengar gripped Cal's arm.

Cal turned to his comrade. Pen put a finger to his lips and they all strained their ears. Cal was about to shake his head and move on when they heard the sound that had caught Pen's attention: A woman's soft sobbing.

Cal examined the various doors along the hallway. They were ornate and widely spaced. To the right of where they stood, the nearest door showed Lerric's hunting dog emblem emblazoned in marquetry and gold inlay. To their left, the decoration was of swans and flowers. Realizing these were the private chambers of the king and his daughter, Cal nodded his men toward the sconces in the wall. Those with torches deposited them, leaving their hands free. Cal directed them toward the left-hand door and they approached it cautiously.

Listening carefully with his ear to the door, Cal thought he heard faint movement within, and maybe a soft moan. He drew back, and motioned for Brant, a big, raw-boned man, to open the door. The rest gathered round, ready for what they might find. They were pre-empted. Before Brant's hand could close about the latch, the door burst open and a body of swordsmen came roaring into the corridor, weapons slashing. Brant was lucky not to lose his hand in the first flurry, but the cut across his fingers still severed the last two. He dropped his blade, gasping in pain, but retained enough presence of mind to use his body to barge the nearest swordsman, who was dispatched by another of Cal's men. Furious in his pain, Brant took his sword in his left hand, wielding it clumsily but effectively.

The fighting spilled out into the corridor, Lerric's men pressing hard. One of them, a hulking black-haired man with calloused, meaty hands, fastened avid eyes on Pengar and fought his way toward him. He grinned as he came and Pen gave a gasp of recognition. His blade rang under the large man's assault, but he twisted it aside, bringing it back across the man's belly in a savage cut that should have spilled his guts. His opponent grunted as he dodged, but still found breath for speech.

"Well, if it ain't the other little drunkard!" He aimed a slash at Pengar's face, forcing Pen to duck. "Come back for more, have you? Want some of what your mate got?"

Pen's face went purple and he panted, lunging at the man. "Why did you do that, you bastard? What did we ever do to you?"

The large man grunted, evading Pen's lunge and coming back with his own. The tip of his blade scored Pen's chest, making him yelp. "Oh, nothing. Gave us a good story, though, didn't you? Gave us what we wanted. Gave us your pretty Major."

"*What*?" Pen roared his fury and attacked with speed, hoping to catch the man off-guard. But his enemy was ready for him and sidestepped neatly despite his bulk, slicing through Pen's cloak and opening a gash in his side. It wasn't deep, but the icy pain of it cooled Pen's anger. He realized what the other was doing and made himself step back, forcing himself to calm. He was well trained and this was what he had come here for. He was being granted the opportunity to revenge himself on one of his bitterest enemies and he wasn't going to waste it. He had promised himself for Col and he would not let his friend down.

His opponent saw the change in Pen's face and smiled grimly as he danced back out of the Manor swordsman's reach.

"Your mate thought he could take me, too," he taunted, letting Pen come at him again. He parried Pen's stoke, ignoring the small cut inflicted on his cheek. "Fought well, he did, I'll give him that. Even though his mate was down and there was nothing he could do, still he fought well. But not well enough. I skewered him like a pig."

The strength behind the swing that followed these vicious words caught Pengar by surprise, and he barely saved his arm. He twisted violently to the side, taking the blade on his forearm. The cut went to the bone, but did not break it. The agony nearly sent Pen into a frenzy, but he refused to let it overcome his senses. Remembering his training, he channeled it into strength and came at his opponent with a coordinated flurry of cuts designed to wrong-foot him and place him on the defensive. It was a set piece that would not have fooled a Kingsman, but Lerric's man did not have the benefit of Ardoch's coaching and did not know about the feint at the end of the move. It was so beautifully executed Master Ardoch himself would have found no fault with it. Neither did Pengar, for it opened his enemy's defenses and gave him the chance it was designed to create. He took it decisively, passing his blade cleanly through his opponent's heart, killing him instantly.

Cal saw the killing stroke and briefly wondered about the smile that touched the hulking swordsman's lips as he died, but he had no time to ponder it with the fighting still going on around him. He joined up with Pen, the two of them making short work of their next opponent. The man surrendered, throwing his weapon to the ground, standing with heaving chest next to three others who had also yielded once it became obvious the Kingsmen had won. Cal noticed the dreadful slash on Pengar's arm and took him aside, leaving the others to deal with their captives.

He examined the wound with dismay. "You were lucky not to lose that arm!" He sat Pen on the floor and crouched beside him to bind the arm, noting Pen's look of satisfaction.

"I got him, though," Pen managed through clenched teeth. "I got the bastard who killed Col, one of those who drugged us. Now we need to find the other."

Cal put his hand on Pen's shoulder, glad the man had found some ease. "Don't you worry about that now. You're doing no more fighting today. You just sit there and keep Brant company. Watch over these bastards while we check the rest of the rooms. I doubt we'll be disturbed again."

He left Pen and Brant and called the others over. The four of Lerric's men left alive were disarmed, trussed, and kicked to one side. The six dead ones were left where they lay, their blood soaking into the expensive carpeting. Two men retrieved their torches from the sconces as Cal moved toward the door that he suspected led to Lerric's chambers and flung it open. No one rushed them, and a swift glance into the room showed it to be empty. Leaving the door open, they left these chambers for later and returned to the first one, from which the guards had come. Cal entered cautiously, wary of hidden enemies, but no one rushed them. Cal motioned his men forward. They searched the room, throwing back the shadows with the yellow flame of their torches, hissing in shock when they saw what lay on the great canopied bed.

Chapter Six

Sullyan and Elias led their group as they systematically searched the rooms of the main floor. They heard Dexter's man hammering at the locked door to the stairs and knew that whoever waited for them in the absolute darkness of this warren-like trap was now fully aware of their presence. It couldn't be helped.

Elias identified each room before they entered it, showing Sullyan which were guest-chambers, which were offices, which were drawing rooms. All were investigated and all proved to be empty. None showed signs of recent use, corroborating Lerric's tale of abandonment by nobles who preferred to look after their own estates through this unseasonably harsh winter. As they moved through the dark, neglected rooms, Sullyan wondered what would become of Bordenn once this was all over. Elias would never permit either Lerric or Sofira to remain in power after this latest treachery, so he would have to appoint a governor from among Lerric's senior nobles. There was no one left of Lerric's line save Eadan and Seline.

As they penetrated deeper into Lerric's palace, Sullyan grew more and more uneasy. A strange feeling she could not name gnawed at her senses. Partly it was fury, for this was where her life mate had breathed his last under unspeakable torture, and somewhere in this deadly place lurked the monster who had devoured his soul. Her heart clamored for vengeance; her spirit cried for mercy.

Yet she could not locate her enemy, and this gave rise to frustration. Shielded as she was, still she sent forth probes; slim, delicate slivers of power, just enough to touch a wary mind, just enough to give her that edge. Failing continually, her fury grew.

She also felt dread, fear, reluctance. The more empty rooms they searched, the fewer remained. Their quarry was running to ground, and soon they would unearth him. Except he wasn't running and *they* were the quarry.

This aspect of her growing unease affected her the most. The palace was a trap and she had entered it willingly. She was dancing to another's tune, and her choices were limited. Nevertheless, she advanced, caught in this master's game, compelled by love and justice. Her wounded soul bled with every step she took.

They remained unchallenged and unhindered throughout the length of their search. Nothing moved to dismay them, nothing sounded to alert them. The rooms were all silent, the hallways deserted, no signs of life even in the private rooms Elias had so recently visited. The men of Sullyan's company strode at her back, eyes alert, swords at the ready, muscles tensed for action. Action they were denied until, at the very last, they came to a large iron-bound door proudly displaying the hunting dog emblem of client-king Lerric.

Limp standards hung on either side of the door, luxurious fabrics worked with gold thread suspended from poles of silver. A horn rested in a niche in the wall, just waiting for the herald to sound it. But the herald was absent and the standards hung still, cold air whispering about them.

"Lerric's throne room." Elias's body quivered with tension. He had caught Sullyan's frustration and the futility of their search so far was jangling his overstretched nerves. "Anteroom first and then the main hall. It's large, even by Loxton standards."

Sullyan didn't reply and the King cast her a glance, unwilling to intrude on her thoughts. Her men stood behind her in silence.

Finally, she spoke, her voice sounding distant and ragged. "They await us in the anteroom."

Elias's head came up eagerly, like a hound scenting prey. "The Baron?"

She shook her head, her expression fixed and grim. She brought up her sword. "His guard." She turned to Elias and spoke curtly. "Stay by me. Remember your oath."

It was an unmistakable order and he nodded before turning his attention back to the door. The others shifted behind him, eager for action; anything to end this uncertainty. Those carrying torches left them in sconces or extinguished them. The hallway faded around them.

Wil came abreast of Sullyan and laid one hand on the door, weapon held ready in the other. Sullyan took a deep breath, held it, let it out. On the next inhalation, she nodded to Wil, who took hold of the latch and pushed open the door.

The anteroom was large, as large as Elias's dining hall. Like the rest of the palace, it was in darkness, but torchlight from the hallway flickered faintly on steel deep within the room. The stirring of feet could be heard, the intake of breath. But no one came to challenge them, no one came to fight. Sullyan let her fury build. It would seem she would have to carry the fighting to them.

So be it.

"Gentlemen. Let us make an end."

Her eyes on her foe, she deliberately advanced, Elias at her right shoulder, Wil at her left. The men fanned out to either side of her, forming a line, watching warily as they passed through the doors.

Faint torchlight revealed the force ranged against them. Wide eyes glittered, steel glinted. It was impossible to tell accurate numbers, but Sullyan thought there were more than she had with her. No matter. Her men were well trained and loyal; their opponents were neither. She had no doubt who would prevail. Her only concern was to win through these servants and continue her search. She moved out in front of her band, fixing her eyes on the opposing commander, catching his gaze and showing him her intent.

Captain Bassan stood and waited for her, automatically assessing his chances. Every man at his back was the Baron's creature—he knew that now. He had been shown just how his master ruled them, and he knew his fate should he let the scarecrow down. His thoughts of desertion had faded away, drained from him during those horrific moments in the presence of such powerful evil. He had been touched but not taken, and he knew it was for one reason only: to direct their stand here in this room.

His life depended on his success, but the horror of it was that his death depended on it too. Doomed if he won and doomed if he lost, Bassan had nowhere to go and only a clean death to gain. There was no possible escape for one touched by the scarecrow. His desperation showed on his face, but the gloom of the palace hid it from those advancing on him. He caught Sullyan's gaze and registered her intent. Without waiting for her to signal her men, he raised his blade in a kind of salute and stepped straight into a lunge for her breast.

Ready for the fray, the Kingsmen took Bassan's attack as their cue to engage. Steel rang loud in the silence of the anteroom, gasps and grunts filling the tension with sound. Elias leaped to Sullyan's side as she swung to block Bassan's lunge. Mindful of her unusual talent, he didn't crowd her; many hours of fencing with her under

Ardoch's critical eye had drummed in to him the necessity of giving her space.

It was just as well, for Bassan's first lunge was a feint. The sword that came for her breast twisted aside at the last minute and went for the King. It was only Sullyan's quick reflexes as she changed hands mid-stroke that saved Elias from an early grave. Elias riposted, beating Bassan back with a furious charge. A man to Bassan's right attacked Sullyan, filling the gap left by his captain, and with her attention diverted she had to trust the King to defend himself. He was a creditable swordsman, well able to hold his own, but these men were being goaded and had no fear of death. She could only hope Elias could see that.

✣ ✣ ✣ ✣ ✣

The fighting swayed back and forth, the line of Kingsmen holding, their opponents ragged in turn. Bassan did not impose a strategy on his men. They attacked the line as they could, holding no formation and leaving themselves open to their more coordinated opponents. Fighting in pairs and supporting each other in disciplined movements, Sullyan's company took advantage of every lapse in defense by the enemy swordsmen, often killing the man to their right rather than the one in front of them. Seeing this, Bassan's men grouped closer together as their numbers dwindled, yet this allowed the men in Sullyan's line to surround them, beginning the final attack.

Wil, fighting on Sullyan's left, ran his man through and stepped over the body as he forced his way forward. Lerric's men were being pushed backward as they were herded together, and Wil suddenly found himself facing someone he knew. He had expected this. He had been here with Elias's escort and had played cards and swapped stories with some of these men. Mostly, they were blurred faces behind a sword in the darkness, enemies to be overcome. But this one face was different. This man had meant something, and Wil could not ignore him. He had thought better of Bassan than this. He knew the Captain had envied the Kingsmen, and he suddenly wondered if he had found a way to end this senseless rout.

Engaging the man with defensive strokes, Wil called out Bassan's name.

Bassan jerked at Wil's call and his eyes focused on the younger man's face. Wil saw him go pale and knew he'd been recognized. Yet the Captain's attack didn't falter. If anything, he grew more frantic, throwing himself on Wil's blade as if inviting him to make the kill. The Corporal fended him off, trying to disarm him, and was rewarded with a despairing cry.

"Captain," Wil called urgently, "call off your men! We can end this. There's no need for you to die. It's the Baron we want, not you. Call them off, give the order to disengage, and you'll be spared."

Bassan ignored him and lunged again, a desperate stroke that went wide of the mark. Wil frowned as he parried the clumsy swipe, an automatic response that wasn't strictly necessary. Bassan swung again, with more skill this time, and very nearly decapitated Wil, who had hoped for a better reaction.

"Don't make me do this," Wil pleaded, attacking Bassan's undefended left, his blade blocked by the man's return stroke. "Bassan! Can't you hear me? Don't you want to surrender? Don't you want to join us?"

Bassan gave an incredulous snarl along with a vicious sideways cut. "How dare you offer me such riches! Don't you know I'm doomed? Don't you know I could never take up such an offer? What gives you the right to torture me this way?"

Wil frowned, still parrying Bassan's furious cuts. He could see rage building inside the other man and felt puzzled. He knew it was what Bassan wanted, yet the Captain fought on, roaring in anger, slashing with scant regard for skill or strength. Wil stayed on the defensive, trying to give him time to calm down, but this only seemed to make matters worse. Then, in fury and despair, Bassan lunged hard at Wil, forcing the Corporal to raise his weapon to block. Bassan dropped his own sword at the last possible moment so that Wil's sharp blade, driven with determination, slashed toward his breast, piercing him deeply.

Wil gasped and drew his blade free. Bassan slumped to the floor. Bubbles of bloody froth burst from his lips and Wil knew he was dying. Yet he had no time to curse, no time to regret, for another blade came at him out of the darkness and he moved forward to meet it, stepping over the body beneath him and on into the fight, leaving Bassan to gasp on the floor. Soon, it was over.

✠ ✠ ✠ ✠ ✠

Dexter led his men down the dank, slippery steps behind the doorway Tad had found. It was an unpleasant place. Damp mottled the walls. Slime and mildew furred the mortar. The air was stale and foul, rank with rot and lack of oxygen. The torches guttered and threatened to die. Dexter could hear Tad's harsh breathing behind him and shared the young lad's dread. There was something evil about this place, something ominous and brooding, and Dexter tightened his grip on his sword. Not given to fanciful fears, the Captain had seen and heard enough in his thirty-one years of life to know there were dark things in this realm, and darker still in some of the others. None would take him unawares, nor any of those under his command. Not if he could help it. Wary and prepared, they descended deeper under the earth.

The dark, winding stair ended at yet another door, oak bound in iron, half-open in the wavering torchlight. The bare stone underfoot was puddled with damp, and Dexter heard water dripping somewhere nearby. That and the nervous breaths of the Manor men were the only sounds, although they strained their ears to the limit. After a few moments, Dexter approached the door, taking a burning brand from the nearest man behind him. With a meaningful glance over his shoulder, he stretched out his hand and pushed at the door.

When it finally creaked open, the uncertain light showed a bare and musty cavern carved from rock, empty save for a single chair and a moldering, leather-sprung truckle bed against the far wall.

Torchlight flickered eerily over the body lying on it.

Dexter took a sharp breath, raised the torch, and approached the figure on the bed. The flames lent a ghastly semblance of life to the gray, unmoving face, illuminating the strange wound in the chest and glinting in the dried blood crusting it. Dexter went down on one knee, his outstretched hand feeling for any signs of a pulse.

Tad gasped behind him. "Taran! Oh, gods, Captain, what's happened to him? What has that bastard done?"

Dexter felt Tad's hand on his shoulder as the youth crowded close, the other men peering over him as best they could, muttering their shock and concern. Dexter waved them back, a frown on his face, trying to concentrate on what he was doing.

"Gently, Tad, let me be for a moment. I think I … yes, there's a pulse. Faint, but there. He's alive, Tad. Only just, but still alive. See if you can contact the Colonel, will you? She'll want to know about this."

Tad moved to one side and his eyes lost their focus as he attuned to his psyche. Dexter ignored him, turning back to Taran to examine the wound in his breast. He sucked in a breath as his gaze passed over it. He had never seen anything like it. It wasn't a blade wound, that much was obvious. It was more open and ragged, almost as if something had burst out from the inside, like infection from an abscess. But if that was so, then it was the largest abscess the Captain had ever seen. His eyes narrowed as his senses told him there was something far from normal about this wound. It was deep, but not so deep as to expose the bone. It had bled, but not much, and the dried blood looked clean, not sullied by infection. Clearly, no attempt had been made to treat it or clean it, and he was fairly sure the wound alone would not account for Taran's comatose condition. He straightened and cast his gaze over the rest of Taran's body.

He immediately identified the older wound in the Adept's throat as a knife cut, and not a sharp knife at that. His wrists bore raw abrasions, consistent with him having been shackled—an image of the manacles and chains in the upper room came to the Captain's mind. But the injuries that caused him the most concern, and which probably accounted for Taran's unconsciousness, were two nasty contusions on his head; one to the left temple and one to the right. Neither had driven in bone, as far as Dexter could see, but head injuries were peculiar things and he had only a soldier's basic knowledge of healing. He would leave further investigation to Sullyan.

He turned back to Tad, who refocused and shook his head to clear it. "Well? What did she say?"

"She was occupied. They've encountered resistance, just as we did. All I got was an acknowledgement. How bad is he?"

Dexter shrugged. "Pretty bad. I don't really want to move him, but we can't leave him here. Let's get him up those stairs. We ought to get back to Charrin. I can't leave him too long on his own, either. He might succumb to shock. Ralf, Ardin, take Taran and go gently up those stairs. Tad, you take the torch."

The two men lifted Taran by his arms and legs. The Adept made no sound or movement as they carried him awkwardly up the slimy stairs. His head rolled forward on his chest, his face gray and lifeless. At the top, Dexter sent some men ahead to check that Charrin was still awake and that he hadn't been attacked. He needn't have worried; all was quiet. Charrin's charges lay as they'd been left, and the wounded swordsman was alert, albeit pale. He was pleased to see his comrades, although he tried not to show how much. Concern tightened his face as he saw what the men carried. When they laid Taran down beside him, he paled further.

"Good gods, Captain, he's never still alive? Look at the state of him! What caused that dreadful wound?"

Dexter had no answers. He stripped a cloak from one of the dead men and used it to wrap Taran's partially naked body. The Adept was terribly cold and Dexter knew that shock and cold could kill a man as easily as a sword. He detailed Tad, Ardin, and Gart to remain with Charrin while he took the rest, intending to join up with Sullyan. As they left, Tad took Taran's wounded head on his lap and prepared to reach for his mind, intending to support Taran's life force until Sullyan could see to him.

Chapter Seven

Cal ran over to the great bed, followed by his men. The source of the sobbing they had heard earlier was revealed by the torchlight. Sofira, eyes wide and wild, cringed away from the faces crowding round her. She trembled violently and was clearly unable to distinguish friend from foe. When Cal saw her terror, he motioned his men away from her. It wasn't until he sat on the edge of the bed, hoping to calm Sofira with gentle words, that he realized she wasn't alone under the tumbled quilts.

Reaching out slowly so as not to alarm her, he gently drew back the quilts, careful not to pull on those Sofira held clutched to her breast. Cal's heart lurched as he saw the blonde head, the closed eyes, the drained, pale skin. "Jinny," he murmured, drawing the bedclothes farther back. Jinny was naked, and Cal's eyes widened in shock when he saw the dreadful wound that oozed between her breasts. "Oh, gods, no!"

He dropped the quilts and reached for her neck, placing his fingers on the big vein in her throat. He could just feel a faint, stuttering flutter. Relieved, but unable to do more for her, he covered her and turned his attention back to Sofira, who gibbered in mindless panic, her mind surely broken.

He tried calling her name, but got no response. He reached for her hand, and a shriek left her lips at his touch. Yet her eyes never met his and her face showed no awareness. She was locked within her panic and that was beyond Cal's skills to tend. Hardly daring to

66

imagine what had been done to cause Sofira to flee so far inside herself, he stood and faced his men.

"Some of you go and check the king's rooms next door. The Princess has suffered some kind of trauma to make her like this; maybe Lerric has, too. I'm going to contact Sullyan and then I'll be with you."

The men turned away, still casting glances at the shuddering Princess. Cal stilled his mind, reaching for his psyche, tuning it to Sullyan's as he quested for her mind. Like Tad before him, he found her occupied, and she barely acknowledged him before pushing him away. Catching the flavor of battle from her mind, Cal ran from the chamber and called for his men.

They had found no sign of the aging king, and so, leaving Pengar and Brant to guard the Princess, Cal took the rest of his band and descended the stairs. As they reached the bottom, they found Dexter emerging from the stairway to the lower floor, and each group informed the other of what they had found. Cal was relieved that Taran was alive, but fearful when he learned of his friend's state. Dexter's vivid description of the wound in Taran's chest was all too familiar. Yet there was nothing they could do for any of the wounded, and Sullyan was now their priority. Banding together under Dexter's lead, they made for the depths of the main floor, where the sounds of fighting could be heard.

✣ ✣ ✣ ✣ ✣

With the fall of Bassan, Lerric's forces lost heart. Already bunched together by the tactics of the Kingsmen, they had little room to maneuver and were overwhelmed. Sullyan's company surrounded them and forced them to yield, taking their arms and rendering them helpless. Eight had been killed; the rest were wounded and demoralized, surrendering easily to the Manor swordsmen. Sullyan saw them secured before she turned to her men.

Tending to the wounded, none of whom were seriously hurt, she came across Wil, who knelt on the floor cradling a man's head in his arms. She crouched down beside the corporal, raising her brows in query. Wil glanced up at her and she was amazed to see his eyes were damp.

"Colonel, this is Captain Bassan." There was a hitch in Wil's voice. "He was good to me while I was here and he didn't agree with what he was ordered to do. He would have stopped it if he could, I know he would. He wanted to join us, but he couldn't find a way to do it. He was a good man, Colonel, and I've killed him."

Sullyan looked down into Bassan's glazing eyes, recognizing the approach of death. The man had blood in his lungs; he was drowning. There was no help for him. Yet there remained a faint spark of awareness in his face and she could tell he could hear them. His lips moved and she bent closer to hear what he was trying to say through the bloody froth at his mouth.

"Robin … tell Robin …"

Shock flashed through her and she gripped the dying man's arm. "What, Bassan? Tell Robin what? Where is he? Do you know what happened to him?"

Wil was alarmed by her manner, her seeming indifference to Bassan's pain. Yet Bassan was beyond pain now and did not register her presence. He gazed up into Wil's face with pleading eyes, his hand grasping feebly at the corporal's sleeve.

"Sorry, so … sorry. Couldn't … Tell … Ro—"

His head fell back and Sullyan swore. Wil sighed and laid Bassan down. He stood, nearly colliding with Elias as he turned to move away. The King raised his brows and Wil felt constrained to explain.

"He wanted to leave Lerric's service, your Majesty. He was impressed by the Major when we were here. He wanted to join us. I thought he might help us by ordering a surrender. I offered him a chance, I said we'd take him, but he didn't listen. Instead, he threw himself on my sword. I don't know why. He asked me to apologize to the Major. I only wish I could."

Wil turned away and Elias made to take his arm. Sullyan stopped him. "Let him be, Elias. We have other concerns right now."

She turned as Dexter and Cal appeared with their men, the captains relieved to find the fighting over and all their comrades safe. Sullyan called them over and heard their reports, her face falling ashen at their news. Elias held his breath when he heard of Sofira's state. "But there was no sign of Lerric?" he demanded.

Cal shook his head. "No, your Majesty. His rooms were deserted. There was only the Princess and Baroness Jinella."

Sullyan turned a grim expression on Elias. "And we still have to find Reen." She turned back to Dexter. "Take some of your men and gather the wounded. Bring them all to this floor and tend their wounds as best you can. Get them ready to travel—we may need to leave swiftly.

"Elias, I give you a choice. Either remain with Dexter and help with Sofira, or continue with me as I hunt for the Baron. Which do you choose?"

Elias didn't hesitate. "I'm coming with you. If Sofira's in a state of terror, I'm the last person she'll want to see."

Sullyan nodded and turned to the men, selecting those who would form her hunting band. The rest she left with Dexter to help with the wounded. They herded Lerric's men out of the anteroom and away down the hallway, toward a room where they could be secured. Sullyan watched them go before turning back to the matter in hand. Grimly, taking up torches once again, she and her band continued the search of the palace's main floor.

After a frustrating hour, all the rooms had been searched. She even turned the kitchens upside-down—neither cupboards nor drawers were spared. The few fearful servants they found huddled in their tiny quarters had no knowledge of the Baron or his whereabouts. They said they were forbidden to enter the palace after darkness, and had never descended to the lower floor once it was boarded. They told a tale of locked doors, eerie noises, and screams in the night. From Lerric's chamberlain, Sullyan learned of the king's increasing melancholy and fear, of Sofira's waspish temper, and the strange behavior of the guards. It all increased her conviction that the Baron was here somewhere. His ease in eluding her boiled her blood. She bade the servants leave the palace and return to their homes in the town. They fled with no further encouragement. Once they were gone, she stood by herself, staring at the walls of their quarters and cursing softly.

Once the cursing faded and Elias felt safe, he approached her. "So what now? Where else do we look?"

There was defeat in her eyes as she turned to face him. Killing the Baron would have been the anodyne she needed, a stroke executed to avenge her love, and to be deprived of this tore at her wounded soul. With a costly effort, she composed herself to reply to him.

"We will return to our comrades and see what may be done for the injured. Then we will think again."

They followed her back through the darkened hallways, alert as ever for signs of their quarry, swords at the ready. Halfway back to the throne room, Sullyan halted abruptly, her head coming up like a hound at the hunt. Elias stopped just behind her.

"What is it?" he whispered.

She held her peace before turning her head. Elias stifled a gasp at the fervor in her eyes.

"He is here."

Her voice was low and raw, the hunger and triumph easy to read. All her men heard its echo and snapped to battle readiness.

She felt Elias striving to sense what she had sensed, his own eager appetites rising. "Can you tell where he is?"

"Somewhere ahead. All alert, now! Elias, stay by me."

They crept along the darkened halls, feeling their way, listening intently. Sullyan's powerful senses strained to their limits, but the faint trace she had detected, that single telltale pulse through the substrate, was gone. It was not repeated. Unable to pin it down, she prowled, her extensive training telling her to be wary.

They approached the pitch-dark throne room, the anteroom door still ajar. The bodies of the slain lay where they had fallen, the figure of Bassan staring wide-eyed straight ahead. The wavering torchlight flickered in his dead eyes, seeming to beckon Sullyan on. She followed the line of his fixed gaze, staring straight into the throne room where Lerric's seat of office should have glinted in the flames. Yet instead of the glitter of gold and precious gems, there was only velvet blackness, an impenetrable blot squatting like a toad in the center of the floor. It drew Sullyan's eyes like a lodestone of evil. She took one tentative step forward and saw the blot move.

"Be still."

Her command hissed into the darkness. Her men obeyed her and froze, watching at her back as she walked slowly forward. All of them stared at the featureless blackness. Sullyan's hair, tawny-gold in the flames, was a beacon of brightness against that devourer of light. Red glints flickered down the length of her sword and sparked from the buckles of her harness. No sounds disturbed the silence; not of breath, not of movement. The whole world was held in thrall as she slowly paced the floor.

"Ah, the witch Brynne Sullyan."

The creaking, gleeful voice crawled forth from the Void like a snake from its pit. Waves of evil flooded her spirit, reaching back to her men and shivering their bones. The blot of black resolved itself, became a cowled, robed figure standing before the throne, its cloak of darkness spreading about the floor like a pool of black blood, swallowing all light and casting nothing back. There was something odd about the flow of the fabric that just caught at Sullyan's mind, but she had no leisure to pursue it. Her eyes were held by the face she could see; the dreadfully slumped and melted flesh, the leprous mottling of ravaged, peeling skin, the cracked and ruined lips. Lips that suddenly stretched in a terrible smile, blood and saliva mingling as the skin broke.

"You came then, my witch? I knew you would. I knew you could not resist the message I sent you."

Her heart threatened to burst with fury and her soul screamed for revenge. There he stood, not twenty paces away, at his ease in front of the throne. Every fiber of her body yearned for his blood, every beat of her heart was a hammer in her brain. Yet she mastered her rage and grief and she answered him, biding her time, waiting her chance. She took one pace closer as she spoke.

"Of course I came, my Lord Baron. *I* do not desert my friends; *I* do not betray them."

"I have betrayed no one!" The anger burst from him like pus from a boil. Rage beat about her head and she felt the thrum of Earth power under her feet as the walls of the palace shuddered. The men behind her glanced fearfully around, and some looked upward as if they feared the roof would fall. Sullyan ignored them, although she felt their concern. She kept her gaze fixed firmly on the specter of her enemy.

"*I* was the one betrayed!" he continued, his twisted figure leaning forward, spittle flying with every word. "I was the one abandoned! Accused and cast down by witches and fools. Left to rot on that island, in solitude and pain. Well, there's a price to be paid for my agony, you witch, and I have brought you here to begin your payment."

"I would dispute that, my Lord." She took another slow pace. Her shields were in place, and behind them she built her power, gathered her strength, ready to counter any move he might make. She had to believe he had access to Robin's great forces, and even if he lacked her years of experience, he would possess enough strength to do damage. She had to consider the men at her back—and her King. The Baron would not scruple to attack any of them should he feel it would serve his purpose. She only hoped they had all obeyed her and stayed well out of the way.

✣ ✣ ✣ ✣ ✣

Most of them had. The twenty men at Sullyan's back stood as she had left them and watched for her signal, obedient to her orders. They remained in their groups, watchful and still, their eyes on the figure in black. One of them, however, did not heed her orders. One of them acted alone, detaching himself from the edges of the group and sliding away into the shadows, slinking along the walls. So stealthy was he that it was a few minutes before Wil noticed the King was gone.

He glanced around, searching frantically for his monarch. He cursed inwardly and knew he should not have been so surprised. He should have kept better watch, and Sullyan would have his hide for it. All the Manor men had trained with Sullyan for years. They knew each other perfectly. They were a team, a band, and loyal to each other. When new men joined, they spent many hours in maneuvers, many hours in practice, until the new had meshed with the old and the cracks in their defenses disappeared. But Elias had joined them overnight and was not of their mind. He might have taken an oath to follow Sullyan's orders, but it did not make him one of them, and it did not prevent him thinking for himself. Seeing an opening, sensing a chance, Elias had decided to act.

Wil swore silently. He was the ranking officer among this

band. He would be held responsible for this unthinkable breach of her orders, but there was nothing he could do for it now. Straining his eyes against the gloom, he searched desperately for the King.

✤ ✤ ✤ ✤ ✤

Unaware of Elias's disobedience, Sullyan kept her eyes on the scarecrow, edging closer. If she could keep him distracted and ranting, she might fix his attention on herself alone. To take the brunt of his anger was her purpose; to protect the others while she dealt with him was her hope. He was dangerous beyond belief in his stolen power, with neither the training nor the restraint to control it, and he could well bring the palace down about their ears if he lashed out in uncontrolled rage.

"The debt is yours to pay," she told him softly, "and it grows larger with every death you deal out. You will never find peace in your life. You will never find ease for your pain. You have committed the ultimate sin and only you can atone for that."

The figure by the throne seemed to swell with dark rage and his voice burst from him in anger. "And who will atone for *your* sins?" His ruined eyes glared red. His clawed hands clutched at the air and his long cloak stirred at his feet. "I am doing God's holy work, but God will not forgive you your pagan beliefs. He will not overlook your unnatural powers. How will you atone for those, you witch? How will you cleanse your soul?"

"My soul is my own affair, but at least it is not burdened by the weight of murdered love."

"*Love?*" the scarecrow shrieked, his body going rigid, his cloak stirring strangely about him. "What do you know of love?" The cane in his left hand slammed down sharply on the stone flags and another lurch of Earth power shuddered through the ground. Her men shifted fearfully behind her.

"I know that you destroyed it." She flung her words at him

like daggers, hoping to prick his puffed up rage. "I know you took the life of the one person who loved you, the one who gave his all to save you, the one who paid the ultimate price. The penalty for his death is on your head, Hezra Reen; the penalty for Serrin's murder."

✠ ✠ ✠ ✠ ✠

Silence fell in the throne room and Elias froze. He was directly behind the throne now, in the shadow of the wall, but the Baron had moved slightly and was standing to the right, facing Sullyan. She had her eyes on her enemy and had not noticed Elias. If he could just keep the bulk of Lerric's ceremonial seat between him and the Baron, he could approach unnoticed. He could see that one of Sullyan's men had spotted him and was trying to catch his eye, but he ignored Wil's frantic gestures to return to the group. He was committed. Only a few moments more and he would reach the concealing sanctity of the shadows behind the throne.

✠ ✠ ✠ ✠ ✠

The mention of his young lover's name incensed the Baron further. His flayed face turned puce with rage. His glaring eyes spat red sparks as raging anger beat at Sullyan's mind like cudgels. She tightened her shield and deflected the blows, her attention riveted upon her enemy.

"Serrin!" the Baron hissed, his throat rasping on the words. "You dare speak to me of Serrin? He was another of your witch-kind. He ensnared me with friendship, he tricked me with love. It was he who showed me my doom, that seductive, evil pool! He led me there, damn his soul. He led me to that torment! But he was repaid for his perfidy, for my God saved me from destruction. He gave me the power to overcome the witch's temptation, and instead of weakening me and turning me from the path, the witch-boy's treachery enabled me to triumph over him, to steal his power

75

from him and turn it to my will.

"He wanted to kill me, but instead he met his death. And you should take notice of his fate, witch-girl. For you want to kill me too, I see it in your eyes. Your friends begged me to release them, did you know? They begged me for death. Do you hear me, girl? Yes, even your virile young lover begged me in the end, brought low by my power, destroyed by my will. He could not defeat me, Brynne Sullyan, and neither will you!"

Chapter Eight

Elias used the noise of the Baron's rant to creep ever closer to the back of the throne. He could no longer see the scarecrow, could not even see Sullyan as she stood listening in horror. All he could see was the line of her men, the corporal still watching him, but motionless now and resigned. The King reached the shadows at the rear of the throne and crouched in the darkness, listening, gauging the distance to the Baron, his sword at the ready. One forceful rush was all it would take, before the Baron could muster his defenses, before he could do them more injury. Elias would repay him for the damages caused to his rule, to his marriage, to the people he loved. Repay him for the anguish he had caused Sullyan. He crouched in the darkness and waited, his heart thumping loudly.

✤ ✤ ✤ ✤ ✤

Sullyan's soul turned to ice at the mention of Robin's fate. Her rage burgeoned and its heat stoked her face. She was a contradiction throughout with the ice in her soul and the heat of fury in her breast. There was only one way to assuage this pain: it would die only in the scarecrow's lifeblood. Her eyes spat gold sparks as she answered his taunt.

"I would not be so sure of that were I you."

The Baron ignored her, his terrible smile returning to sit on putrid lips. He licked them deliberately, savoring the flavor of spilled blood. He turned to face her and captured her gaze.

"Oh, but I am sure, witch." He hissed the words, leering through his ruined eyes. "For I have something here, something you want, and only I can give it to you."

"Your death is all I want, you evil creature!" She took another pace forward. Her eyes were fixed on his face, waiting for her cue. She was irritated and mildly surprised by the lack of fear in his eyes, but this only told her he thought he had an escape route. She already thought she knew what it was. Yet, ready though she was with her powers to enmesh him in metaforce, she had grossly misread his intentions. Triumph shone from his eyes.

"Oh, really?" He took hold of his cloak with one hand. "Have I misunderstood you, my dear? I thought this was of value to you, but perhaps I was wrong."

He twitched aside the dark folds and held the cloth wide. Sullyan whimpered in shock and her heart gave a great lurch, hammering painfully at the cage of her ribs. The gasps of her men echoed in the throne room as they saw it too, and some even moaned in dismay. She stared in stunned disbelief at what the scarecrow had revealed.

Crouching naked and filthy at the Baron's feet, Robin stared unseeing at the faces before him. His left hand, torn and bloody at the wrist, curled tightly around the scarecrow's thigh like that of a frightened child.

Totally unaware of everything save the presence of her life mate, Sullyan stared transfixed at the scene before her. Impossible—it was impossible. This was some hideous, cruel joke. She had felt his spirit brush past her, had felt it leave this existence. There was no way she could have been mistaken. And yet here he was, crouching beneath the vulture wings of the Baron's cloak, his naked body essentially unmarked, his dark eyes blank and lifeless.

Her heart throbbed so painfully her throat tightened on her voice. Somehow, he had tricked her. Somehow, he had used the knowledge he had stolen to make her believe Robin was dead. He had used her desperate need for revenge and her care for Taran to bring her running, and now he would use her life mate to force her into surrender.

And she would do it. He knew she could not bear watching Robin languish in her enemy's power, slowly tortured and killed—again!—before her eyes. She would offer herself for Robin in the hope that her greater powers could overcome her enemy where Robin had failed. What this scarecrow creature craved most was her total despair, her utter submission. He wanted to force her to the very depths of desolation and bring her panting to her knees before him, begging him to strip her of life. But before she did, before she succumbed to his mastery, he knew she would use every ounce of her cunning and every one of her powers to defy him. She had her men at her back; the Baron had none. She had her father's sharp sword; he was essentially unarmed. He could not hope to match her in a battle of steel and was unready to test his metaforce. Yet he had no need of it. His most effective weapon was her life mate. A weapon he could—and would—use in terrible ways.

Sullyan narrowed her eyes at the scarecrow and forced her ragged voice to work. "Let him go."

Reen gazed insolently at her, his cracked lips stretched in a grin, his hand resting casually on Robin's dark curls. The drape of the cloak trailed across the Major's naked shoulders, but the young man did not stir. There was something obscene about their pose, something almost lascivious, like guilty lovers caught in some lustful, unnatural act. Bile rose in Sullyan's throat to see the Baron's casual possessiveness.

She spoke again, harshly. "Let him go. Surrender and we will spare your life. Refuse and I assure you, I will personally watch over your torture and death on the Wheel. And no amount of pleading will gain you mercy this time."

Reen's oozing grin widened as he absently stroked Robin's sweat-stained hair. He stared at her, his voice purring sinuously.

"I don't think so, my dear. I have no need of your grudging and conditional mercy. You cannot threaten my life."

She glared at him. "You are too confident. How will you escape us? My men are here at my back; I do not see yours. There is nowhere you could run to, nowhere you could hide where I could not hunt you down and kill you."

"Kill me?" His red eyes stretched wide, unholy glee reflected within. "Ah, but you will not kill me, witch, and I will show you why."

The treacherous Baron's voice slid slyly from his throat and a triumphant leer split his lips. Slowly reaching to his belt, watching her all the while, he brought forth a small knife. Its blade glittered coldly in the torchlight. Sullyan felt her muscles tighten and tension sprang into the men of her command, their instant readiness running through her blood like wire. Her golden gaze fixed on the blade in the claw-like hand, her whole body ready to drive her sword forward should he threaten Robin's life. Yet the Baron made no move toward the Major. Instead, he removed his right hand from the naked man's hair and brought his own forearm close to the knife. He deliberately captured Sullyan's glare and grinned in triumph as he sliced the blade along the desiccated flesh of his arm.

Gasps of shock echoed about the huge and gloomy throne room as not one drop of blood appeared to moisten the wound. The Baron's flesh sealed behind the blade's furrow as water closes over a dropped stone. Yet red blood welled from Robin's right arm and the gash in his skin gaped wide. The Major showed no reaction while the small stream of blood flowed down his fingertips and dripped onto the floor, the sounds preternaturally loud in the shocked silence.

Sullyan's stricken gaze flickered between Robin's wounded arm and the Baron's bloody, confident leer. Reen cocked his head at her and she tasted defeat. He saw it in her face and satisfaction suffused the sullen ruby eyes. She was helpless and they both knew it. If she attacked him now, if she attempted to take him by force, Robin would suffer for it. If she tried to kill him, Robin would die. How he had done this, she could not begin to imagine. It was beyond even her great knowledge. The men of her company saw her sword tip drop to the floor and knew the utter humiliation of graceless surrender.

Elias did not see it. Crouched as he was behind the throne, all he could see was the Baron's stooped back draped by the black cloak with no indication of what it concealed. All Elias knew was that Reen had his back to the throne, vulnerable to attack. Gripping his sword, tensing his body, and fixing his gaze, Elias chose that moment of silence to launch his deadly assault.

Sullyan closed her eyes. She tasted the depths of abject misery as she prepared to concede defeat. Then the sound of a furtive rush and Wil's sudden warning shout snapped her back to the moment and she saw, with utter horror, that Elias's sword was slicing the air with murderous intent, heading unerringly for Reen's unprotected back. The Baron did not move, although he must have heard the King. He merely held her with his taunting eyes and ignored the lethal threat. Robin crouched unknowing, eyes unseeing, his fate resting squarely in the hands of his love.

Shocked to the core, never even having considered Elias might fail her so thoroughly, Sullyan did the only thing she could. Screaming, "Elias, *NO!*" she gathered her powers and launched an unstoppable Thunderball of solid Earth power directly into Elias's chest. The wind of its passing ruffled Robin's hair and swirled the scarecrow's cloak. But its full force hit Elias squarely and punched him backward before he could utter a sound, slamming him prone to the floor. His sword flew from his hand and skittered across the flags, coming to rest against the wall with an ugly clash of steel. When the echo of its fall died away, the weight of the silence returned. There was no sound from the King.

Sullyan stared at the crumpled form of her monarch, the man she had sworn to protect with her life, and panted in an agony of fury and anguish. Her men exchanged horrified glances. The Baron, ruby eyes glinting, began to chuckle. Sullyan dragged her wounded gaze back to him, shuddering at his mirth.

"Oh, my dear," he said, grinning, his lips trailing spittle, "that was very skillfully done. It seems I must thank you for saving my life. That's the second time you've spared me Elias's wrath. Ironic, is it not, that you should be fated to expend your great powers in defense of your bitterest enemy?"

Sullyan glowered at him, leaning on her sword, not trusting herself to speak. She was terribly fearful she had just killed her King. Panic had heightened her unthinking reflexes and her Thunderball had been far too strong. Half the force would have sufficed. Elias lay unmoving halfway to the wall, but she had no time to assess his condition for the Baron was not yet done. Stooping, he unwound Robin's hand from his thigh and dropped it; it fell bonelessly to the young man's side. Reen stepped one pace away from the Major, his cloak trailing over Robin's naked shoulders like a lover's intimate caress. Still holding Sullyan's gaze with deliberate menace, Reen spoke in a vile, echoing voice.

"Enough of this charade! I tire of your presence. Leave my abode and return to your friends. Take your witch lover with you. I have had what I wanted of him, body and soul, and savored the experience. You are welcome to the empty shell that is left. Try to save him, Artesan witch—try to heal him. And when you find you cannot, when you have striven your utmost and failed at the last, return to me. When you are ready to submit to my will, you will know where to find me. When your skills are exhausted and your spirit is broken, I will receive you. Only I can give you what you want. Only I can restore what you have lost. But there will be a price to pay, my dear, a high one, and I do not have to tell you what it will be.

"Do not delay overlong. My patience will not hold forever and the body can only survive so long without a soul. Already it dies, this handsome corpse. But why wait? Why see this body you profess to love so much suffer more than necessary? Come beg me, Brynne Sullyan, come throw yourself at my feet. Grovel in abject misery and sue for my mercy, as once I was forced to do at yours. Then you will see how generous I can be."

As he spoke, the scarecrow moved farther from the crouching young man, his eyes forever watching Sullyan's furious white face. She did not stir; her men did not stir. His words and his aura held them in thrall while his impossible hold over Robin prevented their action. Then he stopped and cocked his head, a knowing smile on those red, drooling lips. "No? Ah well, I thought not." Unhindered, unthreatened, the scarecrow made his move, gathered his stolen powers and his siphoned strength, and opened a rent in the Veils.

The shimmer of the substrate glittered with ruby malice and all felt the weight of its presence. Rattled and wholly unprepared, even Sullyan gasped in pain. She swiftly accessed her powers and flung out a shield, covering all near the structure. Chuckling, the scarecrow stepped from sight, the sullen shimmer fading as he released his hold. The substrate thundered back to seal the rent with a high-pitched shriek of metaforce. The strength of its uncontrolled closing snuffed all the torches and the throne room plunged into darkness.

For some seconds, no one moved. A slight groan in the dark and a stirring of limbs broke the hiatus and light flared again as Sullyan called Fire to rekindle a torch. She ran for the King, terrified she had caused him real harm.

"Wil, see to Robin!" she snapped as she reached Elias and knelt down beside him. A hovering ball of pure elemental Fire appeared at her back, held there by the power of her will as she bent to examine him closely. She pressed her senses into the King, her heart hammering fearfully. He groaned again and she sighed, her skills telling her he was only stunned. With her help he soon recovered, opened his eyes, and gazed into the furious inferno of her outrage. He frowned at her and tried to sit up, one hand to his throbbing brow.

"Brynne," he groaned, "what happened?"

"What happened? *What happened*? I will tell you what happened, you bloody fool!"

Her voice trembled with the strength of her emotion and the King turned pale before it. So deep had been her terror that she poured it out wholesale on the prone and helpless King.

"You disobeyed my direct command, Elias, that is what happened! You broke your sworn oath and you stepped out of line! What the *Void* did you think you were doing? Your actions put us all in danger! Stay by me, I told you, and I gave you that order for a reason. But you thought you knew better. Do you know what you so nearly did? Had I not stopped you, you would have killed Major Tamsen! That sword you had aimed at the Baron would have slaughtered the father of my child! What have you to say to that, Elias? What is your defense?"

Her rage was so fierce, even her men paused to watch. Her temper was legendary among the men of the Manor, and few had faced such wrath and kept their post. Any who deserved such treatment soon found themselves dismissed, or transferred far away where their shame was unknown. None of her company had ever witnessed such a display, and the fact that its object was the High King of Albia made it all the more shocking and potent.

His position and nobility would not protect Elias now. Caught out and forsworn, he had no defense. Spreading his hands, he bowed his head, offering no excuses and pretending none.

"I'm sorry, Brynne." He could not meet her eyes. "You're right, I should have obeyed you. I saw what I thought was a chance and I took it. I was wrong and I'm sorry. But, Brynne," he turned perplexed blue eyes on her, seeing the faint glitter of unshed tears in her eyes and knowing it was fear that had caused such an outburst, "I thought you said Major Tamsen was dead? How could I have killed him?"

The fire of her fury died, exhausted and overcome as she was. She understood little of what had passed here this night, and to unravel its portents she needed time to think. Unwilling to bide longer in the abode of her enemy and urgent to tend to her life mate, she took Elias's hand and hauled him to his feet. Drained and frustrated, she avoided Elias's gaze, turning him wordlessly so he could see the naked form of Robin, standing now but still unresponsive under Wil's care. Elias's eyes widened as he stared at the Major. Sullyan approached her life mate, searching the depths of his eyes while one of the men flung a cloak over his shoulders, covering his shivering, filthy body. Elias stared in confusion at the young man's vacant gaze, the stillness of his limbs, and the drip of blood from his wound. He could find no words.

Sullyan's stretched out her hand, touching the seeping gash, sending out her healing powers. Questing for the familiar pattern of his intimate essence, she recoiled in sudden fear, her anguished cry sounding loud and unnatural in the dark hall. Elias caught at her shoulders as she reeled into him.

"What is it, Brynne? What's wrong?"

His voice was urgent in her ear, his hand clamped tight on her shoulder. She turned to him slowly, dragging horrified eyes from the face of her lover. He gripped her harder as she ground out her panic.

"He is empty, Elias. There is no spirit within his body; no psyche in his mind. I was not mistaken when I felt his soul pass me by, no matter what our eyes might tell us. He is dead, only his body does not know it. The Baron has taken his final revenge and now I understand the words he spoke. Unless I can find a way to undo what has been done—unless I can find a way to restore a dead man's soul—I will be forced to surrender, give up my own life to gain Robin's true and final death. If I do not, Reen will hold Robin's spirit forever in torment and his body will live on, untenanted and hollow, until it withers for lack of a soul."

Her body shuddered and she let loose a sob. "That is why he was so confident in confronting us. Those attacks by his men were a feint to draw us in. He wanted us to find them. He wanted us to have them, ruined as they are. He wants our despair, our anguish, our surrender. And I am all too fearful he will soon have them."

Her words sank like a death-knell into the hearts of the men and they stared at her in silence. The slow drip of Robin's blood was the only sound in the desolate throne room until a sharp, panicked scream rent the air. Elias reacted instantly, his body turning even as he recognized the sound.

"Sofira!" He ran from the room.

"Fetch his sword and go with him, Wil," barked Sullyan, and the corporal obeyed, taking several of the others with him. Sullyan extended her senses, touching the patterns of both Cal and Tad, discovering no threat to their safety. She ignored the screams, pitiful though they were, and turned her attention to Robin.

He stood there immobile, no emotion on his face, no spirit behind his eyes. His image blurred as her eyes filled with tears, seeing his handsome form essentially unharmed yet bereft of all she loved. She stretched out a trembling hand and tenderly brushed his face. He did not even blink to register the touch. Choking down sobs, she took up his hand, intending to see to his arm. The flow of blood had slowed. A cloth binding would see it stop. As she raised his arm he took a step closer, as if pulled by her will. Startled, she frowned, giving his hand another gentle tug. He followed her movement, his steps automatic. Shaking her head to clear it, she gave Robin's hand to Rhyn, who had stayed by her side.

"Bind his arm and then bring him." Her voice was rough and dull. This latest humiliation just tore at her heart and she wanted to strike out, to hurt and to kill. To think that his loving, indomitable soul should have been so cruelly wrenched from him, leaving him to follow at their heels like a worthless cur! Yet even as she raged, she realized it solved one problem: he would not have to be carried like a child.

Unlike those whose condition affected her like a slap in the face as she emerged from the anteroom.

The rest of her company were gathered there, the wounded, including the crippled Charrin, being tended by some of their fellows. Elias sat against the wall, cradling the shuddering form of his former wife, who clung to him like a traumatized child, her eyes wide and panicked. Her frantic screams had dwindled to mindless whimpers and she had wrapped her arms about Elias's neck, pleading incoherently for some kind of succor. Dismayed by her state and nearly unmanned by her panic, Elias comforted her as best he could.

It was not her men's injuries or Sofira's torment that cut at Sullyan's heart. It was the inert and silent figures lying together on the floor, wrapped in blankets and watched over by Cal. Taran and Jinny lay still as two corpses and Sullyan stared at them fearfully.

Cal's dark eyes were full of confusion. He knelt next to Taran, his hand on the Adept's brow. "What's been done to them, Colonel? I can't access his psyche. I can't sense him at all. Tad couldn't either. He's like a void, an empty shell. Where has he gone, why can't we reach him?"

Sullyan closed her eyes, unable to deal with Cal's distress when her own was too painful to bear. To discover that Reen had served Taran as he had served Robin flayed her sore heart like a scourge. She shook her head and turned away from Cal. She found Pengar standing beside her, his arm bandaged.

"I think you ought to see this, Colonel."

She stared at him, desperate to leave this dark place, to run from this nightmare, to return to the Manor and the support of her home. Perhaps this evil would seem less bleak there; perhaps there she could find some small hope. Her desire made her sharp as she answered. "What is it, Pen?"

He bent to one of the dead guards and with the tip of his knife twitched back the man's clothing. Sullyan sucked in a breath, stooping to examine the wound. The stench of rotting flesh assailed her nostrils and she hastily straightened.

The swordsman held her gaze. "They're all the same. All the dead and all the injured carry this wound, although on some it's merely a sore. But that's not all. Look here …" He moved across to Taran, parting the blanket that wrapped the Adept to expose the ruin of his chest. "And I'm afraid the same has been done to his lady."

Sullyan gasped at the damage and turned her eyes toward Sofira, who was still being comforted by Elias. "The Princess?"

Pengar shook his head. "Not that we could see, although we didn't examine her closely. She's so distressed it was hard enough to get her to leave her room."

Elias noticed their regard and raised his head, wrinkling his nose in disgust. "Gods, Brynne, what is that terrible smell?"

Her tone was harsh with fear. "Do you not recognize it, Elias? It is the same smell that pervaded the east wing of your castle, and it originated with the body we found there. It was also present in the ruins of Jinella's mansion. It is the smell of the Baron's contamination, the result of his control over his victims."

Cal stood from his position beside Taran. His voice was rough and unsteady. "But you can save them, right?"

She met his eyes reluctantly. In truth, she did not know. This was outside of her experience and she had no leisure to think. The Baron's confident statement seemed to provide the answer, but she was not prepared to dwell on it now. They had other priorities. She brushed aside Cal's anxiety.

"Up, all of you." Her commanding tone cut through their confusion, restoring some sense of stability. "We must leave this hellhole and find some refuge, a place where we can tend to their wounds and I can assess what has been done to them."

"Are we not going back to the Manor?" Elias was coaxing Sofira to her feet. The Princess's childlike whimpers never ceased.

Sullyan shook her head. "I dare not risk the Veils until I know what afflicts them." She nodded at the men as they gathered up their wounded. Two of them carried Charrin supported over their linked arms, his arms around their necks, his face drawn with pain. Cal reluctantly left Taran to two others while he cradled Jinella, her slight weight no burden on his strength. Rhyn emerged from the anteroom leading Robin by the hand, the Major's arm now clean and bound, his indigo eyes still devoid of life.

Seeing him for the first time, Tad cried out in joy, but his face soon fell when he saw Sullyan's eyes fill with heartbroken tears. Wil moved over and whispered to him, and the young man's shoulders slumped with despair. Cal almost lost his hold on the blonde woman in his arms. Sullyan appreciated how he felt as the pang that had seized her own heart at the sight of Robin was almost too strong to bear. She turned away, walling off her distress.

Dexter approached her. "What about the enemy wounded, Colonel, and those we left tied up?"

Her voice was tight with grief. "They are no longer our concern, Captain. Leave them. Let the Baron take care of his own." She glanced around her band. "Those wounded and burdened to the center, the rest of you form a defense. We cannot relax until we are far from this place."

They moved forward by the light of Sullyan's Fire, which hung like a nimbus above her. It drained her already depleted strength, but light was too important to them now. Despite her conviction that the Baron wanted them to leave, she would not drop her guard. They made their way carefully toward the east tower door, testing each blind turn and darkened hallway, but they were not molested.

As they reached the tower door, she let her Fire die. When Wil put his hand on the latch she stopped him, standing still and closing her eyes. She quested through the substrate for Drum's elemental pattern. Communication with the black stud was chancy and quite unlike communing with a person. Drum could only perceive and respond to emotions and instincts. But she managed to catch his attention and let her need of him filter through his mind, gently lest he panic. She breathed a sigh of relief when she sensed his response. Opening her eyes, she nodded once to Wil and the corporal pushed open the door.

What met them was a howling maelstrom of white-flung wind, bitter, icy, and strong. A blizzard had descended on Bordenn in the night and it snatched at their clothes and stung their eyes, throwing flaying hail and frozen snow into their faces. Staggering back from the force of it, Wil lost hold of the door. It was torn from his fingers to crash against the stone.

"Stay close together!" Sullyan yelled against the howl of the wind.

Surrounding the wounded and those heavily laden, they made their careful way down the snow-blurred steps. Sullyan kept her senses tuned for the Baron, or any other sign of attack, but they remained unmolested. It looked as if the Baron truly was going to permit them to leave.

Reaching the courtyard, they made for the lee of the walls where the murderous howl of the wind was mercifully blocked. A ringing whinny cut through the gale and Sullyan raised her head. The thudding sounds of a beast hammering at the wood of its stall throbbed through the storm, and an answering peal came from outside the palace walls.

Sullyan waved a hand. "Dex, go and free Tobias, and any other beasts inside. Just beware of their heels!"

The Captain forged his way head-down through the snow, battling against the wind. He disappeared into the stables. A short time later, a stallion's angry challenge screamed into the wind, followed by a bulky mahogany body that rocketed into the yard, scattering snow from its hooves, snorting and tossing its mane. Another great cry answered the call from beyond the walls and Sullyan sent one of the men to open the gates.

Ignoring the few horses that had followed Tobias out, Sullyan whistled to the mahogany stallion, calming the angry beast and forcing down her disappointment at the continuing blankness of Robin's gaze. She had half-hoped his beloved horse might trigger some response, but there was nothing. Blinking back tears that threatened to freeze her eyes, she stepped away from the men as a huge black shape hurtled through the gates and into the yard. Drum and Tobias greeted each other loudly, and the rest of the mounts could be heard calling from out in the road.

They swiftly caught and calmed the horses, many hands helping the wounded to mount. Those too injured to ride by themselves went double with friends or were passed up into the arms of those who would carry them. Cloaks were pulled tight against the scourge of the wind and swords settled into place. Glancing swiftly around to check everyone was safe, Sullyan gave the order to ride out. They left Lerric's palace to its brooding black master, pushing the fretful stallions to their best pace. Malice and triumph seemed to gibber at their backs as the howling wind swallowed the spires of the palace.

Chapter Nine

"We have to find shelter soon, Brynne. We can't last long in this dreadful storm."

Sullyan acknowledged the King's words and cast him a glance through the flurries of snow. He rode beside her at the head of the group, Sofira cradled tightly against him, her unbound hair whipping over his shoulder. The others jostled at their heels, the stallions crowding together for shelter, eyes raw from the sting of the wind. The darkness was absolute; horizontal streaks of white were the only visible points against the black rage of the blizzard.

Dexter urged his horse close to Drum. "Shall we make for the barns, Colonel?"

But she was unwilling to rest within the sphere of Reen's influence, unlikely as it was that he would molest them now. She would feel easier the farther they could get. She shook her head, pressing on. Her band battled stoically in her wake, hands growing numb on the reins, feet freezing despite fur-lined boots.

Once they left the environs of Daret she felt more inclined to stop. The horses were tiring of the constant struggle to forge a passage through the clinging drifts. She called Cal and Wil to her, instructing the corporal to take Tad and search to the west, while Cal went with Gart to quarter the east. The rest of them pushed on, Sullyan keeping a link to each Artesan. Twenty minutes later, Tad reported that he had discovered a suitable site to shelter them and she recalled Cal as she swung Drum's head. They struggled through the deep snow until they saw what Tad and Wil had found.

It was a steading, small and deserted. The tiny stone cottage was derelict, but the barns were not, and one was large enough to hold them all. Although the house had fallen into disrepair, the surrounding fields would still be grazed. The animals might have been moved to more sheltered pastures, but the straw in the barn had been left. Sullyan blessed this oversight.

Crowding the horses into the barn, they dismounted on stiffened legs, their bodies relieved of the scourge of the storm. The floor of the barn was hard-packed earth, and snow patched the ground where the roof had been torn. But the strength of the gale was now muted and the holes in the roof did not worry them. They used some of the straw to soften the ground and the company settled into the routine of a makeshift camp.

She sent two men to scavenge what they could for a fire while two others began to dig a latrine in the far corner of the barn where the horses would be. No one would have to leave their shelter in order to relieve themselves outside. They were all exhausted and drained; they needed what comforts they could get.

A pile of salvaged wood soon grew in the center of the barn, placed on the bare, packed earth. Sullyan spared some of her fading strength to call Fire, as the wood was damp and frozen. Soon a bright blaze was doing its best to warm the icy air and bring some cheer to their dismal camp. Those men who were not tending the wounded or the horses set to, melting snow for water.

The wounded were set down close to the fire, on the side away from the door. Elias laid Sofira next to Jinella and the stricken Princess seemed to recognize her, taking up her hand at once. But her eyes were still wild and her words incoherent and Elias was unable to reach her. Taran was laid beside them and tended by Cal. Sullyan needed to examine his wound, but she was exhausted and there was still too much she must do. She raised bleary eyes as Rhyn led Robin over, the swordsman having carried him on his own horse.

Robin did whatever he was commanded, which made things easier. As Rhyn bought him close to the fire, it became evident that his body was completely out of his control as a characteristic sharp smell revealed the extent of his helplessness. Tears sprang into Sullyan's eyes as the depth of his humiliation came home to her, and she could have cried for his shame. But she was spared the necessity of cleaning him up by the appearance of Tad at her shoulder.

The young man reached for Robin's cold hand. "Let me care for him, Colonel. He did the same for me that time Parren half-killed me. It's only right that I return the favor. And I don't mind, really I don't."

Unable to speak for grief and anger, not even to show Tad her heartfelt gratitude, Sullyan gripped his arm. Tad turned Robin and seated him next to the fire. Taking cloths and warmed water, he began his work with no murmur. Sullyan forced down her guilt at Tad's selfless gesture and turned her attention to Sofira and Jinny. If such straits had been forced on Robin, it was likely Jinella had suffered the same, and Sullyan could hardly let the men deal with her.

She ordered two of them to rig up a shelter, cloaks strung on timbers to screen off the women. Sofira seemed terrified of Sullyan and wouldn't let her touch her, but Elias persuaded the trembling Princess to drink some warmed water into which a soporific from the well-stocked medical packs had been mixed. When it finally took effect and the Princess lapsed into sleep, the relief from her constant, mindless whimpering was felt by all.

Once Sofira was asleep, Elias left the shelter, leaving Sullyan to her work. She eventually ascertained that the Princess bore no signs of the wound inflicted on Jinny. It was while she was cleaning the woman that she saw the evidence of a vicious rape, recognizing marks she herself had borne once, and she turned pale, remembering only too clearly what such things could do to the one so assaulted. Small wonder that the Princess had lost her wits. Fearful for Jinella, she made Sofira as comfortable as she could and turned her attention to the younger woman. The blonde Baroness was as still as a corpse and just as cold, but warming blankets were beginning to have an effect. Sullyan, relieved at least to find her free from the signs of rape, examined and cleaned the dreadful wound in her chest, trying not to gag at the smell. She bound it as best she could, the cause of the strange rupture confounding her. She had no energy to pursue it. She placed a hand on the younger woman's brow, and her senses were confronted with the same void she had felt in Robin. She simply did not have the strength to fight this alien vacuum and eventually conceded defeat, wrapping Jinny tightly in blankets and leaving her by the fire.

When she emerged from the shelter, she found hot food waiting. The horses had been tended and the fire stoked. Tad had finished with Robin and the Major lay quietly beside the leaping flames, wrapped in a cloak, eyes closed as if in normal sleep. Sullyan sat disconsolately by his side, averting her gaze from the deception of his state. Elias approached her, bearing a bowl of warmed meat, and he set it down next to her.

"You need to eat, Brynne."

"How can I eat at a time like this?"

Yet she knew she needed sustenance, and when Elias said simply, "You must," she capitulated.

He pushed the bowl of meat toward her and sat by her side while she ate. The aroma of fellan filled the warming air and the men began to settle for sleep. Dexter took on the task of apportioning watches, telling Sullyan she was not required. "You concentrate on the Major, Colonel." She watched him move away with desolation in her eyes.

Cal sat nearby with Taran's head in his lap. He sipped at his fellan and stared at the walls, his eyes distant and bleak. They had come for revenge, avid for blood, but what they had left with was more rage and despair. Struggling to cope with the dreadful fate of their friends, all of them sat in the chill of their thoughts.

Cal suddenly stiffened, staring down at the gray face of the man whose head rested heavy across his legs. His indrawn breath caught at Sullyan's senses and she glanced over, a frown creasing her brow.

"What is it, Cal?"

The dark-skinned Captain glanced at her, apology in his eyes. "I'm sorry, Colonel, for a minute I thought … no, wait … yes! There it is again! He moved, Colonel—Taran just moved!"

Sullyan crossed to Cal's side. Elias, who had retreated to the entrance of the women's shelter to keep an eye on their sleep, leaned forward to hear what was said. Sullyan crouched down next to Cal and placed her hand on Taran's bruised brow. The Captain fixed his eyes on her, too frightened to hope. After a few moments she gazed at him, her eyes alight.

"I can feel his psyche, Cal. I can sense his mind!"

Tad heard her from his seat across the fire and his eyes leaped to Robin, desperate to see some movement from the Major. But Robin didn't stir.

"Move over, Cal, let me take him."

Cal moved out from under Taran's head, allowing Sullyan to slide into his place. She took the Adept's head in her lap, folding her arms about his chest, feeling the swathe of cloth that wrapped his wound. Ignoring the lesion and calming her heart, she concentrated on Taran's complex psyche. Softly, she called to him, deep within his mind, sensing the emergence of his spirit, hardly daring to think what this might mean for what beset her own true love.

The gray of Taran's face changed, the skin taking on a more normal hue. Pale still, he nevertheless lost the semblance of a corpse and gained the aspect of a tortured man. His eyes moved beneath bruised lids, his muscles twitching with returning circulation. All who watched him held their breath as Sullyan called to his psyche. Cal lent her strength when he could, aiding her work with his mind. His gasp of relief when his master's eyes finally flickered open was echoed by most in the barn.

"Taran? Can you hear me, my friend?"

Sullyan's soft voice seemed to reach the suffering man and his bloodshot eyes settled on her face. He took a trembling breath, but was unable to speak. Cal reached for a cup, mixing a pinch of herbs into warmed water. He held the cup to Taran's dry lips and Sullyan tilted his head. Most of the drink went down the Adept's throat; what spilled from his lips, Cal wiped away.

"Give him more, Cal, and double the dose."

Cal complied. Their medical supplies had been packed by Rienne, who always made sure there were restorative herbs. Cal gave Taran the water and he drank it all down.

Sullyan gestured Cal to come and support Taran's back so she could move to face him. His sore eyes followed her as she knelt by his side, taking his hand, still cold from his shock, and pressing it close to her breast. "Taran? Can you answer me?"

She was half afraid he would not be coherent. Whatever he had suffered had been terrible indeed. Yet if he could return from the Baron's torture, then maybe there was hope. She needed to find out how much.

Taran's eyes fixed on hers with a dreadful intensity and he struggled to speak. She smiled for him, encouraging him, but didn't touch his mind. This he must do for himself. Blinking bruised lids, he swallowed, taking another shuddering, rasping breath. "No ... Brynne, no."

She stifled a sob, tears rolling from her eyes. "Oh, Taran, my friend, you are safe, have no fear."

Taran was weak, his voice barely audible, but the terror in his eyes lent strength to his words. Sullyan felt his cold fingers tighten briefly on hers as he struggled to make her understand.

"Go back ... you mustn't ... oh, Brynne, go back!"

Thinking she knew his meaning, she tried to calm him. "We are no longer in the palace, my friend. Whatever you feared, it is gone. The Baron no longer threatens us. We have you all safe— you, Sofira, Jinny, and Robin."

Taran's brows creased and he stared at her. Sullyan feared she had gone too fast for him. Maybe he wasn't as lucid as his words made him seem. Her mention of Robin's name seemed to perplex him all the more and some nameless terror appeared behind his eyes.

She glanced across at Elias and nodded to him. "Elias, hold that screen aside, will you? Cal, let him see."

As Cal turned the Adept's head toward the shelter, Elias held the cloaks aside so Taran could see the women lying peacefully side by side. "Do you see, Taran? There is Jinny, and Sofira with her. And there by the fire lies Robin. We have you all safe."

"Jinny? Robin?" Taran's voice was an incredulous whisper. His eyes struggled back to Sullyan's, confusion and pain crowding their hazel depths.

"But I saw ... but I thought ... was it some terrible nightmare?" His free hand crept up to feel at his chest, and Sullyan saw the moment when the presence of his wound confirmed the reality of his dreadful experiences. His face crumpled and tears welled in his eyes. She could sense the horror and revulsion swamping his heart. His eyes sought hers again, pleading and frightened. "Oh, help me! Gods help me, Brynne, I'm losing my mind!"

His desperate appeal and utter incomprehension cut Sullyan's sore heart like a knife. Devastated as she was by Robin's condition, Taran's return to consciousness had seemed like hope. She really didn't have the strength to deal with this now, but no matter what his confusion, he still held the key. She must know what he had seen. She had to hear what had been done to the Baron's captives if she was to stand any chance of redeeming their souls. Sofira was too far gone in her panic and might well need weeks of careful treatment before she was able to respond. If Taran could tell her what he had seen, she would be better prepared to fight this evil.

She leaned closer and smiled gently, doing her best to radiate calm. "You are not losing your mind, but you have suffered a dreadful experience. I felt your terror when Reen forced you to contact me. You wanted to warn me, I know. You felt you had betrayed me by calling me here, but you must understand that I came of my own accord. I would never have left you there—any of you—if it was within my power to save you. And now you are safe. But I can see you are hurt. I know he did something to you, to all of you, and I need to know what it was. I need to know how to fight it, how to deal with it. Can you help me, my friend? Can you tell me what he did?"

Taran stared into her eyes, seemingly mesmerized by her voice, only half-comprehending the words. It was pain, terror, and the exhaustion of his ordeal. She thought perhaps she ought to let him sleep. After what he had suffered, it was cruel to question him so. Time enough in the morning to see what could be done. Yet the tears welling in his eyes spilled over at her words and he glanced at Robin, wincing from the sight of the still form as if from some monstrous parody of the friend he had loved. One hand stretched weakly toward the still man, then fell back, his eyes closing against the pain of his memories.

"I don't know how to tell you. Oh, how can I tell you what that monster did?"

Her heart turned cold and she shivered. "Let me make it easy for you, then." She spoke as softly as she could, her voice hoarse with fear. "Let me see for myself, Taran. Let me into your mind."

"NO!" His shriek turned heads. Even those who had lain down to sleep were roused by the panic in his tone. "No, Brynne, I won't … I can't!"

Her eyes widened at the horror behind his dread. Whatever had been done to him, or what he had witnessed done to others, had affected him very deeply if he could not bear to accept her touch. Chilled to the bone by the thought of what he had been forced to endure, she laid a reassuring hand on his arm. "Easy, Taran, easy. Tell me what you fear. You are among friends now, no one will hurt you."

The Adept closed his eyes, breathing as deeply as he could. Sullyan watched him striving for calm and exchanged anxious looks with Cal and Elias. She had to know what had transpired in the palace, but all of them feared to hear it. She longed to reach out to Taran, to lend him some strength, but couldn't take the risk of upsetting him again. He had gone through so much, and just telling them of it would be ordeal enough. Once more, she considered letting him be.

"Perhaps you should sleep, Taran," she murmured, increasing her grip on his arm. But he shook his head and opened his eyes, slowing his breathing and gathering his strength.

"No, Brynne, I have to tell you. You have to know what he did, what they suffered. It's just that … I hardly know the words to tell you. It was so vile … so … *evil* … that I don't think I can …"

He lapsed into silence, trembling and gasping for breath, and she gazed at him in concern. "If you cannot accept my help, perhaps you will take Cal's? You are wounded and exhausted. Let him help you."

She felt Cal offering his strength, and this time Taran seemed able to accept. Perhaps her deep grief over Robin had colored her metaforce. Perhaps she gave him pain merely by her presence. But Cal's familiar aura, long used to Taran's mastery, was easier for him to deal with and he soon seemed a little stronger.

"Start at the beginning, Taran," she advised gently. "Start from your journey to the mansion. Tell us what happened to Col."

Despite his shame at the ease of his capture and his obvious grief over Col, this was easier for him to tell. He told of Col's brave fight, and of the callous disposal of his body. Pengar and Dexter listened avidly, their eyes alight with rage and vengeance. The satisfaction Pengar had gained at the death of the man called Varth had been cancelled out by his failure to deal with the murderer's co-conspirator.

Taran told of waking chained in the cell and of Robin's attempts to help him. He recalled what he could of Robin's warnings and told them of the Baron's marriage to the Princess. Elias gasped in shock at this unexpected news, but Sullyan was more concerned by her memory of Sofira's injuries. What parody of a wedding night had the Princess suffered? Whatever she had endured, it had fully repaid her for her misguided succor of a traitor to the realm. She wondered what Sofira thought of her new husband now.

His eyes closed in pain, Taran continued, recounting his failed efforts to contact Rienne. Then his voice faltered and Sullyan's heart grew cold. He was approaching the worst and she did not know how to bear it. She had to remain strong, and if there was to be any hope at all, she could not hide from the facts. With a whisper to Cal, she had him increase the flow of his support. Taran's hoarse voice spoke on, his pale face reflecting the horror of his tale.

"Robin told me what Reen did to the runner who had been taken with him. He feared the same would be done to him. And when they finally came, he fought for his life. He fought them so strongly, Brynne! I could scarcely believe he had that much strength left. We both knew it was hopeless, but the depth of his fear was so great there was nothing else he could do. In the end, it took all of them to hold him. They chained him to the bed on his belly and the Baron sent them from the room."

Sullyan sat stiff-backed, her face white, her eyes fixed in horror on Taran's. He could not look at her, could not look at any of them, least of all the figure lying inert beside the fire. His handsome face and sleek, powerful body seemed so untouched, so unhurt, that Taran's dreadful tale felt like some imagined nightmare. He took a breath—a shuddering sigh—but even with Cal's constant support he could only bring himself to skirt round the words.

"Reen taunted Robin with what he was going to do. He said he'd steal his powers and use them to defeat us all, and there was nothing any of us could do to fight him. He brought out a knife and I thought he was going to use it on Robin, but instead he cut at his leathers and stripped him naked. And then he …"

Taran raised his eyes, looking for the first time at Sullyan's pinched, white face.

"He took his life force, Brynne. I don't know how, but I know that he did it. And as he did it … as he destroyed him … he did to Robin what Rykan did to you."

Chapter Ten

Everyone in the barn felt the shock that pulsed through the air, even those who were not Artesans. Sullyan went rigid. Cal froze. Elias gasped in revulsion, an action echoed by many of the men. Apart from Cal and Taran, the others in the barn knew only the bare details of Rykan's brutal treatment, but they all knew it had included rape. Only Taran and Cal knew the extent of what she had suffered and they had never told the tale.

Sullyan held Taran's gaze and understanding passed between them; she felt his torment, and he knew the depth of her comprehension. Then she dropped her head to her hands and sat there in silence, struggling with her horror and revulsion.

Dexter took control, shoving aside his burning anger, curtly ordering more fellan. Rest would not come easy that night, despite their exhaustion, but the addition of Rienne's soothing herbs might dull the worst of their pain. He placed a mug firmly in Sullyan's hands, wrapping her fingers about it, and waited until she had drunk at least half. Cal did the same for Taran.

When the initial horror and disbelief had turned to vengeful rage, Sullyan's hot gaze met Taran's once again. Her voice was a whisper of restrained fury. "I thank you, my friend. I can only imagine what it cost you to tell me that. I will not ask you much more, but one thing I must know. You said you were both held in spellsilver, that it was on the surface of the manacles. When they chained Robin on his belly, was the silver still in use? And if it was, how did the Baron force his way into Robin's mind?"

Taran shook his head. "I don't know. The silver was still there, that much I can tell you. They only changed the chains, they never removed the cuffs. But the silver seemed to make no difference to the Baron."

"So Robin was unable to fight him, and with the Baron's essence inside him, Reen had full physical access to the seat of Robin's power."

Her bald statement of such a terrible deed was almost worse than Taran's revelation. She raised her eyes, the dark crescents beneath them stark in the firelight, and another horror appeared in their depths. "What of you, Taran? Did he …?"

Taran jerked his hand, as if to push the thought away. "No. No, he didn't do the same thing to me. I must have passed out before he was done with Robin, and when I awoke I was alone. Robin was gone and I thought they had killed him. Someone had half-stripped me, and I feared I would suffer the same fate. When Reen came to me again, I was prepared to fight him as Robin had, but I was not given even that choice. He told me I was to send you a message. He wanted me to call you, and I refused, of course. But then he brought Jinny and I knew I was finished. He had his guards strip her and hold her on the floor. They threatened to rape her, even though she was his niece, and although I agreed to do what he wanted, he still didn't let her go. Afterwards, after I'd betrayed you to him"—Sullyan shook her head, but Taran ignored her, plowing on in mounting distress—"he still didn't let her go. He made me plead for her life. He made me beg him to release her, and all the while she was screaming and crying on the floor. But his idea of release was not the same as mine.

"He had a strange gray cane. He stood over her body and brought that dreadful thing down over her chest and he … The way she screamed … I'll never forget that terrible sound. And the smell, and the burning! And then he came for me and I saw the end of the cane—and it was alive, Brynne, somehow it was alive!—and he pressed it to my chest, right over my heart, and it sucked the life from me. And now he's inside me, and my mind's not my own! I don't know how to bear it, but what can I do?"

Taran's voice grew louder and the tremor of his muscles increased. Panic flavored his tone and his eyes started from his head. Taran's frightened face and outstretched hands that begged for her help cut into Sullyan and flayed her to the bone, overwhelmed and helpless as she was. There was nothing she could do, no hope she could give him, and her failure sent despair swamping through her limbs. She caught at his hands, her heart in her eyes.

"Oh, Taran, my friend, what can I say? You know I will do all I can to help you. But first we must get you home to the Manor. Once we are safely there, maybe I can find the solution. Now, you need to rest; we all need to rest. Cal will watch over you. Let him help you, Taran. Let him help you sleep."

He was reluctant and fearful, but eventually Cal got him to sleep. Sullyan left them, her face stark and pallid, returning to her seat close to Robin. She accepted more fellan from Dexter and drank it unseeing, not even protesting at the huge dose of herbs stirred into the brew. One hand rested gently on Robin's unmoving shoulder and her eyes were pools of despair.

"Is there any hope at all?" Elias's voice came softly to her, reaching through the veils of her fear. "Is there anything you can do?"

She raised her head and the King flinched from the pain in her eyes. He could hardly imagine what she was feeling, hearing of such evil done to those she loved.

"I do not know, Elias. I truly do not know. This is beyond my experience, beyond any horror I have ever even dreamed. I do not even know if we can take them through the Veils. But I cannot think now; I need to sleep. In the morning we shall see. Will you watch over Sofira and Jinny? Wake me if you have need."

She took off her boots and laid herself down, rolling beneath the cloak that covered Robin, taking his unresponsive body in her arms and surrendering to the pull of the herbs. Cal stayed close by Taran, and Elias laid himself across the entrance to the women's makeshift shelter. The barn lapsed into silence, the muted howl of the lessening wind swirling outside. Within the barn, the breathing of the men and the occasional stamp of a hoof were the only sounds in the firelit darkness.

Sullyan slept, but her dreams were troubled by two ruby points of light that glinted wickedly, baleful in the heart of their refuge.

✤ ✤ ✤ ✤ ✤

"Who's going to deal with these, master? We can't leave them here. They're really beginning to stink."

Seth looked in distaste at the bloody sprawled bodies. One of them stared up at him in a stiff parody of a grin and he wondered what Varth could have found to amuse him at the last. The gaping wound in his chest did not seem to Seth like a matter for smiling, but the hulking swordsman had always shown a peculiar sense of humor. Remembering their last strange and uncomfortable encounter, Seth could feel no sorrow at the brawny fellow's death. Turning his eyes away, he bent to untie the final prisoner. The man got to his feet unaided, rubbing at the sores on his wrists.

"The rest of them will clean up."

Seth's dark-robed companion, stooped and sticklike, spared the dead men barely a glance. He glowered at the remaining guardsmen, now freed from their bonds and their prisons, and an unspoken command passed between them. They immediately took hold of the nearest bodies and began slinging them over their shoulders, heedless of the blood. The scarecrow turned away, beckoning Seth with one hand. The tapping of the cane, muted by the thickness of the carpet, was even more sinister as it slid through the gore.

Reen moved toward a door embellished with the hunting motif of Lerric's House. It stood half ajar and he pushed it fully open. "What do you think? Will these rooms serve you after the weariness of your labors? Are they reward enough for the discomforts you have suffered?"

Seth stepped inside and gasped at the opulence. He had never been anywhere half so splendid and the sheer luxury of the furnishings astonished him. Reen smiled at his amazement.

"This is nothing, my faithful Seth. Do you think this is rich? Do you think this is grand? I tell you, when I am done, all the wealth of the realm will be ours, all the riches and all the power. And you will have helped me obtain it. Try as she might, there is nothing that Artesan witch can do. Death alone will release those I hold captive, and only *her* death, only her total and willing surrender, will buy them freedom from my torment. What do you think of *that*?"

"But how did you do it, master? How did you learn? I thought she was the most powerful witch in the realm. How did you defeat her?"

Reen was amused at his servant's puzzlement. The triumph of his plans and the powers he had absorbed all combined to make him lightheaded, and he savored the sensation. He had not felt so fulfilled since sealing his pact with Rykan, but that had been short-lived, thanks to the demon's obsessive lust and Sullyan's thrice-damned interference. Now he had drawn her claws and she must dance to his tune. He threw back his head and laughed.

"Never mind how I did it, Seth. Suffice it to say she is no

longer so powerful. *I* am the master now! And once I have her surrender, once I strip her of her might, then it is *I* who will rule, and none shall stand against me!"

Spittle sprayed from his lips as he indulged himself, and Seth stood watching, amazed and fearful. His master had changed, that much he could see, but quite how deeply those changes went, Seth had no idea.

Reen abruptly sobered and clapped him on the back, startling the manservant. "But first, I have matters to attend. We can leave the rabble to clear up the palace, and the servants will return in the morning, and so you and I can concentrate on matters of importance. I need your aid once again for the next part of my plan, and it is daring and risky. Whether we succeed or not matters little, but I do not intend to give them leisure in which to think, or peace in which to work. We must move on."

He moved farther into the suite, drawing a puzzled Seth with him. It was late into the night, although time meant little in this gloomy, shuttered palace, and Seth was weary. He'd had little rest since his rescue from the castle. He had only the vaguest idea of how the Baron brought him here, and the translation through the Veils had unnerved and disoriented him. He didn't even know what province he was in. What he really wanted was to sleep, but it seemed his master required more labor. Seth's heart fell. He had thought his trials were over. It seemed he was mistaken.

Discerning his thoughts, Reen turned to face him. "Oh come, my faithful servant, do you think I would send you off with no time to rest? It is true, there is somewhere I would send you, and a task I need you to perform, but that can wait. What I have in mind should not tax you too greatly and may even be pleasurable for you. Does that not please you, faithful Seth?"

He indicated Lerric's great bed with a wave of his hand. Seth glanced at him, frowning. The scarecrow almost purred. "Does it not look inviting? Do you not long to try its comforts, to lounge upon its softness? And we have been apart a long time, have we not? Do you remember our pleasures, Seth? Do you ever think of them, as I do?"

Seth moved closer to the bed, comprehension in his eyes. Despite his weariness and the still-present ache left by Varth's powerful but clumsy lust, he found he was not averse to what his master was asking. It was true their past liaisons had not been unwelcome, back when Seth was younger and eager to please his master. And had he not wanted this? Had he not felt cheated by the Baron's exile? Well, here was his chance to resume his dutiful service; here was the opportunity to reaffirm his loyalty and worth. Smiling his willing compliance, he shed his clothes by the bedside, watched in anticipation by the scarecrow's hooded ruby eyes.

✣ ✣ ✣ ✣ ✣

Nothing disturbed the sleepers in the barn; nothing could be heard but the sounds of the storm. Wind still howled in frozen gusts about the abandoned buildings, but it did not penetrate their sanctuary. Its intensity faded as the long winter night wore on, blowing itself out over the land to the east. The fire was kept fed and its warmth soothed their hurts. Gentle snuffling from the horses and the occasional shift of a hoof reassured the sentries there was nothing to fear. The two women behind the screen never stirred through the night, and Elias woke frequently to check on their condition. Cal slept fitfully with Taran by his side. The memory of his master's words echoed through his mind, the horror of his ordeal filtered even through his dreams. But eventually, as the peaceful hours wore on, even Cal and Elias succumbed to their enervation, sliding deeper and deeper into sleep.

Sullyan breathed gently, wrapped around Robin's naked body, her head resting on his shoulder as if they shared a private bed. The

110

cloak that covered them was warm with the closeness of the fire. Despite her despair at the fate of her friends, Sullyan's mind drifted in pleasant memories of Robin, finding much needed refuge from her pain and desolation. Conflicting emotions confused her sore heart. Finding Robin's body alive when she knew his mind had died had sent her into turmoil and caused her to question the fact of her grief. She had felt his spirit shrieking as it fled. She had heard the despair in his cries. She knew full well she hadn't been mistaken, but the breathing, sleeping body next to hers seemed to refute what she thought she had felt.

The warm hand that moved gently against her side and ran down the curves of her flank was just what she was longing to feel. He knew her so well, this mate of her soul, and she stirred in her sleep, murmuring his name. She imagined him turning toward her, his arm coming about her, his body responding to the closeness they shared. The familiar touch of his mind upon hers enveloped her in love and with urgency. She had missed him so much, had so yearned for his presence, that she opened her heart to him and let down her shield.

Warm, loving lips descended on hers and she accepted his kiss. His forearm had moved to lie across her throat and she reached to move it away. As she did so, he pressed down hard and she startled awake, only now realizing something was terribly wrong. The scream that struggled for release was throttled as he bore down on her throat with all his might. She stared frantically upward into a contorted face and terrible, red-flaring eyes as her windpipe was crushed, her cry through the substrate muffled and snuffed out by the willing access she had granted him. She lay trapped by his bulk as he tore at her clothes, ripping them from her in a frenzied attack. She tried to struggle, but he held her firm, his weight pinning her beneath him. With her body so encumbered and her powers enveloped, he was so much stronger than she. She could not even cry out with her throat so damaged, but her instincts screamed as she fought to be free. The folds of the cloak that had kept them so warm now blanketed the sounds of the struggle and hid the desperation on her face.

Locked in her terror, she heaved for breath. He was suffocating her and she was powerless to stop him. As the agony in her chest swelled and a red mist covered her sight, she knew she would pass out. He had no real need to squeeze her throat now—it was already ruined and useless—yet he continued to lean, single-mindedly ripping at her breeches with his other hand, struggling to force them from her, and she knew he would succeed. He was being driven to commit a terrible act and she was helpless, choking, the pain in her lungs and her heart overwhelming. Her vision went black and she collapsed as the tearing hands grappled her unresisting limbs. A rough hand parted her legs and she shrieked inside as his powerful body lunged forward to enter her.

The crush on her throat intensified abruptly, as did the weight on her chest. She was dying in blackness and despair. Then the wrenching hands fell still and she vaguely heard shouting. The weight on her body disappeared and her starved lungs heaved for breath, but her throat was too damaged to let the air through. Hands clawed at her again, pulling her to her knees. Pressure built against her mind, frantically trying to force its way in, and the pattern behind it finally imprinted on her brain. Before she passed out completely, she recognized Cal's pattern and opened her mind to his touch. Relief flooded into her as the pain eased, and her body shuddered as she heaved in desperate, wrenching breaths. Bitter agony ripped through her throat, but her body was starved of air and there was nothing she could do. Shivering and wheezing, retching and gasping, supported only by Cal's strength, she crouched on all fours, intent only on taking in air.

A savage scream filled the barn and men's voices cried out.

Scuffling feet and the nervous whinny of a horse could be heard. A harsh, pain-filled cry was followed by the crack of a hand upon flesh, and then there was silence but for Sullyan's agonized breaths. Gradually, the red mist of her sight began to clear.

Tad knelt next to Robin, tears in his eyes, the knife he had wielded fallen to the ground. Dexter took it up and handed it back to the young swordsman, who accepted it in a hand still shaking with fright. The Captain spoke tersely. "Better keep that safe, lad, after what's just happened."

Tad nodded and gulped down a sob, trying not to look at the blood in Robin's hair. Dexter saw his distress and took him by the shoulder. "You did what you had to do! You probably saved her life, and maybe his, too. Don't blame yourself for what's been done. Now, I think you'd better tie his hands, or who knows what he might do when he wakes."

He knelt down beside Cal, who was still supporting Sullyan. She had to fight for every breath—her face was blue, her agonized gasping through her ruined throat painful to hear. Dexter put his hand on Cal's arm. "What can I do?"

Cal's face was pale with the effort of assisting Sullyan's breathing. It was as much as he could do to answer Dexter without relinquishing his life-giving hold on her mind. "Her windpipe's crushed. Find some of those pain-numbing herbs. If we don't help her breathe, she's going to pass out. If she passes out, I won't be able to keep her airway open and she'll suffocate."

Dexter leapt to his feet, brushing past Tad, who was tearfully tying Robin's arms behind his back, rolling the Major's naked body once more in the folds of the cloak. Ignoring Taran, who had been roused by the screams and the scuffle and was desperately trying to gain someone's attention, the Captain grabbed up the medical pack and returned to Cal's side. Calling for someone to see to Taran, and shaking his head at the confusion in the barn,

Dexter fumbled for the herbs. Sullyan's wracking gasps urged him on. She was only vaguely aware of the uproar around her.

Dexter handed Cal the cup. "How are you going to get them into her?"

Cal's breathing was almost as harsh as Sullyan's. "I'll need your help and it won't be nice. Take hold of her head and push her chin up. Quickly now! And I don't care if she struggles or stops breathing. When I say so, force her mouth open and hold it that way. Ready? Now!"

Cal pushed his fingers into Sullyan's open mouth, forcing down her tongue. She gagged and fought them, but they held on to her and eventually she managed to swallow the thick, foul mixture dribbling down her damaged throat. Cal held fast to her psyche, forcing air into her lungs, just praying the strong herbs would do their work. They were not really intended for internal use and he didn't dare think what they would do to her stomach. But they were potent and effective, and even if she brought them up they ought to relieve her long enough to ease her breathing.

Gradually, the dreadful wheezing eased. Sullyan knelt on all fours with Cal at her back to calm her panic. The shock of Robin's attack and the ease with which she had been overwhelmed brought tears to her eyes. The pain and ruin of her throat was deserved payment for her stupidity. She should have known better, and she should have been prepared. Reen would never have let them go so easily had he not known he could still cause them pain, and she should have realized what his taking of their souls meant in terms of control. What had just happened was her fault, and now she had more guilt to bear.

Trying desperately to rein in her emotions, she slowly came upright and glanced up at Cal, nodding her head to let him know she could cope and gripping his arm in heartfelt thanks. If not for Tad's quick thinking and Cal's emergency treatment, she would now be like Robin—dead, but languishing in the scarecrow's power. Fighting down tears and the ache in her throat, she accepted the jacket he held out to her and covered the tatters of her ripped clothing.

She watched Dexter move over to Elias, and realized for the first time that she had not been the sole target this night. It was Sofira who had screamed so savagely, and if she had not, the King might well be dead, too. The knife she had wielded had been meant for his heart. As it was, the wound in his upper arm was deep and bled freely. Tad was working to stitch it shut. Of all of them, his slender fingers were the nimblest and his skill with the needle, learned from his healer mother, had earned him the gratitude of many of his comrades. The delicate work served to take his mind from the blow he had been forced to deal his hero, and this service to the King might restore his sense of worth. He cleaned and bound the wound when he was done, applying some of Rienne's pain-numbing herbs beneath the bindings, as they were meant to be used.

Sullyan heard Dexter's question as he squatted down next to the King. "What the Void happened?"

Elias spared Sullyan a quick glance as he shook his head, transferring his gaze to the still form of his former wife. One of the men was tying her hands, having heard what Dexter had told Tad, and another did the same for Jinella, although she had not stirred.

The King gave a shrug of confusion. "She just went for me. One minute I was sleeping, and the next I heard her shriek and she was coming for me with my own knife. She must have slipped it from my belt without waking me. Her face was all strange—contorted and sort of desperate—and I could swear her eyes were glowing red. Must have been a reflection from the fire, but it chilled me for an instant and I lost my chance to evade her. If it hadn't been for Aldo here, smacking her face with that great fist of his, she'd have had that knife in my heart."

Aldo glanced over from his work beside the Princess, grinning briefly at Dexter's nod of approval. The Captain addressed his men. "Better keep all weapons out of their reach, even if their hands are tied. Two of you are to guard them at all times and no one is to release their hands, no matter what they might need to do." He turned back to the King. "Will you be all right, your Majesty?"

Elias managed a weak grin. "It's Swordsman Elias, Captain, or had you forgotten? With all that's gone on, I'm more than happy to continue under your command. Yes, thank you, I'll be all right. The pain's going now and so are the shakes. But what about Brynne?"

Dexter turned back to check on Sullyan just as a new commotion broke out. Taran had finally learned what had happened and was terrified he would be forced to commit a similar act. He begged a dismayed Cal to truss him hand and foot. His strident pleas rang through the barn, forcing Cal to swamp his mind to press him into calm.

"You'd better do as he asks, Cal."

The hoarse, grating voice made Cal turned his head, his eyes full of tears. Sullyan crouched behind him, her jacket clutched tightly around her bruised and scratched body. Her eyes were haunted and she refused to look at the figure of her life mate.

Dexter came closer, laid his hand on her shoulder. "Will you be well?"

She didn't reply, but she nodded her head, her breath still rasping dreadfully through the ruin of her throat. Sighing, Dexter knelt and bound up Taran's hands, taking care not to pull the ropes too tight. He laid the distressed Adept down beside the unconscious Robin and gestured for two men to stand guard over them. The rest of them moved farther away.

Elias got shakily to his feet, unwilling to remain by the women. All of them were shocked and dismayed by their enemy's power, disturbed by his ability to turn their friends against them. Needing the comfort of comrades and seeing Sullyan's haunted gaze, Elias could take it no more. The love he bore her and the care she had shown him demanded some expression, and he no longer cared who saw it. Cradling his wounded arm close against his chest, he folded himself down beside her and gathered her to him with his free arm as if he had every right.

She glared up at him, her body stiff, but he didn't give way and soon she relented, melting against his side and giving herself over to the warmth and comfort of his body. Her rasping, painful breathing an ever-present reminder of the hurts they had suffered, they sat wide-eyed and helpless as they waited out the night.

Chapter Eleven

A s dawn spread its light from the east, the dispirited company prepared to leave the dubious sanctuary of the old barn. The snow had piled up against the doors during the night and it took six men shoving with all their strength to push them open. Dexter emerged into the wan daylight to find that the gale had blown itself out and a watery sun could be glimpsed behind a gray mist. The snow lay thick upon the frozen ground. They would have a hard time of it if they had to ride back across country rather than travel through the substrate. He sighed in vexation and went back inside to consult with Cal and Sullyan.

He found her standing by her horse, sipping fellan and grimacing through every swallow. She had spent the last of the dark hours in healing, and now her breath was coming easier, sounding less like a whetstone on steel. She had discarded her torn clothing and put on her spare, and her hair was braided as usual. But she was unable to clear her mind of the dreadful events of the night. Her face was still pale and her eyes were hot and haunted. She raised her head at Dexter's approach, glad for a distraction from the desolation of her thoughts.

He spoke softly. "What are your plans for the day, Colonel?"

She glanced toward the fire, where guards were tending the four they had rescued. With the coming of dawn, they had reverted to their state of the day before. Robin's eyes were open and free of demonic glow, but they were also devoid of intelligent thought. He seemed to have no comprehension that his hands were tied and mechanically took the sustenance offered him by Tad. The young swordsman had cleaned up the fresh wound under his hero's ear and had taken responsibility for Robin's care. The Major's pliant, catatonic state seemed to ridicule the violence he had shown only a few hours before, and Sullyan's eyes filled at the memory of his vicious assault. Although she knew it was the Baron behind the attack, still she could not erase the terror of lying helpless beneath Robin, knowing she would be raped. All the old feelings of terror and despair instilled in her by Rykan's abuse came flooding back. This, no doubt, was the Baron's intention. Knowing he could not harm her himself, he had attacked her through her friends, well aware she would not stand it for long. Already, a fierce and terrible rage was growing in her breast, and the sight of her loved ones' predicament fueled the flames of her vengeance.

Cal tended to Taran. The Adept had woken with a start and a cry, still fearful of being taken over by the Baron. His eyes were dreadfully haunted by what he had endured and witnessed. Sullyan still did not feel able to speak to him again.

Jinella had neither moved, woken, nor made a single sound, and by her sat the whimpering Princess, whose pitiful litany of garbled denials had resumed the moment her eyes flickered open.

Dragging her eyes away from their torment, Sullyan turned back to Dexter. "We need to establish whether we can use the Veils to return to the Manor. Until we know that, we can make no other plans."

"And how will you do that?"

She sighed. "I will have to speak with Taran. He is the only one who can help us. If he cannot bear the touch of the substrate, even with shielding, we will have to ride back the long way. If we are forced to do that, I will send Elias on ahead; I will not risk him further."

Dexter nodded. "Have you contacted the General yet?"

"I have informed him very briefly. I will contact him again once I know our situation."

She finished her fellan and gave Dexter the cup. Squaring her shoulders and gathering her courage, she approached Taran.

"Stay back, Brynne, I beg you!" There was terror in his tone. "I don't know what I might do. I can feel him in my mind, it's not safe!"

Tears blurred her vision as she ignored his request, folding herself down beside him. He reared away, as far as his cramped position and bound hands would allow.

"Please, Taran, I need your help. There is no one else I can ask."

He closed his eyes briefly, pain crossing his features. "What do you want?"

It was so unlike him, this strained reluctance, but she forced it away from her mind. None of them was as they had been before. They were all altered by what their enemy had done. Scant surprise, then, that he should react this way.

"My friend, I need to know if you have control over your psyche."

He gaped at her and his face turned pale. "My mind's not my own, Brynne, you can't ask me that!"

"I have to, Taran, and you have to help us. We need to get everyone back to the Manor. We are injured and weary. Will you force us to ride miles through the snow because you will not try?"

His look of betrayal at the uncompromising tone of her rasping voice stabbed her heart with guilt. She pushed it away. Ignoring his tortured expression, she tried again.

"The Manor is your only hope. I know what you fear, and I fear it too. You saw what happened last night. Both Elias and I could have been killed. The last thing I want is to expose any of us to more of the same, least of all you or Robin. But if we can reach the Manor, the College may be able to help. Remember, the healer suite has walls of spellsilver. It is my hope that the Baron cannot control you once you are within them. You can be free of his threat while we search for a way to rid you of his influence. But if we have to spend more nights in the open, I fear what his power may do. Now do you see why I ask you?"

It was clear that Taran had not considered the spellsilver in the walls of the healer suite. Judging by the expressions of hope on the faces of the men gathered close, neither had they. Sullyan shielded her thoughts very carefully, especially from young Tad, who gazed at her with wide-eyed adoration, his trust in her power implicit. For the truth was, she didn't know for sure whether even the presence of the ore would hinder the Baron's hold. He had survived immolation in a pool of the substance, and Taran himself had told her it had not prevented him from reaving Robin of his life force. Yet it was her only hope, and she clung to it, watching it filter through to Taran, seeing him grasp at it like a drowning man.

"What do you want me to do?"

She hid her heartfelt sigh of relief from the Adept. She needed detachment now, not turbulent emotions. Until they knew what they faced, stark reality had to prevail.

"Can you access your psyche, Adept? Is it under your control?"

Taran closed his eyes and tentatively reached for his psyche. The attacks during the night had affected him deeply and his touch was flinching and half-hearted. There was an alien thread in his mind, a pathway he could not close down, and he knew it led straight to the Baron. But when he tested his control of his power, it seemed to obey him as always. There was no response down the unnatural connecting thread. He opened his eyes and met her gaze. "I think so."

She smiled, but her approval didn't warm him as it usually did. He was too fearful of losing his hold, and he knew she feared that, too.

"Then deploy your shield, if you will."

Doing as she bid, he felt the familiar swell of the shield flood over his senses, blocking out external influences. She enquired as to its strength and he answered that it appeared to be holding. She gestured the others to clear a space of floor around them.

"I am going to raise Earth and form a small portway. If you feel even a moment's pain, tell me."

He nodded and she accessed her force. The shimmer of Earth power began to rise about him, its opalescent gleaming telling him the Veils were being breached. He felt nothing but the tingle of its touch on his mind, and no pain came to break his control. With a sigh of relief, she let the power go and sat breathing carefully, her throat tight with pain.

"I thank you, Taran. That was courageous."

She got stiffly to her feet and began to order the company, the men making ready to leave the barn. She knew her curt tone revealed how greatly she had feared the outcome of the experiment, and she sensed Taran's pang of guilt at his reluctance. He cast down his eyes as Cal aided him to his feet, trying not to look at Robin, who blankly followed young Tad. They were all desperate to return to the Manor, where the security of the healer suite might relieve them of this terrible burden of fear.

✣ ✣ ✣ ✣ ✣

Early it might be, but Rienne was already in the infirmary when Hyram came to fetch her. The General's valet found her deep in discussion with Hanan, the older woman having discovered a simple herb that she thought could be used to counter the effects of the poison that had killed the nursemaid Bessie and so nearly taken

First Minister Levant's life. Despite exhaustive searching, they had been unable to find a single toxin that would produce all the symptoms exhibited by those affected. Hanan surmised it was a combination of substances and, lacking a sample to test, they would likely never identify it.

However, the insignificant herb she had read of in an ancient, half-legible document concerning the treatment of scouring in sheep was credited with being able to counter those exact same symptoms—at least in ovines. They had a small supply of the dried herb in the pharmacy stores, but Hanan wanted to obtain the fresh plant and distil it, to see if refining its essence would render it effective in humans.

When Hyram arrived with the summons from the General, they were discussing how best to increase their stock of the herb, a furry-leafed plant called temany, as it grew best in high country such as the Torlands. More importantly, how they would test its efficacy without endangering the subject.

"They're on their way back," the valet reported when he had the two women's attention. "The General requests your presence, Healers. Colonel Sullyan wishes to make use of the College healer suite."

Hanan and Rienne collected extra medical supplies and followed Hyram. "Are any of them badly wounded? Is Cal all right? Have they found Taran?" Rienne asked.

The middle-aged man shrugged. "I don't know the details, Healer Arlen, I only know what the General told me. They're making their way back right now, and there are injured among the party."

They emerged into the courtyard to see Bull coming their way. Rienne glanced at him then shot him a keener look, noting the pallor of his face and the slight blue tinge to his lips. She frowned. "Are you all right, Bull?"

She had spent most of the previous evening hearing his report to the General about what he and Sullyan had discovered on the clerics' island, and she had checked on his heart and his supply of medication before allowing him to retire. To her relief, all had seemed well. Yet this morning his aspect had changed and her concern for his health returned in force.

Bull glanced down at her and smiled briefly, the expression not touching his honest brown eyes. "Oh, I'm all right, Rienne. But the news isn't good, and I'm feeling very afraid."

She paled. "Cal's all right, isn't he? Oh, have they not found Taran? Please, Bull, don't tell me they've failed!"

Bull threw his arm about her shoulders as they hurried along, unwilling to say any more. "Let's just wait and see, dear heart."

They waited near the College, straining to hear the hoof beats. Hanan went inside to warn Jay'el to keep the children out of the way. Blaine had given strict orders that they were not to see or greet the returning company, at least until the wounded were settled. This worried Rienne even more than Bull's vague information, hinting as it did at sights too awful for the children to see.

Finally, they heard the sound of horses and the low mutter of voices. A group of stable boys came trotting round the corner ahead of the bulk of the riders. Bull sighed with relief when he caught sight of Sullyan, but her expression made his face go pale. She ignored his presence and rode straight up to Rienne.

She slid down Drum's shoulder, and a stable boy led the stud away. After ascertaining that Cal was present and hale, Rienne registered Elias's bandaged arm and the swordsmen riding double. She sent Bull to help with the wounded. Then she came forward to speak with Sullyan, her heart aflutter.

"Brynne, where's Taran? Don't tell me he's dead—I just couldn't bear it!"

"I'm here, Rienne." The Adept's strained voice reached Rienne's ears as Cal helped him off his horse. Rienne ran to him, exclaiming in dismay as she saw the state of his body and the bonds on his wrists.

"Leave him be, Rienne," Sullyan said, more harshly then she meant to. "Help me get them inside the College. I will explain later."

Her rasping voice and cold tone cut through Rienne's distraction. Casting her friend a look of confusion, Rienne responded to the urgency in Sullyan's manner. She put aside her bewilderment and was about to take Taran from Cal when she heard Bull give vent to a vicious expletive. Her head snapped toward the sound and her eyes widened in shock. She stood frozen as Robin walked toward her, led carefully by Tad as if he were blind. The younger swordsman's eyes were filled with tears.

Bull stared between Sullyan and Robin, his face white and his mouth open. Then he strode up to Sullyan and grasped her by the shoulders. "I thought you said he was dead?"

His voice was raw and edged with disbelief, and Rienne knew he was remembering the raging Fire she had set loose with her grief. "How could you have been mistaken about something like that?"

Sullyan spoke hoarsely, tears forming in her eyes. "I was not mistaken."

The big man spread his hands, staring from her to the Major. "But—"

"Just look at him, Bull!" Sullyan's voice rasped out, full of savage despair. "Take a long, close look! Look into his eyes and search for his soul. Reach for his mind and tell me what you see. His spirit has been taken, his soul has been destroyed! Only his body remains to us, but for how long, I cannot say."

Her furious outburst rocked Bull, and he stood dismayed.

Rienne knew how he felt. This was way beyond their experience, way beyond belief. Robin stood there so perfect, so obviously *alive*, yet the blank stare of those indigo eyes was devoid of character and spirit. The truth of Sullyan's words cut into Bull's heart and he clasped his arms about his chest, bowing his head, unable to bear the pain of this cruelty. Sullyan watched him, her ire draining away, her own stiff sorrow returning in force.

"I know, Bull. I know. Better that his body had died too. It is what we all fear and dread, is it not, losing our minds and existing without?"

Bull raised haunted eyes to hers. "So what do we do? What *can* we do? We can't leave him like this!"

Sullyan ignored Bull's question. "Take them into the healer suite and make sure they cannot leave. I must report to the General."

Rienne's face paled when she saw the other two captives, both with their hands bound behind them, but Jinny's inertia and the Princess's moans galvanized her and she efficiently organized their retreat into the College. The King followed them to speak to his children, and the other wounded men were helped to the infirmary. Sullyan left for the General's office, leaving Bull unsure whether to follow her and hear her report or go with the wounded and help Rienne. Seeing his confusion, the healer decided for him. She and Hanan could cope, and he would only get under their feet. Head hanging, he made his way into the Manor, feeling in his pocket for Rienne's packet of heart-calming herbs.

✠ ✠ ✠ ✠ ✠

Sullyan found the General in his office, awaiting her report. She knew Bull had told him the majority of what they had discovered on the clerics' island, and once she had downed the fellan he wordlessly held out to her she ran over it again, making sure he understood the implications of their findings, especially in the light of what had transpired since. Bull arrived halfway through, and he busied himself unobtrusively at the hearth, brewing more fellan and nursing his fears.

General Blaine sat in silence, although the rasp of her voice drew an expression of concern. His eyes widened at the tale that unfolded and the conclusions she had drawn, and he was confused and confounded by the problem they now faced.

Sullyan sat gripping her cup with hands that trembled. "He made it easy for us, Mathias. He wanted us to find them. He wanted us to take them, for he knows how it will hurt me. This is precisely why he left them in this dreadful state of limbo. He has mastery over their minds now, and I hardly know what to do. I very much fear that he has defeated us this time. I very much fear I will be forced to bow to his will."

Blaine frowned. "But why can't we just kill him and put an end to this threat? He cannot control them if he is dead."

She sighed in vexation. "Believe me, killing him is exactly what I yearn to do, and I think he half expected me to do it. He made no move to protect himself when Elias attacked him from behind, and he was most amused when I was forced to use my powers to preserve his miserable life. Had I not been quick enough, had Elias succeeded, I dread to think where the monster's soul would have gone with four empty bodies under his full control."

The General's face turned pale, sickened by what she implied. Sullyan continued. "Besides, he showed me very clearly what an attempt on his life would do to Robin's body …" She paused, something nagging at her as she replayed the scene in her mind, some small discrepancy that, try as she might, she could not identify. She shook her head, resolving to puzzle it out later. "Even putting that aside, if I were to kill him without redeeming their souls, I would condemn them to spend eternity in the sphere of his power. They have no link back to their own bodies; he has destroyed it and forged another, one that he alone controls. They would either be cast adrift, to wander aimlessly until their spirits slowly faded, or be joined to him forever, and then their torment would never cease."

Blaine stared in horrified dismay. "Then what are we to do? We can't suffer him to live, knowing what he has planned! You don't even know that the spellsilver will protect them, not if what Taran told you about Reen's power is true. And I will never let you surrender to him. You know what will happen then!"

"I have not forgotten, General! Did you think I had?"

The acerbic tone of her voice cut through the General's anger. Seeing his chagrin, she moderated her tone, speaking more gently. "I have told Dexter to keep them restrained until we have tested the College's protection. If the spellsilver blocks Reen's control, their hands can be freed, and at least they can move about the healer suite. Once that is done, I will go to Andaryon to consult with my father. Perhaps there is something in his archives to help us solve this terrible dilemma. At the moment, I can think of nothing else to do. I am open to suggestions, Mathias."

If the General had any, he had no leisure to voice them, for a commotion sounded in the corridor outside. The sound of running feet and a young, strident voice reached their ears. Sullyan bowed her face to her hands, recognizing the piercing whine of Princess Seline and knowing who would bear the brunt of the spiteful girl's anger. Somehow, Seline had discovered what had happened to her mother and needed to lash out in her habitual way.

The door to the General's office slammed open and Seline rushed into the room. Hyram appeared behind her, hands spread helplessly, but Blaine waved him away. There was nothing the valet could have done to hinder the Princess's entry. The young girl was followed by Elias and Rienne. The King's face was thunderous, while Rienne appeared anxious and afraid.

Seline, ignoring the General's presence and her father's angry roar, flew at Sullyan, her outstretched hands raking like claws. "What have you done to my mother? You've betrayed us, you witch! You've broken her mind! I want you dismissed—I want you disgraced!"

Sullyan fended off the Princess's attack, holding the girl's wrists and avoiding her kicks. She was stronger than Seline, but the girl was beside herself, sobbing and screaming foul imprecations, not caring who heard her use of expletives. Elias's scowl deepened. Seeing her so violent and Sullyan's reluctance to restrain her more forcibly, the King lunged forward and grasped his daughter firmly by the arms, pinning them to her sides and wincing as he strained his injured arm. He dragged her roughly back and shook her, hard.

"Seline, control yourself! I've already told you this is not Brynne's fault. It's the Baron's doing. He's the real enemy. Brynne rescued your mother and you should be grateful, not behaving like some bawling tavern brat!"

Seline turned on Elias, her face contorted with fury. "Oh, yes, Father, you'd really like us to be grateful to her, wouldn't you! You'd like us all to grovel at her feet and fawn over her every word, just like you do. Well, we're not all blind like you! We've not all been bewitched by her charms, we've not all fallen under her spell. Some of us can see her for the treacherous bitch she is, but you're too full of lust for her, aren't you? No wonder my mother hated her—no wonder you sent her away! You're too busy bedding your little concubine to see what she really is. She's a common whore, and you can think of nothing else than crawling between her legs!"

Chapter Twelve

There was a stunned silence, broken only by Seline's angry panting. Rienne had her hands to her mouth and the General looked appalled. Sullyan had turned white and Bull gaped in astonishment. Elias's face had turned purple and none of them had ever seen such a fire of rage as that which burned in his eyes and caused his limbs to tremble.

Seline seemed to realize she had gone too far for she suddenly took a pace backward, away from his menacing aspect. But she was not quick enough to avoid his cracking blow, and she fell to the ground with a shrill shriek as his hand snapped her head on her shoulders. Rienne twitched, as if torn between offering comfort and striking the brat herself. In the end, her Healer instincts won out and she gathered the Princess into her arms.

Elias regarded his sobbing daughter with unconcealed dislike. He raised clouded blue eyes to Sullyan, as if fearful of her reaction. "I'm so sorry you had to hear that, Brynne. If you want to rescind your Oath to my daughter, I'll not stand in your way. I knew she was jealous, I knew she disliked you, but I never for one moment thought she harbored such notions as these. It must have been Sofira's doing. I know I have done nothing to give her such suspicions."

Sullyan shook her head, too full of her own pain and problems to worry much over the jealousy of one little girl, even if she was Elias's daughter. It did not surprise her that Seline had formed such ideas. She must have heard the rumors that had circulated the castle for years now, spread by those who distrusted an Artesan's motives despite the loyal service she and her kind had given the crown. Sullyan's undeniable part in Sofira's disgrace had validated those rumors in the young girl's mind and fanned the flames of her hatred. Seline would never be comfortable in Sullyan's presence, that much was plain, especially when the essence of her outburst was really no less than the truth. Elias had made no secret of the regard in which he held his colonel. She faced the King openly and waved down his dismay.

"Pay it no heed, Elias. Of course I will not rescind my Oath. She is distraught and afraid, and I understand how she feels. If the healer suite proves adequate protection, she should be permitted to stay with her mother while the Princess is here. It may be that Seline's presence will comfort Sofira." She forbore to add that it might be Seline's last chance to spend time with her mother.

Rienne raised her head from consoling the girl, who had lapsed into shuddering sobs not unlike her mother's mindless litany. "I will take her back to her quarters for now, but before I go, I have a message. Taran has been asking for you. He says he has something to tell you, something you ought to know."

"I will be there directly, Rienne."

The healer encouraged the Princess to her feet and led her out of the room. The girl went without protest, shocked into compliance by the force of her father's blow.

Elias stood shamefaced. "I really am very sorry, Brynne. I couldn't keep it from her that her mother was here, and then, of course, she was frantic to see her. Although I explained what had happened and why her mother was bound like a prisoner, the moment she saw Sofira she just exploded. It was all I could do to keep up with her as she ran here. I knew she would say something stupid, but I didn't think she would accuse us of *that*."

Sullyan shook her head. "Really, Elias, pay it no mind. Seline dislikes me. There is no help for it. It is not so surprising, given what has happened. I fully understand her distress. Now, gentlemen, if you will excuse me, I must go and see what Taran has to say."

Elias reached into a pocket and pulled out a parchment. "Before you do, I think you ought to see this. You, too, Mathias."

He handed her the parchment and she took it to the desk, spreading it out so the General could read it also.

The King slumped into a chair by the fire. His tone was sad. "It was given to me by one of the men. He found it when they searched Lerric's rooms, but didn't remember it until we got back here."

There was silence while they read the letter, and when they were done Sullyan had tears in her eyes. The General's expression was bleak as he stared at his monarch with a hard gaze.

"So, now we know what he wanted to tell us. If only Sofira hadn't stopped him. If only he'd found the courage sooner—"

"If only one of you had noticed his pain and approached him alone!"

Both men started at Sullyan's exasperated outburst, stung by her accusation. The knowledge that Lerric had probably paid for his spinelessness with his life only made her sorrow deeper. They had seen no sign of his body, and she could only hope he had not suffered. Given the Baron's vengeful nature, she had scant reason to put much store by that hope.

She sighed, putting Lerric's profound regrets and useless apologies from her mind. Dwelling on what might have been was counterproductive and would only weaken her further. She eyed the General. "I really must go to Taran, and then I want to spend time with my son. I intend to try for some sleep before night falls, but when it does, I will watch over the Baron's captives until I am sure he cannot harm them. Tomorrow, I will go to my father."

The General nodded and waved her away. He leaned back in his chair, accepting fellan from Bull. The big man also served the King, who took his cup with hands that still shook. Sullyan turned on her heel and left the room, grateful to escape the atmosphere of confusion and hopelessness.

She was keen to make her visit to Pharikian, but had to wait until she knew whether the spellsilver could indeed block the Baron's malicious influence. She knew not whether the Andaryan archives contained a solution to their predicament. Yet if that failed, it had also occurred to her that she might, with Pharikian's help, be able to forge a route through the Baron's control and wrest his captives from him by force. It might be that his mastery was not as complete as he thought. Reen did not have the years of experience she and her adoptive father had amassed, after all. And if she and Pharikian failed ... There were four souls at stake here and she would never forgive herself if she attempted a rescue only to leave some of them stranded. How much more would Reen torture those he had left if she did not succeed in freeing them all? That prospect was too terrible even to imagine.

She walked the College's quiet corridors until she came to the healer suite. Guards stood by the doors, alert and watchful. Nodding, she passed them by, making for the rooms where Reen's captives were quartered and ignoring for the moment the one that held her son. She badly needed rest, having had little sleep for two nights now, and ached to spend time with Morgan—but first she must speak with Taran. She found more guards on each internal door, as she had specified, and entered Taran's room. He glanced up at her, haunted fear in his eyes. Her heart contracted at the sight of his pale face, and the bonds on his hands filled her with sorrow.

"Ah, Taran, if only I could free you from this! I hold myself totally responsible. Had I not pleaded for his misbegotten life and spared him the Wheel, none of this would have happened. Had I not been so urgent to free Elias from Sofira's threat, the Baron would have been long dead. I should have realized she would never have had the courage to act against Elias alone. As it is, all I did was store up trouble for later and leave him free to work his poison."

Taran's hazel eyes were dull with despair. "Don't blame yourself, Brynne, it will only give you pain. You couldn't have foreseen he would come into his powers. You did what you had to, to protect Elias. I sent Rienne to tell you that I believe the spellsilver is working. Since being brought inside the walls, I can't sense him in my mind. The link is still there, but his presence is not. It's left a void, though, and it feels very strange. I didn't realize it was there before, but now Reen's influence has gone, it's obvious. I don't like it. I don't feel … *right*. It's the only way I can describe it. It's like some vital part of me is missing and I can't survive long without it."

Hearing this made Sullyan's blood run cold. The first part of Taran's news was heartening—the spellsilver seemed to be blocking the Baron's control. This would enable her to remove the sufferers' bonds and make their imprisonment in the College more bearable. But the consequences of blocking their captor's immediate control was one she had not foreseen, and the Baron's cruel words came back to haunt her.

"My patience will not hold forever and the body can only survive so long without a soul."

She stared in dismay at the tormented man before her. She could not hide her dread and he guessed her thoughts.

"We're damned, aren't we?" His shoulders slumped and he bowed his head. "He's never going to release us, Brynne, not even if you submit to him. We either stay here and wither for the lack of a soul, or perish by his malice while controlled by his will. And even if you did convince him to trade us for your surrender, once he has your powers at his command, he's eventually going to destroy the world. We all know that's his ultimate aim. Kill all the Artesans and then bring down the Veils. He didn't believe you before when you told him what that would do to the realms, and he's hardly going to listen to you now. Our only hope is that when he does destroy the Veils his hold over us will be broken, and we'll be freed from the threat of Perdition."

Sullyan had no real comfort for him and not much hope in her soul. But until she had explored every possibility, she would not bow to Reen's cruelty. She had to give Taran something to hold on to.

"Do not give in to despair, my friend, not yet. There are powers yet untapped in this wide world of ours and no one has all the answers. I will fight this to the bitter end, whatever that may be, and hope, strength, and love may yet play their part. Do not cede him the victory until the last battle is fought. Remember Rykan—remember the circle! Remember how hopeless the situation seemed then? Answers have been found at the final hour before. Keep praying that they will be again."

He raised teary eyes at the love in her broken voice, longing to hold her and to be held. She was too raw and her emotions running too strong to allow him that comfort, much as they both desired it. There was one other she could offer him, however, and she gave it willingly, thinking that it might even work in their favor. Holding on to what they believed, and the depth and strength of the ties that bound them, might serve to empower their souls and keep them protected from the Baron's evil influence. Turning her head, she called Taran's guard.

Ralf appeared quickly, anxious and fearful, but she put him at ease with a smile. "I think Taran would be more comfortable if he was by Jinella's side. Free his hands so he can tend to her, but I want you to bind him come evening. Until we know for sure that the Baron cannot reach them, we must still be cautious."

She turned back to the Adept. "Are you content, my friend? Ralf will still be here to guard you and you can rely on him to do what is right. But I have a feeling that being close to Jinella may help both of you, and you need all the comfort you can get right now."

Taran bowed his head again and Sullyan had to turn away, her own heart too sore to watch the slow crushing of his spirit. She gripped Ralf's arm as she passed him, a cautionary look in her eye. The swordsman, long used to her ways, recognized and understood her tacit warning. She left knowing he would restrain Taran should the need arise, and that the Adept was safe in his care.

She passed the room where Robin lay on her way to see her son, but lacked the courage to open the door. Tad was inside, caring for his hero, and she let them alone, too weary and sore to deal with her pain. Making her way to the children's rooms, Sullyan spent time consoling her distraught and confused son before lying down to sleep, Morgan curled safe in her arms.

✢ ✢ ✢ ✢ ✢

In a state of euphoria, Princess Lirina sat at her dressing table and watched her maid in the mirror as the girl unbound the priceless fillet from her elaborate curls. It was late in the evening and lamplight warmed the room, reflecting from the fillet's golden wires and jade-pearls. Lirina hugged herself, trying to contain the turmoil of emotions surging through her soul. Her reception at Caer Vellet had been all she had dreamed of and more, and she could scarcely believe her good fortune. She could barely sit still as she recalled the day's events and remembered the plans for the morrow. Her long-suffering maid, after some pointed sighs went ignored, laid down her brush in exasperation and regarded her mistress with a reproving smile.

"If you don't keep still, my Lady, I fear I will damage this beautiful fillet. I know you are excited, but you really must calm down. You'll never sleep if you keep on like this, and then you will not look your best when you greet your lord in the morning."

Lirina caught the girl's hands in her own, her eyes over-bright and her cheeks flushed with emotion. "For goodness sake, Shandra, how can you expect me to calm down? How can I sit still after the night I've just had? Did you see Prince Aeyron's face? Did you see the way he looked at me, the way he held my hand? He didn't want to leave my side the whole evening, not even for his father! And as for sleeping, well, if you felt the way I do, you'd know it is impossible. I don't feel tired, I feel elated! I don't think I'll ever feel tired again, not while I have Aeyron's love to sustain me."

Lirina was twenty-eight years of age. She had grown up knowing her fate was to wed to the advantage of her father's province. She had received suitors aplenty, some she had even admired, but none had come up to her father's high standards. Most were younger sons with little in the way of prospects, and Lirina had resigned herself to spinsterhood.

To while away the time, she immersed herself in her family's shipping interests and soon learned the sea-trade routes as well as any sailor. The Princess learned the value of the cargoes they shipped to foreign ports, and knew exactly what to expect in return. She ran her father's household with her younger sister's help, and saw to the provisioning of the palace. She received the factors in charge of each trade commodity and listened to their advice before placing her orders. She investigated every fluctuation in prices and adjusted her father's accordingly. She was accepted by the businessmen who flourished in the city, and was soon regarded as a shrewd and respected bargainer.

When a dreadful storm struck their coastline, forcing the Hierarch's trade flagship to limp into their port, it was Lirina who ordered Perinath's harbormaster to permit Captain Ky-shan a berth for repairs. And although it was Lord Seyakin who granted Ky-shan an audience on the strength of the Hierarch's seal, Lirina had been by his side to receive the burly sailor and his handsome son, and she instantly recognized the value of trade links with Caer Vellet. She was charmed by the ex-pirate's flattering attention, never dreaming he had more in mind than the furtherance of commerce. The only thoughts of romance she entertained had concerned the instant attraction between her sister and Ky-shan's son. When her father informed her some weeks later that he had received a message from the Hierarch requesting hospitality for his son, the Crown Prince, Lirina had no idea she was the cause of his visit. It had seemed perfectly reasonable that the ruler of Andaryon should send his son to her father to discuss the affairs of trade. The revelation of Aeyron's true interest had set her heart to racing.

Lirina's emotions had deepened and intensified throughout their courtship, and now that she was here in the court of her beloved, with the welcome she had received still resounding in her heart, she could not contain her excitement. Her feelings overflowed, causing her to behave like some silly, foolish girl. The events of the day kept replaying before her eyes: the strange journey through the Veils and the thrill of Aeyron's mastery over forces she could hardly imagine; the royal welcome on the Plains and the stirring acclaim of the Hierarch's forces; her first sight of the Citadel and Aeyron's evident pleasure at her awe; and the cheering of the people as she rode through the streets.

And then the ascent toward the Palace and the knotting of her stomach, trembling anxiety over the reception she would receive from the Supreme Ruler of her realm. Yet he had known exactly how to calm her, that gentle, powerful man, and he had taken her into his arms as if she were his daughter already, murmuring his welcome privately into her ear. He had made her smile with some easy comment, and walked her into the Palace with her hand upon his arm.

She could find no fault with the apartments allotted her, nor the provisions made for her ladies and their security during their stay. The Hierarch's men were unobtrusive yet watchful. She felt as safe here as she did in her own chambers at home. And the banquet they hosted for her! The music, the dancing, the feasting, and the laughing! All had been a revelation and served to make her feel at home. She had been presented to so many people she could scarcely remember their names, but she knew she would be forgiven if she had to ask for them again. No one seemed hostile, no one caused her worry, and the attentions of her handsome suitor were all she could have desired. The love his people bore him was evident, and the fact that they seemed willing to include his intended bride put the final seal on Lirina's hopes of happiness.

Yet now she had a problem, and she couldn't see how to resolve it. They had a full day ahead of them tomorrow. Aeyron had told her of the procession that would take them through the town, and an early start was needed or they would never make it to every district. His obvious pride in her and desire to show her off had warmed her heart as much as his concern for his people. It would be exhausting, and a good night's sleep was essential. Yet how could she manage that when her heart was tied up in knots?

Fortunately, Shandra had come prepared. Although only twenty years of age, she had been with the Princess for five years and knew her mistress well. She had watched the Princess's demeanor change as it went through the various phases, and was not surprised by the intensity of her emotions. Lirina had repressed her desires in line with her father's wishes, but now that love had been seeded within her heart it would sprout and grow tall and bear sweet fruit. Until she learned to weather these emotional tempests, there would be many nights like this. Shandra prepared a soothing drink and brought it to her mistress.

"Here, my Lady, take this. It has relaxing properties and might even help you sleep. The time will go too slowly if you don't try to get some rest. Why not slip into bed? It looks warm and soft to me. I will finish here and come and talk with you, if you find you still can't sleep."

Shandra helped Lirina into the vast, luxurious bed. The powder she had mixed into the Princess's usual drink had her sleeping calmly and soundly before half an hour had passed. The young woman smiled fondly and continued with her duties.

Chapter Thirteen

O nce night had fully fallen, Rienne came to Sullyan and woke her. Preparations had been made according to her wishes and the time had come to test the spellsilver's protection.

Sullyan opened eyes dulled by fear and anguish. Lying curled around her son, she had almost forgotten her friends' terrible plight. Sleep had taken her deeply for once, and her dreams were innocent and formless. Upon waking the memories flooded back and a great lassitude seized her, infusing her bones with dread. She groaned and sat up, and Morgan whimpered softly as he caught his mother's distress.

The healer spoke softly. "You said you wanted me to wake you, but maybe I should have ignored your request and allowed you to sleep a little longer. You look as if you need it."

"There are many things I need, and sleep is the least."

Her broken voice caused Rienne's eyes to mist. Sullyan could not help but sense the storm of rage that swept through her healer friend, a storm that might, under extreme circumstances, render her capable of killing. She also sensed Rienne's shock at this realization.

"Your love for your friends runs deep, Rienne. Be not ashamed by the urge to protect them. It may well be needed before this is through."

Rienne looked startled. "What do you mean?"

Sullyan unwound her son's arms from around her neck. "We have to face hard facts. It may be that this time I will fail. Where, then, will that leave those we love? Could you bear to see them wither, like a flower in summer's drought? Could you watch them fade slowly away? You, who are their healer, may have to make a terrible decision."

"Stop it, Brynne, for god's sake, stop! I won't listen to such talk. This is not like you—I've never heard you sound so beaten. I won't let you give up hope, not while they're still so much alive!"

"Alive? Is that what you think? Ah, well, maybe they think so too, those who *can* think, and I would not take that from them just yet."

Rienne stared in horror, but Sullyan knew she understood her pain. It wasn't only her voice that had been broken by the Baron's assault on her life mate—she and Robin were truly joined in life, and Reen had also raped part of Sullyan's soul. The malicious giving back of Robin's stripped-out shell was the scarecrow's master stroke. He knew exactly how to hurt her. Rienne knew that the wounds and the scars of Rykan's abuse had never fully healed. Forcing Robin to attack Sullyan with the same goal in mind was guaranteed to reopen those wounds. The continuing decline of the friends she loved would also eat into her resolve, sapping what strength she had left. Even if the spellsilver in the healer suite blocked his control, Reen's vengeance would still carry weight.

Rienne said the first thing that came into her head. "Don't give up, Brynne, don't let him win. None of them is dead yet—don't we owe it to them not to despair? Don't hold the wake—"

"—before the bloody funeral!"

They both started at the deep voice by the door. A small smile twisted Sullyan's lips. Bull's solid presence lent her strength, as it always did. He was so dependable, so unflappable, and so necessary to her life. She found it hard to despair when he used his ritual phrase. Even if this time she feared she would fail. She straightened from comforting Morgan and stepped toward the door.

Her young son desperately wanted to see his father, but she knew the experience would traumatize him and she couldn't stand the sight of his distress. Besides, she could only guess at the Baron's triumph should she bring her son into his power. No greater force could he bring to bear to force her to surrender. So the tearful child remained behind, and a swordsman stood by the door to guard him and the other children.

All four of the Baron's victims were now gathered in the main room of the healer suite. It was a roomy and uncluttered space, intended to cater for large numbers of wounded, and had never yet been used. The beds were stacked neatly in one corner, save for four that occupied the center of the room. Each bed had an occupant, and all were fastened securely to the frames by one wrist—even Jinella, who still had not opened her eyes. Taran had the bed next to hers and his haunted gaze sought Sullyan as she entered the room.

Captain Dexter had his men positioned around the walls, there to protect their colonel should the spellsilver prove insufficient. Dexter himself stood behind the bed where Robin lay, his usually cheerful face gaunt and grim. He had ordered Tad from the Major's side, the youth protesting as strongly as he dared. But Dexter wasn't about to trust Tad with what might have to be done should things go awry. He needed to know that the hand wielding the blade was steady and sure, and Tad's might waver at the final, crucial moment. If the only service Dexter could render his commander and friend was the painless taking of his life, he wouldn't balk at the task.

Ralf stood behind Taran, and Elias hovered by Sofira's side.

Sullyan raised her brows at the King's presence. She had specifically ordered he was not to attend. Yet when she opened her mouth to order him from the room, he averted his eyes and took up Sofira's free hand. A look of resigned annoyance crossed her face, but she let him be, motioning Aldo curtly forward to stand behind the King. The swordsman obeyed her instantly, under no illusions as to why he was there. Elias heard the movement behind him and shot Sullyan a grateful glance, which she ignored. His gratitude might be grossly misplaced. She just hoped she would not regret allowing him to stay.

At least the King's presence relieved them of one irritation: with him close by, Sofira remained quiet. Rienne had told Sullyan that the Princess had not ceased her mindless denials for one moment. Elias's touch seemed to soothe her and she had lapsed into silence, her eyes wide and wild, her face bleached white.

Sullyan's gaze turned to Jinella, who lay still and unmoving on the bed next to Taran. The slight rise and fall of her breast was the only indication her body still lived. She had never moved once, nor shown any sign she was anything other than a breathing corpse, and seeing her like that tore at Sullyan's heart. Jinny was normally such a lively woman, so full of life and vitality—the fact she was the Baron's niece, his own flesh and blood, made his malignant act all the more repulsive. As he, no doubt, had intended. Sullyan glanced at the swordsman by Jinny's bed, seeing him ready and alert. Refusing to meet Taran's haunted gaze, Sullyan moved toward the bed where her beloved life mate lay.

She looked down on his handsome face, trying to shut out her last memory—the one of the baleful red glow in his eyes as he crushed her throat and ripped at her clothes. It hadn't been him, she knew that very well, but it was hard to separate her feeling of terror from the sight of his face before her. Raising her eyes to the men of her company, she let them know she was ready. Then she sat down on the bed and took up Robin's unbound hand.

There was no response from the young man, no flicker behind his eyes or pressure on her fingers. She stretched out her other hand and stroked the line of his cheek. Her fingers trembled where they rested on his skin and she made no effort to still them. She concentrated on his face, watching for any reaction. When none was forthcoming, she took in a deep breath and accessed her psyche.

Isolating Robin's familiar, well-loved pattern, she held it before her inner sight as she quested for his mind. Slowly and carefully feeling her way, she cast her senses into him, alert for any signs that he could feel her presence. Yet there was only a void, a great emptiness where his soul should be, and a wail of deepest loss threatened to break free of her iron control. Fighting it down, she tried again. She could hear the beat of his heart and feel the pulse of his blood—not to sense the intelligence that drove them, the essence she loved so well, flayed at the rawness within her. It was hopeless and in vain, and she was forced to pull away, unable to bear the desolation of her heart.

Bull came forward to wrap her in his arms. There was silence in the room as they all brooded on her failure. Many there had trusted she would succeed in recovering her love's lost soul, despite what she had told them. Bitter disappointment settled like a noxious fog over the room.

At length, she pushed away from Bull's arms. Her eyes were dry, but her face was pale, her breathing ragged and rough. She stood and moved toward Sofira, who cowered in the circle of her former husband's arms like a wounded, abandoned child, her wild eyes darting, unable to focus. She didn't react to Sullyan's approach, not even when she sat beside her on the bed. When Sullyan reached for her hand, however, and took hold of the stiff, cold fingers, Sofira's eyes latched onto her face and sanity flashed in their depths.

The shrill wail that ripped from the Princess's throat rang through the College. Before the echoes had died down Sofira resumed her whimpering, though her eyes still held a spark of reason. She stared at Sullyan with an expression of horror, but offered no violence.

"Brynne!" murmured Elias in stricken tones, indicating the Princess's trembling body. She shivered uncontrollably, even her teeth chattering. She seemed to be in the grip of some overwhelming terror, yet there was no ruby glow in the depths of her eyes, and no chance of coaxing coherent speech from her. Releasing Sofira's hand, Sullyan shook her head sadly and rose from the bed.

Sofira immediately collapsed against the King, burying her head in his shoulder and weeping piteously. The intense grief of her sobs brought tears to Sullyan's eyes and she wished their relationship had not always been so cold. She might have been able to cut through the Princess's terror if she had not always been so hostile. Sofira would never grant Sullyan access to her mind, and Sullyan knew better than to force her. The natural shield of the ungifted was the hardest shield of all—not even a Senior Master had the strength or the power to break it. Sullyan suddenly wondered whether that was the Baron's hope. Maybe that was why he had left the woman a shred of her rational mind—apart from the obvious cruelty it inflicted on his betrayer, he might have hoped Sullyan would attempt to force Sofira to accept her. With the lowering of her shield such an attempt would require, he might have hoped to trap her. Sighing in weary frustration, Sullyan moved to the beds where Taran and Jinella waited.

The Adept watched her come, fear and desperation in his eyes. She knew what horrified him most—that he would be the one forced to take her over, that their enemy would use his love and corrupt it into violence. He would rather she ran him through than

146

be exposed to the depths of such shame. She would not take such drastic steps yet, however. Despite her despair and her earlier words to Rienne, she was not utterly bereft of hope. Pharikian might still be able to supply some answers, and she had not exhausted her own ideas. But time was not on their side, as Taran had realized earlier, and she must satisfy herself that all possibilities had been considered. Ignoring the waves of fear emanating from the Adept, she crossed to Jinella's side and sat upon the bed.

Jinny looked close to death; her face was lined and gray. The bindings round her chest that covered her terrible wound could not quite hide the smell rising from the shattered flesh. Rienne had used some freshening herbs, but they had little effect against such a foul miasma. Sullyan ignored the stench and reached for Jinny's hand, aware of Taran's eyes on her and the weight of his frantic fear.

Jinny's response was the same as the Major's: not a flicker of movement stirred the younger woman's hand. Placing her palm on the damp hair over Jinny's brow, Sullyan reached within, questing for Jinny's mind. When she sensed the dreadful void she drew back, knowing there was nothing to be gained by lingering. Before she removed her hand, she gently pushed back one of Jinny's eyelids. The pale-green orb was rolled back in her head, no tinge of ruby marring the iris. Releasing her hold on Jinny's hand, Sullyan left her side and moved toward Taran.

Had he been less in control of himself, she thought the Adept might well have been moaning in his terror as mindlessly as Sofira. Yet she could not afford to spare him this ordeal. It may be that he held the key to this dilemma. But that did not mean she should not try to ease him.

She sat by his side and gazed into his eyes, not touching him, only sending him soothing thoughts full of her love for him. She knew he felt them, she read it in his eyes, but the panic did not lessen and there was not much more she could do. "Try not to fear so, Taran. We are well protected and everyone is alert. You will not be permitted to do me harm. No one will blame you if he takes control, you must know that."

He did know it, but the issue was not the apportioning of blame: it was the Adept's own guilt. Despite his helplessness, he would hold himself responsible due to the ease with which he had been caught. Well, she could do nothing about his habitual self-blame. It was the one lesson his father had taught him better than any other all those years ago. And although his recent experiences had largely wiped it out, it still reared its head when his confidence was low. She had hoped his love for Jinella might finally erase all his guilt, but his part in their recent quarrel had brought it all back again. And now he was sure he would never be able to put that error right.

All these things she knew, and she felt the ache of his pain. But if she was to stand any chance of finding some way to defeat their enemy, Taran had to play his part. So she reached out swiftly, before he could react, and clasped his free hand in her own. He tried to pull away, but it was already too late. She knew him too well, knew the intricacies of his psyche, and she used this knowledge to slip inside his mind while he still tugged vainly against her grip on his hand.

He gasped in outrage, but he was too late to stop her and too weak to force her out. All he could do was glare at her in resentment, for a moment forgetting the root of his reluctance. And when he did remember a spilt-second later, she had already gleaned the answer to her question and withdrew the essence of her life force, smiling as warmly as she knew how.

"There, Taran, your fears were unfounded. There is no presence within your mind. The Baron cannot touch you here."

They all let loose a sigh of relief, although it was but a small success when measured against their enemy's malice. Taran bowed his head, covering his face with his hand, deeply ashamed now of the terror he had fostered. Sullyan moved closer and took him in her arms, much as Bull had done for her so short a while before. She glanced up at Dexter.

"They can all go back to their rooms, Captain, and there is no further need for bonds. But there are to be four men guarding each of them constantly, with two more available within call, and no one is to be permitted into the healer suite alone. Seline may visit her mother and sleep in her room if she wishes. The healers are to have free access, of course, but never without a guard. For the rest, only myself, Bulldog, Elias, and the General should be permitted entry."

"What about Morgan, Brynne?"

Sullyan shook her head, regarding Rienne's anxious face with resolution. "None of the younger children will be permitted to see them. I will explain what has happened to Morgan and do my best to make him understand."

"But he'll be so upset! Especially as he knows his father's here, so close and yet …"

Sullyan remained unmoved. "He is already upset, in case you have not noticed, and he is not alone. I have made my decision, Rienne. Seeing Robin's body will not relieve his grief. Would you have Elisse see Cal in a similar state?"

Rienne cringed at the ice in her friend's harsh tone. The damage to her throat almost made Sullyan sound like an uncaring stranger. Yet Rienne knew better than that, and she realized Sullyan was doing what she could to protect her innocent son. Despite what this trial had seemed to confirm, Sullyan would make no solid assumptions and would continue to distrust what she saw until all other possibilities were either proven or disproven.

A short while later, after a conversation with Morgan that tore her heart, Sullyan reported her findings to the General in the officers' hall. Elias was still in the College spending some time with his furious daughter, trying hard to make her understand. Rienne had remained with her patients, and Bull had stayed with the children as Cal was on guard duty. With Vassa still in Port Loxton, the officers' hall was deserted.

Hyram served them fellan and then went to his bed, leaving a full pot of the beverage within easy reach. Sullyan related the events in the healer suite as calmly as she could, but then fell silent, brooding, turning possibilities over in her mind. The General watched her, seeing her inner turmoil and searching for words that might comfort her. He failed, so he concentrated instead on the next most logical step.

"I take it you'll leave for Andaryon in the morning?"

His quiet voice and resigned manner brought Sullyan out of her absorption. She raised her head, appreciating his easy acquiescence. Considering the pressure they were all under, both in the city as well as at the Manor, he could ill afford to lose another senior officer while she labored to find answers to what might be an impossible question. There was no doubt of his support, and she knew he would continue to give it right up until the resolution of this terrible situation, whatever form it might take. She afforded him a wan smile, the only sign of her gratitude she felt capable of giving.

"Before first light. I would go now, but it is far too late. I will not disturb my father's rest."

"Then you'd better get some sleep yourself." The General drained the dregs of his fellan. "Once you start delving into those archives of theirs, I doubt you'll tell day from night."

She put down her empty cup and stood, on impulse placing her hand on his shoulder. He gazed up in surprise. Rarely did she show him affection, but his wholehearted support touched her soul and she wanted him to know the depths of her appreciation. Besides, there was no one to see should he grow embarrassed.

He smiled slightly and covered her small hand with his own. "Take all the time you need, Brynne. We'll manage here. And don't concern yourself with Morgan's safety. I personally guarantee he'll not be touched. Reen would have to get through *me* first."

She was lost for words, the intensity of his gaze suddenly too much to bear. She squeezed his shoulder in lieu of thanks and left him, going to her rooms to sleep alone. She intended to be gone before first light and didn't wish to disturb her son by such an early rise. The General watched her go, willing her to succeed with more fervor than he would have believed possible.

Chapter Fourteen

"**O**h, they think they've been so clever, using spellsilver to block my control, but it makes little difference to my plans now that I possess their minds."

The gloating, venomous voice crawled out of the dark, winding its way to Seth's frightened ears. The manservant shivered and flinched as it came, pushing himself farther into his corner. The speaker was unaware or uncaring of the young man's fear and hissed to himself in malicious pleasure, spittle dripping from cracked and ruined lips, dusty robes sweeping the stone floor.

"She knows she cannot escape me, she knows she will have to face me again. Not even the combined power of the two of them could force me to give up what I hold, and if I were to be killed, well, they would never be free! So you see, my faithful servant, I simply cannot lose. Her only hope of redeeming their souls is to surrender to my demands. She will come, Seth. Believe me, she will come. I will see her on her knees and watch her beg for my forbearance. She will suffer for her betrayal and for making me grovel in shame. I will visit such agonies upon her that she will plead for the merciful release of death. And maybe I will grant it, but not before I strip her of her power!"

Seth cowered in his corner, listening to this manic rant. Twin orbs of ruby malice glittered and blinked before his face, the only visible indication his master was physically in the room. They were in total darkness—not a single glimmer of light relieved the velvet black. Seth could easily believe his eyes had failed were it not for those lamps of red fury. He watched them, mesmerized with dread. What he had witnessed only moments ago had served to show him just what a monster the man had become, and the manservant now lived in terror of those monstrosities being unleashed on *him*.

His day had begun simply enough, with the Baron's prediction concerning the return of the servants borne out by the appearance of breakfast. Seth had woken in Lerric's great bed, vague memories of pleasure stirring in his mind. Yet when he tried to pin them down, when he tried to remember exactly what had happened only a few hours before, they disappeared like morning mist, leaving him wondering what he had been trying to do. He could scarcely even remember how he came to this grim place, and when he tried to force his brain to think, his memories slipped away and faded even more. It was easier not to concern himself with how things had come to pass. He was here in the service of his master, and that was all he really needed to know.

He had risen feeling languid and partook of the food brought to his room by a vacant-eyed chamberlain. Neither spoke; there didn't seem to be any point. He washed and dressed as he always did, and then left the room to look for his master. He walked the gloomy hallways of the silent, shadowy palace, seeing that the bodies and the blood had been cleaned away. Yet there remained a stench about the place that Seth thought he recognized, although he could not quite remember what it meant.

He passed several servants tending the few low fires that kept the palace air from freezing, and never stopped to wonder why they went about in groups. None spoke to him and he didn't greet them either, although he was one of their number and would have done so ordinarily. He wandered aimlessly through the palace, never once seeing his master, and he felt no summons in the vacant spaces of his brain. It didn't strike him as odd, though. He clearly wasn't required, and so when he found himself quite naturally in the more normal atmosphere of the kitchens, the only truly warm spot in the place, he stayed. There he spent the day, ignored by the servants around him.

He worked at whatever chores he thought it right to do, although no one gave him orders and no one gave him thanks. They all simply stepped around each other, doing what needed to be done, never speaking, never touching, never catching one another's eye. It wasn't that they were hostile, or that they resented his presence; they simply never registered his presence at all. He was accepted and left to himself, as each of them left the others.

As evening fell and the palace servants left, drifting away to their hovels like the shadows they seemed, Seth felt a questing touch in the echoes of his mind. He rose from his chair beside the kitchen fire and took up a lamp. Somehow, that feeble gleam felt like a pair of comforting arms and Seth was loath to leave it, so he carried it with him as he made his way toward the source of the summoning. The call seemed weak, less than sure, and he hastened his steps in case his master was in need. Hurrying through the chilly, darkened halls, preceded by flickering shadows cast by the lamp, he finally came to the curtained doorway leading to the palace's lower floor.

He hesitated. He had been told not to venture down these dark and echoing stairs unless specifically summoned. He had been summoned indeed, of that he was in no doubt. Yet there was a feeling down below, lurking among the shadows, an atmosphere pervading the darkness. Suddenly, descending those stairs was the very last thing Seth wanted to do. He dimly recalled his master's words concerning some task Seth would be required to perform. Although the air of menace did not seem directed at Seth himself, nevertheless he felt his master's hand within it.

Taking hold of his courage and ignoring the tremble of his hand which made the lamplight dance, forming eerie ghosts among the gloom, Seth pushed aside the curtain and descended the echoing stairs.

He moved slowly along the hallway, feeling the icy chill of the air. No servants ventured down here, no torches lit the way. Only the glow of Seth's feeble lamp served to guide him past the doors. He could sense the room where his master was and feel the pull of his will. But there was something else, something strange, and Seth felt his spine creep with dread. It was all he could do to place one foot before the other, so strong was his urge to run. His mind, however, was not entirely his own and the decision not his to make. Reluctantly, fearfully, he walked toward the wooden door at the end of the passage.

His master was within—Seth knew it as well as he knew that he breathed. The hour of his task was at hand and the scarecrow was gathering strength. Seth could feel him pulling it in, swelling his spirit and empowering his will. The task must be something important for him to prepare himself in this way. Seth approached the door, placing his hand upon the wood. Slowly, he pushed it open.

The terrible scream that rent the air beat about Seth's ears and vibrated right through to his heart. With a gasp, he clapped his hands to his head, dropping the lamp, which shattered on the flags. The flame went out at once, but imprinted on the back of Seth's eyes was an image he would never forget.

The swordsman's face might have been familiar were it not engorged with blood and contorted in pain. The throat might have shrieked for Seth's help if the mind had retained some reason. But all that was familiar and everything of reason had fled that chained and tortured shell as its life was sucked out and absorbed by the creature before it, a monster that reveled in the emanations of terror as the lurid cane throbbed in the dark. Seth fled to the corner of the room, cowering down on his haunches, his hands to his ears, unable to block out the dreadful sounds as the monster continued to feed. He could feel the rapacious soul gorging on the gibbering life force, and his body shook with palsied fear when the crawling voice spoke his name. His heart nearly stopped with an icy shudder and he cried aloud when the scarecrow gripped the collar of his cloak.

"Oh, get up, you sniveling coward! Have you never seen a man die? The spirit leaves the body. Surely it is better to use the energy it expends. That peasant no longer had need of it. Do you see what that pagan Artesan witch has reduced me to? No longer able to sustain my own body, she forces me to take life where and how I can. But it doesn't last long. Each time I act, I have to refresh myself, and these feeble wretches of Lerric's guard are all I have at present. But once I have conquered her, once she has breathed her last and surrendered her power to me, I will have no more need of these lowly creatures. Her powers will sustain me and her young energies suffuse my ravaged heart. Her knowledge and her mastery will be mine to use at will, and it will be her everlasting torment that I will use them to destroy her evil kind.

"Forget what you have seen here, Seth, and put aside your useless horror. You are too important for me to use in that way. I have other, more interesting ways in which you can serve."

The shivering manservant felt the shriveled hand slip gently over his hair, almost a lover's caress, as indeed that is what the two of them were. And with the trail of the fingers, now no longer claws, the terrible memory receded, losing its power to appall. He didn't quite forget it, but he could no longer recall why he had feared. He straightened before his master, his eyes becoming accustomed to the dark. Twin ruby lamps shone from the pallor of his face, although he could not feel the glow. He faced the scarecrow, listening intently as he learned his next task.

✤ ✤ ✤ ✤ ✤

It was early yet and still pitch-dark when Maxin left his room at the rear of the royal apartments. He walked through the hallways silently so as not to disturb those still asleep, which was the majority of the Palace's inhabitants at this ungodly hour of the morning. Apart from the guards at their duties, everyone else was abed—not even the household servants had risen yet to tend to the lamps and the fires. Maxin was used to keeping odd hours. In fact, he had begged for this duty, so he could hardly complain, even though he had been given leave to take the day off to visit the Fair. There would be time aplenty for such pleasures once the duties of the morning were complete.

Maxin was the Hierarch's personal page and considered himself highly privileged to be so. He had won his position by merit of his good nature, his diligence, and his loyalty. Yet he suspected he also owed it to the recommendation of his brother, Norkis, who had held the post before him. Many young boys vied for this most prestigious of duties and few were chosen. They entered Pharikian's service at ten years of age and were required to move on when they turned fifteen. The Hierarch generally kept four pages, who shared the rota of serving both their ruler and the Crown Prince, and one of the four became the senior boy whose task it was to organize the others and share out the duties fairly. Like his brother before him, Maxin had caught the Hierarch's eye and had been chosen to lead the group. Full of gratitude and pride, he was determined to live up to his appointment.

When he had learned of the imminent arrival of Aeyron's bride-to-be, nothing would do for Maxin but to be the one chosen to serve her. He would arrange the duty rota to free himself for the task, and his earnest entreaty to his lord had gained him the permission he craved. He was presented to the Princess upon her arrival at the Palace and fell at once under the spell of her charms. He charmed her in his turn. She had never had the luxury of a page as her life in Dalkia had not required it, but the Imperial Palace was a whole world away from the simpler court of her father. Maxin's cheerful grin and unobtrusive presence helped put her at ease in what would become her new home. He was proud to be the one to serve her and he already thought of her as the wife of his Prince.

This morning he was on an errand for the Princess. She had told him she would require extra time to prepare herself that morning, and had asked for an especially early breakfast. Maxin knew that she and Aeyron were making a Procession through the town, and he knew how early they would have to begin in order to fit everything in. These things had their natural order so as not to insult the nobles, and the Procession had been planned down to the finest detail. If anyone should be even a few minutes late, the entire schedule would collapse and the Prince and Princess would be shamed. Maxin could not bear to even consider such a disaster. And so he made his way to the kitchens to check that the kitchen maids were engaged in preparing the Princess's morning meal.

He was nearly there when he saw a figure advancing toward him out of the gloom. The dim lamplight was just enough to let Maxin see who it was. He frowned. The newcomer was buttoning his tunic and he grinned as he came abreast of Maxin, his pale-blond hair and eager face very similar to the younger boy's. Norkis was sixteen and a trainee in the Velletian Guard. He should by rights have been in the barracks. Maxin knew Norkis still had many friends in the Palace, as those who had served the Hierarch with him had stayed on to become stewards. The page cocked his head at his older brother, noting the jaunty angle of the sword belted at his hip, the half-finished dressing, and the self-satisfied flush on his face.

"Aren't you supposed to be on duty?" He kept his voice low.

Norkis grinned wider, infuriatingly smug. "Oh, I have another hour yet before I report to my post. You're the one who's early, little brother. Taking your duties seriously, I see!"

Maxin huffed. "You'd thrash me if I didn't. You told me so, remember?"

"And so I will, if you don't come up to scratch, you scamp. There's a standard to uphold here after all, and family honor at stake, so mind you don't forget it!"

Maxin placed his hands on his hips, eyeing his brother knowingly. "It's not me who should be thinking of honor, judging by the look on your face. You just make sure our family doesn't grow before you're ready to support it. You're still in training, remember? You've not passed your final tests yet."

Norkis spluttered and lunged for his brother. "Why, you cheeky brat! How dare you lecture me about responsibility? You're barely out of swaddling bands! You wait 'til I catch you …"

Maxin dodged the grasping hand, trying not to laugh. His guess was correct, if his brother's reaction was anything to go by, and he wondered who his latest conquest was. Norkis was good-looking and likeable, easy going and generous; it wasn't so surprising the maids found him irresistible. Maxin's impudent warning had been serious, however. If their father should learn that some maid was expecting, Norkis's promising career might be over before it began.

Norkis glared in mock fierceness at his younger brother, who ignored the implied threat. "For your information, little brother, I have things well in hand. It's only a casual alliance. Neither of us is serious. And I've learned enough about my powers to prevent her from starting a child, so you can take that self-righteous look off your face. I'd never disgrace us that way. Besides," his look turned sly, "I have my heart set on a new prize, a greater prize than any kitchen maid."

Maxin stopped abruptly. "Oh yes?" He really couldn't waste any more time, but Norkis's demeanor intrigued him. Something about his brother's manner told him this was important. "So who is this lady who has caught your eye? One of the guest nobles' daughters?"

Norkis grinned irritatingly. "No, dear brother. You must have seen the lady who has caught my attention. That youngest maid of the Prince's bride, the one with the coppery hair. She looks like a grand catch to me, and I'll be doing my best to impress her. So if you want to escape a drubbing in payment for your cheek, you can put in a good word for me and test the waters. Maybe then I'll let you off."

Maxin stared with his mouth open. "Norkis, you must be crazy, she'd never look at you. She's at least twenty years old, and a Princess's maid! A beauty, I'll grant you, but way above you."

"Oh, you think so, do you? Well, thank you for your faith, brother. Now, would you care to put a wager on it?"

"Ha! I'm not that stupid. Just be careful—the Princess will look after her own and she may want better for her pretty young maid than a cocky cadet with more cheek than good sense! Now you'd better get going or you'll be late. It won't do your chances any good if Shandra sees you on punishment detail shoveling horse muck in the stables!"

Norkis swaggered off chuckling, full of his plans for conquest. Maxin continued to the kitchens, hurrying to make up for the delay. He tried to put all thoughts of Norkis's intentions out of his mind for the moment, although he might well explore Shandra's opinions at a later date. He was genuinely fond of his older brother and grateful for his help. If Norkis could aspire to a Princess's maid—and providing he was successful—then Maxin's own chances, when he was old enough to take them, might well be improved by the match. His older brother was an honorable man, despite his brief flings with the maids, and was widely expected to excel in the military and improve his family's standing. Such a match would please their father no end. Grinning to himself and shaking his head for the audacity of it, Maxin entered the kitchens. He glimpsed but did not have time to investigate the brief ruby glow glinting around a doorframe as he passed.

※ ※ ※ ※ ※

The early hour didn't affect the routine of the Manor. Guards were changed and meals were taken regardless of the weather or the hour. The horse lines, the infirmary, the kitchens, all were manned at every moment so that fresh mounts, medical care, or much-needed fellan were always available to those who served their realm. Sullyan entered the bustling kitchens and made for the glowing hearth, accepting fellan from one of the kitchen boys and tearing a chunk of warm bread from a freshly baked loaf. Another of the boys spread honey on it and she savored it absently as she waited for the fellan to cool. The atmosphere of Goran's kitchens was always warm and comforting, especially at this hour when the irascible man was absent. She leaned against the huge wooden table and let her eyes rove around the vast room, memories of time spent helping in here when she was a child drifting through her troubled mind.

It all seemed so very long ago now. Brought here by the General on a whim, she had spent blissful years in discovery, both military and metaphysical. He had given her a life filled with purpose, although that hadn't been his intention. And it had all come down to this. Spite and malice, prejudice and hate. She had endured them all her life; they attended her wherever she went. No matter how hard she tried, no matter what she did, they would never leave her alone. The comfort and support of her friends had often enabled her to overcome them, to hold her head high when they became too strong. Now it was her friends who suffered, and it was all because of her. They were going to die because of her. Not even death would be the end, for their spirits would linger on, held in terrible torture by the master of their souls, who would not let them rest until he had his fill of vengeance.

She shook herself angrily. She would not give in to such defeatist thoughts or his malice, not until she had explored every possibility she could conceive. She would go and confer with her father and enlist Gaslek's help. She intended to scour their archives until every single parchment that spoke of an Artesan's powers had been rooted out, examined, and discarded or kept as useful. Dawn was not far off. It was time to head for the horse lines to collect Drum.

Emerging into the pre-dawn chill, she gathered her cloak around her, settling her sword at her back. She heard Drum's impatient whicker long before she reached the horse lines. He always knew when she needed him. She smiled to see the prick of his ears as she came up to his ebony shoulder, his snuffling breaths as he nuzzled her hair warm on the chill of her skin. She ran a hand along his neck and loosened his rein from the rail. Swinging up onto his back, she nudged him out of the yard.

He never complained, this huge black beast. He was always ready to serve, always eager to bear her wherever she wanted to go. Come rain or shine, his pricked ears conveyed his willing spirit and the greatness of his heart. He was no longer in the first flush of youth at eleven years old, but he was in his prime, as fit and muscular as he had ever been, and his body moved powerfully with his usual supple grace. She let the feel of him soothe her, as it always did, wishing she could indulge in the thrill and excitement of a fast cross-country ride. The concentration necessary to keep them both from harm whilst still maintaining the fastest speed possible was a sure way of clearing her mind; almost as good in its own way as a sword fight, or making love with Robin.

That thought sobered her and brought her back to the present. Robin's spirit was relying on her to save it from eternal torment. She could not afford to linger. Pushing the stud into a ground-eating canter, she rode away from the Manor, heading for open country to effect her crossing.

Chapter Fifteen

The kitchens were well lit and cozy, the servants all busy at their duties as Maxin waited for the Princess's tray. He watched the kitchen maids, trying to discern which one Norkis was bedding, knowing something of his brother's tastes. It couldn't be the one by the window—her hair was too short. Norkis favored long hair, and preferably with some curl. It definitely wasn't the black-haired girl, she was too thin. It could be the blonde by the fire, although she was slightly too plump. He knew Norkis wasn't averse to that, but if slender was available, that would be his choice. That left just two contenders—the brunette brewing the fellan, or the ash-blonde cutting the fruit. Both were slender, the brunette marginally taller than her companion. Both had comely faces and well-shaped eyes and mouths you wouldn't hesitate to kiss. So which one was it?

The tray was finally ready with Maxin none the wiser. Truth was he wouldn't be surprised to learn that Norkis had bedded every one of these girls, although he was probably maligning his brother. Half the stories were barracks talk, designed to impress his peers, but Norkis was good-looking with a mischievous streak and a twinkle in his pale-blue eyes. Many a girl had approached him by the time he turned fifteen. He had never answered Maxin's questions as to whether he accepted any of their offers. Well, it really wasn't any of Maxin's business. What Norkis did was his own affair and Maxin would trust him not to bring disgrace on their family. He knew his brother valued his position too highly to jeopardize it over a tumble.

The brunette motioned him to take the Princess's tray. Maxin took it up, smiling at her as he did so. She averted her eyes, but not before he had seen the pink flush on her cheek and the faint red marks on the pale flesh of her throat. He grinned. So this was his brother's latest love! He couldn't fault Norkis's taste—the girl was really pretty. But he didn't think it would last long, not while there was Shandra to win, and Maxin hoped his brother was right about the affair being casual for both of them. The girl might be only a kitchen maid, but she could have brothers who were in more of a position to avenge a broken heart. Norkis's chances would not be improved by the acquisition of bruises or a bloody nose. Maxin left the kitchens carrying the Princess's tray, wondering how he would feel when he was old enough to be of interest to some pretty maid.

He was immersed in thoughts of love, pondering what little he knew and trying to decide how best to persuade Norkis to tell him some bedroom secrets when he sensed the man behind him. The awkward tray prevented him from swinging round, and the query he intended to utter died stillborn as a hand clasped his shoulder and a ruby glow settled into his mind. Maxin stood immobile, his reason suspended, his eyes blank. He only vaguely felt the strange burning of the other's grip.

Seth smiled as he sensed the boy's thoughts and felt the first true stirrings of his adolescent desire. The lad was good-looking, and had he more time at his disposal Seth could have opened the boy's eyes to the uses and pleasures of his body. A pity, but his master would find him another, should Seth wish to slake his desire. Still gripping the young boy's shoulder and firmly holding his vacant gaze, the manservant reached into his cloak and brought out a packet, given him by his master. He sprinkled its contents over the food, careful not to spill the brownish powder or get any on his hand. It disappeared immediately, absorbed into the food, and Seth stepped behind the boy, releasing his shoulder and retreating once more behind the door that had concealed him.

✣ ✣ ✣ ✣ ✣

Maxin stared around him, puzzled, certain he had heard a sound. Yet the hallway was empty. He frowned, shaking his head to clear it of disquieting thoughts. His body felt odd, too. His shoulder stung as if burned and he felt like he had worms inside his belly. He was uncomfortable between his legs, his breeches were straining and tight, and he felt a hot flush over his face as he realized why. Why he should be embarrassed, he had no idea. There was no one to see him, after all, and he was on the verge of becoming a man. Why should his natural physical reaction to the sight of a pretty girl shame him? Well, he thought wryly as he gathered his wits, maybe that would teach him not to let Norkis distract him in future!

Pushing these thoughts from his mind and trying to ignore the urges of his body, he hurried back to the Princess's rooms, aware he was in danger of being late. Once again, his brief glimpse of a ruby glow disappearing into a strange shimmer was dismissed from his mind.

✣ ✣ ✣ ✣ ✣

Shandra woke early, which was easy to do. For all her advice to her mistress the evening before, the maid was as excited as the Princess. She was Lirina's personal maid and would come to live here with her. She would lodge within the Imperial Palace, in chambers adjoining her mistress's, and would be exposed to all the Caer could offer in terms of its traders and their goods, its social occasions, and its many eligible young men. She had seen a good few of these already in the course of the previous day, and was aware her status would make her attractive. She had been too busy caring for the Princess to take any serious lovers in Dalkia. Now she was glad she had not, for she would have had to leave them behind. It made more sense to make her life here than worry about what had gone before.

She dressed in haste in her plain working clothes, for she would not be part of the Procession. Once she had readied her mistress and the squire came to escort Lirina to her Prince, Shandra's duties would be over until the pair returned. She would be free to amuse herself for the day and intended to visit the Fair in the company of the Princess's other three maids to see what the Caer had to offer. Already she had caught Rigel, the Prince's young squire, glancing her way more than once. She smiled as she contemplated the look in his eye.

She twisted her coppery hair into a mound upon her head and was fastening its curls with a pin when a knock sounded at the outer door. That would be Maxin with their morning meal, and she hurried to let him in. His impish grin greeted her at the door, and he entered the suite and made for the window, setting his tray down on the table that stood there.

"Good morning, Mistress Shandra. I've brought what the Princess ordered. I trust she slept well after yesterday's excitement. She'll need all her stamina to get through the itinerary laid out for today. The whole Caer wants to see her, you know."

"So I've heard. Thank you for bringing the food. I hope we didn't make you rise too much earlier than normal."

"It's my pleasure to serve, mistress. Anything you want, you just call for me. And if you ever need a guide to show you the sights of the Caer, my older brother Norkis, who's training in the Guards, told me to tell you he'd be happy to escort you."

Shandra smiled at the young boy, who ducked his head and

flushed. "If he's as agreeable as you, Maxin, I'm sure he'll be good company. I'll remember his offer, and thank you. But now I must see to the Princess. I dare not let her be late."

Maxin bowed his way out and took up his station in the hallway. Shandra closed the door and checked on the tray, finding everything was as the Princess had specified, although the maid doubted whether she could be persuaded to eat any of it in the excitement of the morning. She took up the pot of fellan and poured out a cup, moving to the door of the Princess's bedchamber and tapping lightly on the wood.

"My Lady? Are you awake?"

There was no response and Shandra hoped she had not given Lirina too large a dose of the sleeping powder. If she had, her mistress would not be at her best and Shandra would be to blame. She pushed the door open and entered the darkened room, placing the cup beside the bed. As she pulled back the heavy drapes to let the gray winter light creep in, she heard her mistress stir, stretching lazily in the bed.

"Oh, Shandra, it can't be morning already? I feel as if I've hardly been asleep!"

She sounded drowsy but not drugged, and the maid breathed a sigh of relief. The Princess's own exhaustion had obviously taken her over and kept her naturally asleep. Lirina pushed herself upright in bed and accepted the cup from Shandra's hands.

"Did you have a comfortable night, my Lady?"

A mischievous look came into the Princess's eye as she sipped the scalding drink. "Comfortable enough, except for one thing. This bed is too large! What it really needs is another warm body— then it might be just right."

"Highness!" The maid's tone was scandalized, but she grinned at Lirina's coy expression. "I think you've been having overly vivid dreams."

Lirina's smiled widened. "If the reality comes anywhere near them, my dear, you won't hear me complaining."

Shandra laughed at the Princess's coquettish smile and went back into the outer room to fetch the tray of food. Lirina's face fell when she saw it, fulfilling her maid's prediction. "Oh, I don't think I want any, Shandra, my stomach will surely rebel."

"Now then, my Lady, I know how you feel and I'm not going to make you eat it all. But you've a heavy day ahead of you and who knows when you'll get time to eat once the Procession starts? If you don't take some food while you've time to digest it, you'll feel faint during the morning, and we can't have that, can we? And besides, we made Maxin get up especially early to fetch this for you, and it's full of the things you like. You can take some of the fruit with you in case you feel hungry during the ride, but I want you to eat this bowlful right now."

Lirina sighed. "Oh, very well, but only if you join me. I'm so full of nerves I need to just sit and talk. Maybe you can help me calm down. Come and sit on the bed here beside me and help me eat. Look at this. Have you ever seen such strange curved fruits before? I don't think I have. I wonder what they're called?" She picked one up, holding it upright in her fingers, her eyes sliding slyly to the other girl's as the flush deepened on her cheek. "Oh, Shandra, guess what that reminds me of ...!"

They sat together, sampling pieces of fruit, giggling and telling stories as they had when they were at home. It was just what Lirina needed, and Shandra saw her begin to relax.

✣ ✣ ✣ ✣ ✣

Sullyan emerged from the Veils on the edge of the Plain. She had only just remembered what day it was, and felt guilty that she would be imposing on her foster father's happiness. The winding file of tradesmen making for the Caer was visible even from where she sat. It was just as well that she had chosen to emerge well away from the Caer. A huge black warhorse appearing from nowhere in a shimmer of Earth power would have startled the most stoic of tradesmen. She hesitated, remembering the Procession planned for the day, and considered returning to the Manor and leaving her father in peace. Taran's words kept resounding in her brain, however, reminding her that time was passing and it was a luxury her friends did not possess. Her feeling of guilt divided between her father and her friends, she touched heels to Drum's sides and sent him on his way, the big stud responding to the urgency she felt.

The press of traders parted when they heard the big black approaching, and she rode in through the east gate to the greetings of the guards standing duty. She acknowledged them in silence, in no mood for their banter, although she wished she could partake of their festival cheer. This should be one of her happiest days, meeting her brother's beloved, the woman who had touched his heart and made a place there for herself. She set her face in resolution and continued up through the town, taking the less-frequented routes where she could and seeing everywhere the preparations for the coming Procession.

She finally reached the Palace and rode into the courtyard, greeted by the Palace Guard. Barrin was there with the honor guard, waiting to escort the Prince and Princess. He held two magnificent horses, Aeyron's chestnut stallion and Lirina's dappled mare, and he gave Sullyan a silent nod as he sent one of the grooms to take Drum. She slid down the stallion's shoulder and returned the commander's curt greeting. He had never become a friend, although she knew he bore her no grudge. It was his nature to be silent, and today he was concerned over the safety of his charges. She couldn't fault him for that. So she didn't approach to ask how he did, as she might otherwise have done, but headed into the Palace, making for the royal apartments. She was halfway to Pharikian's rooms when she heard the terrible cry.

✣ ✣ ✣ ✣ ✣

Maxin heard the girlish giggles behind the door and smiled to himself. Lirina would make a good partner for Aeyron, especially if she could make him laugh like that. Ever since his maiming by the Albian Baron, the Crown Prince had been more withdrawn, more serious than his true nature, although this past year had seen him come closer to the man he had been before. During the long months of his recovery, he only ever smiled when his family was by his side, and particularly when in the company of the Princess Brynne. It would do him good to have someone of his own, and the arrival of children would make his life complete. It was what all Velletians wanted for their Prince, who would be their sole ruler once his father was gone.

Musing on the future and watching the maids trim the lamps and draw back the heavy hangings, Maxin only belatedly realized the laughter had ceased. Perhaps Shandra was dressing the Princess. Time was moving on and it would not be long before Rigel appeared to escort the Prince's Lady to his side. The sound that Maxin heard, though, didn't seem like the murmur of girlish conversation. It was faint and vaguely disturbing, more like a moan or maybe a choke. Then he heard what he would swear was a thud, as if something heavy had fallen to the floor. He stiffened, listening intently, but there was silence within the suite.

He stood irresolute, wondering what to do. Maybe Shandra had dropped something. She would not thank him for disturbing her just to check all was well. Time was running out—if she were engaged in some delicate task, he would be scolded for holding her up. Yet he was troubled by a prickle of worry, a feeling that something was wrong. Well, there were others who could enter those rooms without calling Shandra to open the door, and Maxin stepped across the hall to rap on the opposite door.

A sleepy-eyed woman opened it to stare at the page in surprise. "What is it, boy? What do you want?"

Maxin heard Lirina's other two maids enquiring behind the first, but he ignored them. They had all been given the day to themselves and hadn't expected to be disturbed. He kept his attention on the older woman, trying not to let urgency color his tone. His sense of fear was growing, although he could not say why. "Madam, I wonder, would you check on the Princess? Time grows short and the Prince's squire will soon be here. I don't want to disturb her Highness or her maid by knocking, but I think they should be made aware."

The woman called reassuringly to her two companions and stepped into the hallway. She was clad in a houserobe with her hair flowing loose. Unconcerned by her appearance, she walked across to the Princess's suite and quietly opened the door. She passed within and Maxin heard her footsteps cross the room, heading for the Princess's bedchamber. The dreadful wail that scythed through the air shocked Maxin and he plunged into the room after her.

A terrible sight met his gaze and a putrid smell burned his throat. The maid stumbled backward, her hands to her mouth, her face white as milk. She gagged on the smell and sobbed with hysteria. Turning, she fled the room, offering no help to the page. Even Maxin, trained to serve, stood locked in horrified stasis as he stared at the two stricken women.

The Princess sprawled across the bed, writhing and choking, her hands to her throat, the bedclothes soaked and stained. Shandra lay on the floor, moaning in pain, and the smell of vomit stung Maxin's eyes. Both women had soiled themselves and both were unaware; indeed, Shandra's moaning cries were fast becoming weaker and her eyes were glazed and blind. Maxin stood appalled, not knowing where to turn. Trained to serve he might be, but he had no experience of this. Tears filling his eyes, he hovered on the brink of action, unable to make his limbs move.

✦ ✦ ✦ ✦ ✦

He was saved by Sullyan, who suddenly burst into the room. Taking in the scene at a glance, she struggled out of her sword belt, letting the weapon fall to the floor. She grabbed Maxin by the shoulders and shook the boy hard, jolting him out of his shock. He stared into her eyes, trying to blink back tears as she barked instructions with no courtesy or finesse. Her harsh, broken voice only added to his fear.

"Maxin, listen—I need you to listen! Get Aeyron, Deshan, and Timar. Tell them they must send for Rienne. Tell them to say it is poison—Rienne will know what I mean. Tell them to bring her here *fast*! Get the servants to bring lots of saltwater, and keep everyone else away from this room. Send guards to the kitchens to cancel the meals—no one is to touch any food. Do you hear me, Maxin? *No one*! And no one is to touch that tray! Now go, Maxin, run! Go *on*, boy—*RUN*!"

She gave the page a violent push that nearly sent him sprawling. He regained his balance clumsily and bolted out of the room, yelling for the guards and for the Prince. Sullyan cast him from her mind as she ran to the figure on the bed. She recognized the signs immediately, she also recognized the smell. She saw again Levant's convulsing body and Bessie's dreadful corpse. That wasn't going to happen to Lirina, even if she killed herself saving her. She wasn't going to let Aeyron's lady expire, not when he had only just found her. Praying fervently that Aeyron had not been attacked as well, Sullyan sat on the bed. She had to ignore the poor maid, as she only had enough energy for one, and even that depended on Lirina's ability to let Sullyan help her. The Princess was far gone in pain and delirium and she didn't know who Sullyan was. The Artesan could only hope she could reach the woman. She took the stricken Princess's face in her hands and stared deeply into her unseeing eyes.

✤ ✤ ✤ ✤ ✤

Maxin ran as he had never run before, dashing for the Prince's suite. All the Guards were out in the courtyard, ready to escort the Procession, and the maids he encountered were useless. Desperate to reach the Prince, Maxin shoved them aside in his haste. Cries of anger and of fear followed him as he fled, but he ignored them all, skidding round the final corner that led to the Prince's rooms.

He nearly cannoned into Rigel, who was just coming through the door, sent by the Prince to request her Highness's presence. Maxin flailed for his arms, grasping Rigel hard. The squire stared at him in shock, seeing the state he was in, but the page couldn't get his breath and his few choked words made no sense.

"Calm down, boy, calm down! What's got you so panicked?" Rigel shook Maxin much as Sullyan had done, beginning to fear the worst. The door to the suite was still open behind him and Aeyron appeared from within, looking resplendent in his parade-clothes, a pale frown marring his face. Sensing Maxin's panic, he took the page's arm from his squire, fear making him harsh.

"What is it, Maxin? Tell me!"

The boy forced down his tears, gulping air to speak. He finally forced out Sullyan's message and Aeyron's face turned white. "Rigel, fetch Deshan, send him to the Princess! Maxin, run to my father and tell him the same! I'll contact Barrin and General Blaine in Albia."

Aeyron gave Maxin a shove in the back and the panting boy sprinted away, Rigel hot on his heels.

✤ ✤ ✤ ✤ ✤

Sullyan sat very still on the soiled, sweat-soaked bed, her head bowed, her eyes closed, her breathing tight. The Princess's body convulsed with pain, her mind completely overwhelmed by poison and fear. Her reason was fading, her muscles were weak, but Sullyan knew she felt the hands that cupped her face, the force that sought to aid her. Sullyan's power flowed into her body, lessening the pain, and Lirina gradually dropped her resistance to the probing thoughts and yielded to the control behind them.

Lirina had no gift and no influence over her own life force. And although she had let Sullyan in, there was little the Artesan could do. She had no saltwater for purging, and no Taran to help and support her. There was no point in strengthening the Princess's spirit while the poison raged unchecked through her system, but she couldn't tackle the poison without releasing her hold on Lirina's soul. Either way, the woman could die. It was vital that the toxin's hold on the Princess's body be lessened, and there was only one way to do that, only one way to prevent the Princess from receding too deeply before help arrived. She shrank from it, but she knew she would have to shoulder some of the burden if Lirina was to survive. Taking a deep breath and holding it fast against what she knew would assail her, Sullyan surrounded the Princess's life force with her own and accepted the poison's lethal effects into the depths of her psyche.

All at once she was drowning in pain. She felt her body wracked by agony, ripped in two by the toxin's action. Antithetical to moisture, the poison attempted to drive out every drop of fluid within her, forcibly expelling it. Sullyan had known what to expect—she had seen the results, after all—but she had thought she would be able to contain the pain, as she didn't have the substance within her own physical body. But the violence with which it attacked her and her own already weakened state rendered her helpless against its aggressive potency, and her mind convinced her body that the poison was rampaging within. She slumped forward onto the bed, senseless and heaving in the toxin's thrall.

Chapter Sixteen

Rienne was just waking when Cal's arm tightened around her waist. She murmured a sleepy protest, but the pressure did not abate. She tried to twist round to look at him, thinking he was in the grip of a dream, but the look in his eyes took all thoughts from her mind. "What is it, Cal, what's wrong?"

"Trouble at Pharikian's Palace." He flung back the bedclothes and started pulling on his leathers. "The General has had word from Prince Aeyron—Sullyan says his intended bride has been poisoned. They want you to go there now. They're sending Barrin for you."

Rienne gasped and slipped from the bed, reaching for her clothes. "Dear gods, not again. Where is all this going to end?"

He didn't answer and she glanced up at him, noting the way he avoided her gaze. "Is there something you're not telling me?"

He faced her, reluctance in his eyes and something else lurking beneath. She frowned, not liking what she saw, and held his gaze as she forced him to answer.

"I don't know where it will end, but I do know one thing. I don't want you to go to the Palace."

She hadn't expected that. "What? But I have to go. They need those herbs and a healer who knows how to use them. If I don't go and help them, the Princess may die! This isn't like you, love. Why are you saying this?"

Cal came closer and took her in his arms. "Just take a moment to think. How do we know this is a genuine call? You said it yourself—where will it end? Remember how Robin was trapped by the Baron, called away suddenly by a plausible emergency, not given time to think? If he hadn't been so frantic to rush to his mother's side, perhaps he would have taken someone with him and they could have fought off the Baron's men. What if this is the same, Rienne? What if it's a trap?"

She froze, staring at Cal. She had not considered this possibility and was taken aback. Why should the Baron want to hurt her? She wasn't an Artesan; she was no threat to him. But, said a voice of cold reason inside her mind, she was a close friend of all those who *were* Artesans and they all relied on her skills. The man was obviously depraved and deranged. Why would he balk at killing even her? Anything he could do to harm Sullyan would further his cause and force her more surely into his power.

Yet, argued Rienne's healer side, if this was a genuine emergency and the Princess had truly been poisoned, any prevarication could seal her fate. Rienne knew all about the toxin's effects and knew that time was vital. Surely the General would hear the lie, if there really was no such emergency? He wouldn't pass on the call if he suspected foul play. That fact made up her mind.

She shrugged into her cloak. "I'm going, Cal. Blaine wouldn't have contacted you if he suspected a trap. Speak to Sullyan if you're worried, but I'm going with Barrin."

"Then I'm coming with you." Cal reached for his sword. "Remember what Sullyan said—none of us is to travel alone."

"You can't come, love, you're on duty. And besides, who's going to look after the children?" Rienne rummaged in her bag, swiftly checking her medical supplies. "And I won't be alone, Barrin will be there, and I doubt he's come without a guard. You do trust Barrin, don't you? If I'm not safe with him, there's nothing you can do." She heard Cal's exasperated sigh, for she was right. He opened his mouth to make a final attempt to dissuade her when the blankness of his gaze told her another message had reached him.

He spoke roughly. "Barrin's waiting for you by the horse lines. He says to hurry, it may already be too late."

Rienne flew from the room, Cal following. She made a swift detour to the College pharmacy and gathered every bit of dried temany she and Hanan had managed to find. It wasn't much. Looking at the small package clasped in her hand, she could only hope it would suffice. As Cal held the door for her and relieved her of her bag, she had a sudden thought. "Contact Barrin and get him to pass a message to Deshan. Ask him if they have an herb called temany in their stores, and if they do, tell him to gather every shred he can find—dried, fresh, or powdered, it's all the same."

Cal's eyes glazed as he obeyed her command and she ran for the doors, pulling her cloak about her to ward off the early morning chill.

Barrin waited impatiently at the horse lines, his men hovering at his back. He looked relieved when he saw her. "Healer Arlen, ride double with me—we don't have time to saddle you a mount."

He boosted her to his saddlebow. Cal handed up her medical bag and watched as the commander settled himself behind her. She barely had time to raise her hand in farewell before Barrin wheeled his mount and raced it out of the yard. His men streamed behind him, leaving Cal alone.

Rienne twisted to see Barrin's face. "How bad is it?"

"I don't know, Healer, I was only told to fetch you. I'd say it was pretty bad. I've passed your message to Deshan."

Barrin's tone was grim and Rienne felt her stomach tighten. She was very fond of Aeyron and knew how this would affect him, especially if they were too late and the Princess died. She doubted he could stand such a blow. Barrin prepared to open the Veils and Rienne shielded her mind as Sullyan had taught her, forcing down her questions until the crossing was over.

Having emerged onto the Plains dangerously close to the battlemented walls, they galloped through the Citadel gates and thundered up to the Palace. Everywhere, Rienne saw preparations for the day. She had forgotten that Aeyron intended to show off his bride to his people—the fear he might never do so grieved her. She would do all she could to prevent such a tragedy.

They clattered into the courtyard and Barrin reined his mount to a haunch-skidding stop, sliding down from the beast before it had halted. He swung Rienne to the ground and escorted her into the Palace, her bag slung across his shoulder. His men hastened after them, weapons ready. They hurried through hallways full of silent, anxious servants, finally reaching the suite allocated to Lirina. Barrin opened the door for Rienne, but didn't enter behind her. He had his hand to his mouth as he passed her the bag and then retreated back into the hall. She heard him barking orders as the door swung closed.

The living space was deserted, but Rienne heard voices in the bedchamber. She crossed the room and stopped in shock just through the door. The smell was overwhelming and she had to force bile back down her throat. Every breath threatened to make her heave, but she knew if she did, she was lost. Assuming a professional detachment, her only defense against such things, Rienne shouldered past a weeping Maxin and came toward the bed.

Sullyan's unconscious body lay next to another woman's. The bedsheets were in a terrible state, but no one worried about that. The Supreme Ruler of Andaryon sat among the mess holding Sullyan's hand, his eyes closed as he gave her support. His breathing was ragged and strained. He didn't react to Rienne's arrival. His son, the Crown Prince, was similarly engaged, cradling Lirina's limp form to his chest. The Princess gasped and labored for breath. Rienne didn't care for the sound, or for the color of her face. Aeyron's eyes were open but unseeing, so deeply was he involved in his task, and he didn't register Rienne's approach either, nor feel her hand on his arm. She turned to where Deshan knelt by a younger woman who lay unmoving on the floor. The two servants beside him followed his commands, mixing saltwater and dribbling it into the stricken woman's mouth. The Master Healer glanced up as Rienne knelt down beside him, relief and welcome evident on his face.

"Rienne. I got your message. There's a healer on her way with what temany we have. We only keep it for use on our livestock, so she's had to run to one of the traders. Do you think it will help against this poison?"

Rienne leaned forward to examine the unconscious young woman. There was blood mixed with the fluids her body had expelled. "We've only just discovered its properties ourselves. I won't mislead you, Deshan; we've not tested it yet. Our records that mention it all pertain to scouring sheep, and you obviously use it for the same purpose here, but the symptoms it's said to counter are identical to those induced by this poison. How long have they been like this, does anyone know?"

Deshan waved toward Maxin. "Not too long, thanks to the quick wits of this page. He heard a strange noise and alerted a maid, who entered and found them like this. Shandra was well when he brought the food earlier."

Rienne smiled at the boy, but Maxin just stared with tears of horror on his face. Rienne frowned to see his shocked state. "It'll be all right, Maxin, they're in safe hands. You can leave the treatment to us. Why not go and get something hot to drink? You've had a nasty shock."

"The kitchens are closed, Healer," the boy murmured automatically, not really hearing his own words. "The poison was in the food."

Rienne's eyes swung to the disarranged tray, the nibbled fruit. She glanced grimly at Deshan. "Just like Loxton Castle. I trust someone's looking for the culprit?"

Before Deshan could reply, the boy's mechanical voice came again.

"It was me."

Their heads snapped up and Deshan glowered, but Rienne got there first. "What was, Maxin? What do you mean?"

"It was me." The lad's tone was flat and cold. "I brought them the food. I caused all this. I'm to blame."

Rienne wanted to protest, to go to him, but running footsteps sounded in the hall. Before she could speak, a servant girl rushed in, bearing a box in her arms. She gave it to Deshan, who glanced at the contents, showing the jumble of fresh and dried leaves and parchment twists of powder to Rienne. "Will this be enough, do you think?"

"I have no idea. It will have to be, won't it? I've brought everything we had at the Manor."

She began to instruct the Master Healer in how to prepare the herbs, praying with all of her loving heart that people wouldn't prove to be so different from sheep. Ignored and forgotten, Maxin slunk from the room.

✢ ✢ ✢ ✢ ✢

Pain and sickness swamped her. She was conscious, but elsewhere, her senses refusing to work. Holding on to Lirina's fading spirit, Sullyan doggedly endured. Although the poison couldn't touch her, leaving her physical body essentially unharmed, her mind suffered the full effects and her grip was losing its strength. She needed something to help her, something to override the pain, something to latch on to that wouldn't distract her from her task.

The one thing that had always flowed constantly through Sullyan's soul and needed no encouragement to surface was music. Music was in her blood, passed on through the seed of her sire, the spirit of the bard in her heart. Music had often soothed her when troubled; it buoyed her and calmed her mind. One song above all others had been with her all her life—sung to her in the womb by her mother, recognized throughout each of the Five Realms, its strains ancient, its origins unknown. She had never yet found a clue to its source and concluded that it was one of those primeval tunes whose airs are essential to life, woven deep into the thread of existence, with no beginning and no end. It seemed right that it should come to her now, when life was at its lowest ebb.

Earth speaks in tones of soil, wood, and stone
An echo that runs through all that we are.
Its presence and power sustain on their own
But your love gives life meaning, your heart is my home.

Its gentle refrain rippled through her mind, needing no thought to sustain it. It swept her along with a life of its own, carrying her deeper and away from the pain. She allowed it to transport her, not fighting its calming spell, wrapping its familiar strains around her and finding some ease. All other concerns dropped away from her thoughts and the milky swirl in which she moved became a balm to her hurts.

There were words to the song and she knew them by heart— had known them even before she could talk. They were not Albian words, yet they spoke to her heart, and they surfaced in her mind with no effort, before she even knew they were there. She caught hold of their meaning, the love they expressed, and bathed herself in it, feeling warm and alive.

Water's music gives birth to the soul
Its essence surrounds us, feeds all that we are
The hard rain, wild sea, the softness of snow,
Run deep within us, as Love itself flows.

They were not so ancient, these words of true love, but they carried the weight of many hearts. Penned in veracity, honesty, and a need for expression, they conveyed more than their author had dreamed of. The magic of his skill had entered his words and imbued them with a primal spirit. They had become the anthem to her life, and they were also a link to her past. She had sung them for comfort in her lonely childhood, and had learned of their meaning by pure chance. The Sinnian bard Fiann, greatest of his kind, had heard her by chance, and once he recovered from his surprise at hearing the long-dead tongue sung by a young human child, he told her their language and explained what they meant. Once he started translating, she recognized the words, as if their meaning had already been there but was locked behind a door to which Fiann was the key. Since that time she had sung the words often, and they were embedded in the core of what she would become—their significance ever dearer once she learned who had made them.

Fire of the sun pours warmth through the leaves
Life's cradle of heat gives us all that we are
Light for our eyes and the life that we see,
Kindling true friendship, your love kindles me.

She heard them now and they enveloped her mind, soothing

the hurt and calming her fears. As always, they led her to thoughts of her father, who had penned them in praise of her mother, and she fancied she could hear his well-trained voice as the much-loved song unraveled through her mind. She drifted in a haze of white, just listening and hearing the love, disembodied and protected from the trials of the wider world. Her concerns for her friends and her devastating grief over the terrible death of her life mate seemed to lose their sting, as if conflict had no meaning and life itself no power to harm. She gave herself over to the skill of her father and lay as if wrapped in the protection of his arms.

Air with a soft sigh, or raging with force,
Filling the spaces of all that we are.
Tempests and zephyrs, the clouds upon their course,
Its voice sings so sweetly when Love is the source.

A door to her mind slid open, and a presence made its way through. It was one she felt she should acknowledge if only she knew who it was. And yet she did know, she sensed him, and greetings were said, although not in words she remembered. His soul merged with hers and she felt the depths of his love, and she smiled in the haze that surrounded her. She sensed a sudden urgency, a desire to convey, but no matter how hard she tried, she could not understand. Part of his meaning came through to her, but part of it was lost. It was as if a barrier existed, flimsy and permeable, yet inflexible and strong. The barrier floated between them, like the Veils between the realms, and she did not possess the knowledge to pass from her side to his. Frustration gnawed at her spirit and she pushed even harder to reach him. She felt him responding, encouraging her efforts, and sensed that she might even succeed. The sound of the song that had drawn him flared in the caverns of her mind, fueling her struggles and empowering her.

She called to him, and he to her, but their outstretched hands never met.

Spirit rise up and join all these as one
The core of our being, of all that we are
The source of all loving, the heart's labors done
When two spirits join, when two souls sing one song.

Suddenly, the world turned bitter and the strains of the song faded away. The haze of her milky surroundings became tinged with darkness and she shrank from the shadows in alarm. There was a vile taste in her mouth and she struggled to spit it up, but fingers clamped over her mouth and prevented her. She was forced to swallow the stinging mixture and she felt her stomach rebel. The milky haze vanished and she vaguely heard a voice crying urgently in the distance, exhorting her to remember the words, desperate to make her understand. But it faded and vanished and the vile taste came again, and then her body struggled against strong arms and voices called her name.

She opened her eyes to the flare of bright light, the pain of it piercing her muddled mind. Half of her still resided in the song and she resisted the pull of the herbs. Yet someone—Rienne—forced her mouth open and poured more liquid in, demanding that she swallow, pleading with her to be all right. She heard disturbing noises around her and other voices raised in fear, and then the bitter tang of the herbs swept through her body and cleared the confusion from her mind. She turned her gaze to Rienne's pale face and slowly nodded her head.

"Let go of her, Timar, I think she's all right."

The grasping hands loosened their hold and Sullyan leaned forward, wrapping her arms about her aching belly. There was still a powerful urge to vomit, but it was only in her mind. She knew

186

the toxin was not inside her and spoke sternly to her senses, ruling her reactions and forcing out the pain. She was able to straighten then, and smile tentatively at her adoptive father, who hugged her tightly to him, murmuring words of grateful thanks.

✢ ✢ ✢ ✢ ✢

Rienne turned to Aeyron, who still supported his princess. Lirina was unconscious, white, and violently shaking. Her clothing was badly soiled and soaking wet, but she was alive and would recover, although it had been a very near thing. Aeyron stared at Rienne, unable to voice his emotions. He took hold of her hand and squeezed it hard, the only acknowledgement he was capable of giving. She stood and gripped his shoulder, passing him a dampened cloth so he could cool his lady's face.

She turned her attention to Deshan, who still knelt on the floor. Poor Shandra was still in the throes of purging, but at least the blood-flow had stopped. Rienne thought she would probably survive the ordeal, although there may be some internal damage. But that remained to be seen. The one thing they needed to focus on was that, this time, the Baron had failed. No one had died and their skills had proved sufficient—all thanks to a weed that cured scouring in sheep. Rienne shook her head at the ridiculous thought as she sank to her knees to aid Deshan.

Sometime later, the servants left quietly, bundles of soiled bedding and clothing in their arms. The floor had been scrubbed and dried, the fires tended and fed. Fresh herbs lay strewn on the floor and scented candles bobbed their flames as the door to the suite finally closed. Those who remained within were dressed in fresh clothing, Rienne having borrowed a robe from one of Lirina's maids. The comforting smell of strong fellan chased the lingering foulness away, and Rienne stirred the pot, wafting the smell as she listened to Sullyan's husky voice.

Aeyron's princess was sleeping in a freshly made bed, her face regaining color as her body slowly recovered. Her intended lay wakeful beside her, holding her in his arms, watching over her sleep with a lover's anxious protectiveness. The door to the bedchamber stood open so he could hear the low voices coming from the other room, but he was too fearful and angry to take part in the conversation. The copper-haired maid had been placed in her own bed in the rooms across the hall where her three companions watched over her rest. She had not regained consciousness, but Rienne wasn't worried. She was only exhausted and would recover given time. The Albian healer glanced across at Sullyan, who only needed fellan to complete her own revival.

The Artesan woman sat curled on the couch, her hands around her cup, her legs tucked beneath her and her hair lying over her shoulders. The midmorning sun, weak though it was, fell on her face and warmed her skin to pale gold, the amber of her eyes flashing in the light. She huddled within a blanket, although the room was warming nicely now the fires were well alight. Pharikian sat beside her, sipping from his own cup, his eyes hot with rage as he heard all she had to say.

The conversation had moved on from his ranting against the Baron's vengeful actions and the heartfelt thanks he had directed to both Sullyan and Rienne. Now Pharikian listened in horror to his adopted daughter's harsh, choked voice as she told him of the Baron's brutal abuse of Robin and the results of his malicious revenge. He sat silent through it all, his expression clouded and troubled, and when she finally lapsed into silence he regarded her from dangerously glinting eyes, knowing and feeling the gaping wound Robin's fate had left in her heart.

"You cannot let him live, Brynne."

The implacable tone of his statement fell like a weight of lead into the room. Rienne shivered despite her proximity to the fire,

188

fear and denial in her wide gray eyes. She knew that to kill the Baron was to pass a sentence worse than death on those he held captive, and although Robin may be only a shell and Jinny in a soulless coma, Taran was still too alive for her to even consider such a dreadful fate. She could still see the terror in the depths of his eyes as he'd realized the hopelessness of their enslaved state.

Sullyan bowed her head, and Rienne knew her emotions were mirrored in her friend's soul—sharp fear, cold rage, and a great, ravening fire yearning for vengeance warring in her aching heart.

"I know, Father, believe me, I know. He has become too powerful if he can reach even here. I cannot take the chance that he will strike us yet again. I came here today to request the freedom of your archives. I need to satisfy myself that there is no known way of releasing those he has taken before I confront him and kill him. He has power available to him that none of us can counter. He can move between the realms before we are even aware of his presence. He has Robin's knowledge and skills. He can influence the minds of others—even those we might think would be safe— and cause them to act against us, whether they will or no. It is impossible to guard against that. I know he will continue these attacks until I am forced to surrender. If I kill him, I condemn those I love to torment eternal. If I suffer him to live, how do I take onto my conscience the deaths of those who would oppose him, let alone innocents such as Lirina?"

There was movement by the bedchamber door and their heads turned that way. Prince Aeyron leaned against the door jamb, his face white and drawn, his eyes full of fury. His hands were clenched into fists and his body trembled with the force of his rage and the effects of his fear. He stared at his sister with feverish eyes, a light flickering behind them that was not wholly sane.

"Why?" he rasped, his voice shaky and strange. "Why did he not attack me? Why did it have to be her? Why can't he leave us alone? Hasn't he hurt us enough?"

Pharikian closed his eyes at the terror in Aeyron's voice. Rienne knew he feared this would prove too much for the injured spirit of his son, so fragile and maimed since his ordeal in the circle. Given more time, and the support of his bride, those wounds would finally heal, but now they all saw how lasting the effects of them were, and Rienne doubted Aeyron would ever be whole. Lirina had survived this time, but if anything else were to happen, she feared Aeyron would not.

Sullyan captured her brother's tortured gaze and reached out with her strength. He blinked as he sensed her touch and the tinge of instability faded. He drew a deep breath and straightened from the door, crossing to the fire where Rienne silently handed him a cup. His hands shook as he took it and he nodded absent thanks, a measure of his distress. He sank down on the couch next to his father.

Sullyan spoke deliberately. "Aeyron, have you not realized the poison was meant for you? Reen has Robin's knowledge of the servants and the layout of the Palace, but he could not have known Lirina would be here, or that Maxin would serve her. His target was you, or your father. Had either of you died, it would have gladdened his black heart, and both of you together would have filled him with glee. We are fortunate indeed that Maxin kept his wits, and that the women were not very hungry and ate little."

Sullyan watched this register with Aeyron and then turned to Pharikian. "Has Barrin not found the lad yet? We really need to speak to him. If we can discover how this was accomplished, it might help us guard against more of the same."

Rienne saw Pharikian's eyes glaze as he contacted the commander, who was heading the search for the missing page. Lord General Anjer had gone down to the town to cancel the Procession and inform the lords. The Fair would proceed as normal, but the town would be subdued and fearful as the news of this terrible attack spread among them. Anjer would also discreetly search the town, and the guards on the gates had their orders.

Sullyan was deeply concerned by Maxin's disappearance. He was their only link to understanding this attack. She doubted the Baron had captured him because Barrin had thoroughly searched and sealed the Palace as soon as he delivered Rienne. Rienne had seen Maxin in this very room, so he ought to be somewhere close, although he obviously didn't want to be found. Rienne had told her of the boy's desperate words and how he blamed himself for the dreadful attack.

Pharikian stirred as his eyes cleared. "There's no sign of him yet, and no evidence of any intruders. Deshan is scouring the kitchens, checking all the food—he will personally oversee the preparation of all meals. He has devised a way of testing for toxins in the food, so we should have some safe refreshments before much longer."

Rienne knew that food was the last thing on Sullyan's mind. She had told Rienne how urgent it was that she begin her search of the archives. Something was nagging at her, telling her there was a clue to be found, some possible course of action she had to uncover. It was a new sensation, this urge in her mind, and where it had come from she simply did not know. She kept feeling a phrase trying to surface in her thoughts, plaguing her like an irritating itch that was just out of reach. The more she tried to pursue it, the further it receded, and she confided to Rienne that reading the Palace's archives might bring it to the fore. But Rienne knew she really wanted to speak to the page, to see what his memory of events could tell her. Besides, they all were concerned for his safety.

"Has anyone asked Norkis?" Sullyan said. Pharikian shook his head. "Then tell Barrin to enlist his help. He knows his brother best. If anyone can find where he's hiding, it is Norkis."

Chapter Seventeen

axin sat in darkness, cradling his head in his hands. He simply couldn't get the dreadful smell out of his throat and his stomach threatened to heave with every breath. He clasped his hands over his nose, forcing himself to breathe between his fingers, but it did no good. His hands, his clothes, his hair—all seemed to be impregnated with the vile smell, and everything he touched seemed tainted by it. The sights and sounds that his mind kept replaying tormented him with his shame.

Tears stung his cheeks and a sob welled deep in his throat. They were going to die—they might already be dead. Surely no one could survive such virulent poison, least of all those fragile women. His Prince's bride, the one he had searched so long to find, that gracious, beautiful creature wracked and tormented by terror and pain. The pretty young maid who had caught his brother's fancy, writhing in convulsions on the bedchamber floor. He had seen the pleading look in her eyes before she was overcome, desperation for help he couldn't give—and a terrible accusation for the agent of such betrayal. He was convinced she had known, she guessed it had been him, and he fled the scene of his terrible crime, intending to punish himself, remove himself, and in so doing atone at least for some of his guilt.

It should be him dying in agony, not those innocent women. *He* was the one who had brought this to pass. *He* was the one who had been lax in his watch. All the Palace servants had been warned by the Chief Steward to be on their guard and to report anything odd. Any strangers in the Palace, anyone prowling the grounds, anything at all that seemed out of place. Yet Maxin had relaxed his guard and let the enemy in. Distracted by pride in his duty and by inappropriate thoughts, he had allowed himself to be duped and had become the carrier of death.

His hands beat out his shame on the stone seat, and he felt the damp creep into his bones. He sat in a disused storeroom, musty and dark. No warmth entered here, no light from lamp or torch. It was as lonely and cold as a newly dug grave. Maxin wiped his eyes and reached to his belt, the movement aggravating the pain in his arm. The burning sensation made him frown and pause, and he took his hand away from the hilt of his knife. He explored the painful shoulder with his other hand, finding it sore to the touch and bruised beneath the skin. He couldn't see in the unlit room, but he could feel the skin was raw. He wondered at it. He could not recall injuring himself, and certainly not enough to break the skin, but the evidence of his nerves was irrefutable. Perhaps he had done it as he ran, obeying Aeyron's orders to fetch his father. He must have struck his shoulder on a door frame, or grazed it on the wall, but it hardly mattered now. Forcing down the tearful lump in his throat, he reached once again for his knife, bringing it before his eyes and testing the edge against the ball of his thumb. He held it in trembling fingers and tried not to think.

✣ ✣ ✣ ✣ ✣

Norkis raced through the hallways, bellowing Maxin's name. Barrin ran behind him, following his lead. As soon as Norkis heard what had happened, and how the poison must have reached its victims, he knew where his brother would be. He would have retreated to his secret hiding place, where he always went when he needed to think or to hide from trouble. Maxin was slightly built and his position had attracted some envy—he had endured a measure of bullying from some of the older boys. Norkis had given him advice, but refused to fight his battles, saying he ought to learn to defend himself now he was no longer a child. Instead, he gave his brother a dagger and began teaching him how to use it. Maxin had told him where he went when he wished to avoid a fight. Knowing how deeply the boy felt his duty and desperately hoping he was only hiding his tears, Norkis led Barrin and his guards down to the servants' floor.

✢ ✢ ✢ ✢ ✢

Maxin gasped in pain as the blade bit into his flesh. He was proud of his brother's gift and had learned how to keep the knife oiled and sharp. He never thought to use it in such a way, or to use it at all, if he was honest. Although he listened to Norkis's advice and practiced the moves his brother taught him to deflect and defend, he had only accepted it as a means to frighten his tormentors. It was enough to be seen with it in his possession, and to show he knew how to use it. To be left to his duties in peace was all Maxin desired. His future lay among the Palace staff. He would leave the swordplay to Norkis, who seemed to have an aptitude. Maxin simply wanted to serve.

Yet now it had come to this. His desire to serve the Princess had led to the woman's death, not to mention the anguish of the Crown Prince, whom Maxin loved so well. He couldn't bear being the one to destroy Aeyron's life, couldn't live with the guilt and shame, and so he took the knife in his hand and laid its bright edge to his wrist. His hand was shaking and he nicked the skin, the blood mingling with that from his thumb. Well, at least he knew the blade was sharp. One deep slice was all it would take. When he had done one, the other would not be so hard. The pain would be great but fleeting; it would soon drain away with his life.

His shame roaring in his ears, he took a grip on the hilt of the knife and drew it sharply across his wrist.

Light burst into the room, blinding him. A cry rang in his ears, sharp with the panic of love. Pain lanced up his arm and hot blood spurted; the knife fell from nerveless fingers. He felt himself grabbed by the arms and lifted from his seat as other hands grasped at his wrist. There were voices shouting and bodies crowding in— he felt dizzy and sick with confusion.

✜ ✜ ✜ ✜ ✜

"Quick, someone, get me a cloth!"

At Barrin's roar, Norkis flung off his tunic and ripped the shirt from his back, thrusting the linen at Barrin. The commander bound up the boy's arm, ignoring the spurting red shower. He clamped his strong hands on the wound, forcing the bleeding to stop. His furious face was inches from Maxin's and his pale-brown eyes bored into the boy's.

"What the hell do you think you're doing, you stupid young fool? How dare you try to take your own life? Were those your instructions, once you'd poisoned us all? Well, you'll not get the chance now, you little traitor! We have other ways of dealing with the likes of you."

Norkis started in alarm at Barrin's vengeful words. He had not realized the commander held Maxin responsible. Norkis knew there was no possibility of his brother being a traitor. If indeed he had been the carrier of poisoned food, Norkis was certain he'd had no foreknowledge. Yet Norkis was only a cadet and Barrin was Commander of the Velletian Guard. There was no way Norkis could contradict him. And Maxin's actions did seem to indicate guilt, although Norkis would stake his life that it was Maxin's sense of shame and not fear of discovery that had driven him to this desperate act.

He followed discreetly when the commander picked up the

young page, gripping his arm in a bone-bruising vise and carrying him back to the Hierarch.

✣ ✣ ✣ ✣ ✣

"Good gods, Maxin, what the Void have you done?"

Rienne ran to the boy when Barrin entered the room, exclaiming in dismay over the red-soaked cloth still gripped in Barrin's hand. The commander shouldered her aside and strode toward his ruler, who stood to face him, concern in his eyes.

"What's happened, Commander, how was he wounded?"

Disapproval saturated Barrin's curt tone. "By his own hand, Majesty. He was attempting to take his own life. We only just stopped him, but perhaps we shouldn't have bothered. It would have saved you the expense of a trial."

Rienne sucked in an astonished breath and the Hierarch narrowed his eyes. Sullyan dropped the blanket from her shoulders and stood, approaching the commander with a stern look. "Well for you that you did save him, Barrin, for not only is he innocent of any guilt, he likely carries information as to how the crime was committed. If we are to protect the Hierarch and his son from further attacks, what Maxin can tell us will be vital. You would have been guilty of two reckless acts had you allowed him to die."

Barrin flushed at her tone, looking to the Hierarch for confirmation.

"I asked you to find him, Commander, not judge him," said Pharikian, and Barrin's flush deepened.

Rienne's immediate concern was for the boy's injury, not his guilt or innocence. If his wrist was not seen to soon, it would become a moot point. "Set him down over there, Commander, and keep a firm grip of his wrist."

Chastened and silent, Barrin obeyed, laying the semiconscious boy down on the table. Pharikian caught sight of Norkis by the door, hovering uncertainly, and waved the former page into the room. "Norkis, come and relieve Barrin of this task. I believe there are more important matters for him to attend. I trust you will release Maxin to me, Commander?"

Barrin bowed low, not trusting himself to speak as Norkis took over his hold on Maxin's arm. He strode from the room, calling for his men, and the Hierarch watched him go.

Rienne worked on the cut to Maxin's wrist, with Sullyan helping to stem the blood-flow. The knife had not bitten too deep, thankfully, and the artery was not severed. Rienne soon had it stitched and then bound the wound securely. Maxin recovered slowly with the help of some red wine. He choked a little on it, unused to the rich, sweet taste, but its reviving properties soon took effect and he was able to sit and face their concern.

He was red-faced and mortified, unable to bear that he had botched the attempt. Now he had two sins to carry. Although Norkis tried to comfort him, his shame did not abate. It took Pharikian's embrace and sternest order before the boy would listen to his ruler's words.

"Maxin, you are *not* to blame, do you hear me? You had no knowledge of the poison, we all know that. Do you think you would have been permitted to serve her Highness if we did not trust you implicitly? You are the finest page we have, lad. Never doubt our faith in you."

"But I *am* responsible, Majesty. It was me who brought the food!" Maxin's voice was strained and his pale eyes shimmered with tears. He found it impossible to meet his sovereign's gaze and positively flinched from the sight of Aeyron's white face.

Pharikian knelt beside him and took up the boy's uninjured right hand, clasping it tightly. He spoke in low, earnest tones. "Do we blame the blade that takes another's life? Or do we blame the wielder, who sets it to the throat? You have been used like a tool,

Maxin, and cruelly. But the man responsible has had no victory here; his purpose did not bear fruit. We have *you* to thank for that, brave page, for you used your wits and ran for help. You did the right thing, and you are responsible for saving both their lives. If not for your sharp ears and commendable common sense, those two women would have been beyond our help. So you are not to blame for what happened here, and I forbid you to mention it again! Am I understood?"

"They live?" Maxin stared dumbly at his lord's kind smile and nod, and tears trickled down his face. When Aeyron stepped close and laid his hand silently on the young lad's shoulder, his sobs finally broke free. Rienne let him weep for a moment before handing him a cloth for his face. He gulped in a shaky breath and took it with a faint nod of thanks. When he was calmer and could look them in the eye once again, Sullyan took the Hierarch's place.

"Maxin, I must ask something of you, if you will. We need to know how this was done, how the deception was accomplished without you being the wiser. There is only one way to do that, and so I must ask for your help. Will you allow us to look within your mind, to see if the poisoner has left us any trace?"

The young page spoke earnestly. "Of course, Highness." Sullyan smiled at him. She held her hand out to Pharikian and the Hierarch sat beside her, merging his mind with hers. As yet, Maxin had shown no signs of developing an Artesan's powers, but both his father and brother were gifted so it was almost inevitable he would eventually show the gift. For now, his willing compliance was all they needed, and he sat still and passive as their combined powers settled on his mind, as gentle and welcome as warm summer rain, and sank within his consciousness, peeling back the layers of memory.

It didn't take them long to find those innocent thoughts of love, the momentary distraction that left his natural shield weakened. The Baron's entry to his psyche had been tuned to that adolescent desire, and Sullyan felt furious that such guileless wonderings had been so foully corrupted. It fed her desire to exact retribution, but she forced down her rage and continued her search.

There was only a brief memory of the sight of Seth's face before the pain in his shoulder snatched Maxin's senses away. That transient flare of agony cut into Sullyan's soul, echoing in her mind like the sound of Robin's death cry. Tears prickled her eyes, and the Hierarch swiftly soothed the aching despair away. She sifted through Maxin's memories, realizing that his brief lapse of consciousness was all the Baron's minion had needed to put the poison in the food. Once his hold over Maxin was removed, the boy had been too full of embarrassment over the state of his rampant young body to remember the encounter. It was cunning and it was evil, and it left a foul taste in her mouth.

She and Pharikian came back to themselves, grim-faced and angry at their enemy's low tactics. She shared a glance with the Hierarch as she reached to Maxin's shoulder, drawing down his tunic.

"Did you find what you needed, Highness?"

The angry red patch she revealed drew a breath of surprise from Rienne. The healer came closer to examine the strangely altered skin.

Sullyan watched Rienne's questing fingers. "Yes, lad, you were most helpful. Your mind gave up all its secrets, and now we will be on our guard."

She was pleased to see that her deliberate phrasing drew no blush from the boy. She had carefully erased the memory of his shame. It was the one thing she could do for him, to remove that taint of evil. Maxin would be a good catch some day. The last thing he needed was a maliciously planted sense of shame to spoil, and perhaps pervert, the innocent delights of awakening desire.

Rienne straightened from her probing and glanced at Sullyan. "You know what this looks like?"

Sullyan met her gaze. "It is the same as the wounds inflicted on Taran and Jinella, only less severe."

Rienne reached for some salve to rub on the outraged flesh, and Maxin sighed in relief as the sting was soothed. "I really ought to get back to them. Taran is not coping well with his fear."

Sullyan's eyes clouded at this reminder of their plight and she turned to the Hierarch. "I must get down to the archives, Father. It will take me many hours to sort through them. Can you arrange for Rienne's return, and an escort for her safety?"

"Of course, child, consider it done. I will call Barrin to escort her home. And Gaslek will help you in the archives."

For the rest of that day, Sullyan pored over texts, surrounded by piles of parchment. Caer Vellet's extensive records were housed beneath the Palace, in caverns hewn out of the rock. The echoing place was dry and cool, its atmosphere maintained by its depth underground. The heat of summer never reached so far and the ice of winter was held at bay by the insulating rock. It was a silent and peaceful place. She sat shoulder to shoulder with Gaslek, the little secretary as eager in the search as she. News of the attack on Lirina had purpled his face with anger. He threw himself into the task, his encyclopedic knowledge of the contents of the archives and where each parchment could be found proving once more invaluable to Sullyan as they steadily worked through the texts.

She began by scrutinizing every reference to the powers of Liyan Tamilane she could find. He was one of Pharikian's distant predecessors and the only Supreme Master Artesan of whom they had more than passing knowledge. She chose to start with him because he was reputedly able to influence Spirit, that mysterious co-adjuvant of life, and this was what Sullyan was urgent to explore, to see if she could unearth any shred or hint of hope that there might be a way to free her life mate's consciousness from the Baron's control. She was desperate to sever his hold on the souls he held before she was forced to destroy him. The knowledge that she would be responsible for damning them to Perdition if they were still in his grip when he died tore at her aching heart. As he, no doubt, intended. However, he had stolen the powers he used; he did not have her skills. Surely, she pleaded in the depths of her desolate soul, surely he had overlooked some flaw. Surely there must be a way? Yet no matter how many texts Gaslek found, how many references to Tamilane's talents they uncovered—and there were few enough three hundred years after his death—they found nothing to indicate he'd had any experience of the situation she faced.

She flung down the last of the parchments and spat a pithy barrack-room curse, dropping her head to her hands. Gaslek, well used to her occasional foul language, stared at her with weary sympathy, neither desiring nor expecting an apology for the lapse. He was surprised, therefore, to receive one, and to see the tears shimmering in her eyes.

"I must beg your pardon, my Lord Baron. This search is obviously hopeless. I fear I have wasted your time."

Gaslek leaned back in his chair, stretching the kinks from his spine. "I never consider searching though the archives a waste of time, Highness. I spend a great many hours in solitude down here. I find it relaxing and peaceful. My only regret is that we have not been successful, although, in truth, I am scarcely surprised. We have only ever come across these few ancient texts from Tamilane's tenure here. We are probably fortunate to have even these."

A thought pricked Sullyan's mind and she gasped, her face tight with new hope. "My Lord, are you saying Tamilane was not Velletian?"

Gaslek paused briefly before replying, his eyes widening as her meaning sank in. "No, Highness, he was not. He came originally from Quarlock, and resided here only after he acceded to the throne."

"What age was he when that occurred?"

The Baron's voice gained a note of excitement. "He was in his early thirties. The date 7002 refers to the year of his birth, not the commencement of his reign."

"And was he already Supreme Master when he became Hierarch?"

"He was, Highness. He was considered extraordinarily gifted, even in those days."

She quelled the premature elation that struggled for release. "So there could be records in the place of his birth. I take it he was nobly born?"

Gaslek nodded. "The Tamilanes were a powerful family who ruled the entire northeast, incorporating Quarlock, Lythe, Radnar, and even reaching as far as the island of Wyx."

Sullyan's eyes felt like they were afire. "My Lord Baron, please tell me Kethro respects the ancient records!"

"As far as I am aware, he does. But what his father may have done before him, and his ancestors back in time, none of us can say."

"I must go and see him! Would you be willing to accompany me to Quarlock?" She was already moving toward the stairs, drawing the little round man in her wake. She had never personally set foot in Quarlock, but she knew its youthful lord, having helped expose his father's treachery and seen the son declare allegiance to the Hierarch. Gaslek puffed along behind her, more than willing to lend his aid. The history of their realm was a passion of his. Any opportunity to learn more was not to be missed.

It was already long after noon when they hurried back to the Hierarch, finding him resting in his rooms. He had dealt with a succession of worried nobles, alarmed by Anjer's news and the cancellation of the day's Procession. The increased armed presence around the Palace had unsettled the Caer's inhabitants. Every noble family, keen to demonstrate their loyalty, sent a representative to tender their good wishes and to elicit more details about the attack. Wary of fostering panic, the Hierarch answered them carefully, forcing his son to face them also to quell any gossip.

The elderly ruler received the news of Sullyan's failure with weariness, but acknowledged the sense of her plan. "I will contact Lord Kethro immediately and request that he open his archives. I doubt he will have any objections. He remembers you with fondness."

Sullyan gazed at her adoptive father with concern, hearing his exhaustion. This day should have been so joyous, but it had been disfigured by pain and fear. "I am a little surprised he is not here, Father, given his loyalty to your son."

Pharikian smiled faintly, a pleasant thought soothing the lines on his face. "He is recently married, Brynne, and his wife is expecting. But he will receive you with welcome and so will his bride. She is a very pretty girl and worthy of his love."

His obvious emotional and physical fatigue caused Sullyan's heart to fall. He had borne so much, this powerful man, and he was coming to the end of his life. His decision to share the burden of rulership should have relieved him of much of his care. Yet their enemy would not let them rest and his strength was slowly eroding, hastening his decline. Once he had departed, she would lose her last link, the last living person she knew who had intimately known her parents. The love she felt for this gentle man went far deeper than gratitude. His caring heart had enfolded her soul and they were closer than ever these days. His wholehearted inclusion of her and her son into his family had touched her to her very bones. She now considered herself his child indeed, as much as either Aeyron or Idrimar. To see him so weary and to feel so helpless just tore at the roots of her love.

Impulsively, she knelt at his side and clasped his veined hands, gazing into his yellow eyes with intensity. "I will see him pay, Father. I will see him destroyed, of that you may be sure! He has worked his last evil on those we love. Whatever I find in Lord Kethro's records—even if there is nothing to find—this I will vow and aver. The Baron is living the end of his days. There will be no mercy when I take him. If I have to, I will choke out his breath with my own hands!"

The fury in her low, strained voice brought Pharikian to his feet. He swept her upright and enfolded her in a tight embrace, swamping her psyche with love and sharing the depths of her pain. His fear for his son matched her anguish over Robin and they were both overcome by their rage. Helpless and torn, they supported each other while Gaslek shifted uncomfortably where he stood by the door. It took his discreet and diffident cough to bring them back to themselves.

Chapter Eighteen

Sullyan stepped away from her adopted father. Their faces were pale, their eyes damp. Only at times like this was it possible to see the blood that bound them, as their shared heritage shone forth in the similarity of their eyes.

The Hierarch's eyes glazed as he contacted the young Lord of Quarlock. He smiled as he ended his communication with Kethro and turned his gaze on his daughter. "Lord Kethro grants your wish to examine his records. He will give you any aid you might require. He awaits you at the gateway to his residence, and will personally guide you to the archives. Do you wish me to open the way for you, or shall I show you his location? Brynne?"

Sullyan didn't hear him. His words had triggered a flash of recognition that punched through her body like a lightning bolt. Her wide eyes stared at nothing, her face turned chalky-pale. Alarmed, the Hierarch took her shoulders, turning her to face him. Her pupils were widely dilated, but he knew she expended no power. Realizing the futility of normal speech, the Hierarch reached for her mind.

All at once, he was sucked into her struggle, sensing the force with which she strained. She was desperate to capture a thought or a phrase, and he lent her his power to bolster her own. But she was trying too hard and losing the fight, and he could feel what she sought slipping further away. Taking control, he soothed her mounting frustration, pushing her psyche lightly aside. She reluctantly gave way, permitting him to root through her thoughts, granting him access to her most private sanctum where even Robin had rarely ventured.

He found it eventually, although it was buried very deep, planted in her subconscious by one he knew well. His startled surprise filtered through to her and dissolved the shield she had erected against the pain of his probable failure. She sensed the surge of his emotions as he recognized that frail impression, and demanded answers before he had even withdrawn from her mind.

What is it, Father? What did you see?

Pharikian declined to reply until they were separate. He had tears in his eyes and a smile on his lined face as he took her by the shoulders once more and gazed into her avid eyes. "I think you know, my daughter."

An image of her sire swam into her mind. She berated herself for not recognizing him sooner, but Pharikian was having none of that. There was too much self-blame in her already for him to countenance her adding any more.

"The image was buried too deeply, my child. You would never have retrieved it alone. I wonder if he planned it that way, so you would be forced to ask for help. We will probably never know. And I have no idea of the significance of the phrase. That is something we must trust will become apparent in time. But Morgan would not have been permitted to breach the barriers this way unless it was vitally important."

She felt him opening a door in her mind and heard the well-loved voice. The tones of her father the bard echoed about her soul, exhorting her to remember *"the Gateway, and the Guide."* Pharikian's innocent earlier use of the word "gateway" must have triggered the imprint of the memory, but not enough to make it accessible without his help. She pondered the possible significance of this, but came to no firm conclusions.

"I have no idea what it means, Father. If his intention was to offer me aid, I wish he had spoken plainer."

The Hierarch regarded her. "Perhaps he was not able. Perhaps it was not permitted. I know little of the worlds beyond the Void. You have more experience of such matters than I."

She glanced up at him, remembering her strange visions during the birth of her son. She had seen the revenants of those she had loved and lost, had spoken to them and been led away by them from her determination to relinquish her life. They had seemed so real and natural at that time, but had faded and lost their meaning with the passage of the ensuing three years. She rarely thought of those visions now, and had almost come to believe they were the product of her own distress and the yearnings of a broken heart. Yet she could not deny that there had been many times in her life when she had felt a presence hovering just behind her mind, a watchful and protective force that had comforted her when troubled. She had instantly recognized that presence in the spirit of her father, confirming what she had always known, deep in her heart. So she could not dismiss this message as a consequence of her fears, especially with her adoptive father so ready to accept it. He had known her sire well. If anyone could confirm Morgan's touch on her mind, it was Timar Pharikian.

"Well, whatever it was he intended to convey, I will have to wait to be shown. At least that nagging sense of having forgotten something vital has now been explained. I will watch for those words and take note of them if I come across them again. However, I see no reason to change my plan. I will accept Kethro's generous opening of his archives."

After taking an affectionate leave of the Hierarch, Sullyan led the way out of the Palace courtyard, Gaslek's stocky dun pony following close on Drum's ebony tail. She fixed the Hierarch's directions firmly in her mind as they rode through the darkening streets of the lower town and out through the southern gate. The merchants of the Trade Fair had swelled the Citadel's populace, but the coming of the evening and the unsettling events of the day had cleared the stalls of patrons and so the traders had packed up early. The streets were almost deserted and the taverns would be doing brisk trade as everyone drowned their unease in ale. The increased presence of the Velletian Guard, still visible about the streets, was a constant reminder of the fragility of their safety. But there was nothing she could do other than continue her search. And whether this foray to Quarlock proved fruitful or not, her path ahead was plain. The Baron had to be killed or his malevolence would continue to spread. She only hoped she could do her duty without being distracted by the dreadful fate of her friends.

She and Gaslek emerged onto the Plain in the twilight and heard the harsh, reassuring clang of the southern gate as it was secured behind them. They traveled a safe distance from the Caer and she turned in her saddle to check how far they had come. The Citadel was stunningly beautiful when viewed in this transient light. Its slim, soaring towers and flickering amber lights appeared ethereal against the aquamarine sky. The Hierarch's Imperial pennon, flying from the tallest spire, rippled in the breeze like some beckoning hand, exhorting her to return, saluting in farewell. She couldn't bear to think all the love and friendship she had found here, so unexpected and so selflessly given, could be destroyed. Sighing and setting her face resolutely to the fore, she warned her companion to be ready, and opened a passage through the Veils.

Lord Kethro awaited them as promised by the ornate white entrance gate to the vast walled gardens of his mansion. His gate guards presented their arms smartly as Sullyan and Gaslek rode out of the gloom, and grooms ran forward to take their mounts. Gaslek dismounted awkwardly, his bulk not suited to riding. Sullyan slid easily down Drum's shoulder and rubbed his nose. As grooms led the horses away, Kethro came forward, bowing low and smiling his welcome. He was not much changed from the last time she had seen him. He was still tall and thin, although he had gained muscle. His pale-brown eyes were friendly and clear, his unruly dark hair reminding her of his treacherous father. Yet the air of rebellion and discontent that had always surrounded Lord Corbyn was absent from his son, and Sullyan detected maturity in the twenty-year-old Kethro that probably had much to do with his recent marriage and impending fatherhood. She held out her hand in greeting and Kethro gallantly kissed it.

"It is good to see you so prosperous, my Lord. I gather I must congratulate you on your marriage. I believe you are expecting a child?"

Kethro's pleasant face flushed as he straightened and she saw the pride in his eyes. "I thank you, Highness. You are most welcome here. We are indeed awaiting the arrival of our firstborn, and my wife, Lady Orwen, sends her regrets that she cannot greet you in person. She asks that you grant her the pleasure of your company if your errand permits you the time."

"Send her my greetings, my Lord, and tell her I will do my best. But my errand is pressing and the hour grows late. Might I prevail upon your offer to show us your records?"

Kethro bowed them through the gates and led them through a vine-covered colonnade toward the house. It was a large and attractive building, constructed mainly of delicate white stone carved into swirling designs. Surrounded by a high stone wall, it sat in park-like but secluded gardens. Elegant, willowy trees with papery white bark swayed in the chill wind, their buds still tightly furled against the frost that crisped the air. Quarlock was far to the northeast of Caer Vellet and its lands higher by some thousand feet. Spring was still some way off in these colder, northern climes.

They approached the slender porticoes framing the main

entrance and guards stood aside for them, bowing their heads. Sullyan acknowledged them, more at ease now with her adopted royalty and finding it simpler not to dwell on it but to accept it for what it was. She preceded Kethro through the delicate tracery of the tall, elegant doors, Gaslek close behind. Emerging into a long hall warm and bright with firelight, they both looked around with interest, admiring the stylish tapestries and the air of simple comfort. Nothing was overstated, nothing lavish or overly ornate, yet the residence exuded peace and contentment and it suited Lord Kethro well.

He led them through various hallways and down a sweeping fall of stairs. They approached a wooden door on their left, set back within an arched embrasure, and locked by a huge brass key. Kethro turned the bulky key in the lock and then pushed the door back for them and waved them inside. Stepping in, they found a huge vaulted room, surprising in its size, packed with dusty shelves bursting with parchment and vellum. Gaslek wrinkled his nose, making his spectacles flash in the lamplight. His disapproving eye took in the disheveled state of the chamber and its contents, and he failed to suppress a sneeze. "Your servants have long neglected this room, I think, my Lord."

Kethro blinked and ducked his head, ashamed to admit he was right. "I have not yet paid much attention to the archives, my Lord Baron. After the … death … of my father, I was much occupied with learning how to run the province. Once I became confident in my management, I turned my thoughts to more pleasurable topics. But now I am settled, and with the succession about to be assured, I will be free to set things to rights down here and begin to make sense of this jumble of records."

Gaslek stared in dismay, his fleshy fingers plucking at each other. "Are you saying there is no system here, my Lord? Have you no index, no catalog, no lists?"

Kethro reddened under the Baron's criticism. Sullyan sympathized, although she shared Gaslek's dismay. If they were forced to trawl through every individual record in this vault-like room, the task could well take days. Time was a commodity her friends could not spare.

Kethro spread his hands. "If there are such things, my Lord, I have never seen them. This place hasn't been touched since long before I inherited. I have discovered to my cost that my father's administration left much to be desired, and not only in the area of the archives. But I am willing to lend you my aid for the evening."

Sullyan intervened before Gaslek could comment. "We thank you, my Lord, and accept your generous offer." She glanced meaningfully at the little secretary. "Shall we begin?"

They selected places at the huge central table, which Kethro swept clean with one arm—to Gaslek's silent but no less obvious disapproval—and the Baron took control of the search, apportioning them each a section of the walls. Sullyan instructed Kethro to lay aside anything relating to Liyan Tamilane, and to watch particularly for the words 'gateway' or 'guide.' Servants brought them fellan and a selection of cold meats, and soon the only sounds were the rustle of ancient parchment and the occasional rattle of a cup. The rich aroma of fellan chased away the musty smell of the records and hung about the room like a warm, comforting presence. They worked long into the night.

It soon became apparent that the section Kethro had drawn contained the vast majority of references to the man they sought. For every parchment the others found mentioning the long-dead Hierarch's name, Kethro found two. Although none of them, as yet, were of any significance as far as Sullyan was concerned, she and Gaslek eventually abandoned their own shelves and concentrated on Kethro's. The young Lord and the Baron restricted themselves to separating out the relevant texts while Sullyan sat with a growing pile at her elbow, scanning through each as swiftly as she dared, terrified of missing something vital. Servants continually refreshed the fellan pot, for which she was grateful, and also trimmed and filled the lamps. Gaslek and Kethro worked tirelessly, despite sore eyes and aching backs. And in the end, their persistence paid off when Kethro raised his head from a scrap of ancient, expensive vellum that he had found among a sheaf of lesser quality parchment.

The light of hope and excitement shone in his eyes as he called her name. "Brynne, here is something I think you should see."

Her head snapped up from the text she was reading, her neck protesting the cramp in her spine. He walked the few paces to hand her the scrap.

Looking at its faded and sometimes illegible lines, she thought he had probably found part of some kind of journal. This was rare, for most of the other texts were accounts and household records, detailing matters pertaining to the running of the province. The script that formed the neat, faded lines was different to the rest and Gaslek, peering at the text over Sullyan's shoulder, said, "That is not a scribe's hand. I wouldn't be surprised if that was written by Tamilane himself."

Sullyan knew he could be right. Every trained scribe or archivist in Andaryon was taught by the same method and formed letters in much the same way. Even scribes taught in Albia would recognize the forms, although some of their capitals had slightly different styles. But Tamilane's hand, if indeed this was his, was very different, his unique script not as clear or defined.

The fragment of vellum was small, hardly larger than her two palms placed together, and showed the letters on only one side. It was also fragile and inclined to tear, and the inks had lost much of their color, rendering parts of the text completely illegible. She glanced up at Kethro. "Would you continue your search, Kethro? There may be more of this."

The young man would clearly rather have helped read the script, but he went back to the search with good grace. After a moment, Gaslek joined him, both of them stirring up clouds of dust, eager to uncover more of the same. Sullyan bowed her head and focused on the ancient vellum. Strain though she might, certain words and letters were too faded to read, only a small portion of the text having survived. A momentous success had been recorded, that much was clear, and the brief account made Sullyan's spine tingle with suppressed excitement.

Today I fin... ... my goal; I ... the region bey...nd... Void, where it is po... to spea... to the ...rits of the depar... Op...ng the Gatew... I ... the mists, using ... powers ... push back ... guar... ... But I could... ... further ...out ... guide and ... I unders... her parting ...rds. She was waiti... for me ... that ... place, as she had ... ... would wait, and she offer... to take me ... I ... ... go. I was fear...l at first and inclined to mis... but she ... me and I ...endered myself ... her hands. We are now ... as one fore... and I am her ...gth; she my liais... among the ... ... dead.

Sullyan sat lost in thought as she mentally inserted words and letters to fill the blank spaces. Although initially elated at finding something that mentioned the words her father had planted in her mind, she had to admit that they seemed to offer little in the context of her problem. However, what was clear from the fragment of journal was that Tamilane had succeeded in entering the realm of Spirit, and that he had been forced to find some form of guide. He must have formed the gateway himself using his Master-level powers, and it seemed that he already knew the one who had been his guide. That gave her pause for thought and the beginnings of understanding—or at least encouragement—formed in her mind.

She shook herself out of her reverie, painfully aware of the late hour but avid to explore the possibility that more of this journal might be stored in the chamber. Even the smallest phrase might help her understanding. Exhorting her companions to search ever harder, she worked feverishly alongside them, ignoring her weariness.

After another back-straining hour, they had uncovered nothing more exciting than an order from the Hierarch to his horsemaster concerning the breeding of a favorite mare. It was not what Sullyan had hoped for, but it did confirm that the scrap of journal had indeed been written in Tamilane's hand. Once Gaslek pronounced himself satisfied as to the provenance of the journal scrap, Sullyan called a halt.

"I thank you for your unstinting efforts, gentlemen." Her raspy voice was weary, and she leaned her weight upon the table, gesturing to the vellum. "Without your aid tonight, I might never have found this."

Kethro slumped thankfully into a chair and stretched his legs out before him, trying to suppress a yawn. "But how does it help you, Brynne? It doesn't say much at all."

"That is true, but it does tell me that Tamilane succeeded in finding a way to communicate beyond the Void, and so it gives me hope. If I can do the same, I may find answers to some unsolvable questions. All I need now is to discover how he opened this Gateway he speaks of, and how he obtained the services of a Guide."

Kethro shook his head wryly. "Is that all? Well, I wish you luck. Do you want me to assign servants to finish searching this lot? See if any more of that journal is hidden away somewhere?"

She smiled at his offer, unwilling to turn down his generosity.

"Only if you have them to spare. Time is of the essence, and if I have not the skill to emulate Tamilane's achievement, even the most explicit instructions will not avail. Yet I believe I now have a basis to work from, which I lacked before. Your aid may well prove decisive in this, Kethro. I am forever in your debt."

The young lord flushed at the warmth in her eyes. She pushed herself upright. "I will keep you from your rest no longer. It is far too late already and your lady will not thank me for keeping you from her side. Please convey to her my deep regrets that I was unable to visit. Perhaps when your child is born I may come here again."

Kethro gained his feet awkwardly. "Of course, Brynne, you're always welcome in my house. But it is far too late to return to the Caer now. I have had chambers made ready for you and the Baron. Won't you take some rest and leave in the morning?"

She shook her head. "I appreciate the offer, my Lord, but I must decline your hospitality. I must return to my home. I have much to think on before I make any decisions, and my own son has done without me for far too long. With his father taken from us … well, I am sure you understand."

Kethro's protests died in the face of her obvious pain. Bowing his head, he led them from the room. He escorted them to the outer gates and watched until they were swallowed by the darkness.

Sullyan and Gaslek rode out into clear countryside before Sullyan opened the Veils. She led the way through into Albia before forming a second passageway back into Andaryon, watching Gaslek protectively as he nudged his pony through. When he turned and waved his thanks, she collapsed the portal, leaving him to ride on to the Citadel while she made her way to the Manor. Giving Drum to the night duty lads, she reached her own rooms unmolested and sank into an exhausted sleep, theories and murmured phrases tumbling through her troubled mind.

Chapter Nineteen

As he had been instructed, Seth stood clear of his master in the darkness, listening to the terrible, pleading cries. No shudders of revulsion wracked his youthful frame, no abhorrence shadowed his eyes. Seth was past caring now. The horror could touch him no longer. The Baron's hold on his mind, untested and light though it was, insulated Seth from what took place in this dreadful room. The compassion or pity he might once have felt for the scarecrow's victims was missing from the manservant's heart. It suited the Baron that this should be so.

The pathetic remnants of Lerric's palace guard waited outside like cattle, each held immobile by the power of the Baron. Summoned to the lower floor by their master's merest thought, they lined up with panic-stricken eyes, unable to move or to run. The knowledge that they were fodder, mere sustenance for the Baron's evil deeds, their life forces about to be wrenched from their bodies by the parasite feeding within, was all part of his plan. Reen could have rendered them senseless, could have spared them this agonizing wait, but he fed off their panic as surely as he absorbed their gibbering souls—he delighted in the surge of mortal terror each new victim felt.

He had told Seth he intended to take them all this night. He needed all the energy he could muster to face the witch. He could sense the deep hatred within her and knew she was coming to confront him. This connection was merely one of the benefits Reen had gained when he pillaged Robin's dying mind. He now knew every secret Robin had known, and he knew Sullyan's psyche well. He could read its emanations and feel her churning thoughts just as her life mate had been able to do—while she, of course, had no access to his. It was partly why he had gone to such lengths to secure the handsome young Major, and why he had taken such pleasure in the manner of his death. The young man's priceless knowledge was the key to the Baron's success. His other captives had fed his need for revenge, and each brought their own unique use, but his gleeful capture of Robin was the seal on his ultimate triumph. The Major's close bond with the Artesan witch would enable Reen to defeat her and take over her sundered powers.

He had explained this to Seth at a basic level, and the manservant understood. What he was still unclear about was how his master intended to survive once his supply of servants was gone. Their life forces only sustained him so long. If he exerted his stolen powers, his body weakened considerably. Seth understood that he needed more strength in order to defeat the witch, but once he had what he wanted of her, what then?

The scarecrow had deliberately left this gap in Seth's knowledge. The manservant had no knowledge of the transfer Reen was certain he could effect, nor the use to which Robin's body would have been put had Elias succeeded in his murderous assault during the confrontation in Lerric's throne room. Reen had not furnished his servant with this information to prevent him from inadvertently giving it away and jeopardizing Reen's careful schemes.

Seth was also mercifully unaware that he was his master's contingency plan—although mercy had played no part. Seth's younger body could also serve the scarecrow, even though the manservant himself had no Artesan talents. Had the Baron possessed the metaphysical strength, Seth's body might even now be playing host to the brooding parasite. Despite his acquisition of Robin's Master-level skills, Reen knew that the voluntary separating of his own soul from its weakened, tortured body was, as yet, beyond him. He would need to suffer the anguish of being killed before he could wrench his psyche free and use his knowledge to invade another. So Seth was spared that ultimate horror, at least for now, and if events continued as Reen hoped, Seth might prove more useful as he was. His life force would always be available.

Swelling obscenely with stolen vigor and exulting in the flood of terror pervading the atmosphere around him, Reen beckoned to the final swordsman. The poor wretch staggered into the room. His eyes nearly started from his head and his clothing was drenched in sweat. His lips trembled with the strength of his fear as he garbled faint pleas for mercy. Reen, eager to complete the rite, had no use for mercy. Drinking in his victim's terror, he gestured and the man began to strip.

Clothing rank with the results of mortal fear fell in a sodden heap to the floor. The man stood naked and defenseless before the Baron's malice, his red hair dark with sweat and his normally ruddy face sallow with fright. Held immobile by the Baron's will, muscles shivering violently, he watched the slow rise of the cane, the tendons standing out like hawsers in his straining throat.

Reen smiled his cat-like grin, reveling in the miasma of horror. It enveloped him, soaking pleasurably into his peeling, livid skin, seeping inward to saturate the lining of heart and lungs with the leaping energy of fear. This one was strong indeed, the instinct for life still vital despite the dreadful sights the bloodshot eyes had seen. Reen could feel the frantic pump of blood surging through the veins and tasted the salt of sweat oozing from every pore. He gestured the man to his knees.

✛ ✛ ✛ ✛ ✛

Unable to refuse, Othal sank to the floor, straining frantically against the hold on his mind. He had watched his fellows murdered, and now their twisted, terrified faces loomed madly behind his eyes. He knew he stood no chance against this evil, and that his resistance only fed the creature, but he could not stop himself fighting his fate as the dreadful cane drew closer. The tip began to glow red and Othal felt the heat of its power. Silver-gray wood seemed to writhe in anticipation as it merged with the flesh of the claw that held it. Othal saw the way the fibrous nails flowed into the cane's substance, how the bones of the hand became gnarled, like knots of wood. The skin of the Baron's hand and arm, leprous and rotting at best, took on the sheen of the strange gray wood until neither could be told from the other. The cane was an extension of the scarecrow himself as the tip came to rest over its victim's pounding heart.

Othal howled in agony as the wood sank deep into his chest. Flesh parted like sluggish water, blood boiled and hissed into vapor. His eyes were blinded by the red mist as his lifeblood sprayed into the air. He was transfixed by a spike of maliciousness as it wormed its way to his heart. Terror burst from his soul in a violent leap and shot screaming into the room, only to be absorbed with gleeful ease by the parasite's sucking maw. He felt his soul invaded and knew he was lost.

✣ ✣ ✣ ✣ ✣

Reen withdrew the bloodstained cane from the remnants of the corpse and watched impassively as the silvery wood absorbed the fluids. The intense red glow of his eyes faded to a satiated glimmer and the flesh still covering his tortured bones creaked and swelled with life. His hand returned to normal, giving up the semblance of wood, and the scarecrow straightened as he turned dismissively from the remains.

"Clean this lot up."

He passed the silent manservant and Seth bent to the ruined body, catching it by desiccated wrists. The sounds of dragging followed the scarecrow down the hall.

✤ ✤ ✤ ✤ ✤

Despite her exhaustion, Sullyan rose before reveille, feeling scratchy-eyed and worn. She intended to spend the morning with the General, discussing her findings and her next move. All she had was a moment of clarity that had come to her in the night, that and an overwhelming conviction that in order for her to succeed the treacherous Reen must first die. Her avowal to the Hierarch had been a spontaneous act, and there was no doubt that killing Reen was the strongest wish of her heart. Yet the desperate plight of her friends' and life mate's souls had clouded her capacity to think.

The image of the Baron slicing his own arm while Robin suffered the wound had played in her mind and convinced her the scarecrow should not be killed. During the night, however, realization had come to her—the resolution of a puzzle that had nagged at her since that terrible encounter in Lerric's throne room. The image of Reen's sneering face, his cracked and bleeding lips, had played before her mind, contrasting sharply with Robin's visage. No cracks had marred *his* lips; no blood had stained his face. Therefore, the wounding of Robin's arm had been a sham, a clever charade to make her believe Reen must not be killed. Had he not even used that same word? And it had worked. Clearly, the man could influence Robin's body. He had absorbed her life mate's essence and could work his will on his victim's flesh. Yet they were not inextricably linked, otherwise Robin's body would have mirrored every mark on Reen's, even down to those suppurating lips. Providing Robin was kept within the healer suite's protective spellsilver, and providing she could keep the scarecrow distracted while they fought, she should be able to disregard the Baron's charade.

She turned it over and again in her mind, searching for flaws in her reasoning. She was too close to the problem to objectively seek them out, and knew she needed help. Blaine would help her, but before she was free to consult him, she must visit the healer suite and spend time with her son. Heart heavy with uncertainty and the necessity of shielding her thoughts from Morgan, she dressed and left her rooms, heading for the College.

Rienne was up and dressed, supervising the children's breakfast. Morgan squealed when his mother appeared and ran to her arms, tears in his eyes. She hugged him to her, sending him waves of soothing thoughts and letting him feel her love. When Elisse crept forward to join in the hug, Sullyan swept her up too, valiantly striving to hold back her fears. She glanced at Rienne over their heads.

"Where is Eadan?"

"With Elias and Seline," Rienne responded tonelessly. "The King persuaded his daughter to leave her mother for a while to eat with him and her brother. He's desperately trying to heal the breach between them, but the girl's wearing the mark of his slap like a martyr's robe. I think Elias hoped Eadan's presence might make her remember they're a family. I doubt the girl will forgive him. She's very full of bitterness for one so young."

"Sofira's spite saw to that." Sullyan released the two children. Morgan stayed close by her side. "Seeing her mother in such straits has only fueled Seline's hatred." She smiled absently down at Taric who sat gurgling among toys on the floor, and leaned down to run her hand through his soft, dark hair. The baby made a grab for her fingers but missed, tumbling onto his side. He wailed in indignation and she scooped him into her arms, tickling him under the chin and making him chortle. "How are they today?"

Rienne knew she didn't mean Elias or the children. "There's no significant change in either Robin or Jinny, and Sofira still moans to herself, although she spends more time asleep now." The healer's voice was devoid of inflexion and Sullyan knew she was protecting herself by drawing her professional calm over her emotions. "But Taran seems to be fading. His condition worries me."

That was a gross understatement, thought Sullyan, catching the gleam of tears in Rienne's gray eyes. The healer had known Taran for six years now, and counted him as close as her life mate. The stealing of his spirit preyed on her heart. Sullyan's fledgling plans would not allay those fears one bit, so she decided not tell the healer what she intended. She would not tell any of them, save the General and the King.

"Would it help if I spoke to him?"

Rienne shrugged. "I don't know what will help him. He's terrified his body will fail while the Baron still holds his spirit. I can't tell if that's why he's weakening, or if it's due to that terrible wound. We're doing all we can to keep his strength and spirits up, but still his condition worsens and I feel so helpless to aid him. I'm concerned about the state of those dreadful lesions, Brynne. Neither Taran's nor Jinny's are showing signs of healing. They're both still weeping and as raw as the day they were inflicted."

Sullyan winced, although Rienne's words were not unexpected. "These wounds are unnatural. Perhaps whatever method Reen used to cause them is preventing them from closing. I doubt they will heal while their spirits are absent."

"So they'll either die for lack of a soul, or from the effects of those wounds." The quiver in Rienne's voice betrayed the flatness of her tone. "Which will overwhelm them first? I have a right to know."

222

Sullyan faced her friend openly, her honesty the only gift she could give. "I cannot tell you that, Rienne. I am as helpless as you. All I know is that while even one of them lives I will not cease striving, no matter how black the future or how futile my efforts!"

Her vehement words and broken voice melted the bitterness in Rienne's loving heart. She turned wordlessly and flung desperate arms about her friend, the children looking on with wide, frightened eyes.

"I'm sorry," murmured Rienne, sniffing as they pulled apart. "It's just so hard seeing them, you know? So hard watching them fade and knowing there's nothing I can do—"

"What you can do is keep them alive. Do all you can to ease them until all hope runs out. Hard enough, I know, but essential. You must hide your own fear, and never let them see you despair. That is a sickness that will destroy their hope sooner than any wound. Even Jinny's and Robin's spirits may hear our hearts and know we still harbor thoughts of success. We must do everything we can to nurture that belief. Rienne, I have to go now. I must talk to the General and discuss my next move. I will be with him all morning and possibly all day. Can I leave you to inform the King? He may wish to join us once he is free."

"So you're not going to see them?" Rienne's tone told Sullyan she was not really surprised. Sullyan's pale face and reluctant demeanor would already have shown Rienne the delicacy of her courage. The sight of their friends' state would be too much for her aching heart to bear. She cancelled the question with a wave of her hand before Sullyan had time to reply. "I'll tell Elias. Go to General Blaine."

Sullyan left after giving Morgan a final hug, thoughts of her dead father running constantly through her mind. The slight hope she had was based mainly on his words, but how much faith could she realistically place in the advice of a shade? Plenty, she told herself sternly, when that shade was the essence of a Senior Master, and one who had breached all the rules to place these seeds in her heart. She knew he loved her with a powerful strength and would never knowingly lead her astray. She would sink her faith and the fate of her life mate and friends in her father's brief message of hope, and trust that the idea she had spawned in the night would save them from the scarecrow's malice, even if it could not save them all from the separation of death.

✣ ✣ ✣ ✣ ✣

It was just past midday when Bull finally completed his morning duties. As he was free until his teaching session in the College later that day, he made his way to the General's office to see what had been decided. Rienne had told him about Sullyan's return and that she was in discussions with Blaine and the King. He had hoped she might call for him, but that hadn't happened, and he could contain his anxiety no longer. He was very much afraid she would do something rash, knowing how distressed she was at the torment of their friends. He felt it himself, of course—everyone did—and it had affected him so much he was even reduced to asking Rienne's permission to increase his dose of herbs to sustain his limping heart until the crisis was resolved. She had stared at him in misery, knowing there was no way she could refuse. He would only go behind her back and do himself gods knew how much damage. Better that she kept control of his usage, even if it did mean allowing him more than she wanted. Rienne had other things to worry over than Bull's ailing heart.

He left his rooms having taken the herbs, feeling the welcome ease of the strain in his chest. Most days it didn't trouble him much unless he overexerted himself. He had learned how to pace his physical exercise so no one could tell he was unfit. Drilling the cadets in their swordplay was one of the ways in which he served, but with Falkerk and Ramsy on hand to do the energetic stuff, showing the cadets the moves, Bull merely watched over their practice, making comments and guiding their arms. He rarely had to swing his own sword these days, except in quick demonstrations, and these simple exercises kept up his strength without putting a strain on his heart. Falkerk was well aware of his state, but chose to keep quiet about it. He knew the big man had never been happy just sitting behind a desk.

Bull approached the door to Blaine's office, greeting Hyram who was stationed outside. The valet often served as both manservant and guard. "If you're going in, sir, I'll go fetch more fellan. I expect they've just about exhausted the supply by now. They've been in there for hours. Tell the General I'll order some food as well."

Bull could hear the muted murmur of voices behind the door. He rapped softly and lifted the latch without waiting for a reply. Hyram would not have left his post if the meeting was private, and Bull was desperate to hear what might have been decided. The men of Sullyan's company were just as concerned. They were all awaiting her orders to return and finish what they had left in Bordenn. He stepped into the room and closed the door.

At his entry, Mathias Blaine looked up from his seat opposite the King, who slouched in a chair on the other side of the room. Elias's long legs were stretched out to the fire, his bandaged arm cradled in his lap. His sandy complexion was pale and his blue eyes lacked their usual luster and piercing gaze.

The General appeared no better, his stern features stony and grim, but he nodded to Bull as if he were expected and waved him to the couch. The big man acknowledged the invitation and crossed the room, passing Sullyan and laying his hand briefly on her arm.

She covered it with hers and glanced up at him from tired eyes, shaking her head at his concern.

He dropped his heavy frame onto the couch. "Hyram's gone to organize fellan and food," he told General Blaine. The General nodded but didn't reply. His eyes had returned to the King. Elias had ignored Bull's arrival beyond a flick of his eyes. His attention was on his colonel and Bull sensed the tension in the room. It seemed he had interrupted a disagreement between Sullyan and her King, and Elias continued the conversation as if they were the only two present.

"I don't like it, Brynne, and I've a mind to forbid it. We all have too much to lose." His tone was impatient and his clouded eyes held a hint of reprimand.

"You have no say in it, Elias," she retorted immediately, her broken voice sounding harsher than she may have intended. Or not, Bull thought, watching the drama unfold.

The King leaned forward in his chair, his dislike of whatever she had proposed overcoming his reluctance to oppose her. "You're still my colonel, Brynne Sullyan. You're still under my command."

"And I am still your only hope against the strongest enemy your rule has ever faced! You and Mathias have both had your chance, and both of you failed. Who else will you send against him—who else can meet his threat?"

The King's face flushed and even the General winced. They all knew the truth of her words, and Bull knew that Blaine felt the consequences keenly. Elias was quicker to anger and his temper was already aroused. Her disrespectful attitude did nothing to calm his concerns. Then Bull saw Elias's expression change as he slyly tried another tack, knowing her temper was the equal of his.

"But if he kills you, who will take over as General-in-Command of my forces when Mathias retires?"

She stiffened immediately. "What?" Her eyes flashed with anger as she glanced from the King's face to Blaine's. "When was this decided? You never consulted me!"

The General looked uncomfortable and shot his unrepentant monarch a pained look. "It's only been discussed, Brynne. We weren't going to mention it yet."

She narrowed her eyes at both men, infuriated by this extra complication and the totally inappropriate timing of Elias's revelation. She stared archly at her monarch. "And what about Jerrim? Have you discussed this matter with him, or were you just going to cast him aside?"

Elias refused to rise to her challenge. "Vassa doesn't want command. I've known that for a long time."

She sat glaring in silence. She had far more important things to think about than what might happen in ten years' time. Finally, she spoke. "This makes no difference to my decision, Elias. If I do not deal with the Baron, you will have no forces to lead. You will have no kingdom, my Lord High King, and probably no realm. At any rate, all your Artesans will be dead."

Elias threw up his hands, his final argument lost. Bull didn't know why he had thought he could win. He ought to know better by now. "At least get some rest before you go." The King's exasperated tone caused Sullyan's eyes to narrow. "You were up all night reading those texts. You can't have had more than three hours sleep. You can't seriously consider facing him until you've had adequate rest."

Bull turned on Sullyan before she could respond to Elias. "You're never going *today*?" He read the confirmation in her eyes and hissed a breath. "But you can't have informed Dexter and the lads yet! They'll need time to re-allocate the guards, time to—"

"They are not coming with me."

Her bald statement brought him up short. "What? Whyever not?"

She shook her head, irritation making her sharp. "Because they can do nothing to help me. The Baron has other defenses

CAS PEACE

against which swords are useless. This will be a battle of metaforce and cunning, not physical weapons."

He took a deep breath. "Then you'll need someone to stand for you. I suppose it had better be me."

He watched her emotions rise at his casual offer of his life. He would give it, too, she knew that. He would gladly lay it down for her. It was why he existed.

There was a moment of silence before she answered. "No, Bull." She held up a hand to forestall his next words, knowing full well what they would be. "I will not risk your life against the Baron, my friend. I know how it would please him to hold another of my loved ones against me. I will give him no more than I have to, and I will face him alone. I will face him and defeat him, or die in the attempt."

Chapter Twenty

Sullyan retired to her rooms to rest while she could and muster her reserves. She had forbidden the three men to mention her plans, knowing how they would be received. The dismay of her friends she could cope with if she must—the betrayal in the eyes of her men, she could not. She knew they would demand to accompany her at any cost, but she could take no chances that the Baron might capture them and use them against her to compel her surrender. Defeating him would be tricky enough, but her intention was to force him to yield her the souls he had taken control of if she could. How this would be accomplished, she had no firm idea as yet, but it would be impossible should the scarecrow get his hands on more hostages. She was under no illusions about what he might do to her men if he got them into his power.

She slept as much as she could, going through what she knew in her mind. She took time to contact Pharikian to find out how Lirina was and to discuss what she and Gaslek had found in Kethro's archives. The news on the Princess was good; both she and her maid were improving and Deshan reported they should make a full recovery. Aeyron was still angry and fearful, but hid his feelings well. On the subject of Tamilane's journal and the idea she had birthed in the night, the Hierarch's thoughts coincided with hers, but their conclusions remained to be tested. That testing could only happen once the Baron was dead, and may not be necessary at all if she could force him to yield her the souls. First, however, she had to overpower him, and to do that she must get past his cane.

The cane had worried her since hearing Taran's story of how it had been used on him and Jinella. The Adept's terrible experience and his vivid description of its power had turned her blood cold. She could only speculate on what manner of object it was, and how it had acquired its lethal effects. The only thing even remotely similar in her experience was Rykan's spellsilver Staff, but that had been metal and ceramic and had required a powerful Artesan for its manufacture. Sullyan knew from Patrio Ruvar's accounts of Reen's incarceration on the island that the cane had been with him for some time—certainly before he killed his young catamite, and long before his terrible transformation. She could only conclude that the cane had somehow become altered during his ordeal, but what its full potential might be and how it could be dealt with, she had no firm idea. Her only hope would be to part him from it, but she was not even sure she could. Such alien things had a way of cleaving to their masters, and this one obviously defied natural laws.

So much of her plan was conjecture. Much depended on her conviction that Reen had no real knowledge of the powers he had usurped, but the cane was one area where he was more experienced. She had no choice but to face him with only her love and resources to aid her. With her adopted father's loving thoughts and admonitions resounding in her mind, she slept until dusk, when she finally rose from her bed and left the comfort of her rooms, nurturing murder in her heart.

She took no leave of the General or the King, having said all that was needful earlier. Once she had made up her mind to confront the Baron alone, a swift and silent departure was her only option. The last thing she wanted was a scene before she left. She also forsook her father's sword, leaving the weapon hanging in its straps, turning her eyes resolutely from it as she closed the door on her chambers. She could not afford to kill the Baron too soon, and the lure of its lethal edge might just be too much when she had her enemy in sight.

Trying to stay focused on the task ahead, and pushing a strong sense of guilt right to the back of her mind, she made her way to the ground floor of the Manor as stealthily as she could.

Fortune, however, was not on her side.

"Are you heading for the College, Colonel? Are you going to speak to the company? Have you decided when we're going back to Bordenn?"

Her heart sank as she recognized the eager, youthful voice behind her, and she turned as Tad increased his pace in order to catch her up. The avid light of revenge sparked in his gray eyes and she cursed under her breath. Of all those she most wished not to see, Tad came high on her list. Yet he had seen her and she was trapped. She would have to explain now.

She faced him, wondering what she could say. She was spared the effort of finding the words, though, for he guessed her intent, reading her expression and divining her purpose with a flash of intuition that did his burgeoning powers credit.

"You're not heading for the College, are you, Colonel? You're going to face the Baron. You're going back to Bordenn alone!"

Unwilling and unable to give him a lie, she answered him squarely. "I am, Tad, yes."

He stared in disbelief. "But you can't! You can't go back there alone. Gods, you're not even armed! Colonel, let me alert the captains—we've been waiting for this all day. We can be ready to ride as soon as you wish. We all want to repay him for the evil he's done to the Major and the others. You don't have to walk in there unprotected, and you can't deny us our chance of revenge."

She shook her head as firmly as she could, holding his eyes, seeing the alarm and anger mirrored within them. She really didn't blame him for his uncomprehending fear. Every one of them had been affected by what they had witnessed in Lerric's palace. Yet she had no time to explain so she fell back on his training to gain his compliance.

"Swordsman Graylin, I am going to give you an order, and I expect it to be obeyed. Do you understand?"

Tad came to attention at the sharp tone of her voice and she blessed the tight discipline instilled in her men. They knew when to relax with her and when they must obey.

"This is not something any of you can help me with. You are not to alert the company, nor tell them where I have gone. You are to continue with your duties as if you had not seen me here. I need you here to guard the Baron's captives. I will return as soon as I can, and it is then that I will need your help. But until I do, you are ordered to remain. Is that clear, Swordsman?"

Tad swallowed, his face pale, doubtless thinking of what Dexter would say when he found out. Not even Dexter would dare argue over such a clear-cut order, but to see her go off alone and unarmed went against all their strictures and training. Unable to refuse her directly, Tad nevertheless tried his best. Dexter would expect it of him, and so would Robin, had the Major been in any position to say so. There was a slight tremor in his voice as he spoke.

"Does the General know of your plans, Colonel? Do you need me to inform the King?"

Sullyan's resolve nearly gave out then and she smiled at the anxious look on his face, proud beyond measure of his courage and care. She could not be angry with him while his feelings were so plain. He had already lost Robin, his greatest hero, whom he had worshipped for more than five years. The thought that he might lose his other hero was a pain he found impossible to bear. She turned away from the struggle in his eyes, wishing she had left ten minutes earlier. It would have saved them both much discomfort.

"The King and the General already know, Tad, and if it makes you feel any better, they did not approve either. I thank you for your loyalty and concern. The Major would be as proud of you as I am. But my orders still stand and you must continue with your duties. It is time you returned to the College."

The young man turned away, his shoulders slumped in defeat, but then she saw him straighten and her heart raced with dread. He spun on his heel and faced her again, a desperate look in his eye. "I just can't let you do it, Colonel. I can't let you go alone! What would the Major say if he was here? He wouldn't be proud, he'd flay me live for not going with you! At least take me to stand for you, if you think I'd be no use guarding your back."

"Oh, Tad. Do you think I *want* to do this? Do you think I want to go there alone? And you know what I think of your excellent swordsmanship. It is not for lack of skill that I must refuse you. I cannot fully explain why I have decided to go alone, so you will just have to accept it and trust me. Now obey my orders and return to the College. Take care of your charges; I entrust them to you. And believe me, I am not giving you the easy option."

Tad made no further protest as she turned and walked away. She felt his gaze boring into her back as she went out into the freezing gloom. She had to dismiss his disappointment and resolutely put him from her mind. He may have a worse time to come if this mission turned out as she thought. Watching warily for others who might waylay her, she slipped unnoticed through the Manor grounds, waiting until she was well away from the buildings before she opened the Veils. Still, Tad's accusing stare refused to be banished. It filled her mind and saddened her heart as she walked through the shimmer of Earth power and left the Manor behind.

It was full dark when she neared Lerric's palace, having crossed the Veils through Andaryon. She slipped cautiously down the deserted snow-covered road toward the unlit building, remembering the last time she had come this way. The road was as empty now as it was then and there was no sign of recent footprints. She released a sigh of relief that the inhabitants of Daret seemed to be avoiding the place. She turned her gaze toward the palace, seeing the looming towers outlined sharply against the indigo sky. She shivered—nothing to do with the cold—feeling an unfamiliar void at her back and reflecting wryly that she felt more naked and vulnerable without her father's sword than she would have without clothes.

Loosening the dagger at her belt—the only edged weapon she had brought—and casting aside these unsettling doubts, she made her way toward the gates, which stood as wide open as when she had ridden through them three days ago with her company at her back. Squaring her shoulders and sharpening her senses, she ghosted into the courtyard.

It was devoid of life and silent as the grave. The snow in the yard still bore traces of their passage, even though the blizzard had dumped more on the ground. She was sure no one else had been through this place since then and was glad Dexter had opened the stalls to free the palace's horses.

Standing by the wall at the foot of the icy stairs, she gazed up at the eastern tower. As expected, no lights showed behind the boarded windows and she heard no sound but the sighing of the wind. Did he know she was here, her black-hearted foe? Could he sense her bloodlust and eagerness to kill? Reaching deep within her psyche, she surrounded herself with metaforce, drawing on her mighty skills to shield and protect. The amber power flooded out at her merest touch, holding itself ready for attack or defense, her trained and honed reflexes sensitive to the smallest threat. Hooding herself with her power, she mounted the tower steps.

The tower's interior was as cold and dark as the night outside, only the lack of fresh air betraying the presence of walls. She waited for her eyes to adjust to the blackness, but she was already using her other senses to search the stygian dark. She felt no signs of life nearby and no hints of ambush or trap. Unwilling to push farther and alert her enemy too soon, she pulled her powers back and advanced slowly down the echoing hallway, questing for his aura in the fastness of his lair. Her reason told her where she might find him, but she was unwilling to rely on that. He was wily and he was waiting for her and she could not afford complacency. She was halfway down the hallway when she heard the agonized scream.

✣ ✣ ✣ ✣ ✣

Rienne closed the door on Sofira's chamber, leaving the Princess and her daughter within. Seline had accepted the supper tray with her usual silent nod. Her demeanor with Rienne marginally less sullen than with her father or the guards, yet she could not be described as friendly and Rienne left her alone as often as not. She was anxious enough for her charges' well-being without dealing with the young girl's spite.

She left Sofira's day-to-day care in Seline's hands, grateful for her help. It gave the young girl something useful to do and also freed Rienne of the menial task. Sofira wasn't noticeably soothed by her daughter's presence, but neither was she disturbed by it, and so Rienne left well alone. Still, Seline's constant air of sullen disgruntlement dragged on the healer's nerves.

She looked in on Tad and Robin, seeing the bruises of exhaustion under the younger man's eyes. She was becoming worried over Tad's low spirits, and she thought he seemed even more depressed tonight since returning from his brief break. He glanced up at her and gave her the ghost of a smile before returning to his task of feeding Robin. Rienne frowned as she noticed the tremble of his hand.

She came farther into the room. "Tad, are you all right?" When Tad ducked his head, she was sure she saw the glitter of tears. Her own eyes stung as she sensed his grief and she put her hand on his shoulder. He turned to her and she hugged him. But he didn't give way to the tears he held in, merely took comfort from her warmth, and she soon heard him sigh as he pushed himself away, mastering his weakness with an effort.

"I'm all right, Healer Arlen. I expect we all feel the same."

She had no words to encourage him, for he was correct. The same bruised weariness could be found on everyone's face. Not one of them was unaffected by the plight of Reen's victims. Still, she ached to offer him something and she searched her heart for hope, remembering Sullyan's determination when she left earlier that day. She was about to mention it to him when she heard the urgent shout.

Tad's head shot up as hers did and he started to his feet. "No, Tad." She spoke tersely, pushing at his shoulder. "You have to stay on guard. Leave me to find out what's wrong. There are others I can call on if I need help. You must stay at your post."

Tad subsided and Rienne ran for Taran and Jinny's room, from where the shout had come. Ralf, Taran's guard, was in the corridor, waving at her to hurry, and she wasted no time joining him, her face pale with fright.

"What is it, Ralf, what's happened?"

The swordsman urged her into the room and she entered, seeing immediately why he had called out. Jinella, who had shown no sign of movement or consciousness since her rescue, writhed in apparent pain on her bed. Taran kneeled by her side, trying vainly to soothe her. Yet the Adept was little better himself, being weak and ground down by his fear, and Jinny was too much for him as she thrashed in some hell-induced agony.

"Ralf, get help, we need to restrain her." Rienne heard the man calling for back up as she reached for the herbs in her bag. "Stand away, Taran, there's nothing you can do to help her. Let me deal with this."

Taran did as she bade him, his haunted eyes dark, and Ralf came to stand by his side. It wasn't for comfort, they both knew, but in case Taran should be taken over and used to harm Rienne. Sullyan's conviction that the Baron could not reach them here had not relaxed her men's vigilance. Now that prudence was paying off, for something was certainly torturing Jinny. As two others of Sullyan's company ran into the room, Rienne was already preparing her drugs.

She got the men to hold Jinny's arms to prevent her from hurting herself. Her struggles were weakened by her emaciated state, but she could still do damage if unrestrained. Rienne used the respite to administer the drugs, hoping the soporific might render her quiescent, but they would take a few minutes to work. She glanced up as someone else came to the door and met Bull's alarmed gaze. The big man had come to see his friends, as he always did at the end of the day. Catching his eye, Rienne snapped urgently, "Get Brynne, Bull. She should know about this."

His frowning evasion startled her and she straightened, realizing something was wrong and knowing instinctively what it was. A curse hovered at her lips. "She's not here, is she? Where the Void has she gone now, or do I need to ask?"

The big man could not meet her eyes and the curse slipped free, no one noticing the expletive in the tension of the room.

"Don't tell me she's gone to confront him! Dammit, Bull, why couldn't she have said? Did she think it wouldn't affect us? Did she think they'd be safe in here? You know what will happen if she kills him, don't you? This will be only the beginning. They'll all suffer and die in horrible pain. I can't *believe* she didn't tell me! And you're no better, if you knew of this. When I think of what I've done for you, how I've deceived her and gone behind her back …! And for *what*, Bull? For you to deceive me, too? Well, thank you for your concern! Thank you for your trust!"

Rienne fell into furious silence and Bull came toward her. "Oh, Rienne, dear heart!" She batted angrily at the arms he held out to her, not wanting his comfort when she felt so abused. He ignored her feeble protest and enfolded her anyway, forcing her face up to his. "I hear what you're saying and I understand your feelings, but I was sworn to say nothing, as others were. She had her reasons, as you ought to know, although I admit, I'm surprised she didn't warn you. But are you certain this is the Baron's doing? Perhaps Jinny's just coming out of her coma?"

Scarcely mollified by his words, Rienne freed herself. He had reminded her of her duties and she turned back to the woman on the bed. Jinny was still moaning in pain, although her struggles had eased. Her face was white and bloodless. Taran, however, showed no sign of being affected by whatever afflicted Jinny.

Rienne spoke with heavy conviction. "No, Bull, this is no recovery. She's still deeply unconscious. It's her spirit that's being tormented, and we all know who's behind that."

She glanced meaningfully at Ralf, who understood. He guided Taran back to his bed, producing padded wrist shackles with which he rendered Taran unable to attack. The Adept suffered the binding, his sweating face frightened and pale, his hazel eyes fixed on Jinny's tormented figure. Rienne's soporific herbs had eased her limbs, but it was clear her mind was under attack.

Rienne turned to Bull. "Seeing as Brynne isn't here, you'd better alert Cal and Dexter. I think they ought to secure the others in case they are attacked too. Someone will have to fetch Elias.

Seline can't stay where she is. And the General should also be told, although I presume he knows Brynne has gone?"

Ignoring the ice in her tone, Bull left to carry out her orders.

Chapter Twenty-One

Sullyan froze as she heard the scream, her head swinging toward the sound. She thought it came from the upper floor, but couldn't be certain due to the echoing nature of the empty stone palace. It was a woman's scream, but whether it was real or designed to distract her was impossible to say. She decided to ignore it and resumed her careful advance.

The cry came again. It shivered through her bones, for this time she recognized the voice. Jinny was calling her name in a pleading wail and Sullyan gritted her teeth. She could not afford to be diverted, no matter how pitifully Jinny screamed. She knew the girl's body was beyond the scarecrow's reach, yet Jinny's mind was his captive and could still feel pain, so Sullyan had no doubt the screams that tore through her were real. She yearned for her sword, burned to strike him through the heart. She had come unarmed but for a knife for this very reason, fearful that he might drive her to take his rotting life before she had forced him to yield his captives, thus damning her friends forever.

A strange thought surfaced with a frisson down her spine. Might this be what he wanted—his own premature death by her hand? Was that why he had taken those closest to her heart? Not only for his malicious revenge, but in order to goad her into killing him? Was there some way his twisted spirit could gain if she were to reave him of his life? Was it not simply her surrender he craved so deeply, but her murderous anger as well? It would certainly explain some puzzling events, not least his lack of self-defense when Elias launched his attack, and she mused on the possibility as she edged her way through the dark.

She reached the open hallway where she had split her forces. The huge space was cold and silent, Jinny's sobbing wails having faded, and she stood with her back to the upper stairway, straining her ears for the slightest sound. There was nothing to be heard and she was about to continue on when another scream sounded from above—not Jinny's voice this time, but one she recognized nonetheless. Sofira shrieked in anguish in a chamber over Sullyan's head, and despite her intuition that this was a trap, she cautiously followed the lure her enemy had laid out. She could not afford to ignore it, as doubtless he knew well, so she climbed the stairs and emerged silently onto the upper floor.

She sent her senses out, finding nothing to alert her defenses. There were now two different sounds, coming from two separate sources. One was a harsh, masculine sobbing, a sound of deepest despair, and the other was Sofira's voice, not shrieking now, but murmuring with pleasure, which was almost worse. It came from the suite of rooms nearest where Sullyan stood.

Ignoring for the moment Sofira's low, seductive tones, Sullyan moved to the farther door, the one decorated with Lerric's hunting hound motif. Pushing the door lightly with her hand, she leaned against the frame, regarding the figure seated within illuminated faintly by flickering candles. His head was bowed over his hands upon the desk, his body shaken by his sobs. He did not react to her presence until she uttered his name.

"Lerric."

She spoke softly, but it jolted him nonetheless. The quill fell from his palsied hands, ink splashing on the desk. His aging eyes stared into hers, filled with self-blame. The parchment he had been working on fluttered to the ground and he got jerkily to his feet, holding out his arms in supplication.

"I didn't want him here!" The client king's whiny voice begged for understanding. "She pleaded with me, played on my love, and I never was able to rule her. I tried to warn her, tried to stop her, but she just wouldn't listen. And then it was too late, he became too strong. When I heard Elias was coming, I knew I would have to betray them. I knew it had gone too far. But he already had his claws into her, that filthy, treacherous creature, and she … she was always the stronger and she made me follow her lead. I tried to warn Elias, I really did try! But I knew what that vulture would do to me—what he would do to *her*—and I just couldn't tell him. So I wrote it down, my weakness, my cowardice, so he would know I didn't willingly go against him …"

Lerric's echoing voice faltered and he glanced over his shoulder. There was nothing behind him, not even a shadow, but he crossed his arms over his head as if to ward off a blow and sank to his knees, gibbering in panic. There was the sudden stench of burning flesh and Lerric emitted a dreadful shriek of pain that cut right through Sullyan's mind. She started forward involuntarily, but Lerric crashed to the floor, his body spraying fluid as his ravaged chest exploded.

Sullyan jumped back, cursing as the putrid liquid splashed at her feet. Her heart thumped, ready for action, but the vista before her had vanished; there was nothing in the room to threaten her, not even the ghosts of the candles remained. She turned to face the hallway, but nothing lurked there either. Blinking, she looked back into Lerric's suite. All was silent. Her heart heavy for the aging king's dreadful fate, and for his useless remorse, she closed the door on the memory and moved to the second suite.

The seductive voice still murmured within, now echoed by another. Reluctant to see what he intended to show her, yet knowing she must learn all she could, Sullyan pushed gently at the door. As she had expected, it swung open, revealing a shadowy chamber. A woman stood by the bed, her head thrown back in sensual pleasure. Sofira whispered soft words of love as the scarecrow caressed her neck, but Sullyan saw the red gleam of his eyes in the murk. Shivers ran down her spine. Before she could move, the scarecrow had his queen on the bed and Sofira's anguished cries spiraled once again as he used her body for his evil revenge. Her muscles locked into a horrified trance, Sullyan was forced to watch as her nemesis drank Sofira's terror and took his pleasure. Raping the shocked woman's mind as surely as her body, he left her gibbering in senseless fright.

Sullyan's hand clenched the hilt of her knife as both figures faded into the gloom, the echoes of the Baron's final exultant cry lingering like a rotting smell. Trying not to retch with the horror of his acts, Sullyan slammed the chamber door on the terrible vision. She was trembling as she leaned her back to the wall.

Forcing her heart rate to slow, she gritted her teeth and pushed away from the cold stone. She methodically searched the upper floor, finding no traces of life and seeing no more visions. Satisfied that the rooms were deserted, she left them to their ghosts and descended the stairs to the silent floor below. Standing motionless in the utter dark, she awaited her enemy's next move.

Jinny subsided after those initial frightening throes, but whether from the effects of the drug or from lack of outside stimulus, Rienne did not know. She left the woman in Ralf's capable care, the swordsman grimly securing her wrists, and went to check on the other captives. She felt guiltily grateful to escape Taran's rank aura of fear, although she carried her own terror with her. She was angry, too, and deeply hurt that Sullyan hadn't seen fit to warn her of her departure. Why else was she here if Sullyan couldn't trust her? She muttered curses under her breath as she went from room to room.

Tad's white face begged her for reassurance when she visited Robin's bed, but she left the young swordsman in silence, having none to give. Dexter had appeared to lend Cal his support, although he was obviously angry too at their exclusion from Sullyan's plans. His capable presence gave Rienne some courage, although she didn't think swords would prevail in this instance. Still, he was there to lend support when Sofira's tortured screams shrilled through the building, turning their blood to ice.

Rienne sprinted for the Princess's room, Dexter at her heels, both of them cursing. Sofira had been secured as all the victims were, yet she still thrashed and writhed uncontrollably. Aldo, her guard, was reluctant to lay hands on her. Rienne sent Dexter running for the King.

"Get someone else to sit with Seline," she barked, "and tell them to make damned sure she stays in her room. We can't have her seeing this."

Dexter left with no demur and Rienne blessed his instant understanding. She reached to her bag for more of the soporific and dispensed it into a glass. When Elias appeared at the door with Dexter behind him, she tersely instructed him to hold Sofira's head. The High King did as he was told. Rienne poured the liquid down Sofira's rigid throat, praying the drugs wouldn't enter her lungs. The woman's reflexes saved her, however, although she spluttered and spat before the drugs went down. Rienne told Elias to hold her tightly and try his best to calm her until the soporific took effect.

While she waited for the drugs to work, Rienne sent Dexter to the infirmary for Hanan and any other healers she could spare. She had a nasty feeling they would all be needed soon. Then she mixed more of the sedative, intending to administer it to all the captives to minimize the danger to themselves and others. She didn't leave the King until the Chief Healer arrived, when she took Hanan aside to fill her in on the latest developments. Both healers turned in anxious surprise when the Princess's struggles suddenly ceased, and Elias stared up at them in dread.

"Oh, Rienne, she's not dead! Please don't tell me she's dead."

One part of Rienne's brain registered amazement that Elias still cared. She checked the woman's pulse, which was weak but steady, and placed her hand on Elias's arm, trying to hide her own fearful tremor.

"No, she's not dead, but she is very weak. Her ordeals have drained her and she's now succumbed to the drugs. Hopefully, they'll give her some respite from the terror in her mind. Maybe if she stays this way she can recover some strength."

Elias didn't believe her, that was evident from his eyes, but he stayed with his former wife while Rienne and Hanan conferred. The Chief Healer agreed to remain with the King, and Rienne left to check on the others. Dexter shadowed her constantly, for which she was grateful. Bull reappeared as she made her way back to Robin, telling her that Blaine was safeguarding Seline and the other children in Seline's room and had asked to be kept informed.

Rienne's fright frayed her temper. "*He* wants to be kept informed? He should be so bloody lucky! When *I* find out what's going on, *he'll* know, and not before!"

Bull wisely held his peace.

✣ ✣ ✣ ✣ ✣

Sullyan stood alert in the lightless hallway, straining for the slightest sound. Her instincts still tugged her in one specific direction, but she doubted she would be permitted to follow them until Reen was done with his games. Trying to harden her heart and strengthen it against his assaults, she waited motionless in the dark, reluctant to move until she knew what he had planned.

Behind her, some distance from where she stood, the curtain

covering the entrance to the lower stairwell moved in some unfelt breeze. She sensed it rather than saw it in the murk of the neglected palace. Yet nothing emerged to disturb her, no presence impinged on her mind, and she dismissed the movement as natural, caused by some gelid draft from the lower floor. She turned her senses from it, irritated by the distraction, knowing she could afford no lapses. He was probably waiting for her to make such a slip and she didn't want to give him that satisfaction.

She was alerted by a low keening that only faintly reached her ears. It affected her heart like a hammer blow, sending adrenaline pounding through her veins. Her stomach lurched in dread as she recognized Robin's voice, and she could not keep herself from turning toward the dark stair from whence it had come. The groan sounded again, weak, agonized, urgent. She felt her face drain of blood as she crept forward in the darkness until she reached the curtain that had stirred in the phantom breeze. Tentatively, she stretched out her hand and snatched back the folds of cloth. No assailant jumped out to attack her. No light shimmered on the stairway, no firelight flickered below. As she set her feet to the midnight-dark stairs, she summoned a glow to the nearest torch and it brightened. Taking it down from the sconce, she held it before her like a shield, watching the play of shadows as they retreated before her. Like fearful foes they slunk from her path, drawing her ever on, and she followed their beckoning movements, trembling with anger and fear.

The groan sounded again when she left the last step, coming from farther along the hall. There was a miasma down here, a charnel reek her senses recognized, but it was old and fading and she paid it no heed. She knew some of Lerric's palace guard had been killed here when her men searched the rooms on this floor. It was likely their bodies still lay here, left to rot in the dark. The moans drew her on, past the doors on either side, her instincts honed and ready for the ambush she knew was being set. Robin wasn't here. Whoever was using his voice was hoping to put her off guard. He had underestimated her, if that's what the Baron thought, and her powers were just waiting to be used in her defense as her hand came to rest on the latch of the final door.

She jumped back reflexively at the shock of pure terror that merely touching the door sent racing through her. It was as if many voices had screamed their agony all at once, released by her powerful touch, and a curse escaped her. She took a moment to compose herself, to calm her thundering heart, but she was given no respite as the sounds of a scuffle came surging to her ears. Expecting attack from some of Reen's men, she gathered her powers in an offensive shield and shoved hard at the door.

It crashed open on an appalling sight. A filthy bed sat in the center of the floor with her life mate chained naked upon it, wrenching with all of his mighty strength at the iron that held him fast. Over his writhing hips crouched the grinning scarecrow, red eyes blazing into hers as he mounted the struggling man. She heard Robin's agonized scream as his flesh suffered the Baron's burning sear, and once again she was locked in a vacuum of helpless rage as she witnessed Reen's vicious rape. Bands of steel seemed to clench at her muscles as she screamed and threatened revenge, but still the relentless act went on and she was forced to endure it to the bitter end.

Her enemy's triumphant, climactic howl resounded about her brain as her life mate's soul was torn yet again from its roots, and the demonic, twisted body finally withdrew from the flesh it had consumed. A crowing, gibbering specter of ragged black shot past her in a blast of charnel air, slamming her paralyzed body to the floor, great sobs wracking her as the terrible image burned into her mind. She struggled to all fours, retching, heedless of what dangers might be around her in the suddenly silent dark.

At length she straightened and wiped at her mouth, taking tremulous, shuddering breaths. Small wonder Taran had balked at the task, when asked to tell her of this. With such a fate dangled before his eyes, how the Void had he kept himself sane? She staggered to her feet, hugging herself, shaking and crying. Her left hand had been cut on some broken glass, and she stared blindly at the shards on the floor before sealing the cut with a thought. The filthy bed met her hot stare before the prick of tears blurred her sight. With a great cry of rage, she called Fire, and an inferno of ravening hate bloomed over the site of Robin's death. The acrid smoke rising from the bed caused her sore throat to constrict and she forced herself out of that monstrous cell, slamming the door on her heartache and grief. Yet the terrible image refused to fade and the sound of Robin's death cry beat frantically against her ears. She bolted for the higher floor, fleeing the place of his murder.

Flinging the curtain aside, she burst into the hallway and stopped to gather her breath. She ought to have been ready for that, but Reen's viciousness had taken her by surprise. She had not thought he would be able to master such detailed illusions, even though he had Robin's powers at his command, and Robin's intimate knowledge of the vulnerable parts of her heart. Acknowledging her failure and her enemy's victory, she knew she would have to be prepared for a true Master's skills and harden her soul against the unguessable depths of his spite. He would dredge up every pain his twisted heart had inflicted and parade it before her eyes. She would have to do better than this or she might as well kill herself now.

Drawing slow, shuddering breaths to steady her, she shut away her grief and pain and moved away from the stairway. Her eyes became gems of fiery fury as she went hunting the killer of her heart.

✤ ✤ ✤ ✤ ✤

Rienne struggled to hold back her tears at the desperation in Robin's cries. Tad, unable to stand the tortured sound, had fled the College, unmanned and ashamed. Rienne sent Bull after the lad, fearing what he might do, and the big man went without a word, also worried by the youngster's state. Rienne strove for outward calm while her inner voice cried in the caverns of her mind. How much more damage could the vengeful Baron do them?

She used a cool cloth to soothe Robin's brow, but she doubted he even felt the sweat. Sullyan had told her he was not really alive, animated only by the Baron's will. This latest torment seemed to bear that out as his wasted body struggled in its bonds.

Cal and Dexter stood behind her, watching the terrible scene and trying not to break down in the face of Robin's suffering. Both captains had tears in their eyes, for they loved this wreck of a man just as much as Rienne. His cries and contortions hurt them as deeply as they did the healer. Their helpless rage intensified with every new scream, and Rienne felt her own heart tearing in two.

Just when she thought even she would be forced to leave, unable to bear any more, the straining muscles abruptly relaxed, the writhing body collapsing to the bed as the raw throat ceased to cry out. Dexter exclaimed and moved closer, but Rienne put out a hand. She stared down at Robin with a frown, watching for signs that his heart was giving out. Yet when she checked the limping thread of his pulse, she found it beginning to steady, and she allowed herself to slump to the bed, holding Robin's trembling hand in her own.

Cal's normally dark face was ashen with distress. "Is it over?"

Angry at the question, and angrier with herself for feeling so frustrated, Rienne didn't trust herself to answer. She stared up at the pair of them and helplessly shook her head. She wanted to lash at them in her despair—how was she supposed to know?—yet it wasn't their fault that they should look to her in this terrible situation. In the years she had been working here, they had all come to rely on her skills and practical good sense. She could hardly blame them for needing reassurance now. It was only that she was so *helpless*, and the only one who might have been able to give her the answers she craved was far away and out of reach, fighting the evil that beset their friends and by no means certain of victory. Dashing tears from her eyes, Rienne pushed up from the bed and left the room, speaking curtly as she went.

"Watch over him."

✣ ✣ ✣ ✣ ✣

The Baron did not currently inhabit the lower floor of the palace; of that, Sullyan was certain. Although she could sense his malignant spirit seeping from every stone, it was only the echo of his will, the power he had used for his illusion leaving an imprint in the substrate. Once her emotions were back under control, she cast her own powers out, searching the palace for traces of his aura, some clue to lead her to where he hid. Her instincts still nagged at her, drawing her to one place, and now she determined to follow them, despite what he might throw in her way. These cruel visions were his way of weakening her, his opening moves in this final battle for her fate. Gathering her powers about her in a strong defensive shield, she used the knowledge he had inadvertently given her to protect her from his attacks.

She hoped he would not realize it, although the information was there in Robin's mind, but each new use of his power gave her insights into his technique. His overriding control left imprints in the substrate, clues a skilled Master could read that would contribute to her picture of his psyche. She might not have as clear a view as he would have of hers, but nevertheless she was becoming familiar with the patterns of his psyche. Patterns that would afford her pathways of attack. No matter what he had absorbed, what skills he had purloined, she was still two levels above anything he could achieve, and she wielded the mightier force. The only unknown that still nagged at her mind was the potential contained in his cane. Pondering its possible uses, she advanced cautiously through the lightless halls.

No more sights appeared to assail her, no tortured cries to catch at her heart. Only silence and blackness met her advance, the heavy weight of anticipated conflict gripping her shoulder like the hand of the dying. She moved quietly through the abandoned palace, retracing her steps of three days ago.

Past empty chambers, guest rooms, and halls, she moved determinedly toward her goal. She was certain now where she would find him: at the site of his victory over her, the place where he had revealed his triumphal vengeance and thrown down the terms of her defeat. Trying not to recall those cruel terms, she approached the iron-bound door flanked by its silver poles, and stood staring at the inlaid scene on the surface of the wood, her eyes hot for killing. Her heart blazed within her and she once again forced it into calm, knowing that what she needed was cold and calculating courage, not the reckless heat of vengeance. Her heart rate eased gradually and she drew a deep breath into her lungs. Checking her defenses one final time, she pushed at the door to the anteroom and stepped through it, past Lerric's redundant flags.

The large chamber was just as they had left it, apart from the bodies that had littered the floor. Although the corpses were missing, their odor remained. It pervaded the atmosphere of the anteroom, rank and cloying in her lungs, the necrotic reek of Reen's parasitism rising from the stone beneath her feet. The same stench hung about her friends, where they languished back at the Manor, but this thought was too painful and she deliberately pushed it from her mind. Allowing cold hatred to suffuse her veins, she crossed the anteroom floor, moving toward Lerric's throne room where she expected her foe would be found.

The vast ceremonial chamber was empty, however, devoid of his malicious presence. Frowning in confusion, she stood framed by the huge double doors, staring outward into the echoing chamber toward the ornate throne in the center of the floor. Keeping her senses about her, she cautiously sampled the substrate, seeking a certain aura and wary of its absence. Of course, he had done this to her before, the first time she had come, forcing her to search for him until he was ready to be found. Well, she wasn't going to play that game, not this time. She had listened to his distractions and watched his evil visions; she'd had enough of being led by the nose. She would let him come to her.

Chapter Twenty-Two

Sullyan walked boldly into the center of the throne room, hearing the echoes of her own steps. She found herself wondering why it had been built on such a grand scale when the rest of the palace was modest. Bordenn had never been truly wealthy and its history was nondescript. It had always been a client state, controlled by its larger neighbors. Only since the civil war had it acquired a lord of its own. Perhaps whoever commissioned the building had had aspirations toward the High Throne, but if that was so their plans had failed, leaving only this memory of majesty.

She approached the throne, watching the deeper shadows for movement. She couldn't help but see ghostly echoes of her previous visit, remembering the triumph in the scarecrow's eyes and her own distress when Robin's body was revealed. Visions of what she had witnessed in that chamber far below crept under her hardened defenses and taunted her with unbearable scenes. Her life mate's dreadful torment and the destruction of his valiant spirit tore once more into her heart like a dagger, bringing hot tears to her eyes. Her body began to tremble with outrage. Why would he not face her, this stealer of souls, when he was so confident of her surrender? This continuing game just frayed at her nerves and eroded her steely control.

She moved past the heavy ceremonial chair and paced out the rest of the room, sampling the substrate with her metaforce and finding nothing worthy of note. Her failure to sense him pricked at her, and suddenly she could stand it no longer, certain he was laughing at her efforts. She could almost hear his mocking tones and feel his fetid breath on her neck. Her control snapped and hot anger welled up into her throat.

"Where are you, you evil monster?" she cried into the dark. "Show yourself! Come face me, and let us make an end!"

A low chuckle behind her made her spin to face the throne. A shroud of dense blackness huddled there, impenetrable even to her augmented sight. Twin lamps of ruby malice glittered from within the mass, and a rounded voice crept out into the freezing air.

"You disappoint me, witch-girl. I had thought you more powerful than that."

She took two involuntary paces closer before she stopped herself, hiding her chagrin, her heart thumping loudly. How the Void had he deceived her so when she had been ready for his tricks? How had he appeared so silently behind her when she had searched the room so thoroughly? She sampled the substrate, finding no trace of his passage. Meeting his red eyes with confusion and anger, she read his aura of sly amusement. He was vastly pleased with his subterfuge and she was forced to revise her opinion. She must take nothing for granted. He had powers she didn't fully understand.

Despite the darkness, she could see him well through the medium of her metaforce attuned to his. Something about him was different somehow. Something had changed. As he sat there matching her scrutiny, locked with her stare for stare, she suddenly realized what had pricked at her senses. His twisted, ruined body was no longer emaciated. He appeared almost obscenely fleshed, as if he had stolen someone else's skin.

He continued to stare at her, chuckling, his damaged eyes useless in the dark. She knew he could see her regardless. Light was unnecessary to him, but it might be a weapon to her. She was aware of his sensitivity to it and intended to use it against him if she could. She decided to play him out awhile and see what move he might make. Risky it may be—and against her instincts—but then, he was no ordinary foe.

She forced her trembling to calm. "You cover your movements well." His cruel smile widened. Flattery had always moved him. Her unexpected failure to sense his whereabouts might now work in her favor. If she could convince him of her weakness, she might overcome his twisted strength.

He watched her with gleaming red eyes that never left her face. "I had to master my new skills swiftly. But then, I've had some very good teachers, although they didn't all impart knowledge willingly. I had to 'persuade' them to teach me, and they all gave up their secrets in the end. *I* enjoyed the lessons, even if some of them did not."

Sullyan gasped as a vision swam into her mind: a dark, terror-filled chamber, two men chained to the wall. Roamerlings by their appearance, and one with an Artesan's strength. She saw the scarecrow take him, saw him imbibe the man's powers and suck the carcass dry. Suddenly, overlaid on the Roamerling's face was another face she knew well, and Robin's terrified indigo eyes stared pleadingly into hers.

With a curse, she slammed him out of her mind, strengthening her shield against his cunning trick. Stunned that he had got past her so easily—and for the second time—she backed away from him, feeling her confidence deflate.

"You cannot dismay me so easily, Reen. Your visions have no real power. I know he is dead and that you can do him no more harm."

Reen watched her with amusement, a small smile hovering about his fleshy lips. "Dead?" he hissed, his red eyes boring hatefully into hers. "Oh no, my dear, you are wrong. Your precious life mate is not dead. The part I allowed you to take away, yes, that is dead. But the part I retained, the essence of the man, oh, that part is very much alive. Impotent, maybe"—he leered as if at some pleasing, private joke—"but very much alive. And you are sadly mistaken if you think I can cause him no more harm. Despite the spellsilver that surrounds them, I can harm each one of your captive friends, as I have already demonstrated for your entertainment."

He grinned wider at her sudden start, pleased at catching her out once more.

"Did you think I didn't know? Did you think your simple precautions could stop me from reaching their souls? Then you are not as knowledgeable as your vanity makes you think, for while they reside within me, they are under my control wherever they are."

A terrible image formed before her eyes, an image that wavered and ran. Four bodies writhed in torment on their beds, their faces contorted in pain. Once again, her mind was invaded and the shock of his strength coursed through her. With a superhuman effort and a hoarse cry, she thrust him out of her mind once more and dropped into a crouch. Panting, she turned to stare at him, hopelessness rising within.

His voice crawled sinuously toward her to taunt her with evil glee.

"What's the matter, witch-girl? Is my power so much of a shock? I know you intimately, don't forget. I know all your weakest spots, whereas you, of course, are completely ignorant of mine. Well, I will teach you to know me, as I have taught many others. I will show you some of my power, and we will see who wields the superior force. And in the end, *Artesan*, you will bow in abject surrender at my feet."

Hot tears pricked Sullyan's eyes. "I will never bow to you, traitor!" She barely felt the tears slide down her face, shed for the memory of Robin's death, for she was already preparing her defenses, gathering her forces for the kill.

The scarecrow's taloned hand flowed and blended with the wood of his cane. Its strange gray shimmer gleamed in the red mist that covered her sight. As the tremor of Earth heaved beneath her, as it surged and responded to her controlling touch, a flow of solid blackness erupted from the end of the cane. The vast Thunderball of power she directed toward the throne was easily deflected and sent hurtling back at her. So swiftly was it thrust away that she was totally unprepared, and her own forces caught her squarely, slamming her into the wall.

She had never experienced her own powers turned against her. The nearest she had come was when she encountered her cousin Huw's great forces, so similar to her own. Her shield went down instantly, not designed to protect against itself. She lay gasping for breath, her sight flickering with jagged light, while her enemy made no move save for a low chuckle of amusement. Slowly, painfully, she rose to her knees, drawing in shallow breaths, shocked to the core by his ability to turn her forces so effortlessly aside. He considered himself invulnerable, wrapped in his blanket of black, and she would have to be more cunning with her next assault.

Forcing her heart to a steadier rhythm, she raised her head as he waited for her to admit defeat. She held his red gaze in defiance, refusing to be dismayed. He must have a weakness that she could exploit. She studied the aura around him, trying to penetrate the pool of black. Perhaps it concealed something he didn't want her to see, something she could use. She would try to force it aside, cause him to defend himself again. Maybe she could wear him down, catch him out, if she kept him at work.

Not giving herself time to think, and with no warning to her squatting foe, she formed a shaft of purest elemental Fire and flung it toward the throne. It flared into brightness and stung her eyes, although she was ready for that, and she heard, with the ghost of a satisfied smile, the suggestion of a panicked cry as the flaming spear cut through the dark. Pushing with all her might, she sped it toward its mark, but a mantle of gloom bloomed and enveloped it, swallowing the brightness whole, engulfing it and extinguishing it, sending it back through the substrate from whence it had come.

She gasped with the pain of its passing as it was wrenched out of her control, but she also heard heavy breathing and knew she had stung him, at least. Throwing off the ache in her furious mind and determined to press her attack home, she called Fire once more to her will and shaped it into a mesh, casting the glittering network over the seething puddle of black. The Firefield sputtered and spat as it grew, filling the vast room with leaping amber light. She could hear the scarecrow cursing and she fed her creation extravagantly with her own strength. The darkness contained inside it roiled with rage until suddenly a figure loomed into her sight. She felt her forces weaken, drained by dread as she saw who it was, although she was sure that what she was seeing couldn't possibly be real. Her life mate stood there, tall and alive, staring at her with paralyzed fear, and she watched in dismay as his flesh turned to wax, running in the heat of her Fire. His shrieks spiraled out of the darkness as he lifted his burning arms. His charring hands held a sword of red flame, and he cut through her net with a single powerful stroke. Pieces of the Firefield cartwheeled away, sparking and hissing as they died in the cold. She felt a searing thrust to her heart and cried out as her beloved was consumed by the flame.

The freezing darkness returned once more, unaffected by the display of elemental Fire. Hoarse breathing was the only sound in the room, and it came from two separate sources. Although she could not see her foe, hidden as he was in his shroud of black, she knew he was also feeling the strain of their conflict and that she could not give up now. Robin had a Master's skills and that meant he could master Fire. But he did not have mastery over Air, and that was where she might prevail. Using a little of her diminishing power to shore up her trembling heart, she banished the ache of her body and gathered the strength of her force. Before Reen could recoup, she surged upright and flung her senses through the substrate to fasten on the element of Air. Calling with all her desperation, she whipped up a storm of wind, casting its buffeting powers toward the center of the room. Icy shards were bound up within the ferocious gale, and they shredded the darkness over the throne and swept it upward, away from his reach.

Now she could see him clearly as he stood leaning on the strange cane. His eyes flared in malice as he gathered his force to answer hers, and she saw the gleaming of the wood he held. His hand had fused so completely to the substance of the cane that she could not tell one from the other. A glimmer of understanding slipped into her mind and eroded her courage still further. Yet she had to concentrate on the forces of Air, had to retain her control, for the elemental strength she had unleashed was tearing at the fabric of the palace, shuddering the walls and weakening the stones.

The shrieking of the tornado, contained as it was within the room, was almost too much to bear. Pressure built up against her eardrums until she could have cried with the pain. The flailing, pounding winds threatened to tear her from her feet, despite the shield of metaforce she cast around herself. She could hardly keep her eyes open against the tumult as her hair was whipped and flung about like an aura of tawny fire. She felt a sudden stinging blow against her arm and realized pieces of masonry were tearing loose.

The far wall was beginning to collapse and she directed her windstorm into the breach that was forming, whirling up the stone as it cracked and fell. The smaller pieces became lethal missiles as she flung the cyclone toward the Baron.

The figure in tattered black seemed untroubled by the shrieking tempest. He raised the cane high over his head and swung it in a wide arc. A translucent shield of shimmering gray appeared at the tip of the cane and spiraled down to cover his form, protecting him, making him inviolate against her attack. Small blocks of masonry, flying chips of stone and gritty plaster all shattered harmlessly on the shield and fell to gather in a windswept pile around his feet. The winds of Sullyan's fury were beaten aside and funneled away from where he stood to spend themselves in useless battering on the already perilous structure of the walls.

She couldn't believe it. Her final efforts were futile, her strength fast running out. Sweat beaded her face as she increased the power of her attack, but the scarecrow just stood there grinning as his cloak stirred faintly about his legs. He watched her struggle with the cruel reality of his supremacy and exulted as she lost control. Her fading dregs of strength gave out at last, and the ravening cyclone of Air shot free of her restraint to rocket upward in a violent, destructive surge. The triumphant Baron threw back his head and let loose a peal of mocking laughter as a huge section of ceiling gave way and fell to the floor in a thundering cloud of debris.

The winds died abruptly and the din faded away, leaving the freezing air clogged with settling plaster dust. Sullyan, her strength and courage exhausted, crouched wheezing and coughing in the murk. Desperate for air, she pushed to her feet, intending to flee the room, but the Baron's voice checked her and his power flicked out to grip her mind like a vice.

"Oh no, my dear, you can't leave now. I haven't finished with you yet."

She struggled against his grip, trying to fling off his hold, but she was just too weak. She had expended too much power and she had no resistance left. Unable to deny him, her muscles refusing to answer her will, she found herself drawn inexorably nearer the throne. The shimmer of the cane's shield mocked her with its strength, its scarecrow master scarcely out of breath. The malignant aura of his evil pierced her soul with despair as she felt herself forced to her knees.

He stared down at her, a cruel smile on his lips, bloody spittle trailing over his chin. His hand gripped the cane and flowed within the wood. Her head fell to her breast, unable to bear his gaze, and heavy, frustrated sobs welled into her ravaged throat. Her lungs were full of powder and she could hardly breathe. Defeat and desolation beat together within her heart.

She couldn't believe her powers had failed her, that he had beaten her so easily at the end. She had never really troubled him, despite her vaunted skills. Whatever the source of power contained within the cane, it fed him and sustained him and she could not match its might. It seemed inexhaustible. How could she hope to counter it? The sour bile of defeat made her stomach cramp and heave and, unable to prevent the reaction, she bent low to the gritty floor, retching in misery at the scarecrow's feet.

Above her, she heard his rumble of pleasure to see her brought so low, and she resolved then to give him no more than he was able to take. She might have failed to save her friends, but she could still deny him his prize. He would never have her powers to add to his stolen hoard. Her friends' souls were his to torment; she could do nothing to alter that fact. But she could deprive him of his deepest desire, and was fully prepared to die while he strove to take it.

"I told you you would bow to me." His loathsome voice crawled over her skin like slimy snakes. "I swore I'd see you grovel, as I was forced to do. How does it feel, pagan witch, to know yourself defeated? How does it feel to have to surrender, to beg at my feet for mercy?"

Her rasping voice contrasted harshly with his oily tones. "You may have won this battle and shown yourself the stronger, Reen, but you will never hear me beg at your feet, nor have the pleasure of my surrender."

His black-clad body stiffened, and she slowly raised her eyes. The aspect of his livid face, seen closely and without its concealing dark shroud, caught her attention and she frowned at the changes she could see. Gone was the unnatural fleshiness, the stolen health that had swollen and plumped his skin. His frame was once more sticklike, covered with peeling, leprous hide. The dreadful face was slumped, its features slewed to one side, the lips cracked and torn, and she realized their battle had exhausted all his usurped strength. He was being sustained by the cane alone. It was his lifeline and his source of power. If only she could separate him from it, she might yet have a fighting chance. Yet that was hardly possible while his hand was fused so completely with the wood.

He leaned over her, spraying bloody spittle from broken lips as he spoke. "So, you're still not ready to acknowledge me, not even to save your friends? You astonish me, witch-girl, you really do! I thought your kind placed great store in loyalty, in standing by each other. Instead, it seems that you're willing to abandon your friends just to salvage your contemptible pride."

"My pride has nothing to do with it, you parasite! Do you think I would hesitate to sacrifice myself if I thought for just one moment you would keep your faithless word? I know you have no intention of setting free the souls of my loved ones. You will take what you want from me and then renege on your word. And I will not see my powers used to destroy the Veils, and thereby the world, even though its destruction would also mean the end of your miserable life."

He snorted, a guttural sound. "Oh, spare me your altruistic carping. You've tried that lie before. Don't forget, I have your life mate's knowledge now. You can't fool me with such doom-laden tales."

Sullyan raised her head higher, staring him squarely in the eyes, her husky voice charged with desperation as she willed him to see the truth. "Then look inside his mind, Reen. Make use of the knowledge you stole. For pity's sake, man, *he* can't lie to you when you have control of his thoughts!"

The mad red eyes boring into hers flashed with fury and the strange cane moved fractionally, flicking out toward her face. She recoiled with pain and shock as his power stabbed into her, doubling her over with roiling sickness. His voice raged again, echoing in the darkness.

"You will address me as *my Lord*. Don't forget who is master here!"

"You forsook all rights to that title when you attempted the life of your King! You—" Her retort cut off with a cry as he assailed her with agony again.

"I place no store in empty titles, nor in the life of that misguided fool. I was born into lordship. It is mine by right. I am also the uncontested ruler of this wretched province, through my marriage to its princess. So you will afford me the honor due my nobility or suffer the consequences!"

Hot agony seared through her belly yet again, threatening to swamp her mind. She was loath to access her metaforce lest he be able to leach it from her, so she endured the pain by clasping her arms across her belly and raised her furious eyes to his face.

"Very well, but it is the last thing you will force from me, *my Lord*, for hear me well: I will cast off my own life before I see you take my power."

Her snarling words gave him pause. She could see the flash of uncertainty in his eyes. It pleased her that he had forgotten just what she was capable of. Any Master Artesan could freely give up their life, and she was a Senior Master. It would be a simple process for her. He might have mastery over her where sheer brute force was concerned, but without a means of blocking her metaforce, he was powerless to take her against her will. She was fully prepared to suicide if he attempted to overwhelm her mind. Rykan had shown her the way of it, and she had never forgotten that terrible time. The scarecrow's one and only hold over her—his threat to torture the spirits of her friends—she had thrown back in his face. He had lost all chance of gaining her might by her refusal to play his game. In showing himself untrustworthy he had actually stabbed himself in the back, and she saw his livid face turn purple as he realized the import of her words.

Yet she had underestimated the depth and breadth of his reach. Even as he absorbed her words, she felt the stir of his power. Alarmed, she glanced about, trying to prepare for another attack, but he had no intention of harming her. He had another plan entirely. He turned his mad red eyes on her and smiled a slow, cruel smile.

"So, you don't believe that I mean what I say, witch? You don't trust me to release your friends' souls? And you won't sacrifice yourself to save them, as you always said you would. Well, perhaps you would care to tell them why. Perhaps they should hear for themselves just how shallow your vaunted loyalty runs. Perhaps one of them should be here to see just how faithless you really are!"

A sharp warning stab thrust at Sullyan's mind and she instinctively raised her shield. The uncontrolled opening of the Veils in such close confines was capable of causing considerable pain to anyone nearby. As her vision cleared and her shield took effect, she heard a masculine voice groan behind her. Her heart clenched with fear and her blood turned to ice. She trembled as she turned her head, already knowing what she would see, even if she couldn't believe Reen had the power to do what he had just done.

Lying on the rubble-strewn floor was a man she knew all too well. Weak, wounded, and moaning in pain, he raised hopeless hazel eyes. Her throat tightened painfully as she stretched out her hand.

"Taran! Oh, dear gods, no!"

Chapter Twenty-Three

Rienne glanced up as Bull appeared in the doorway. The big man's mouth was set in a grim line and Rienne's heart skipped a beat, but Bull shook his head. "It's all right, dear heart, I found him. He was down by the horse lines petting the Major's beast. Gave him some comfort, I think, to be near something Robin loved. I told him not to be ashamed, that we all felt the same, but I don't think he took much notice. He kept muttering about not being strong enough, not having the courage of his convictions, but he wouldn't tell me what he meant. I left him alone to get on with it. There wasn't much more I could do."

Rienne sighed and bent her head. "Poor Tad."

Bull came nearer the bed, wrinkling his nose, his eyes searching for the invisible source of the smell he had detected. "Gods, Rienne, what's been burning?"

"He has."

Bull frowned, puzzled, as he followed Rienne's weary gesture to the figure on the bed. Robin lay much as the big man had last seen him, sweat-drenched, manacled, and unconscious. Cal had taken Tad's place as the Major's guardian and he met Bull's gaze with hard, dark eyes, but volunteered no explanation. Bull stared at the Major's body, seeing no clues as to what Rienne meant. "I don't—"

"Neither do we, but nevertheless, the burning smell is coming from Robin. He started thrashing and crying out again, although he said no recognizable words. Then he started screaming, and his body just ... began to smoke. It was as if he was surrounded by fire. We could even feel the heat of it. But then it all went quiet again, and he hasn't moved since. There's just this faint smell left."

Bull's face paled. She knew he felt drained, frustrated, angry, and useless—each and every one of them felt exactly the same. There was nothing they could do to help, except stay by their friends' sides. The only one of the Baron's victims who even acknowledged their presence was Taran, and although he was fully conscious, he was in no fit state to appreciate it.

Bull clearly had the Adept on his mind, too. "What about Taran?"

"What about him? He's just the same. Terrified of dying whilst still under the Baron's control."

"Is he, though?"

Rienne lifted her head, turning her face to Bull's. "What do you mean?"

The big man came round the bed to stand before her. "He's not been affected at all so far, has he? Unless something happened while I was looking for Tad, he's not been attacked by the Baron."

Rienne's brow creased and she stared at Bull from bloodshot eyes. Cal sharpened his gaze and listened intently. "No," she said slowly, "he hasn't."

"So maybe he won't be. Maybe the Baron can't touch him. Didn't Taran tell Sullyan he couldn't sense the Baron's control once he was in the healer suite? Robin wasn't ... capable of telling us what he felt, and neither were Jinny and Sofira, not that they'd have known what to look for anyway, so we don't know if it was the same for them. Perhaps Reen's hold over Taran is not as strong as the others'. Perhaps he'll be safe from all of this."

Bull's voice was eager and his reasoning plausible, yet even if he was right, it didn't really help. Even if Bull was correct and

Taran was spared what the others had suffered, his ultimate fate hadn't changed. He was still linked to the Baron in a way that transcended death. Staying in the healer suite would not save him from Reen in the end.

She was about to point that out when Ralf's sharp cry ripped through the air. She shot Bull a look of accusation before she fled for the door, as if it was his fault for tempting fate. He spat a curse and pelted after her as she disappeared into Taran's room. Even before they arrived, they could hear the Adept's cries. He was struggling wildly, his eyes wide open, begging the empty air to leave him alone. Rienne covered her ears, unable to bear Taran's hysteria. Ralf stood awkwardly beside the man's bed, wanting to restrain him, but frightened to even touch him. Bull mouthed an obscenity and made straight for the bed, taking the Adept's arms, trying to force him to look him in the eye.

"Taran! Taran, fight him! Don't let him take you over. Use your shield to force him out of your mind. Use your power against him!"

Rienne and Ralf stood staring while Bull tried to reach Taran, willing the Adept to hear him, willing him to succeed. But Taran didn't respond, he didn't even seem to see Bull. His eyes started in terror and he moaned over and over, "No, no! Oh, gods, please no!"

Bull eventually released him and stood away from the bed, unable to meet Rienne's agonized gaze. But then she slipped her arm around his waist and laid her head on his chest. She felt his ailing heart jump as he wrapped his arms about her. "Oh, Rienne, I'm so sorry," he murmured, lowering his face into her hair. "I wish I'd never said anything. Why couldn't I have kept my big mouth shut?"

"Hush, Bull, it wasn't your fault. We all know who's to blame. Poor Taran, I know he was dreading this. I'd better see if I can give him some more of that soporific."

Bull released her and she reached for her bag, bringing out a packet of herbs. Ralf found a cup and filled it with water, and Rienne tipped in the dose. The swordsman took it to Taran and managed to get the panting Adept to swallow some of the mixture. His moaning had subsided, and his hazel eyes seemed fixed on one spot. Rienne turned away from him to scrutinize Bull.

"What?"

She cocked her head. "You're a bit blue around the lips. Do you need more herbs, too?"

He huffed, irritated with himself for causing her more worry. "Is it that obvious?"

She handed him a twist of parchment. "Here. I brought some with me, just in case. The last thing I want is you passing out on me."

He smiled faintly and took what she offered, more relieved than he cared to admit to have her permission. The events of the past few hours were taking their toll, and with the outcome of Sullyan's mission still hanging in the balance, rest for any of them could be many more hours away. He tipped the herbs into a spare cup and drank the mixture down, then moved closer to Rienne once more and passed his arm around her waist. She leaned into him again as they stood anxiously watching the face of their friend.

✢ ✢ ✢ ✢ ✢

Sullyan knelt among the rubble, staring with horror into Taran's terrified eyes. He lay sprawled upon the floor, unable to rise, too weak from his recent ordeals even to crawl toward her. She longed to reach for him, to hold him in her arms, but the scarecrow kept her kneeling where she was, her muscles locked, as he slowly moved from the throne. He approached the stricken man with deliberate steps, absorbing the flow of his panic, watching the tremble of his stricken body with malignant delight.

"You bastard, Reen, you evil, evil bastard." Sullyan panted, straining for all she was worth against the will that held her. How had he been able to bring Taran here? Rienne and the men of her company would never have allowed Taran to leave the healer suite, not even for a moment. Somehow, the scarecrow had breached the spellsilver, as he had when he had taken Robin's powers. He must have found the secret of circumventing its paralyzing touch, which she had striven so long to find. Yet another indication of his supremacy.

Taran whimpered as the black-cloaked figure came closer. He was helpless to move from the Baron's path and stared like a trapped animal at his feet as they stopped close by his head.

"So, witch-girl," the Baron purred from ruined lips. "I have brought you one of your friends, the one who had the temerity to be my niece's lover. I have brought him here to witness your betrayal. He can watch while you refuse to save his life. How do you think he will feel about that, knowing you have the means to save him yet have decided to decline? What will he think as you sit by and watch me torture him, knowing you have the power to spare his pain? Will he think your ideals worth it? Will he gladly endure an eternity of my company with only your empty principles to sustain him? Or will he renounce your worthless friendship, your pretense of loyalty and love?"

The man on the floor stirred faintly, turning his head so he could see her around the Baron's legs. He drew in a shuddering breath as he strove to speak. "Brynne! Please—please, Brynne!"

She could hardly face Taran as his hoarse pleading reached her ears. He was terrified beyond bearing. The Baron drank it in, feeding on the energy it gave him, and Taran grew steadily weaker, losing more of his essence to the creature. She could not stand it.

"Leave him alone, you bastard! Torture *me* if you need gratification. You have already taken all he has. Can you not see he has suffered enough?"

The scarecrow roared, startling Taran into a cry. "Suffered enough?" The tattered robes flared as he whirled on Sullyan. "His suffering could *never* be enough to repay me for what I suffered at that travesty of a trial! Where I was forced to grovel and plead for release, as this useless wretch begs now. Where you shamed me and made me beg for your mercy after you brought me so low."

Sullyan schooled her voice with effort. "And mercy you had, if you remember, my Lord." She tried to shut out Taran's fear, to concentrate on her enemy, but it was well-nigh impossible with her friend's hazel eyes fixed in such terror on hers. "Have you forgotten I saved you from the Wheel and argued for a merciful exile in comfort, where you had more freedom than your treachery merited?"

"Don't turn my words back on me!" the scarecrow screamed. He whipped the cane toward Taran, who convulsed with a hideous shriek of pain. His panting breaths tore at Sullyan's heart and tears welled in her eyes. This battle was over, the scarecrow had won— she simply couldn't endure any more. He possessed the strength to bring her friends to be tortured before her eyes. She had never expected such a level of skill and had no way to counter it. Yet one final slim hope remained, and she embraced it with all her guile.

"I surrender!" she cried into the dust-laden air. "You can have my power if you release him, and I hope it chokes your evil, black heart!"

There was silence in the throne room apart from Taran's sobbing breath. The scarecrow stood immobile, his back to her, savoring her words. Yet when he slowly turned to face her, there was cunning in his eyes, and her heart fell to see it. This was the weak spot of her ploy. Why should he accept her at her word when she could not accept his?

He paced a few steps toward her, staying out of her reach. Although he controlled her muscles for now, he clearly didn't trust her quiescence. Would he chance invading her on her word alone?

271

"Oh, that was music to my ears. The great and powerful Brynne Sullyan, Senior Master. There she kneels, at my mercy, where she swore she'd never be, offering words of surrender and acknowledging my superior powers. Well, I accept your surrender, witch-girl, and to prove I can keep my word, I'll permit you to comfort your friend there and say your final farewells. But don't be too long about it. He is fading for want of his soul, so I suggest you waste no more time."

Sullyan's muscles turned to water and she nearly slumped as he released her. She braced herself with one hand on the floor, and slowly straightened her back. Taran watched her from a few paces away, breathing heavily and trying to move. He couldn't speak and she saw the effort it cost him just to stretch out his hand toward her, palm outward, trembling fingers splayed wide as he strove to convey what he felt. Forcing her aching body to stand, she staggered across the floor, stirring a cloud of plaster dust with each dragging step.

He closed his eyes as she reached his side and knelt, taking hold of his hand. The black figure by the throne stood and watched them in silence. Sullyan gathered Taran to her, embracing him and giving him strength. She realized he was trying to refuse her. He must have sensed how drained she was. She could feel the Baron's overriding control, squatting like a toad over Taran's shuddering mind, and something else she couldn't identify lurking deep within.

"Oh, gods, Brynne, I'm so sorry!" Taran choked in a fading voice, using the strength she had lent him to speak these urgent words. "Please forgive me. I never wanted this! I tried to fight it, I really did, but I'm just too weak."

"Hush, Taran, hush, there is no blame. I know you did what you could. You know that I love you, my friend, and I always will. No matter what befalls, I love you. Always remember that."

"No, Brynne, you don't understand—!"

At his whispered words, she stared down at his face and saw it contort with effort and fear. She could feel a struggle warring within him, and she frowned, confused. The flesh of his face seemed to flow and transmute; even the color of his eyes was changing. She heard a cry, far away and faint, his voice screaming out a warning. Before she could react, strong arms gripped her fast, and a terrible numbing lethargy invaded the fastness of her mind.

Spellsilver!

Her senses screamed, but it was already too late, and the last thing she saw as she fell drowning in the ore's unbreakable grip was the face of the manservant Seth, grinning down at her in triumph.

✠ ✠ ✠ ✠ ✠

Ralf and Bull stood back from the bed as Taran's struggles finally ceased. Both men were sweating with exertion and breathing heavily from their efforts. Rienne hovered fearfully behind them, trying to see what was going on, and a small knot of swordsmen had clustered by the door, brought running by the Adept's terrible cries.

Rienne pushed at Bull's arm. "Let me by, let me see to him."

Bull moved aside just enough to allow Rienne access to the bed. He and Ralf had to stay close in case Taran's convulsions started again. The healer sat by Taran's side and placed her hand on his brow, wiping away beads of perspiration and murmuring soothing words. The suffering man made no response and Rienne became fearful. "I don't like the look of this. What's happened to him? What do you suppose it means?"

Bull had no more idea than she did and shook his head. Rienne resumed stroking Taran's brow, watching his pale, lined face. She drew in a sharp breath and Bull leaned closer. He sucked in air of his own as he saw Taran's eyes flicker open, glazed and bloodshot as they were. The Adept's gaze strayed around the room, seemingly searching for something, or someone. Not finding what they sought, they came to rest on Rienne, and everyone heard the deep, wrenching groan that welled from the Adept's raw throat.

"Hush, Taran, you're back here with us now. Try to rest, love, you're exhausted."

Rienne's calm and soothing tones did nothing to soften the terror lurking in Taran's eyes. He glanced from her face to Bull's as tears welled.

Bull laid a hand on the Adept's shoulder. "What is it, lad? Can you tell us?"

Taran swallowed with an effort and Ralf handed Rienne the cup. She tipped it to Taran's dry, cracked lips and he managed to take a little water. Feeling the pressure of his fingers on her hand, she set the cup aside and leaned over him, straining to hear his failing voice.

"It's over, Rienne, the Baron's won. He's captured Brynne and now we'll all die."

Rienne turned white and dropped her head to her hands with a cry. Bull and Ralf stared at each other in horror. The big man pulled himself together and gripped Taran's shoulder, hard. "Tell us what happened, lad, can you do that?"

Taran turned his eyes to Bull and his voice, although faint, was full of gall. "He used me, Bull. He used me to trap her. He made her think I was there and then he attacked me. He forced her to surrender to save my life. This is what I feared all along, that he'd use our love against her. But I never even dreamed I'd be the one to finally cause her destruction!"

Taran's halting voice staggered into silence as his overwhelming grief took hold. He shuddered with misery, but there was no one to comfort him—they were all far too distressed.

Bull's legs refused to hold him and he sat heavily on the bed, gathering Rienne's trembling body in a bear hug. Ralf moved to the doorway and told the gathered men what Taran had relayed, sending one of them to Cal and Dexter, and another to General Blaine to inform their commanders of this fateful development. The two men departed, sick at heart, and Bull sighed, exchanging a look full of bleak foreboding with Ralf before turning back to Rienne.

✣ ✣ ✣ ✣ ✣

The blankness receded as Sullyan opened her eyes. She had only blacked out for a moment as the spellsilver entered her brain. She could feel the sting of a flesh wound somewhere high on her left arm, and the sight of the bloodstained knife in Seth's wavering hand told her she was right. The lurching nausea afflicting her had not come from that blunt silver knife, however. Its source was a pair of manacles that encircled her wrists, bound securely behind her back. She wasted no time testing their hold. It was futile, as she was too sick to do more than raise her head. Her unsteady gaze met the grinning visage of the scarecrow, who was seated once more upon Lerric's throne, his dusty black cloak flared out around him like the wings of some carrion bird.

"You thought to trick me, girl, didn't you?" His gloating voice penetrated the humming in her mind like maggots burrowing into a carcass. "But you were the once who was tricked. Did you like my little charade? I must admit, I'm surprised it fooled you so thoroughly. But then, you're too softhearted—I've always thought so. Well, love has been your downfall, Artesan witch, and I shall take great pleasure in tormenting you and your friends with the consequences of your failures while I slowly destroy the rest of your kind."

"Go to Perdition, Reen!" she spat, valiantly trying to control the heave of her stomach. But the vehemence of her reply upset what balance she had left and she vomited bile onto the floor.

"Oh dear." The scarecrow chuckled as he rose to his feet, his dusty cloak sweeping the ground. She heard the inexorable tap of the terrible cane as he approached. "See how low she has been brought, Seth? This is the great and powerful Colonel Brynne Sullyan, King's Envoy and Senior Master. She can't even hold on to the contents of her stomach, much less defeat a poor, weakened wretch like me."

Sullyan squinted up at him, licking bile from her lips. "Get on with it, you parasite, if you still think you can. But I warn you, my spirit will not be cowed as you have cowed my friends. I know all sorts of ways to make your life a torment, and this I vow: you will never know a moment's peace once you open yourself to take me."

His face grew thunderous and he swept down on her where she knelt and backhanded her across the mouth. She fell back into Seth without a sound, determined not to show her pain, but the silver in her blood churned and boiled, causing her to black out once again. It was fleeting, as before, but it weakened her further and made her heart race as she struggled for equilibrium. The manservant roughly shoved her back to her knees, and she knelt quietly, head down, breathing deeply, while she waited for the Baron's next move.

He had stepped back and seemed to be studying her. He made no sound and she raised her head, not wanting to be caught unawares when the moment of her death arrived. Two glowing red orbs met her unfocused gaze, and a third red glow was centered at the tip of the shimmering cane. It was strangely mesmerizing, the way the wood seemed to shift in the flicker of its own glow, and she wrenched her gaze from it with an effort. The Baron leaned both hands on the wood, his left still fused with it, and she saw the energy pulsing upward into his arms. Somehow, he was able to draw strength up out of the wood.

He saw her frowning and smiled cruelly. "Are you regretting your surrender now, witch? You didn't mean the words you spoke, did you? They were a ruse to placate me, and you intended to rescind them once I was within your mind. But it backfired on you, I'm afraid, and now it doesn't matter whether you yield to me or not. With that spellsilver on you, I don't need your acquiescence to relieve you of your powers, and that's not the only thing I intend to take over once your life force is under my control."

She regarded the evil delight in his eyes and wondered what he meant. She still didn't understand how he could do what he claimed while she still had spellsilver in her blood. Why didn't the ore affect him, as it blocked and affected her? The only way she had ever discovered of circumventing the silver's null field was when she'd had Rykan's essence inside her and Rykan's silver on her skin. Her success in the burning circle on the Baron's land did not count, because she had used Morgan's unfettered mind. She didn't think the Baron possessed the level of control over his power prerequisite to imbuing spellsilver with his psyche, even if he did have the knowledge after stealing Robin's life force. And she had seen no evidence yet that he had even tried to assimilate everything Robin knew.

What she had seen so far was a show of brute force. He had used no finesse or subtlety to defeat her, only metaphysical brawn and an unbreakable shield. Yet according to Taran, he had long been able to brush aside the silver's blocking effects, as he hadn't had to free Robin before invading her life mate's mind. So how was his essence linked to the ore? What was his connection to it, apart from his immolation in the pool on the clerics' island?

Her eyes strayed once more to the shimmering cane, and the hand-become-wood. A sensation of dread crept down her spine and she shivered.

✣ ✣ ✣ ✣ ✣

The scarecrow watched the play of these thoughts across her face with hunger in his eyes. She was no longer able to hide her confusion, and her ignorance fed his swelling pride. She wasn't so high and mighty, kneeling there at his feet. He had finally triumphed over her and all his plans would now be fulfilled. Her assertion that his interference would eventually destroy the world carried no weight in his mind. He gave no credence to anything she said. Her threat to disrupt him from within once he had claimed her power had not been an idle one. He knew he could never trust anything that had its origins in her mind. Yet other parts of her could serve him well, and would enable him to disguise his true intentions once he had effected the transfer. He smiled as he imagined Blaine's and Elias's faces when they realized just what he had done. His mind in Sullyan's body could wreak much havoc before the terrible truth was discovered. And with the energies he could channel through the cane, he was sure he would have the strength to switch his consciousness from his failing body to hers. Even if he didn't, he only had to allow her to think that she might overcome him. Just give her one moment of opportunity and she would kill him without a thought, and that would leave his spirit free to settle in its newly subjugated home. How she would rage at his deception when he denied her escape once more! The anticipation of her frantic resistance made him drool with lust.

✣ ✣ ✣ ✣ ✣

She felt the change come over him and knew the moment was near. Despite the roiling of her stomach and the incessant drumming of the silver in her ears, she could feel the heat of his craving and her muscles tensed against what was to come. Useless, she knew, but she simply couldn't help herself. She watched Reen as he advanced on her, her eyes on the glow of the cane, rearing backward from the glittering red tip and the menace contained within it. Reen saw this futile evasion and his cracked lips slewed back from his decaying teeth. "Hold her, Seth."

She felt the manservant's hands clench painfully on her shoulders, forcing her to remain in place. She was trapped and helpless under his hands, too weak now even to cry out.

The dreadful cane drew so close its heat stung her face. The Baron aimed it squarely at her thundering heart, his evil essence pouring down the wood, flowing from his hands as he prepared himself to feed. She could feel the lust of his emanations pulsing through the heat, reaching out to take her, to reave her spirit from her flesh. The essence of the cane was changing, becoming the embodiment of the Baron's will, and a wild and blinding hope suddenly flashed into her frantic brain.

The spellsilver—the cane! *His essence!*

Her analytical mind screamed at her, years of living with military tactics surging to the fore. Grasping the thought intuitively with no time for reason, she allowed her eyes to widen in shock and gasped, staring past the approaching scarecrow. She yelled at the top of her lungs.

"No, Elias! *Get back!*"

Chapter Twenty-Four

As tricks went, it was one of the oldest, and the Baron didn't fall for it—at least, not completely. Still, the unexpected nature of her words caught him unaware, prepared as he was for struggling, or maybe cursing or pleading for mercy. He could not prevent the twitch of his hands as he stopped himself glancing over his shoulder, and that slightest distraction gave Sullyan her chance. Seeing the tip of the terrible cane waver for a split second to the right of her heart, she lunged toward it with all her failing strength and clamped her teeth on it, hard.

Her surge of movement took Seth by surprise and he lost his grip on her shoulders. He could only watch in amazement as she ground her teeth into the wood. Reen roared in fury and tried to wrench the cane free, but he only succeeded in twisting it in her mouth, accomplishing what her weakened muscles could not. Blood ran freely from her lips, splinters embedding in her gums. White fire seemed to blossom inside her head as the scarecrow's second wrench loosened her grip, and the tattered figure took an involuntary step backward with the force of his jerk.

That second of lost balance gave her the time she needed to clear her head, and her powers sprang forth at her call. The spellsilver field was thrust to one side as the forces of Earth surged and heaved, and the manacles fell from her wrists as she instantly melted the ore. She flung an elemental barrier at the Baron that slammed him against the throne with bone-crushing force, and immediately called Fire to flood the room with blazing light.

The Baron screamed in rage and agony and a pool of inky blackness erupted from the end of the cane, but now Sullyan's mighty forces, linked to the same infinite source as the Baron's, were unaffected by the shroud. Her Fire cut through it and pierced the scarecrow's body, sending a plume of acrid smoke into the dust-laden air. Another shriek of pain burst from the fallen man and she could see him curled beneath the smoking ruin of his robes. Bone shone briefly white before he scrambled to his knees, and she knew that one leg, at least, was broken as he attacked her once again.

Fire met with Fire in the raging heat of the ruined throne room, amber power blazing through black as the opposing forces met. A shocking detonation crashed around their ears and yet more masonry fell, showering them with stone that was pulverized in the fury of the Fire. She was vaguely aware of Seth crawling away, frantically trying to find shelter, but she dismissed him from her mind as she called for the forces of Air. Holding on to her ravening Fire, which was slowly overcoming the Baron's, she funneled a vicious tornado toward the center of the room. The flames whipped and gyred around the throne, fanned by the whirling winds, and within the terrible inferno she heard a despairing scream. The black Fire wavered and vanished, leaving her power suddenly unopposed.

A desperate attack from behind surprised her, causing her forces to falter as she whirled to meet the new threat. The terrified manservant, whom she had supposed to be crawling away, had crept up at her back and snatched the knife from her belt. The sound of it leaving the sheath, faint though it was, alerted her senses and warned her of the impending assault. She reached for strength to empower her muscles and ducked swiftly to the side, avoiding Seth's panicked thrust to her back by inches. The tip of the knife drew blood from her arm, but she ignored the pain, twisting round to grapple the young man and bear him to the floor. A well-placed blow to his windpipe had him gagging for breath and defenseless as she turned her attention back to her real foe.

When she examined the room, his aura had vanished. She quelled the powerful elements and dismissed them back whence they had come, standing in confusion in the ruin of the empty room. Lazy smoke drifted up from the cloak fragments lying at the foot of the Fire-blackened throne, and she stirred them with her boot as she swept the substrate with her mind. She eventually found his trace, concealed within the black Fire. He must have goaded Seth into attacking her to deflect her attention and make his escape. Where he had run to, she had no idea, and now must start over again.

With furious, deliberate slowness, she turned back to Seth, who lay choking amid the wreckage on the floor. He watched her approach with dread in his eyes, not attempting to escape. He had nowhere to run to and no master to help. He had been abandoned and he knew it.

She wiped blood from her lips. "Where is he?"

Her menacing voice cut through Seth's quailing thoughts. He had one hand clasped about his bruised throat, the other he stretched out as if to ward her off. "I don't know!"

She was in no mood for games. "Oh, come now! I know he controls your mind."

"Yes, of course he controls me, but that doesn't mean I know where he is."

She regarded him, noting how his pulse raced. He was looking on the face of death whilst knowing it would not release him from the torment of his soul. He had been taken over just like her friends—he would be as terrified as they.

"But you know how to find him, do you not?"

The implacable tone of her voice froze him. He knew how mighty she was. Hadn't he just seen her defeat his master, despite the awesome power of the cane? Seth began to shudder with primal terror as he stared into her eyes.

Snatching up her knife, Sullyan dropped her weight onto Seth's heaving chest. She held the wickedly sharp point against his throbbing jugular, her eyes fixed furiously on his. He struggled to breathe with her knees pressing down on him, whimpering deep in his throat. She snarled as she pricked his skin with the knife. "You will locate your master for me, or you will feel the bite of my steel. Make up your mind swiftly, you sniveling wretch. My patience grows thin."

Seth could hardly think for terror. Sullyan saw the roll of his eyeballs as he began to faint. She realized what she was doing and briefly closed her eyes. Heaving a sigh and removing her knife, she got to her feet with an effort. She took a firm hold of her fury, reminding herself that she only killed her enemies when they were trying to kill her. She did *not* kill their tools or cat's-paws, or those who had acted under duress. If she did, she would be no better than Reen and would profane the very principles by which she lived her life.

She crouched down by the shuddering Seth, careful to sheath her knife. She placed her hand on his clammy brow and soothed his damaged throat, using her intimate knowledge of Reen's essence to reach that of his servant. His eyes widened in shock at her unexpected help, and while she waited for him to recover, she picked splinters from her mouth, spitting them out on the floor as she worked them out of her teeth. Her torn lips and wounded arm she healed without a thought, glancing back at Seth as he slowly levered himself up on one elbow, making no sudden moves. She twisted her mouth in displeasure as she saw the mistrust that clouded his face, but she could hardly blame him for it.

"Be easy, Seth, you have no need to fear me. I do not intend your death. If you will let me, I can help you, but I need your assistance first."

Seth's terror did not abate. "I'm not going to find him for you, Colonel, no matter what you do. You know how he'll torture me, even if you kill him. If I help you, he'll know, and it'll be the worse for me. I'll never be free of him, and neither will your friends."

She spoke softly, holding his gaze. "That is not necessarily the case, Seth. There is an outside chance that I can free all of you, once the monster is dead."

"I don't believe you!" Tears formed in Seth's eyes. "That's a cruel thing to taunt me with. Why would you bother to free me, even if what you say is true?"

She sighed. "I am not being cruel, and I will not deceive you. The chances of success are slim. My hope is based on no more than a fragment of an Artesan's journal. But I do have hope that I can free my friends, and I swear to you that this is true. However, I can only attempt it once the Baron is dead, and for that, I need your help. Break free of his influence for once in your life and do what you know to be right. You have seen the atrocities he's committed; you know he cannot be permitted to live. The very fabric of our existence depends on my ability to kill him. He is going to end up dead, my friend, whether you help me or not."

"How do I know I can trust you?"

Despite her impatience, Sullyan gazed into Seth's frightened eyes and gave him a sympathetic smile. "I do not blame you for your caution, and I will not force your help. I will not hold you to ransom, no matter what you decide. But this I will tell you, and you will know it for truth. The longer the Baron is permitted to live, the more your body will fade. My chances of returning your soul to you lessen with every passing hour. I know you feel the draining of your energy. I can see it in your face. It is also happening to those I love, and I am desperate to help them if I can. Your spirit will be trapped in the same place as theirs. Aid me and you aid yourself."

She watched Seth struggle with his loyalties and the truth he could hear in her words. He was squaring what the Baron had told him of her with the reality of her beside him. He could sense no deception in her, and he badly wanted to believe. Yet too many things had happened to Seth for him to trust her just like that.

"It's not only my master who has committed atrocities, Colonel. I'm not innocent myself. I've committed murder. I cut the throat of Lady Jinella's housekeeper, Alice, on the night Lady Jinella was taken. What will happen to me if you succeed in killing the Baron and restoring my soul?"

Sullyan wanted to scream at him, shake him into compliance. There was so little time and so little hope. She had no patience with his fears, but she had given her word not to force him, and she would keep it. His question signified a wavering in his caution, a crack in his doubt.

"You can atone for Alice's murder, Seth. Countless souls will be saved if you help me, not just yours and those of my friends. I think, under the circumstances, if you were to choose to leave here and make your life somewhere else, no one will come looking for you. We will have more important things on our minds than what becomes of you."

The honesty in her voice settled Seth's concerns. He really had nothing to lose, after all. The Baron already possessed his soul and would punish him for failing to kill her, no matter what he did. She represented Seth's only chance of avoiding that terrible fate. If he chose to ignore this opportunity, it would be tantamount to slicing his own throat. He closed his eyes while she seethed in frustration.

When he finally opened them and looked at her, he had an answer.

"I can't give you an exact location, Colonel. All I can see is rock and a strange silvery light. Does that help you at all?"

Of course! He had gone back to the island, to the pool that was the source of his power. She leapt to her feet, startling Seth, who cringed. She laid her hand on his shoulder to show her gratitude. "Indeed it does, and I am much indebted to you. Now, if I were you, I would make myself scarce. This ceiling looks none too safe."

Seth stared after her as she ran from the ruined throne room, bemused by her exultant tone. He felt a brief stab of pain and gasped in shock, terrified the Baron had discovered what he had done and was about to punish him. A gray shimmer flared beyond the charred wood of the double doors, and when it faded, Seth's pain faded too. In the ensuing silence, he realized he was completely alone in the palace. The darkness closed around him and he glanced up at the invisible ceiling. He shivered. Panic nipped at his heart, telling him to get out, fast.

He obeyed it as swiftly as he could.

It was still dark when Sullyan stepped out of the Veils onto Andaryan soil, and the stars glittered like ice crystals in a patchy sky. She glanced up at them, trying to gauge the hour. She thought dawn was not far off. Her search and subsequent battle in the ruins of Lerric's palace had taken up more of the night than she had thought. Yet another day of torment faced her lover and her friends unless she could overcome the scarecrow once and for all.

Despite the incessant urge pricking at her heart, she took a moment to compose herself. It was far too early for any of the clerics to be abroad. If she used the island's little landing stage as her point of arrival, Frar Varian would not thank her for rousing him from his bed to let her in. Instead, she decided to arrive just inside the gate. It was far enough from the dwellings that no one would be roused. And even though she was fairly sure Reen would sense her coming, the fewer people who knew of it the better. Fixing her intended spot firmly in her mind, she constructed the smallest portway she could fit through and parted the Veils.

The faint susurration of waves upon rocks was the first sound to greet her ears as she closed the portway. The narrow passage of solid rock let little starlight through, even though the night sky here in northern Albia was clearer than in Andaryon. The moon had already set and no lanterns relieved the darkness. She moved silently through the passage, ghosting past the guest cottage where she, Cal, and Tad had rested when first they came to the island. Her feet found the smooth path that led toward the clerics' dwellings. No lights showed behind any of the windows. The clerics were all sleeping soundly until the hour of the Sunrise Paean. She hoped she could conclude her business here with none of them being the wiser, but was realistic enough to know the hope was probably forlorn.

She left the above-ground dwellings behind and made her way to the narrow steps that wound down between the rocks. The going was slippery with a rime of frost and she put a hand out to steady her passage. She couldn't afford to slip now she was so nearly there. She saw the wooden door ahead, closed against the cold, and experienced a sudden fear that it would be locked. Irrational, she knew, as with the island so well guarded and so infrequently visited the clerics had no need to bolt their doors. Nevertheless, she breathed a silent sigh when the latch turned under her hand. She stepped inside out of the biting cold and pulled the door closed behind her, allowing the warmth to infuse her bones.

She stood for a moment listening to the volcano, hearing the lazy beat of its potent heart. The gentle red glow of the lava tube walls gave her Earth-attuned senses all the help they would need. Her entire body recognized this warm, womb-like passage; she did not need eyes to guide her to the pool.

Laying one hand upon the rough wall of the tunnel, she began her downward journey, questing ahead as she went. She passed the frequent doorways until she came to the one that opened onto the Baron's erstwhile chambers, and although she didn't expect him to be there, she probed within. As she had thought, there was no imprint, and she continued down the passage. The rough walls were now bare of doors and her only concerns were for the unpredictable vents that she knew lay up ahead. She kept her senses attuned to the flow of Fire within the volcano, feeling its slumbering violence roiling very close beneath her feet. As before, the choking smell of sulfur began to trouble her lungs. She had not left the outer door open as she had the last time, and there was no flow of air to ease the sting of her throat. She found herself regretting this as a pocket of pure sulfur wafted down around her, and she covered her nose with her hand as she reached out to call Air.

Her call died before she could complete it as a vent of superheated steam shot without warning from the wall. A tiny fissure had given way before the force of the eruption and the jet spurted toward her with terrifying speed. With hardly a thought, she tapped into her metaforce, slamming her shield up even as she took hold of the heat within the jet. Her forces dealt with the Fire it contained, leaving only a blast of warm air to buffet her body, but even so, she was shaken by the power of the blast.

Leaning into the wall for support, she took a moment to calm herself, thankful the vent had at least cleared the sulfurous ooze. Then she bent her senses toward the newly formed fissure and confirmed her suspicion. That waft of sulfur was no stray occurrence, and the jet had been directed to that crack. Well, she reflected, that answered her query as to whether Reen expected her. At least now she would be on her guard against more such surprises.

Suppressing a desire to curse, she crept farther down the tunnel. The rock changed color as the heat's intensity grew. Oxygen was even thinner here, but she regulated her breathing and examined each magma chamber minutely before passing it. No more jets threatened her, although she heard more than one behind her, but these were all natural pressure releases, the gentle exhalations of the sleeping volcano.

Reaching the left-bearing branch in the downward sloping passage, she stopped for a moment to breathe in the fresher air. If she listened carefully, she could just hear the buried fires roaring, although she had been feeling them for some time through the sensitive bones of her feet. As she had on her last visit, she wondered why the air was fresher here when she was deeper underground. The sulfur reek still lingered, but now it didn't dominate, and she could only surmise that there must be a chimney or a crevice somewhere, up to the open air.

Pushing away from the wall, she took the left-hand passage, walking warily and noting the golden color beginning to appear in the tunnel up ahead. The roaring of fire was now constant in her ears and if she concentrated on it she could feel the pull of the spellsilver pool. This was where she must be constantly on her guard, for although she was stronger here, so was her enemy. He could not overcome her now, not in a trial of metaforce, but there would be other ways in which he might prevail. He only had to catch her off guard or distract her with some trick, and the consequences didn't bear thinking about.

She saw the sharp right-hand curve ahead that protected her from the full influence of the pool and her muscles tensed with anticipation. She stretched her senses outward, disguised within the spellsilver, but she could catch no hint of his presence in the cavern of the pool. That was not so surprising, as he was linked so closely with it. He would be able to hide himself better here than even she could. She would have to be supremely careful.

Sliding up to the angle of the bend, she flattened herself against the wall and steeled her mighty shield against the siren call of the pool. Reminding herself of the wreathing steam that hid the pool's treacherous edge, she moved forward until she could see around the rock. As before, the beauty of the place astounded her with its dancing golden flames and the silver wreaths of steam bending continually through and around them. The slender ribbons of condensed ore spiraled lazily down from the roof, swaying and curling most curiously over the sluggish pool. All was as she remembered it, with no sign of her enemy.

The cavern was hazy with moving steam and more than half of it was obscured. The swaying curtains drifted this way and that across her sight, drawing the eye and confusing the mind. She could not examine the place in its entirety due to the changing clouds of steam, and her only option was to move farther in. He had to be here, somewhere close. He would not want to move too far from his source of power. She knew she had frightened him badly back in Lerric's throne room. He had allowed himself to relax too soon and he would not make that mistake again. Although he had lost his chance of obtaining her great powers, he could still triumph by killing her, and go on to destroy the Veils. She simply could not let that happen, no matter what the risk to her friends. She could only hope they would forgive her if her hopes were not fulfilled.

Slowly, testing every step, she moved out into the cavern.

⁜ ⁜ ⁜ ⁜ ⁜

The jump Reen had made from the throne room had taken him directly to this place. Still ignorant of the theories, he didn't realize he had done the impossible. All he knew was that he'd had to escape before the witch could press her advantage, and he had followed the pull of the spellsilver blindly through the substrate to its source. Now he crouched in the shadows across the cavern, concealed by a curtain of steam, using the pool's tremendous energies to support his failing strength. She had hurt him sorely in her attack of Fire and Air, and it had taken him some time to heal his broken bones and seal the burns on his skin. Unskilled in the finer points of metaphysical healing, he had not done a good job, but it would be enough to sustain him. Once he disposed of her, he would have his pick of victims to feed on. None of the clerics on the island would be able to resist the force of the cane. Squatting awkwardly in the fluctuating shadows, the cane's tip resting in the molten ore, the scarecrow waited for his moment, red lust gleaming in his eyes.

✣ ✣ ✣ ✣ ✣

Sullyan skirted the pools' narrow edge with care and made her cautious way around it, scanning the changing vista as she went. There was only one opening onto this cavern, the one by which she had entered, so she knew no one would be menacing her back. Still, there were plenty of scooped-out hollows in the encircling walls, niches gouged by the molten silver when the primal forces below it stirred into life, causing it to surge and throw up superheated gouts to relieve the mounting pressure. Any one of them could be hiding the Baron. She still couldn't sense his presence and was resigned to waiting until he chose to show himself, readying her shield for the attack she was sure would soon be launched.

✣ ✣ ✣ ✣ ✣

She was halfway around the edge when he made his first move. He had seen her enter the cavern and tracked her progress through the dancing steam. He watched her as she picked her cautious way forward. He was aware she could not sense him and knew her shields were ready. He would have to distract her somehow to stand any chance of success. Drawing the dripping cane out of the sluggish silver, he tightened both hands on it and grasped hold of its molten strength with all the power of his will.

It wasn't easy to wield the stuff. It was viscous and unresponsive and it was heavier than he had thought. Nevertheless, he achieved his end, and a huge, swelling bubble started to push at the surface tension. He thrust at it with his augmented might and it grew even larger, fed from below by the volcano's awesome heat. She had not noticed it yet, intent as she was on locating him, and he couldn't afford to alert her before he was ready to strike. So he eased back on the pressure, holding the bubble firmly within the pool, and concentrated on her next few steps as he prepared to spring his trap. The small spout he commanded was easier to manipulate and he timed it precisely to coincide with her steps. As she reached a certain point where he knew the edge was less than stable, he flung the spout of silver upward into her face.

Chapter Twenty-Five

Sullyan felt the surge of power even before she saw the flash of molten ore, and she was ready for it as it splashed over her feet. It bit into the lip of the pool and rock began to crumble. A section of the edge gave way, and she was forced to leap sideways to avoid slipping into the pool. As she steadied herself against the wall, a huge bubble of spellsilver surged upward with terrible speed. It burst free of the liquid around it to splatter against the cavern roof, exploding and disgorging its contents with a deafening roar.

The curved shape of the roof splayed the deadly metal outward and it fell in a terrifying rain. Anything mortal caught in its path would be instantly flayed or melted. Sullyan flung herself to the ground, deploying the mightiest shield she could form. Even so, parts of her clothing were singed and she felt small burns prick her skin where droplets of molten silver splashed under her shield. These tiny burns were more of an annoyance than a danger. A flick of her power healed them.

"Is that the best you can do?" She injected a note of mockery into her voice as she raised herself from the floor, casting her sight and senses about for her foe. A scrape of wood on stone caught at her ears and her eyes fixed instantly on a vague humped shape across the cavern. She peered at it through the wavering curtains of steam. It was not the signature black she had come to associate with the Baron, but a crouching, pale form that shifted oddly against the wall. When the concealing vapor parted briefly, she saw his naked body huddled low, scuttling spider-like to avoid her prying eyes. One leg was bent and crooked and his spine didn't look quite right. She assumed they had been damaged when he had slammed into Lerric's throne. The peeling, mottled skin was even more ragged than before and a large part across his shoulders seemed to have fallen away altogether, the ropy muscles beneath exposed to the open air.

However, his wounded and pitiful state didn't soften Sullyan's resolve. She only had to consider her life mate to quash any sympathy she might feel. The Baron's dusty black robes might have been burned away in their conflict, but his charred, blackened heart still beat vengefully in his breast.

"Give it up, Reen," she called. "You know you cannot defeat me now I have your essence in my blood. Spare yourself more agony and surrender to Elias's justice. I cannot let you leave this place unless you yield."

"Surrender to Elias's justice?" he shrieked, his furious, snarling voice full of hatred. "Surrender to you, you mean! I know what your justice is worth, you pagan witch. I will not grovel at your feet again. I will see you die here. Don't think I'm finished yet!"

"It is over, Reen, can you not see that? What can you hope to achieve? My powers are greater than yours, as you know, and I can access the spellsilver just as well as you. There is nothing more you can do, no further damage you can cause."

He spat. "No?"

She felt him drawing once more on the silver, knowing intuitively what he planned to do. Desperate to stop him, to save her friends further pain, she flung a powerful Thunderball at him to force him to defend. As she had hoped, he was not adept at controlling two actions at once, and he howled in frustration as he punched her power away, losing his hold on his psyche as he dealt with her attack.

"I can keep that up forever, with this source of strength to draw on," she called, seeing the bitterness and fury seething in his ruby eyes as he realized the truth of her words. "You cannot win, Reen. Give it up."

The sound of her confident voice, so full of power and authority, seemed to snap his feeble hold on reason. A rabid berserker rage burst from his ruined body with sudden, shocking violence. Screaming in defiance, incoherent with apoplectic anger, he straightened his crooked spine and raised his fleshless arms, uncaring of his nakedness as he attacked her with Earth and Fire.

✣ ✣ ✣ ✣ ✣

Cleric Patrio Ruvar opened his eyes in the darkness and took a moment to stretch beneath the fur coverings before swinging his legs from the bed. He sat on the edge and yawned in the predawn chill, then padded to the banked fire to light a taper. He kindled his lamp and carried it into his small cooking room, where he took warm water from the kettle hanging over the cook fire. Divesting himself of his thick nightgown, he washed his dark skin and refreshed his sleep-heavy eyes, dressing in his robes of office before the chill of the air pimpled his flesh. By the time his ablutions were over, Varian was at the door.

"It'll be a fine clear dawn, Patrio."

Ruvar nodded at Varian's murmured greeting, the only words the Frar was likely to speak at this pure and holy hour. Ruvar closed his door, following in Varian's footsteps as they slowly trod the path to the volcano's star-crowned crest. Wrapped in thick woolen cloaks against the frost, they were as anonymous as those who joined them, and the order progressed in silence as they meditated on the dawn.

Halfway up the path, Ruvar stopped, lifting his head to the gradually lightening sky and narrowing his eyes. He could hear the thrumming hum that signaled the beginning of the Paean, but it was not the ritual chant that prickled at his mind. He was used, by now, to the constant tremble of the dormant volcano's heartbeat, as they all were; it ran through their marrow and shivered through their lives. He knew each nuance of its fluctuations and could read its changing nature. He was as attuned to this living island as surely as Sullyan was attuned to her psyche. Something was different this morning, something wasn't right, and his spine stiffened with a feeling akin to dread.

He noticed that Varian had also stopped, and that the elderly cleric was staring at him from the hollows of his hood, no doubt wondering what was holding the Patrio up. He must be in his place before the true Paean began. His was the voice that sang the Greeting to the Sun. He forced his reluctant feet to continue up the path, beginning his own low chant, and the familiar rhythmic cadence soothed his sense of unease. Reassured, Varian turned and completed the hike to the summit, moving around the crater's rim to take his place among the rest. Ruvar walked beside him, turning to face the east.

Varian's prediction proved correct; the sky was perfectly clear, the last bright star just beginning to dim as the Paean gained in strength. The swelling, harmonized voices touched the magic in Ruvar's heart, stirring his senses as they always did with the majesty of this hour. No other service affected him as deeply as Sunrise, and no other Paean was as glorious as this. Ruvar raised his voice with his fellows as they prepared to greet the sun.

✣ ✣ ✣ ✣ ✣

Chunks of rock and gouts of Fire cavorted with lethal chaos in the cavern as the Baron attacked Sullyan. He lashed out indiscriminately with no thought or finesse, insanely desperate to finish her off and uncaring of his own safety. He stood inviolate within the storm, safe beneath a shimmering shield, although Sullyan was doubtful whether he could maintain it in the face of such an extravagant expenditure of power. Despite the pool's resources, infinite and potent though they were, Reen's own concentration would suffer the longer he kept this up. His fragile, ruined body could only take so much channeling of power. It would give out on him eventually, and his psyche would collapse.

Yet could *she* hold out that long? Rocks bounced heavily off her shield and ricocheted off the walls and floor to splash into the roiling pool. Steam shot upward with terrifying force, pummeling the cavern roof, and gouts of golden flame roared and whooshed with fury. The friable rim of the pool was being eroded by the bombardment. Soon she would have to move or risk immolation. The niche where she had taken shelter was too shallow to protect her for long, and her enemy showed no signs of letting his fury fade. She would have to make a run for it, holding her shield in place.

Casting a swift glance at the naked madman across the pool, she saw him gather his malignant forces for yet another attack. One clawed hand grasped the cane as the tip sucked up silver energy with horrifying speed. It was like some kind of Powersink activated by the spellsilver, and as long as its master commanded it, its forces would never run dry. Although Sullyan had told him she could hold out against him indefinitely, her lover and friends did not have infinite time. He knew this, of course, in the raging maelstrom that was his unhinged brain. He would do his utmost to detain her, to wear her down, to break her spirit and force her to yield.

Shaking her head to cast these thoughts from her mind, she left the shallow niche, running nimbly around the crumbling edge of the pool toward the exit tunnel. His offensive efforts, when not randomly indiscriminate, clustered thickest near the entrance to block her escape, and she couldn't afford to ignore them or permit them to shatter her shield. She was not invulnerable to his forces, despite what she had told him, and the energy from the pool would only sustain her for so long. Like his, her mind would tire from the concentration and begin to lose its grip, and it would only take one tiny flaw to see her shield destroyed.

She reached her destination—a hollow not far from the tunnel—and ducked inside just in time as yet another salvo was unleashed. Great lumps of rock tore from the walls, crashing to the floor with a shudder, and as the noise faded she felt him reaching down to the forces of the volcano far below. Its powerful, rhythmic thrumming surged through her bones and she shivered in sudden fear, wondering whether she would be able to prevent him from triggering an eruption. The destruction of the island would gratify his vengeful heart, and the energy within his cane would enable him to escape. She would be helpless to aid the clerics and would be forced to save herself, adding to her sense of futility and weakening her spirit further.

Full of fear for the innocent clerics, she attuned her senses more closely to the island, delving deeply with her metaforce to probe the volcano. Perhaps if she could block the Baron and thwart his intended eruption, she could infuriate him further and prod him into a fatal slip. Yet when she touched the island's molten heart and sampled the flow of its fiery lifeblood, she found no explanation for the droning in her skull. It wasn't the lava pulses that beat incessantly through her body, but some other outside influence singing the volcano's puissant song.

She frowned in confusion before she realized the origins of the elemental song. How could she have forgotten? Dawn must be closer than she had thought. The clerics would be giving throat to the Paean to the Sun. Her sense of fear heightened, thinking of them somewhere above her head, standing in mystical meditation, unaware of the impending horror her enemy strove to unleash. She had no time to ponder how the chant could reach her here, for the Baron was moving, creeping along the wall, and she centered her wayward attention on the aura of his force.

Leaning out from her hollow, she charted his stumbling progress, reading determination in the chaotic signals he gave out. He was completely insane now, all sense of reason gone. The only thing he cared about was the destruction of his foes. How she wished she could take her knife from her belt, her wicked, foot-long blade, and weigh its killing edge in her hand. She longed to draw her arm back and send the well-balanced knife toward his heart with deadly accuracy. Death would be a mercy for his tortured soul, although not for those he held in the fastness of his mind. If she could not force him to release his hold on his captives, a steely knife in Reen's rotting heart would just as surely kill her love. She was helpless to mete out such a death to him while he controlled Robin's soul. All she could do was wait and pray his endurance would burn out.

As if he discerned her thoughts, he stopped and turned his blind red eyes toward her, knowing where she was by the aura of her fear. Flayed lips peeled back from rotten teeth in a dreadful, leering grin, watery blood running down his chin to drop hissing on the floor. He held his barrage of offensive metaforce in rigid check, but she could feel the flow of its violence as it seethed under his skin.

"Had enough yet, pagan witch?" He watched her slyly with twitching eyes, his subsumed hand pulsing with the cane's flow of silver. She had launched offensive moves of her own, all aimed at parting him from that cane, but it was fused too deeply to him and she knew she would never succeed. She doubted she could even cut it from him, were she to have the chance, and had decided to discount it, concentrating her efforts instead on preventing him from torturing her friends. What they were experiencing, held within his mind, she hardly dared to think. Her only hope was to keep him diverted from causing them further harm. That and holding out until this endless conflict ceased.

"Give it up, Reen." She kept her voice soft and unthreatening, its measured tones echoing around the cavern. "I know your mind is tiring. Your body is damaged and full of pain, yearning for rest. You cannot achieve your purpose here, you must have realized that. You have had your revenge and repaid me for the humiliation you suffered. Why torture yourself with the impossible? Why force me to take your life?"

He crouched awkwardly against the wall, squatting close to the pool, the tip of the transformed cane just dipping into the silver. He stared at her with baleful eyes, the dreadful sneer still on his lips, and she could feel him sucking up power as a leech absorbs blood. "You cannot take my life, witch, your powers are not great enough for that. And you know what would happen to your precious friends if you could. So don't bother with your meaningless soft words, don't try to distract me with offers of mercy. I know they hold no truth. I will not give up this fight, not until I have eradicated every one of your evil kind from the world. I have a God-given purpose, and His strength to carry it out."

She sensed his preparation and was ready for the move, but still the force of his Firefield came as a shock. He must have been considering how to form it even as he spouted his pious rant, and it rushed toward her through the cloying steam with commendable cohesion. It was not perfectly formed and would pose no immediate danger to her. Yet as she directed metaforce to block it, she felt another surge through the substrate and realized this attack was a feint. Splitting her attention, she snapped the Firefield away, preparing the rest of her awareness to defend against the Thunderball he launched in its wake.

She had long ceased to be surprised he still attempted these futile attacks, powerful though they were. His mind was incapable of reason now and he acted on instinct alone. Yet as she reached out to surround the missile of Earth and push it aside, it veered sharply and she gasped, her eyes widening as she divined the scarecrow's true purpose. The power was not meant for her at all, but another target entirely, and she made a superhuman leap toward the tunnel in the rock. She heard the scarecrow's triumphant scream and an ominous cracking roar, and jolted to a halt just as a whole section of the roof fell in. She flung herself against the wall as a jagged boulder missed her head by inches, and then she was forced to brace her shield against a splashing surge of molten ore. Dust and grit obscured her sight, mixing with the wreathing steam. When she could finally see and hear again, her heart quailed in her chest.

✣ ✣ ✣ ✣ ✣

The chanting only faltered minutely as another tremor ran through the clerics' feet. They were used to such tremors and paid them no heed. Ruvar was proud of the way the chant resumed with no direction or reassurance from him. There had been many such tentative shivers this dawn as they stood around the summit, and he wondered what made the volcano stir. He normally received warnings when the flow of lava changed, and the members of the order knew to take them in their stride. The sun was approaching the horizon now, the pale sky heralding its rise. It would be a portent of the greatest evil if the Paean were to fail at this point. The swelling voices held steady and he raised his arms high and wide, joining with the order in this gesture of reverence and joy. The cowl of his hood fell back from his head, leaving his dark head as the unseen burning disc lifted higher, preparing to send its first bright ray scything across the peak. Ruvar's greeting sprang full-throated from his exulting soul.

✢ ✢ ✢ ✢ ✢

Sullyan raised herself painfully from the ground, shaking grit from her eyes and hair. Her ears rang with the shock of the tunnel's collapse and her clothing was full of dust. It took her a few moments to realize her enemy was laughing.

"What chance is there now, witch? You're trapped in here with me. The Holy Power of God's retribution means I can stop you from leaving if I choose. I can draw on His strength to keep you from the Veils, and you will never see the sun again unless you yield to my control."

His hideous drawl slid effortlessly from his tongue and his ruby eyes glittered as he drank in her fear. She was all too aware that his boast was not idle. His symbiosis through the cane gave him greater affinity with the spellsilver than she had. It was part of his body now, part of his soul, and he would deploy it swifter than she could ever hope to do. She may have taken in some of his essence with the splinters of cane, but he'd had months to accept its total fusion with his blood. Without even knowing it, he had learned its enhancing effects, and the gruesome experiments she knew he had conducted must have bonded it ever more firmly to the patterns of his brain. Unless she could bring about his death without recourse to hard steel, she was trapped for as long as she could survive in this underground hellhole with its curtains of dancing steam.

Dancing steam?

She snapped her gaze to the rockfall, ignoring the Baron's incessant taunts. His voice spiraled into hysteria as he gloated over his triumph. She feigned defeated submission as she scanned the pile of rock for gaps or cracks and finding none. So where was the air coming from that stirred the wafting steam?

She could not use her metaforce to probe for the signature of Air. He was bound to sense that. Although whether he would guess her intention was beyond her powers to know. Instead, she used her normal senses, those of smell and touch, trying to feel the direction from which the draft entered the cave. It had to be somewhere higher up, for she had seen no fissures in the wall, and as she watched the flow of the wreaths of steam, she gained a rough impression as to where to direct her gaze.

She could still hear the chant of the Paean and knew it was nearing its joyful climax. The sun would rise any minute to cast its piercing rays over the volcano's rim. Her panic rose too, knowing she had but one slender chance, and her eyes finally lit on the thinnest of fissures high up in the cavern roof. Praying for fortune and guidance, she used a tiny burst of elemental power, one she hoped the Baron would not detect. It confirmed what she had hardly dared to believe, but she reined in her surge of hope, knowing she was far from safe and her precarious plan far from assured. Thrusting her doubts to the back of her mind and concealing her working as best she could, she readied a needle of power as she turned back to the ranting man.

✣ ✣ ✣ ✣ ✣

Ruvar gave throat to his Paean, exulting in the day, sending thanks to his deity for the renewed Turn of the Wheel. The sudden lurch of the crater's rim, more powerful than those before, hardly registered as he communed with the force of the sun, and the voices of the order didn't falter. Ruvar concentrated on timing his sun-song precisely with the first golden ray, and his voice changed in pitch, spiraling jubilantly upward as the ray struck his figure.

The voices of his fellows, due to weave and mesh with his, were marred by a discordant shrieking as rock suddenly punched out of the side of the crater, arcing into the air over the bowl and falling like slingshot into the volcano's maw. The rim of the bowl sagged and slipped right from under Ruvar's feet. He was only just saved from a fatal plunge by Varian. The elderly cleric dragged him away from the fall, and both men stared in appalled fascination at the doorway-sized hole that had opened up in the side of the crater's bowl.

Ruvar shouted frantically for the members of his order to leave the crest. Shoving away from Varian, he directed the man to his right, trusting the formerly battle-trained cleric to know what to do. Ruvar himself went left, shepherding his people away, all the time mindful of the slippage and the cavernous, gaping rent. Thick white steam billowed from the hole and Ruvar feared an imminent eruption, although the tremors he could feel through the rock weren't quite right. Side vents had been known to form, however, and the Cleric Patrio feared they were witnessing the birth of one of these. He was still overseeing the flight of his people when a terrible scream froze everyone in their tracks.

✛ ✛ ✛ ✛ ✛

Sullyan strained her ears to hear the clerics' song, channeling it through her bones, striving to keep the purpose from showing in her eyes. This could be her final chance to halt the Baron's threat and she nursed the powerful needle of force as she timed the Paean's chant. She must not move too soon or he would have time to react and form a shield, but one second too late and the power would mute. She must hit him with its full primal force if her desperate ploy was to succeed. The strength she spent to rein in her hope caused a trembling in her limbs.

The scarecrow watched her as he continued his taunts, pleased with the fear he could taste in the air. The submissive angle of her head hid the tension in her quivering body. And when she stood and raised her eyes to his, tears standing in their depths, she sensed his malignant joy as she held her hands out, palms open toward him. He recognized the gesture of surrender, as she was sure he would. He had been too long at Elias's court not to be aware of the codes they followed. Grinning, his ruined eyes red with lust, he faced her across the pool.

"So, witch-girl, you finally acknowledge me and accept you cannot win? What a shame it took you so long to realize I was right! You could have saved yourself much effort if you had listened to me before. Maybe then I would have been merciful in the manner of your death." His useless eyes narrowed with the anticipation of what was to come. The thought of what he would do with her body and strength stretched the rictus of his lips, sending fresh blood trickling down his chin.

"But you pushed me too far for mercy with your futile resistance and petty attacks, and now I am not disposed to make your passing easy. However, if you kneel to me and acknowledge me as your master, I might just make it swift. Which is it to be, Artesan girl? The choice is yours, but do not delay."

Sullyan did not—the moment was upon her. She fell to her knees on the silver-splashed stone, holding out her open hands as if in supplication. She saw his lustful sneer at this gesture of capitulation, but it turned to fury as her needle of force punched out. He screamed in rage as it arrowed toward the roof, seeking the tiny fissure and the opening to the sky. He thrust down with his cane as the Earth force cracked the solid rock, blasting through the fissure with unstoppable might. But the cane never touched the molten ore and his scream gurgled horribly in his throat as a pure ray of blinding sunlight streaked unerringly toward his breast. It struck him in the heart and tore through his fragile shield, ripping at his essence with elemental force. Then it flashed on downward and struck the molten pool, turning the dancing golden flames into an inferno of raging hell.

Sullyan ducked her head, making herself small, covering her eyes with her hands and frantically trying to save herself from the chaos she had released. She dimly heard the scarecrow bubble a hideous cry as the skin that remained on his crooked bones was flayed and shredded by the light.

Burning agony assailed her as the flames consumed the ore, vaporizing the silver in great geysers of exploding power. The rock that formed the cavern, solidified lava from far below, melted and slumped once more in the swiftly intensifying heat. Panic engulfed her as her shield began to fail, and she scrabbled at the jagged floor, desperate to escape. But the Baron had blocked the entrance and the hole she had made was too high. She was trapped inside the chamber with the terrifying forces of the sun. She clawed painfully toward the rockfall that barred the tunnel's mouth and curled up at its base as tightly as she could. With her arms wrapped around her head and her legs drawn against her belly, she tried to use her metaforce to mute the inferno's effects.

The scarecrow was unrecognizable, a jumble of wet, bloody sticks, but the red malice still bloomed from his eyes. He shrilled in agony, mindless and deranged, and the transformed hand still clutched the cane, which inched fatally toward the pool. The blinding light muted as the rising sun's rays drew away, and the chaos of the vaporizing spellsilver slowly waned. The gleaming wet bone that housed those ruby eyes turned on a grisly neck to stare across the pool. Gasps of malignant fury issued from the dripping throat as the all-but-destroyed body dragged itself closer to the edge. The cane touched the surface of the sluggishly rolling ore.

The final ray of sunlight flashed out of existence, catching a stray droplet of spellsilver balanced on the lip of the treacherous pool. The heat and light of that last ray caused the droplet to explode, and it shot up into the cavern roof with a faint pop. The rock that hung above it, right in the projectile's path, had been loosened by the maelstrom and it quivered from the impact. It fell lazily, striking the silver surface and sinking without a trace. The ripples of its fall lapped at the pools' fragile rim, eating more rock away. The stone that supported the scarecrow crumbled at its touch, tipping the dying creature gently over the edge.

Sullyan uncovered her head as she heard a hideous, gurgling scream and cast her gaze across the pool just as the scarecrow slipped within, catching the final, terrible gleam of his eyes before the spellsilver closed over his dissolving bones with a heaving, sucking hiss. The transmuted cane appeared briefly out of the dripping ore before vanishing into the depths with no sound.

She glanced around, seeing the total ruin their battle had made of the cavern. The walls had melted and slumped, and the roof looked none too safe. She couldn't see how to escape this prison of juddering rock. There came a faint, hissing rumble somewhere far below that shivered menacingly through her nerves, bringing a fresh stab of fear to her heart. She turned to face the pool once more and her eyes widened in shock. The entire silver surface was bulging upward with alarming speed.

She cast frantically about for somewhere to shelter, for if the viscous liquid should geyser and burst, its power would be too much for her weakened shield to handle. She could only just maintain it as it was, and she had no strength left to form a portway. But there was nowhere to run to. All the niches and hollows had disappeared when the rock had slumped. She was totally exposed and vulnerable to the spellsilver's destructive force. All she could do was curl up as before beneath what shield she could maintain with the remnants of her waning strength.

As the vast upwelling of molten spellsilver ruptured, punching into the air with an ear-shattering roar, she could swear she heard the scarecrow scream.

Chapter Twenty-Six

Ruvar and Varian only just got their people clear before the terrifying, majestic silver geyser shot up towards the sun. The initial small hole in the crater's side was utterly destroyed by that savage, vengeful blast, and huge projectiles of jagged rock flew hundreds of feet into the air. The screaming clerics covered their heads and fled for what shelter there was, hearing the ominous rumble that heralded the rim's collapse.

A cacophony of destruction beat about their heads as the heavy molten silver fell back toward the bowl, splattering steaming droplets over a wide area. Dust obscured the sun, still so newly risen, abrading exposed skin and clogging the clerics' lungs. A deafening roar signaled the crater's collapse, and when the din died away, desolation met their sight. A whole section of the rim had given way, falling down upon itself through the ragged hole left by the geyser.

✢ ✢ ✢ ✢ ✢

After his ordeal at the Baron's hands, Taran had mercifully fallen asleep. Exhausted by fear, by his terrible wound, and by the betrayal he had been forced to commit, his shattered brain could take no more and simply shut down, hiding him away from the terrors he had seen. His friends sat watching him, trying to come to terms with what he had told them. After a long time, it was Rienne who finally found the courage to speak.

"Do you think there's any hope?"

Her toneless, fatigued voice tugged at Bull's heartstrings. He felt his eyes prick with tears for the fear he saw in her face. He sat by her side, on the edge of Taran's bed, his arm around her shoulders as much for his comfort as hers. Ralf and Dexter stood by the doorway, their faces shadowed.

Bull kept his voice low so as not to disturb Taran, although he doubted the Adept would wake for hours—if indeed he ever did. "Oh, dear heart, there's always hope." He tightened his hold on Rienne, pulling her against his chest. She allowed herself to melt into him, grateful for his steadfast loyalty. "Don't write her off just yet. She's come out of other situations as grim as this, and you know which ones I mean."

Rienne sighed, but Bull knew his words gave her no strength. How many times could one woman overcome such insurmountable obstacles? Luck had played its part in many of her successes. Sooner or later, Bull's commonsense told him, the luck would surely run out.

"How will we know, Bull?" Rienne whispered into his chest. "And what do I do if it all goes awry?"

He turned to look into her face. The pallor of her skin accentuated the soft gray of her eyes, huge and dilated in the shadows of the room. "What do you mean?"

She glanced up at him. "They're my responsibility. What do I do if the Baron gets his way? How can I watch them slowly fade before my eyes? How can I stand it if he torments them before they die?"

Bull closed his eyes, hearing Dexter and Ralf's soft gasps. None of them had dared to think about the consequences of failure. Rienne, ever practical, ever capable and caring, had clearly been sitting there considering what they might be forced to do. His admiration for her increased by several bounds, high though it already was.

"I'm not giving up just yet." He held up a hand against her protest. "But I'm not dodging the issue, either. If it comes to it, you can rely on us to do what's necessary. None of us will see them suffer, I can guarantee you that. Although all we can do is relieve the torment of their bodies, for if the Baron overcomes Sully, their souls are truly damned."

Rienne ducked her head at the bald truth of his words, unable to think the unthinkable, and wiped angrily at her eyes. She drew in a deep breath and seemed to come to a decision. "I want them all together, Bull." She pushed free of his arm and he looked up at her as she rose from the bed. "If the Baron has captured Brynne, the end's not far away. Whichever way it goes, I'd rather they were all together where I can watch over them, even if I can do nothing else. And it might make things easier if you have to … you know."

Nothing could possibly make such a terrible deed any easier, Bull thought grimly. Yet he couldn't deny that Rienne's decision felt right. All of those involved in caring for the captives would derive comfort from being together, and Rienne might not feel so alone with the other healers in the room. He nodded and left the room to organize the move.

It didn't take long to move the four victims' beds back to the main room of the healer suite. With the press of men and healers, the vast space seemed cramped and crowded, but Bull found it perversely comforting after the quiet of the smaller rooms. All the beds were close to each other, with Jinny and Taran side by side, Robin next to Jinny, and Sofira on the end. King Elias, drawn and weary, still cradled his former wife, and Aldo stood beside him as he had done all along. Ralf stood close by Taran, with Wil attending Jinny. Cal sat on Robin's bed, watching the Major's face.

Tad hadn't returned after his tearful breakdown and Bull couldn't blame the lad for not wanting to witness the end.

Once he had seen the Major settled, Cal reported that Robin had been murmuring vague, distressing half-cries. Now, however, the Major was silent, his weakened body barely breathing. Even Sofira had ceased her incessant, mindless moaning. They all seemed far too silent for Bull's liking. Hanan accompanied Rienne as she took their vital signs, counting each shallow inhalation and each thready pulse. They pulled back eyelids and watched the jaundiced orbs, clearly not liking what they saw. Bull waited as anxiously as everyone else in the room. They all involuntarily held their breath as Rienne faced them once she was done.

"They're all lapsing into coma." She spoke tonelessly, her eyes betraying nothing, but Bull could sense the fear she tried to hide. She glanced at Hanan as if for confirmation, but carried on before the Chief Healer could react. "Taran and Jinny are fading faster due to those dreadful wounds, but by my estimation … if things continue as they are, chances are they'll all die before noon tomorrow."

There were murmurs and a shifting of feet as the men took this in. One of them, Rhyn, cleared his throat, his manner diffident.

"You said noon tomorrow, Healer Arlen, but which tomorrow do you mean? It's dawn already. I pray you don't mean noon today."

Rienne stared at Rhyn in utter dismay and Bull realized she'd had no idea of the hour. They all saw the draining of her already pale face and read the defeat in the slump of her shoulders.

"Is it dawn already?" she whispered, turning to the silent victims. "Well, if Brynne fails to defeat the Baron, this is the last day they will ever see."

In the ensuing shocked silence, Bull once again gathered Rienne to him in a bear hug. She clung to his arms, muffling her sobs against his chest while Cal looked on helplessly, unable to leave his post.

Bull was jolted from his despair by the terrible screams that burst simultaneously from each of the captives. They echoed about the treatment room like a thousand dying banshees. Everyone jumped and the guards leaped to subdue them as they writhed on the beds, their bodies helplessly caught in the torment of their minds. Rienne and Hanan rushed to administer what soporifics they could, but before they could prepare the infusions, the tumult stopped. Four bodies went as limp as death, heads falling back, faces drawn and white. Rienne and Hanan approached them fearfully, almost reluctant to check for signs of life. Those standing by held their collective breath once again, eyes fixed firmly on the healers' faces as they did their work.

Hanan and Rienne exchanged glances, neither wanting to admit what they both knew, and it was Rienne who eventually faced them, her voice trembling with tears.

"They're not dead yet, but they soon will be. Something has happened to either the Baron or to Brynne, maybe to both of them. They only have hours left—possibly less if the Baron has won and no longer needs them alive. There's nothing more we can do for them now, except be here at the end."

Shoulders slumped and faces fell, a few tears were wiped away. No one wanted to show weakness while their friends were still alive. Many of the men slid to sitting positions against the wall, their legs unable to hold them. Bull detailed one of them to run to General Blaine with the news. He accompanied the man to the door and slipped through it after him. There was something he had to do and he daren't tell Rienne what it was.

He strode down the corridors and emerged from the College, reaching immediately for his psyche to quest for a well-loved pattern. The spellsilver in the healer suite had prevented him doing this before, but he *had* to know for certain what had become of her. He held her pattern before his eyes and cast it through the substrate, desperately calling, pleading for her to respond.

His heart felt like a lead weight within him when the substrate over Lerric's palace yielded no sign of her pattern. There was recent disruption; he could read that much, but not enough to tell him what had happened. He could sense a variety of intense emotions, but the maelstrom of emanations only confused him. He was so involved in his search that he didn't hear the running footsteps, nor did he register the shallow, breathless voice. It was only when he felt his shoulder gripped that he was distracted from his search, and he returned to himself with an effort to see Tad standing in front of him. The young swordsman's face was pale with fright. He gripped Bull's shoulder with tense and urgent fingers.

Bull frowned at the state of him. "What is it, lad, what's happened now?"

Tad swallowed, visibly trying to steady himself. "It's Drum, the Colonel's horse. I was passing his stall when I heard him squealing, and I opened the top door to check on him. He was dripping with sweat and circling restlessly, and when he saw me he just went mad! Plunging and kicking and trying to jump over the stable door. Solet heard the noise and came running. He vaulted over the door and tried to get a twitch on him, but Drum wouldn't let him near. He kicked him pretty badly—I had to help him out."

Bull huffed sourly. "I'm not surprised Solet got kicked if the idiot tried a twitch. Serves him right! What happened then? Did the beast calm down?"

Tad shook his head, uncertainty in his eyes. "No, he didn't. If anything, he got worse. He was whirling round in the stall, screaming and bucking, doing his damnedest to break down the walls. I've never seen him like that before—I've never seen any horse so distressed! I was frightened he'd hurt himself, so I opened the door and let him out."

Bull didn't like the sound if this. "What did he do?"

"Shot off down the track as if all the devils in Perdition were after him. He's disappeared over the ridge. I heard him screaming that war cry of his for some time, but then it faded. The gods know where he's gone." The lad turned frightened eyes on the big man, desperately fearful of what he might hear, yet compelled to ask the question. "Why would he suddenly turn mad, Bull? Has anything happened I should know about?"

Bull was only too afraid he knew the reason for the stallion's distress. Sullyan had hand-raised him from a newborn foal when his vicious dam nearly killed him. The two of them were linked in a very special way. Her death might just drive the stallion to burst his faithful heart.

Bull's own heart clenched as he told Tad what they knew— Taran's enforced betrayal and the captives' weakening condition. The young swordsman turned even paler and swayed on his feet. Bull placed a hand on the lad's shoulder to steady him.

"Go back to Robin, lad, if you can stand it. It might be the last chance you get. I think he might still gain some comfort from sensing you're close. We'll all need whatever support we can get if what we suspect comes to pass. And if the Baron has killed her and taken her power, some tough decisions will have to be made. I'm counting on you to be a part of that. They're our friends and it's a responsibility none of us can shirk."

Tad stared at Bull from huge, despairing eyes, looking as if he was about to be sick, but then he nodded and turned away, heading into the College. Bull stood locked in place, his eyes dry and sore, his heart aching fiercely with every labored beat. It was an ache that had nothing to do with the current state of his health.

✢ ✢ ✢ ✢ ✢

Ruvar glanced up from the man he was tending as Varian ushered in yet another casualty, this one a young woman. The elderly cleric helped her into a chair and called for the healer, who answered irritably from another room. The community only included one trained healer, and although he had assistants, they were already stretched to their limits. It was fortunate none of the injuries was life threatening.

Varian reassured the woman and left her nursing the angry red burn on her leg where the exploding ore had splashed her skin.

"Are there many more?"

Varian replied gruffly to his Patrio's question. "None serious enough to need the attentions of a healer. The rest are treating each other, mainly for bruises and scrapes. But they're all frightened. I've heard some muttered comments about punishment and retribution."

Ruvar's dark brows rose. "What do you mean, retribution? They're surely not saying the eruption was chastisement for something we've done?"

"Something you've done, to be precise."

Ruvar froze. "What?"

Varian steered him out of the healer's cottage. There were too many flapping ears and rumors were quick enough to spread as it was, even among such a silent Order. They emerged into the chilly dawn, wind whipping at their robes. The early sun did nothing to take the frost from the air. They walked toward the small cluster of houses and Ruvar rounded on Varian as soon as they were out of earshot.

"Come on, old friend, just what are they saying?"

"They're saying it's because of the Baron, because you allowed him to be imprisoned here. They're also questioning your wisdom in permitting Brynne Sullyan to come and investigate his death. They're saying Elias has no jurisdiction here, that Artesans have caused this, that their powers are an abomination and that we as a Holy Order should have nothing whatever to do with people who profess to control the forces of nature. The crater's collapse right under your feet was a sign of God's wrath. They're saying these things because they're frightened."

Ruvar could understand their fear. The volcano was a mighty force that should not be taken lightly. Yet to tie this relatively small event to the powers of Artesans, or to things beyond his control, or to his conversations with Brynne Sullyan, was taking it just too far. The trouble was the volcano had been quiescent for so long they had all forgotten what it could do. In years past it had been more active, making regular minor eruptions, mainly of steam, and issuing small vents underwater that bubbled and frothed the sea. For decades it had held its sulfurous breath. Now, when it let forth a tiny belch, they saw portents of doom and divine retribution.

Still, he was the Cleric Patrio and it was his duty to soothe his people's fears. If that meant facing their criticisms, so be it. His guidance in the ways of their faith had never been questioned before. He had to make them realize this was just one more turn of the Wheel. The volcano would erupt in earnest one day—it was simply part of the natural cycle.

He turned to Varian to tell him his decision when a startling scream rent the air. "What the Void is that?" he blurted.

Varian's face was a picture of amazement as the strident blaring sounded again. The older man turned shocked eyes on Ruvar, his mouth hanging open.

"Unless I'm much mistaken, that's the cry of a very angry stallion!"

Varian had experience with horses, although it was many years in the past, and he ought to recognize one when he heard it. Yet it simply wasn't possible for a horse to be on the island. Even if one had been brought over by boat, there was no way it could have climbed the stairs from the landing. Ruvar felt fully justified in his scorn. "Don't be ridiculous! It can't be a—"

"Look out!" Varian thrust him roughly aside as the deafening clatter of hooves on stone heralded the appearance of a huge, dark, flying blur. It burst around a corner of the track leading down from the crest, feathered hooves skidding on the frost-rimed rock and showering them both with grit. It belled its furious call once again, eyes and nostrils red and wild, and Ruvar covered his ears as it thundered past, heading toward the stairway leading down to the magma passage.

It would surely fall and break a leg, he thought as he and Varian started to follow. Then a dark-robed cleric raced into view and Ruvar stopped as he heard his name called.

"Patrio! Did it come past here? Where has it gone?"

Ruvar indicated the steps between the rocks, where the chaotic clatter of iron-shod hooves on stone suddenly changed to the booming of wood under attack, punctuated by screams.

"Where did it come from?" he demanded, grabbing the cleric's arm. The man turned rolling eyes toward him, gasping for breath.

"It appeared out of thin air right in front of me! Nearly knocked me into the crater as it barged past. It ran toward the slippage, screaming that awful noise, and then turned around took off down the track. It nearly trampled some of us and I think one of the younger boys was kicked. None of them will come down here while it's rampaging about like that. Is it some kind of demon, Patrio? Has it been sent to destroy us?"

Ruvar chose to ignore the impossibility of the creature's presence. "No, of course not, Emer, it's just a horse!" He waved Varian toward the steps. "Now go back and check on that boy, and keep everyone else away. Varian and I will deal with this. Go."

318

Emer turned to retrace his steps while Ruvar followed Varian to the top of the stair in the rock. "You sound very confident," the elderly Frar said dryly. "Just how do you propose we 'deal' with that?" He jerked a thumb in the direction of the booming cacophony coming from below.

Ruvar started down the stairs. "You know about horses. Can't you think of anything?"

"How about a throwing knife or a crossbow?" Varian's muttered sarcasm was drowned by the enraged stallion's screaming. Setting his mouth in a grim line, he followed Ruvar down.

They could see skid marks on the steps where the iron-shod hooves had flailed, and when the beast came into sight, its legs were running with blood from scrapes in its ebony hide. None of the cuts was serious, judging by the way it used its heels. Ruvar could hardly credit the door still held under the frantic pounding. He stood back to let Varian come past him, the elderly cleric looking apprehensive. He made soothing noises as he approached the plunging beast.

The stallion's eyes were wild and rolling, the whites showing starkly against the black. His muzzle dripped foam that streaked his chest and his sleek neck was frothy with sweat. Fury personified, he did indeed look like a demon from the netherworld.

To Ruvar's amazement, the horse ceased his determined pounding and tossed his magnificent head, belling an urgent cry to the man approaching him. Varian, encouraged by the sudden calm, stretched a cautious hand to the damp nose and gently stroked the velvety skin. The horse snorted and took a step forward, butting Varian squarely in the chest. The elderly cleric staggered under the force and Ruvar's heart stopped, but the horse made no move against Varian, instead backing up once more to the door and executing another savage buck, thudding both hind feet into the wood.

319

"I think he wants to get in there," Ruvar said.

Varian shot him an irritable look. "Whatever gave you that idea?" He shook himself and approached the door, murmuring to the horse. He had to pass its considerable bulk to release the latch and Ruvar held his breath, mindful of Emer's comment that the beast had kicked a young boy. Yet the horse stayed still while Varian squeezed past, merely turning his head to watch. His dripping mane hung in rat's-tails and his breath heaved in his chest. As soon as Varian pulled the battered door open, the stallion squeezed awkwardly round and shoved past the cleric into the tunnel.

Varian gave a grunt as he was squashed, but Ruvar didn't stop to check how he was. He ran straight past and followed the charging beast. The hooves sounded louder than thunder in the confines of the tunnel and Ruvar was amazed the horse could fit down this narrow space. Indeed, the rock showed smears of blood from scrapes to its hide, but it didn't falter or slow. It even miraculously avoided three venting fissures as it careered toward its objective. Ruvar pounded after it, Varian wheezing in his wake.

They heard the stallion's shrill scream of fury when the rockfall came into view. The incredible sight of the enraged beast literally pulverizing rock with its powerful forefeet would stay with Ruvar forever. Small chunks and gritty powder shot out from under the horse's frantic, stamping hooves. Ruvar had to shield his eyes from the flying debris. Varian puffed up behind him, transfixed by the beast's single-mindedness, and he didn't immediately hear Ruvar when the Patrio spoke in his ear.

"What?" he exclaimed when Ruvar repeated his order, shouting over the noise. "I've nearly killed myself following you and now you want me to run back up there to fetch more men? How much breath do you think I have?"

"Unless you have the communication skills of an Artesan,

your legs will have to cope. That horse is convinced there's something or someone buried under that rockfall, and I have a terrible suspicion who it is. Now will you go?"

Varian raised his eyes to the ceiling, but forbore to comment, turning on his heel and sprinting away. For all his age and complaining, Ruvar knew he would cope. Varian kept himself fit, a hangover from his swordsman days. Ruvar dismissed him from his mind and turned back to watching the horse, marveling anew at how much rock those powerful hooves had already turned to dust.

Chapter Twenty-Seven

arian soon returned with ten men from the order, all of them young and fit, all of them concerned. The morning's events had been strange enough. Shifting rock at the behest of a horse—which shouldn't be here at all—was just one more impossible occurrence. Varian didn't let them dwell on the peculiarities. He and Ruvar directed them in the shifting of the rock, mightily relieved when the horse stayed out of the way once it realized the fall was being removed.

The lava rock was mercifully light, although jagged and awkward to handle. The men made a chain down the tunnel and piled the loose rock to one side. Dust and pulverized pumice filled their lungs with every breath and the sulfurous tang to the air added to their discomfort. They made slow but steady headway, removing much of the collapsed tunnel roof, although they could see that the cavern behind was also filled with rock.

The extent of the devastation alarmed Varian. "How far are we going with this, Patrio? We can't clear the entire cavern. It would take weeks!"

The clerics ceased their labor as Ruvar straightened his own aching back and wiped the sharp dust from his hands. Like them all, his robes were impregnated with powdered rock, his hair and skin coated with it.

"We'll just—" He got no further, for the stallion stamped his forehoof and belled a plaintive cry. Ruvar would have taken no notice, as it was not the first time the horse had done such a thing. Every few moments he stamped and called, deafening those trying to help him and making the more nervous clerics jump aside. This time, however, Ruvar froze, holding up his hand for silence. In the ensuing quiet, he heard the faintest of sounds. "Did you hear that, Varian?"

They watched the stallion closely as he pawed urgently at the rock. He snorted at the ground, snaking his head down close to the rocks, putting his muzzle to a tiny chink and blowing through his nose. Ruvar pushed past Varian and went down on his knees beside the snuffling nose. "Brynne? Brynne, can you hear me?"

Varian frowned." What makes you think it's her?"

Ruvar waved an impatient hand. "Damn!" He climbed to his feet, ignoring his clerics' scandalized expressions. "I'm sure I heard her voice, although I can't hear anything now. But this black beast knows there's something there, so let's get this lot shifted. Concentrate on this side, close to the floor, and watch out that none of the rest of it falls on our heads."

Another fifteen minutes of effort saw the majority of the rock shifted out of the way. The black stallion grew more and more agitated, and Varian left the heavy work to try to calm it down. The horse kept trying to barge past the clerics as if he thought they weren't working fast enough, and Ruvar was concerned someone would get hurt. He was also worried the horse might bring down more of the roof with his pawing and stamping, but try as he might, Varian could not persuade him to back away. The beast simply dug in his heels and refused to budge. Instead, he stood in front of those lethal iron-shod feet, just daring the stallion to trample him, and the horse finally quieted except for his incessant, plaintive cries.

"Patrio!" It was a man closest to the rockfall who shouted, and Ruvar scrambled forward to see what he had found. Peering through a small hole between the rocks, he could just make out burnt clothing and a tumble of tawny hair. There was no movement and no sound. He beckoned to the men, urging them to hurry as he lifted off another rock. They all bent to it with renewed energy and soon had her uncovered. It was left to Ruvar to lift her in his arms.

She was unconscious and barely even breathing. Her combat leathers and linen shirt were burned almost through to her skin. Her face was covered in scratches and blood mixed up with grit and dust, and globules of molten silver had solidified in her hair. Yet she was alive, and the stallion belled out a greeting, trampling one of Varian's feet as he surged forward to nuzzle her arm. The cleric gasped and shoved frantically at the horse's shoulder, cursing.

"I've got to get her into fresh air. Just make sure the fall's as safe as it can be and then get yourselves out of there!"

Ruvar strode back up the tunnel, the stallion walking almost on his heels, dusty black muzzle thrust over the Patrio's shoulder. Varian prevailed on one of the younger men and used his shoulder as a crutch, swearing under his breath and hobbling on his bruised foot as he followed the stallion's tail. He was careful not to get too close to its powerful hindquarters, despite being sure the beast meant him no harm. He had seen too clearly what those muscles were capable of to take any liberties now.

They avoided the venting fissures and emerged back into daylight. Most of the order awaited them, grouped around the stair. There were gasps and mutters of consternation as Ruvar emerged, but he ignored them all and made for the healer's cottage, disappearing inside. The horse's bulk blocked the doorway and he would let no one else by, but he didn't attempt to force his way through the narrow door, contenting himself with pushing his head in as far as it would go.

The healer gave the snorting black head one single disapproving glance before turning his attention to the burden Ruvar carried. "Put her over there." Ruvar laid Sullyan down where indicated, standing back to let the healer do his work. He caught sight of Varian's face at the window and gave his friend a grateful smile. The elderly cleric merely grimaced.

The healer checked Sullyan over, looking for broken bones and internal bleeding. He clucked his tongue and shook his head while he worked. For all that her clothes were burned completely through in places, it seemed she had escaped serious injury. He looked down at Ruvar, who was using a dampened cloth to clean her face. "Are you sure she was actually under the rockfall, Patrio? There were some hollows in the walls of the Holy Cavern. Perhaps she'd taken shelter in one of those? If the roof had collapsed as you say, perhaps you didn't realize how far inside you had gone?"

Ruvar shrugged. "She was lying on the floor in what would have been the entrance, Cael. The rocks were lying directly on top of her."

Cael shrugged. "Then she's an incredibly lucky young woman. There are no breaks and no bleeding, as far as I can tell. But I really ought to do a more thorough examination. Perhaps one of the women would—"

He broke off as Sullyan stirred under Ruvar's ministrations. She gave a breathy groan and opened her eyes. Cael jumped in alarm as the stallion suddenly shook his tangled mane and let loose a deafening whinny, ending with a vast snort that sprayed the healer with foam.

"Drum?" Sullyan's voice was husky with dust and barely audible, but the stallion heard her. He rumbled deep in his chest, bobbing his head. Her sore eyes looked past Cael's figure and she smiled when she saw the black bulk filling the doorway.

Cael slapped angrily at his spattered robes. "I would be much obliged to you, young woman, if you would persuade your beast to withdraw from my house. This is a place of healing and that animal is hardly hygienic!"

Ruvar made a noise of protest, but Sullyan managed a weak smile, waving an exhausted hand in the direction of the door. "Drum, out." The huge beast withdrew, the clatter of his hooves mixing with exclamations of alarm from those outside who had crowded too close. "My apologies, Healer."

Cael nodded, dismissing the incident. "We need to get you cleaned up and out of those ruined clothes."

Sullyan forestalled him by struggling to sit. Ruvar, whose first instinct was to restrain her, found himself helping her instead, his arm under her shoulders. She looked him over. "Ruvar? Are you quite well? You seem very pale."

Ruvar gave a snort of laughter, not sure whether she was joking or confused. "I've just spent the best part of an hour digging you out of that cavern! What with the effort and the dust, I think I'm entitled to look pale. You don't look so good yourself, if you don't mind me saying. Are you going to tell us what happened down there?"

Sullyan clearly wasn't listening. His first sentence had pierced her exhaustion and her ashen face drained still further as his words registered. She stared at him from huge, fixed eyes. "What hour is it?"

He frowned. "What?"

She gripped his arm hard. "What hour is it? How long after sunrise?"

He glanced at Cael, who shrugged. "About two hours after dawn, I think, maybe a bit less."

"Two hours!" She groaned, pushing herself from his arm. "I have to go ..."

"You're not fit to go anywhere."

Ignoring Ruvar's protest, she struggled to her feet, the scorched remnants of her linen shirt barely covering her body. Her jacket was burned beyond repair and lay in tatters on the floor.

"I have to, Ruvar. You do not understand. Help me to my horse, will you?"

Ruvar could see she would struggle there by herself, so he passed an arm about her waist and helped her hobble to the door. She was weak and exhausted from her ordeal and she barely had the energy to stand. She would need all the help she could get. She leaned heavily on Ruvar as he guided her through the door.

Drum whinnied softly as she emerged into the sunlight. Ruvar put his free hand out to ward the huge beast off, but Drum only extended his nose to gently brush her arm. She stretched out a hand and grasped his mane, holding herself steady by leaning against his neck. "Help me up, Ruvar."

Her voice was a whisper, still gritty from dust, and Ruvar looked hard at her before doing as she asked. "Are you sure this is a good idea? You don't look like you'll be able to stay on. It's a long way down from up there, you know."

She managed a wan smile. "I have no choice. Drum will not let me fall."

Shaking his head, Ruvar boosted Sullyan up to Drum's broad back. She clung with both hands to his tangled mane and gave the worried Patrio a grateful smile. "You and your clerics have my heartfelt thanks. If I can, I will return and explain myself to you, but for now, forgive me. I must go."

Drum whinnied again and moved off past the dwellings, heading for the track that led to the volcano's crest. The gathered clerics hastened out of his way and Ruvar stood and watched as he bunched his powerful quarters, springing into a gallop at his exhausted rider's request. He disappeared around the rocks, the thunder of his hooves loud in the morning air, and then abruptly there was silence.

Ruvar knew they had gone. Staring up the track in the direction of her passing, the Cleric Patrio remained standing long after his clerics left.

✠ ✠ ✠ ✠ ✠

Sullyan hung on to Drum's powerful neck, trusting the stallion to bear her safely. She had no energy left with which to part the Veils and left their passage to Drum, blessing the beast's inherent instinct to guide them back home. There was none of the preparation she always had to make. Drum merely scented his home and followed his nose until he got there.

When she first discovered he had inherited this talent from his sire, she attempted to probe his equine mind, looking for the mechanism that permitted him to part the Veils. An animal's brain, however, differed too fundamentally from a human's. Drum didn't analyze what he could do and she had to resign herself to accepting she would never know. Such thoughts were far from her weary mind now, however. She was too full of concern for her friends and the very real fear that she was already too late. Clinging to Drum and urging him to speed, she prayed as hard as she could.

Drum emerged from the shimmer of his passage and the Veils closed behind him as if they had never been rent. He careered up the lane leading to the horse lines, belling his challenge and rousing the entire herd. Even the brood mares in the farthest pastures heard his calls and threw their heads up, answering, as their herd leader thundered past. The youngsters at their flanks squealed and kicked their heels, prancing in gangly fashion across the frost-rimed grass. The black stud ignored them all. His calls were not for them. Neither were they for the stable lads, who ran yelling from the barns. He rocketed past the stables, leaving them wide-eyed in his wake, the hobbling stablemaster glaring angrily after him. He continued up to the Manor, blaring his clarion-call, and scattered gravel in a widening arc as he slithered to a stop outside the College.

One of the students heard the commotion and flung the College doors wide. As soon as she saw the snorting beast, she ran for the healer suite.

✥ ✥ ✥ ✥ ✥

Rienne sat with Cal's arm around her waist, silently watching over the comatose bodies of their friends. Not one of them had stirred or made a sound since dawn, and they were visibly fading. The men of Sullyan's company were ranged about the room, some sitting on the floor, some standing, all grim-faced and pale. The healers hovered among them, unsure how to help. Hanan stayed close by Rienne, watching over them all.

Elias sat cradling Sofira, her limp body cold in his arms. He sat on her bed with his eyes closed, an expression of deep sorrow on his lined and weary face. Tad clutched Robin's hand, his eyes despairing and red. Every now and then he would sniffle and wipe his nose on his sleeve. Taran and Jinny now shared the same bed, their hands laid close together. Rienne had insisted they be side by side, for what comfort it might give. But there was no comfort and no hope. None of them could possibly survive. They were too far gone in decline.

Bull stood with his back to the door, brooding on what he knew. He had not said a word after his abortive search, not to Rienne and not to the men. He couldn't bring himself to tell them her psyche was nowhere to be found. He couldn't be the one to admit the Baron must have triumphed at the end. He stood with his eyes downcast and his hand gripping his sword, preparing himself for the inevitable and trying to control the pain in his chest.

The door burst open behind him, taking them all by surprise. It thudded into the big man's back, nearly knocking him off his feet.

Wil, who was closest to him, caught him before he fell and steadied him. All heads snapped to the doorway, the sound of several swords being drawn shockingly loud in the room. The young girl who stood there was transfixed by the sight, momentarily as stunned as the rest, but then a raucous whinny broke the stasis, echoing imperiously from outside.

Bull spun on his heel, his face paling. "Drum!" He shot from the room, followed by several of the men. They brushed past the girl and Rienne came to her feet. "What is it, Carid, what's happened?" She grasped the girl's trembling arm. Her eyes widened in disbelief as the girl blurted out what she had seen, and Rienne turned to Cal as the import of the news thudded home. Yet she could sense Cal didn't share her hope, not with Taran lying so still. If the Baron was dead, then so was his master, even if Sullyan still lived. Rienne's flare of hope died and she let Carid's arm drop as she came back to her life mate's side.

They heard voices in the corridor, excited, confused, and overwrought. The incomprehensible babble died down as the approaching footsteps grew louder, and then General Blaine entered the room, followed by Bull and the men. Rienne's eyes lit up at the sight of Sullyan in Bull's arms. She ran across to hug her as the big man set her on her feet.

"Brynne, I don't believe it! We all thought you must be dead."

"So did I." Sullyan's words were barely audible as she returned Rienne's embrace.

The healer stood back to look in her eyes, not quite knowing what to hope for in her friend's answer. "Did you kill him, then?"

"He is dead, although not by my hand. It was sunlight that killed him, but explanations will have to wait. I was unable to force Reen's surrender. There is no time to waste."

A puzzled mutter ran round the men as Rienne led Sullyan toward the victims' beds. "I fear we are already too late. Taran and

Jinny are almost gone, and Robin and Sofira are deep in coma. None of them have stirred since dawn."

Sullyan stood staring down at her friends, her heart lurching painfully as her gaze lingered on Robin's face. Elias looked up wearily from his position on Sofira's bed, and Tad watched her expectantly, as if waiting for her to produce a miracle. His unquestioning faith in her ability to save them sent knives stabbing into her heart.

"Is there anything we can do?" The gruff voice behind her made Sullyan turn as the General approached her.

"There is, Mathias. I do not know if it will work, or whether it is too late or not. All I know is that I must try. But my reserves of metaforce are fearfully low after defending myself from Reen. I will need the help of every Artesan here to stand any chance at all."

The General looked around the room. "You have it, of course." Each Artesan murmured their assent.

She watched their faces. "It will be very draining, and maybe even too much. Mathias, if you intend to instruct Vassa to stand the Loxton garrison down, I suggest you send your messenger now. You may not be capable once we are done."

The General nodded and beckoned to Wil and Rhyn. He steered Carid out of the room with him, saying to Wil, "I want you to go to Andaryon, Corporal."

Sullyan silently thanked him for thinking of Pharikian and Aeyron. It would ease her brother's heart to know Reen was no longer a threat.

Rienne turned from the swordsman she had been talking to and he left the room at a run. "What are you planning to do exactly, Brynne?"

Sullyan seated herself wearily by Robin's side and absently stroked his hand. Tad rose and stood by her shoulder, not taking his eyes from her face.

Sullyan glanced at the swordsman standing by Elias. "Aldo, get some help and bring five more beds over here, please."

He turned wordlessly to carry out her request, many hands making quick work of the task. Sullyan turned to look at Rienne, the depth of her exhaustion plain in her eyes. "I intend to try to reach their souls, but I am not confident of success. I only have a phrase to go on and a feeling that was imparted to me by my father's spirit. I will be attempting something only a Supreme Master has ever done before, and relying on the love of old friends to make the impossible come true."

Rienne frowned in confusion, but Bull gasped in alarm. "You're going to attempt to enter the Spirit realm? Sully, no one even knows if it really exists, let alone if it's possible to enter it! And you know what all the legends say ..." He trailed off and flushed deep red, averting his eyes from the accusation on her face.

The damage had been done, though, and Rienne was no fool. She stared hard at her friend. "Well?" she demanded, hands on hips, a flash of her usual acerbity coming to the fore. "What do the legends say?"

Sullyan sighed, wishing Bull had thought before opening his mouth. "The legends say there is no way back. They say that once a soul has crossed the Void, it can never return to the world." She ignored the murmurs of concern that ran around the room, giving Bull a hard stare instead. "But I am not going to let that stop me from trying."

Chapter Twenty-Eight

Light running footsteps heralded the arrival of the children. With the Baron no longer a threat to them, the General had removed their guards. Morgan, Elisse, and the King's two children came bursting into the room.

"Was that wise, General?" murmured Rienne as Blaine passed her. He glanced at her and shrugged his shoulders.

"They have a right to see those they love, Healer, and it may be their last chance. I don't like it much, I'll admit, but I couldn't deny them. Would you?"

Rienne shook her head, tears in her eyes. She bent to Elisse's upheld arms, enfolding her daughter in a protective embrace and taking comfort from her warmth. She nodded thanks as Blaine told her Carid was looking after Taric. Eadan ran to his father, who scooped him up onto the bed, but Seline just stood staring at her mother's face, her hands clenched into fists at her side. The young Princess's eyes were full of tears and her mouth was a line of fury. She glared at Brynne Sullyan with hatred.

Sullyan didn't see her. She was preoccupied with her son, whose huge blue eyes were fixed in puzzlement on his father's unmoving face. "Why is Papa asleep, Mama?" Morgan stretched out a hand to touch Robin's. Sullyan was too slow to stop him and the child recoiled in shock, turning to his mother with fear shimmering in his eyes. "I can't feel him! Where is he, Mama?"

Sullyan swept him up in both arms, hugging him close. "Hush, Morgan, hush. Your Papa is ill and lost, and we must go on a journey to find him. It may be difficult and it may be dangerous, and I shall need you to be very brave. Do you think you can do that, Morgan? Can you help me bring Papa home?"

Morgan nodded and she embraced him once more, aware of Rienne's presence hovering behind her.

"Is that really such a good idea?" the healer murmured. "What if you can't do it? What if the legends are true? What if none of you can return?"

Sullyan raised her eyes over the crown of Morgan's head, gazing frankly at her friend as she hugged her tearful son. "I will see no harm comes to him, Rienne. I will take no more than he can give and he will be protected with my life. I will not permit him to travel too far. I would never see him trapped. But I believe his presence will call to Robin like a beacon to guide him home, and I can think of no stronger reason for a man to return than for the love of his only son. Can you?"

Rienne could think of another love that might prove as strong, but she merely bowed her head in acceptance. She glanced down, aware of Elisse pulling urgently on her arm. "Mama, Mama, I want to help Morgan bring Papa Robin home. Please, Mama, please!"

Rienne looked over at Sullyan, lips pursed. She didn't want to take the time to explain to Elisse why she couldn't help. Instead, she stared at her friend. "She will be in no danger? You swear it?"

Sullyan smiled encouragingly at Elisse. "You have my word." The little girl ran to her and grabbed hold of Morgan's hand.

"Papa, my mother's lost and ill, too. Will she be coming home?"

Elias tried to smile for his son. "I hope so, Eadan, I hope so. Brynne will do her best."

Seline made an angry noise and Elias's head snapped up. But

what he might have said to his daughter died on his lips as the young Prince followed his peers' example and demanded to be allowed to help. Elias shook his head, unwilling to give his permission, and Sullyan could see Eadan's disappointment.

"Let him play his part, Elias." Her soft voice drew the King's gaze. "He has a right to be involved, and he may not forgive you otherwise. The same principle applies to Sofira as to Robin. She may be drawn to the presence of her child. She has hungered for them so strongly that I doubt she could resist their call."

Seline exploded, fists clenched, her face a white mask. "And whose fault is that? I don't believe you're going to help her, you witch. Why should you? You've hated her for years and I don't trust you. It's your fault she's dying!"

Elias's eyes flashed in anger. "Seline, mind your manners! Brynne represents the only hope your mother has. Don't make her regret her decision to help by spouting this vicious nonsense. If you can't be civil, then be silent. And if you can't be silent, I'll have you removed!"

Seline glared at her father, tears of fury in her eyes, hardly able to credit the humiliation and cruelty of his threat, yet knowing he would carry it out. Sullyan watched in sorrow and sympathy. All this anger was exhausting her further and time was running out.

"Elias, make your peace. This conflict is doing no good. Cal, get the children together on one bed, then you, Tad, and Mathias take one each. This will be draining for all of us and we will need all the support we can get."

The swordsman Rienne had dispatched earlier returned. He carried a fresh shirt and breeches, which he held out to Sullyan. She gazed at them in puzzlement until Rienne came forward to help her, only then realizing the state her current clothing was in. She smiled in thanks as the healer helped her change.

"Where do you want me, Sully?" Bull asked.

"I cannot accept your help, Bull. Not with the state of your heart."

The big man looked as if he had been punched in the gut, and his florid face drained to white. Those in the room held their breath as he struggled for composure. "You're refusing me? How can you *do* that to me?"

Sullyan closed her eyes against the pain of betrayal in his tone, hating herself for wounding him when all he deserved was her love. "How can I accept when you are not fit? How can I risk your life? Please understand, my friend; I cannot take that chance! Would you have me distracted by concerns over your health?"

"No, but you would have *me* molder away in retirement until I died of boredom and uselessness?"

The vehemence of his tone cut through to Sullyan's heart, knowing as she did the truth of his words. He was not made for retirement, for safety and old age. She knew that his dearest wish was to die in some worthwhile battle, defending those he loved. She was well aware of the steps he had taken to prolong his useful life and the covert assistance he had found in achieving that desire. She could not, in all conscience, deny him this trial, as much as she wished to. His love for Robin and Taran was every bit as great as hers. She sighed and glanced at Rienne, who watched through narrowed eyes.

"What do you say as his healer, Rienne? Is he strong enough? Has he taken enough of those herbs you prescribed? I cannot take the chance that his heart will give out before I have done what I can."

"His heart should be strong enough to cope with it, Brynne. He took a booster dose about an hour ago. He shouldn't need another—Oh, I don't believe it! How long have you known?" Rienne's indignant outburst was loud in the quiet room, and heads turned to watch as Bull lowered his gaze.

Sullyan gave them both a weary smile. "You should know me better than that. How many times do I have to tell you that nothing is hidden from me? Bulldog, especially, should have known. Bull, how could you have thought I would not understand?"

Bull shifted his feet, unable to look her in the eye. "I didn't want your pity. I didn't want pity from anyone."

Sullyan shook her head. "Ah, Bulldog, you bloody great ox, you have never had pity from me!" She sighed and smiled at him. "Very well. I cannot deny I would welcome your strength if you are sure you can cope, but I warn you now. One sign of distress from that faithful heart of yours and I will dismiss you from my mind." Bull nodded. He had expected no less. "Well then, we shall make a start. Bull, give Morgan and Elisse to Cal, and you lay by Eadan's side. Rienne, Hanan, we will be relying on you to care for us all while we work. Have healers standing by to help the others. I recommend you prepare supplies of sedative as well as restorative herbs. Their bodies are already weak, and I dread to think what state their minds will be in, having been separated and tormented for so long. They may well be traumatized when they awake. If they wake. Gentlemen, are you ready?"

The Artesans signaled their agreement and closed their eyes. Sullyan lay down on the final bed, trailing one hand along Robin's cold cheek. She immediately wished she had not; his flesh had the feeling of a corpse. Pushing that terrible thought far from her mind, she stretched her bruised and aching body full-length upon the bed, sensing the healers about their work and her men gathering close, their hopes and prayers buoying her mind. Taking a deep breath, she closed her own eyes and reached out through her psyche, melding with the life forces that her friends and colleagues offered her.

She felt Morgan first, her son nestling into her mind like the part of her he was, bringing his fresh and innocent strength, and his simple childish determination to find his father. Elisse and Eadan added their youthful hopes, supporting each other, never doubting her for a second. Cal's Journeyman skills increased her power, the dark-skinned young man giving control to her with the ease of familiarity and practice. Tad also relinquished control with no reservations, although his surrender was tinged with relief. Her overriding mastery flooded him with faith that his hero would return.

She had more difficulty assimilating Mathias Blaine's power, for he was unused to subsuming his psyche and found it hard to release his hold. Sullyan's touch was sure and gentle, and once she helped him through the process his Master-level powers added greatly to her store. And Bulldog, faithful Bulldog, her truest, most loyal friend, gave up what power he possessed more completely than all the rest. She felt him offer it and hardly even had to take it. The two of them were so closely linked that his life force within her felt as natural as her own. She took one fleeting moment to check the state of his heart, finding it beating quite normally and in no danger of giving out. She was suffused with relief, hardly willing to admit, even to herself, how alone she would have felt without him by her side. Now she could begin the greatest test she had ever faced. Feeling empowered and strengthened and full of purpose, she gathered their patterns and went to work.

✣ ✣ ✣ ✣ ✣

The words of Tamilane's journal drifted through Sullyan's mind as she cast loose her hold on her consciousness and sank deeper into her psyche. The twists, spirals, and helixes of her vast and intricate pattern glowed and flared and looped around her, binding her closer and closer with those whose life forces she drew on to empower this uncertain endeavor. She hid her doubt from them as she tried to hide it from herself. She had to believe she could save her friends or she was defeated before she had begun. Using her anger and despair at their suffering, she bolstered her weakened spirit, drifting further into her metaforce and calming her fears.

There was only one method she knew that might help her attain her goal, and she felt for the strains of her soul song as she let herself float far out of time. The ancient, haunting melody came instantly to her mind—familiar, comforting, and strangely powerful as it twined through her being. Yet the refrain itself was not sufficient to afford her access through the Gateway. She had known that from the beginning, when she first conceived this tentative plan. The words of the long-dead Tamilane had planted this idea in her mind, an idea that had taken root and developed during her sleeping hours a day and a half ago. She needed information in order to pass the Gateway into the realm beyond the Void, and a guide to aid her after that, to help her find the souls that were lost.

Whether she would be able—or permitted—to return with them once she had taken that step was irrelevant. She was quite prepared to give up her life in order to see them returned to theirs. She had a unique link to one of the spirits residing in that realm and hoped with all her being that her father could be her guide. Why else had he striven so hard to contact her?

It was not the first time they had spoken. She had met his shade three years earlier, while giving birth to his namesake. He was surely the most natural choice to be her guide, and he would recognize the words he had made, so she opened her soul to the words of the song, the expression of love her father had penned, and flung them out like an invitation, begging him to respond.

Spirit rise up and join all these as one
The core of our being, of all that we are
The source of all loving, the heart's labors done

When two spirits join, when two souls sing one song.

There was nothing in the substrate, no answer to her call, and she intensified her longing, directing her thoughts toward her father's soul. The words of the song echoed hauntingly all around, the substance of this limbo place resounded to their rhythm, but when they faded and fell into silence, they were swallowed up by the vast emptiness of the Void.

Disappointment threatened to distract her from her task, but then she remembered her life mate's love and renewed her resolve. Too many loved ones were relying on her skills, too many trusting her to succeed. She couldn't give up at this first setback. Drawing on the life forces of those bound to her, she tried again and again, pushing back the boundaries and refusing to be refused. At last, her efforts were rewarded, although not in the way she had hoped.

It was the faintest of sounds and at first she didn't recognize it, too intent on the words of the ancient song to hear it. But then it wove with her melody and took on its natural sound: the rippling notes of a beautiful harp, softly and skillfully played. It entered her mind and her memories, taking her way back in time, back to the very first day she had met him on the Downs where once she had lived. That early summer's day with its promise of warmth and sun came flooding back, making her smile as she remembered the encounter. She saw him as she had seen him then, sitting calmly with his harp in his lap, playing the notes of that melody in a way she had never heard before. She drifted closer to his seated figure, never tiring of hearing him play, and he raised his eyes to hers as his mouth curved into a smile.

The majesty of him took her breath away, revealed as he was. She had always known him to be a lord of royal lineage, but he had never paraded his nobility in life. The circumstances of his exile had taught him the value of humility. He preferred the semblance of a humble bard to shield him from his shame. Death, however, had stripped all pretenses away and revealed his true sovereign state. Now he shone with white light and magnificence, and his music cut through to her soul.

Through the misty vapor swirling around her, she approached and bowed before him, meeting the love in his eyes. She spoke his name in greeting and held out her hands.

"My Lord Fiann."

He laid aside his harp, but the music lingered, brought forth from the delicate instrument by the controlling power of his will. He stood and paced toward her, holding out his arms. She stepped within his embrace as if she were coming home.

"Brynne Sullyan, why have you come here?"

His deep voice was as she remembered it, but it wasn't the sound of his voice that made her gasp. The last time she had seen him—near to death herself from childbirth and spiritual sickness—he had not been permitted to speak to her, only to communicate through the music of his harp.

She lifted her head from his chest and gazed up into his face. "I have come to redeem the souls of my friends, souls ripped prematurely from their bodies and sent here to suffer. I need to pass the Gateway, and I need the services of a guide. It was my intention to contact my father in the hopes that he could guide me. Can you help me, my Lord Fiann? Can you bring me to him?"

The regal spirit stepped back a pace and laid a hand on her shoulder. She felt its weight like a feather touch on her skin. His doe-like eyes looked deep into hers and she saw the sorrow within them. When he spoke, his grieving voice rolled over her like a balm for all her fears.

"It is not within my power to convey you through the Gateway, nor am I permitted to summon any who reside therein. But your call rang through our domain like the trumpet-peal of

Judgment. If your father's spirit could have attended you, he would surely have done so by now."

An icy shiver of dread slithered down her spine, freezing the hope in her heart and weakening her resolve. "So why has he not answered me? What could prevent him from coming, when he managed to reach me before?"

The bard's eyes widened and his face became more sharply defined, his brows drawing down as he registered her words. "He managed to reach out to you? He breached the guardian boundaries of our realm?" Sullyan nodded as Fiann stepped farther back. Alarm seeped from his aura and his eyes showed his distress. "Then he will not be able to attend you, Brynne Sullyan, for his spirit will have been banished. We are not permitted to communicate with the living in this way."

She stood aghast, all her hopes and plans in ruins. If her powerful father could not help her, what chance did she stand? "What will happen to him, Fiann? Where has he been banished to?" She couldn't bear to think of him suffering for trying to aid her in her plight.

The bard shook his head, unable or unwilling to answer her plea. She bowed her head in failure, feeling the despair of those who supported her. It was their collective desolation that made her try again.

"I *have* to pass the Gateway, Fiann. I have to find my friends. If I must do it without my father's help, then I will accept that condition, but I will not give up trying until my strength and my life runs out."

She turned from the regal figure and faced squarely into the mists, calling up the strains of the elemental song like a pathway into the Void. She put all her force into her voice and flung the anthem out, offering it like a paean to the uncharted lands of this realm. Following where it would lead her, she forged her way ahead, pushing back the misty vapors with the powerful forces of her mind. She sensed the shining figure following her, his curiosity plain.

All was white about her, all silent but for her song; no light, no features, no guidance to steer her in her quest. Direction was meaningless here in the Void. It was only the strength of her will and the courage of her heart that held any relevance here. She kept a vision of her life mate and friends very firmly before her eyes, and the intent of her whole being to rescue them suffused her soul. The substance of the Void kept beating at her mind, flowing and ebbing around her, refusing to part for her passage. She used every skill at her disposal to fathom its nature and essence, but it was totally unlike the Veils and responded to none of her calls. She stopped before exhaustion overcame her, and stilled the strains of the song, realizing it had no effect on the mists she was attempting to part. With the spirit of the bard still lingering at her back, she took stock of her surroundings, wondering what she had missed.

The partial words of Tamilane's journal emerged within her mind and she let them roll around her, musing on their meaning. She had interpreted the blank spaces as best she could, and now thought she had the full context of his words. She repeated them in sequence in the fastness of her mind, offering them to those who supported her, for any insights they might have.

Today I finally achieved my goal; I entered the region beyond the Void. Opening the Gateway, I stepped through the mists, using my powers to push back the spirits.

She could almost hear his voice as she formed the dead Artesan's words, latching on to that final phrase as it echoed through her mind: ... *using my powers to push back the spirits.* She paused, suddenly struck. Was Tamilane intimating it was the spirits themselves that blocked the Gateway? If that was so, then she was treating these mists in completely the wrong way, thinking

343

they were a natural barrier like the Veils when, in fact, they had once been living souls. Fiann had called them "guardian boundaries," which would seem to corroborate this theory.

She glanced over her shoulder at the indistinct figure of the bard, who had not spoken or otherwise reacted since her song had ceased. He did not react now, but she was sure she sensed something about him, some tension in his regal stance, blurred though it was by the mists. She turned away, excitement building within her and echoed by the minds of those she carried with her. She stretched out her senses and delicately probed the mists, looking for traces of psyche patterns or echoes of past lives. Gently, mindful that these might once have been living people with loves and emotions of their own, she sought for the residues of their existence, clues that might lead her to the truth.

Here again, music helped her, for within the confusing jumble of sensations that suddenly assailed her came unmistakable snatches of melody, disjointed refrains, soaring arias, and deep, sonorous dirges. Tiny fragments only, heard and then abruptly absent, as if she had passed through the trailing thought of a drifting mind. But they were definitely there.

Triumph flashed through her psyche, shared and enhanced by her supporting friends. Not aware of their surroundings as she was, they nevertheless felt what she felt and experienced each emotion. They sent her encouragement, renewing her strength and determination to succeed, and she faced the swirling multitude with knowledge in her eyes.

Music was still the key, of that she was sure, and music was her vehicle for communicating her desire. She would not attempt to force them, these ancient, fading revenants. She sensed they were conditioned to repulse any such invading purpose. Yet she could request and convey her wishes, and she could do that through her music, sending her thoughts and desires couched in a form they could accept.

She delved within her memories, sorting through the strains she knew until she realized that what she needed was a song that had its origins within herself. Once she realized that, there was only one she could offer: the tender, sweet lament that had come to her after the death of Robin's sister, Jessy.

When springtime's freshness found you, tiny blossoms made you fair.
The young sun shone, the warm winds blew so gently through your hair.
Come eventide the shadows grew, we watched them cast their shade.
Farewell, my heart, in dreaming dwell, so must all beauty fade.

The gentle tune ran from her mind almost without her volition, seeding itself through the substrate, twining among the mists. For long heartbeats it sounded alone into the silence of the Void, but then she began to hear muted whispers that grew until they seemed to come from a multitude of throats, as though many millions of voices had taken up the strain. Encouraged by this acceptance, she began to sing the words, and before she had reached the final verse, she sensed the barrier begin to part.

Then summer came, its golden days our growing love revealed.
Upon your face that early trace your youthful joy concealed.
But noontide passed and all too soon the twilit evening fell,
Its purple gloaming dimmed your sight. Farewell, my heart. Farewell.

With autumn's gold and slanting sun, your smile lit waning days.

On gentle spirit, bravely borne, the shadow cast its haze.

And then we knew, with heavy heart, your path would turn away

From ours, and we must part, as night-time follows day.

Now winter's icy tempests blow across an empty space,

But springtime's warmth awaits its chance to take white winter's place.

And though fond hearts are filled with pain, our grieving cannot last,

For soon the Wheel will turn again and Love unite the past.

It was a thinning of resistance, an acceptance of her soul, and all at once she began to see features among the white. She could hardly call them landmarks, as strictly speaking there was no land, but there were thinner and denser patches of white that stayed fixed when she moved tentatively forward. The song drifting from her lips, she moved through the vaporous mists, heading for what seemed to be a clearer space ahead, vaguely shaped as an arch and suggestive of a portal.

As she neared the edges of this wavering phenomenon, she felt a touch on her arm and turned to see the smiling face of Fiann at her shoulder. His liquid eyes were filled with pride and his figure shone dazzling white. She heard the haunting notes of his harp repeating the melody of her lament.

And though fond hearts are filled with pain, our grieving cannot last,

For soon the Wheel will turn again and Love unite the past.

He nodded once and released her arm as he began to move away, the harp still sounding strong. Now, the murmuring voices swelled into joyous being around her. She no longer needed to sing. The song shivered all around, and there before her wondering eyes was an open, inviting Gateway. Alone now but for those she carried, she reached out a hand to the mists. They parted before her, and she stood beyond the Void.

Chapter Twenty-Nine

The mists were behind her, hanging at her back like a curtain of soft rain, and she knew she only had to turn around to pass back through. Yet she must venture farther ahead, and it was a daunting prospect. At her feet there was nothing, not even the shifting substance of the Void, and the only way forward was over a slender, insubstantial bridge. The shimmering structure arced far away into the distance, its end impossible to see, looking too fragile to bear a feather's weight, let alone hers.

She felt the trepidation of the minds within her as she gazed on the terrible vacuum below the bridge. She knew with utter certainty that this was the final bulwark between life and death, and that once she set foot upon the Bridge, there was no possibility of return to the realms of the living. This was where she needed a guide, a messenger to the dead, but her father was prevented from coming to her and Lord Fiann was gone. She was alone in this limbo with only herself to rely on, and she had come too far on this journey of hope to turn back now. Taking a deep breath and refusing to think of what she was giving up, she prepared to free herself of her burdens before crossing the final divide.

She had hardly formed the thought when a presence made itself felt, a weighty pressure bearing down on her psyche, so strong she could barely stand against it. The menace of its regard was plain, but it made no move against her, merely held her powerless in an unbreakable grip. She offered no resistance, knowing how futile it would be. The pressure was simply too great for any mortal strength to oppose. Instead, she waited and wondered and controlled her fear, trying to focus on the will behind the force.

Who are you and why do you come here?

The multilayered voice boomed directly into her brain, making her gasp with the pain of its pressure and nearly causing her to black out. There were voices within that chorus that had not uttered for a millennium or more, and they had no care for mortal ears. The frailty of the human body had long ceased to hold any meaning for them. Sullyan put up her shield as best she could, and directed her own voice into the vacuum, hoping she would be heard.

"I am Brynne Sullyan, Princess of the royal House of Andaryon, King's Envoy to Elias of Albia, and Artesan Senior Master. I have come seeking the souls of my friends whose bodies have not yet died. They were sent here against their will through unnatural means, and should be returned to the living world."

There was utter silence once her voice died away, yet the pressure bearing down on her did not ease. All she could do was wait and hope she would be granted the access she needed.

The unseen multitude boomed again, making her cringe in pain. *Brynne Sullyan, we acknowledge you, although your earthly titles have no meaning here, and neither do your wants or desires. A Master Artesan's powers are respected in this realm, and so you will be heard. But you must be aware that no departed soul can ever return from the vacuum of Death.*

Her heart faltered as her hopes were crushed, and tears pricked sharply at her eyes. She had not come this far and against such odds to accept this without a fight. Fighting for what she loved and believed in was what she did best.

"The souls I speak of have not died. Their bodies still live and breathe. They should never have been forced to cross the Bridge of Death. They do not belong in the realms of the dead. All I ask is the chance to find them before the strength of their bodies gives out."

Her lone voice, flat and thin after the sonorous tones of the ancient Dead, fell into the vacuum at her feet and was swallowed up in silence. The dizzying abyss yawning below beckoned and pulled at her soul, threatening to swamp her courage with its nullifying non-existence. It was all she could do to keep her feet and not cast herself into its maw.

The wait seemed interminable and she was terribly aware of the passage of time, even in this timeless place. The rhythm of human life meant nothing to those who opposed her, but it was everything to her, especially because she knew it was fast running out for her friends. Every moment spent in deliberation, every second that passed in the world, meant less chance to save them and release them from their thrall. She wanted to scream, but she knew she must rein her impatience or risk angering these gatekeepers. She bowed her head to the pressure and ran through the words of her lament, letting the intensity of her feelings drift outward over the bridge. Perhaps those trapped in this meaningless realm would feel her psyche. Perhaps they would sense the love in her heart and know she had tried. It was all she had to offer, if she was prevented from offering her life.

Very well, Brynne Sullyan. The booming conglomerate voice startled her out of her thoughts. *There is truth in what you say. There are indeed those among us whose corporeal bodies still live. The one responsible for their condition but recently passed over the Bridge. He will not be capable of opposing their departure until he has integrated into our realm. But the time spent in integration is often short for one such as he. His evil is unbounded and he retains the powers he absorbed in life. If the captive souls are to escape him, they must do so without delay, for once he accepts the fact of his death, his strength will increase a hundredfold. Powerful as you are, Senior Master, you would be as a lamb before the tangwyr compared to such forces as he would wield.*

The ponderous weight of their verdict landed in her stomach like a punch. She had never dreamed death would actually empower Reen, and the prospect turned her heart to lead. She simply *had* to release his captives, whatever the personal cost, and she began casting loose the minds she carried with her even as she formed her reply to the Dead.

The life forces of the children were the simplest to put aside, as they did not fully understand her intentions and trusted her too implicitly to resist. Tad didn't put up much of a fight and Cal was too frightened for Taran to argue long with her commanding touch. Blaine, however, was a Master and his powers could not lightly be dismissed. Despite his infrequent usage, he knew the scope of their strength. His deep love for her, repressed as it was, was no less powerful for being hidden and she could not ignore his distress. She spent some precious time convincing him before he reluctantly stepped aside.

There was one, however, who refused to let go, and he was the one she feared most to hurt. Loyal Bulldog clung on grimly, like the creature she had named him for—tenacious, loving, and faithful. She found him the hardest to deal with as she pushed him out of her mind and, knowing exactly what she intended, he argued with her to the end.

But you can't *offer your life for theirs, Sully—just think what that would mean! You'd be leaving Morgan without his mother, and you know what that's like. I can't believe you're even considering it. And Robin—what will he say when he finds you've bought his freedom at the expense of your own? How's he going to cope after all this if you leave him on his own? Not to mention Taran. He feels guilty enough as it is! How will he live with the knowledge that he's responsible for your death? The man will never recover! Even Elias will be deeply affected, and the gods know he's been through enough.* Think, *Sully, take time to think, and you'll see that I'm right!*

Bulldog, there is no time! she replied urgently, thrusting the big man away. She could feel the depths of his desperation as he struggled against her will. *I hear you, Hal, my truest friend, and I understand your concerns. I have considered all your objections, believe me, but I have made up my mind. Morgan will still have his father, and I will always be close to their hearts. Robin can even choose to follow me, if he finds he cannot live for our son. Rienne and Cal will take care of Morgan, so he will never know the loneliness I knew. Taran will have Jinella, and they will rekindle the spark of their love. Taran has outgrown the self-blame his father planted in his heart. And Elias will have Sofira, and the love of his two children to sustain him. So you see, my loyal friend, this is the only way. I cannot leave them trapped here to be tormented by the Baron, and you heard how much more powerful he will be once he comes to terms with his death. I did not go through all that conflict to yield control to him now. So you* will *obey me, Bulldog, and do as I ask of you. It is the last request I will make of the friendship and love we have shared.*

Without waiting for his reply and knowing she had hurt him deeply, she shut him firmly out of her mind, careful to keep all of them from falling into the mists. They would hover in dreamless limbo until her soul had passed over the Bridge, and when her ties to them were severed, they would find their way back through the Void. Blaine and Bulldog would see them all home, she had no fears on that score, and they would have to find their own forgiveness for her actions. It was a possibility they all lived with constantly, this painful parting of friends; the life they lived made it inevitable, and they would have to face it as best they could.

Now that she was free of her commitments, she turned once again to the waiting presence and indicated her intention to cross the Bridge of Death.

"I am ready," she murmured, knowing they could hear her thoughts, and she felt the massive weight of their regard as they accepted her offering of her life.

Brynne Sullyan, you understand the conditions? You accept you can never return? The sonorous voices sounded strangely ritualized now, devoid of inflexion.

"I understand and I accept," she replied, her steady voice belying the thunder of blood racing in her ears.

Then we grant you access to the Bridge of Death, to be a Guide to the souls that are lost. But we warn you: do not set foot upon the Bridge as they make their crossing back into life. Once you have walked the span you are denied the Void, and denied access to the Gateway, save only if summoned by the strength of a Master who has the power to deal with the Dead. Do you understand what you have undertaken? Do you willingly surrender your life?

She took a deep breath, held it, and let go, at peace and perfectly calm.

"I do. I willingly surrender," came the irrevocable reply.

✣ ✣ ✣ ✣ ✣

As his deep voice sounded behind her, Sullyan nearly leapt from her skin. Her own reply died in her throat and she spun on her heel, eyes flying wide, despair and denial wild in her heart.

"No, Bulldog! I forbid it!"

But she was too late. The big man had made his reply and the

Dead accepted his freely offered choice as easily as if it were hers. His body was even there beside her, as physically present as she. She cried out in rage, clenched her fists, and sank to her knees, appalled by what he had done. "No, *no*, you cannot accept him!" she screamed into the abyss. "The agreement was with *me*! I forbid you to accept his surrender. He does not understand what he has done!"

The Dead remained silent, unmoved by her protests, and Bull refused to retract. His looked down on her grief-stricken face and knelt beside her, taking hold of her trembling hands. Unclenching her fists, he gathered her fingers to his chest and stared earnestly into her eyes.

"Don't deny me this, Sully," he pleaded, his bass rumble deep and soft. "Don't take this chance away. It's right that I do this for you, don't you see? This is what I was born for. I always knew there was something special between us, something deeper than love, and now I know what it is. This is the one thing I can do for you that no one else can do.

"You know how unhappy I've been of late, wondering what my future would be, how much longer I could carry on fooling people—fooling myself. You knew I would never retire gracefully. I'm just not the type. And I couldn't go on much longer taking those herbs of Rienne's—they were only prolonging the inevitable, I always knew that. And so did you, didn't you?" He shook his head, grinning ruefully. "I wish you'd told me you knew. It would have saved me a lot of skulking around, begging poor Rienne not to tell you. When I think of the grief she gave me for making her go behind your back …!"

"It was no more than you deserved, you deceitful ox. You should have known better!" Sullyan's reply broke the stasis of their position and the tears came in earnest. They fell into each other's arms, not attempting to stem the flow, their emotions overwhelming as they sat on the brink of Death.

Yet time was running out and they both knew it. Bull climbed to his feet, drawing Sullyan with him, both of them wiping tears from their eyes with hands that shook. Bull looked out over the Bridge of Death, facing the consequences of what he had done.

"Find them, Bull. Release them and guide them safely home," she whispered.

The big man turned and caressed her cheek, feeling the warmth of her skin one final time. "I will, dear heart. You can count on me."

He turned away from the love in her eyes, which threatened to weaken his resolve. He had to believe he would see her again—he had to believe this would work. He had taken this step to save her from death, as he had done before, but this time it wasn't a sword he could block, or a wound he could help heal. This was so much bigger than anything he had ever faced, and yet he instinctively knew he could do it. It was the purpose for which he had been born and the reason the two of them had met.

He stepped away from her and set his foot to the Bridge, its fragile substance gaining solidity as it accepted the weight of his soul. He gave one final backward glance, his eyes full of love, and then he set his heart to his task and walked out onto the Bridge of Death.

✢ ✢ ✢ ✢ ✢

"Why is nothing happening, Dex? What's taking them so long?"

Rienne sat on the edge of Cal's bed, wringing her hands and watching the faces of her loved ones. She felt very alone with all the Artesans gone. Seeing them so still and inaccessible made her realize just how helpless she actually was. Her empathic skills might allow her a greater insight into their thoughts and emotions, but it didn't permit her to share in something as risky as this. The thought that they might all perish tore at her soul and it was as much as she could do to keep from crying out.

Dexter stood behind her, his hands on her shoulders, painfully aware of his own inadequacy in a situation such as this. He had lived, trained, and fought with Artesans for most of his life and was used to their strange, unfathomable ways, but this was way over his head. He had no comfort to give, but Rienne was relying on him while the Artesans did their work. Cal and Sullyan would expect him to do his best, whatever his state of mind.

"Give them time, Rienne. We knew it wouldn't be easy and that there was no guarantee of success. You know Sullyan. She won't give up while there's the slightest shred of hope, and we must do the same. Keep your faith and keep praying—it's all we can do."

Rienne glanced up at him and tried to smile, sensing he was as frightened as she. All the other men shared the same expression of tense worry ill-concealed behind hopeful faces. The healers stood clustered around the Baron's captives, eyes fixed on their still forms, alert for the slightest of movements. The vigil went on, a heavy weight of anxiety bowing their spirits down.

✤ ✤ ✤ ✤ ✤

Sullyan had expected to lose contact with Bull's mind as the big man stepped on to the Bridge, but instead she was carried along with him, feeling his physical weight drop away as his soul crossed the border between life and death. The corporeal aspect of his psyche faded too, as if he had passed through a gauzy veil, and suddenly Sullyan saw through his eyes as he walked the narrow span, seeing it widen and strengthen and take on solid form. The yawning abyss below ceased to register in Bull's mind. As far as he was concerned, he was walking a broad, smooth road.

Sullyan relaxed and let him carry her, unsure if he knew she was there. His mind had taken on a different shape as the realm about him changed, and she was subsumed into his being. She

356

could no longer feel his emotions or sense his psyche pattern. He was in a transitory state, all functions suspended. It was unnerving and uncomfortable, but she endured the strange sensations, knowing that her own route back was secure inside her mind.

✣ ✣ ✣ ✣ ✣

The Bridge had seemed interminable from just inside the Gateway, but as soon Bull stepped upon it, its end came into sight. It was closer than he would have thought and he strode eagerly down the Bridge with a buoying sense of purpose, a feeling of strength and confidence that had been missing for far too long. He felt much as he did before a fight, when he knew his skills would protect him. If the souls of his friends could be located, he knew he could return them. Finding them in the first place would prove the trickiest part.

As he reached the far end of the Bridge, a vista stretched before him, and he stepped unhesitant upon the solid ground of his spirit's final home. It looked much as he had always expected it to: not so different from what he was used to, except that the air had a lucid quality he had never experienced before. He didn't feel very different either—maybe a bit fitter, a little stronger—and he sucked the elemental air into appreciative lungs. It seemed to feed him as he inhaled, flooding his being with vitality, and he knew food would be unnecessary if the air always tasted this good. But there would be time for savoring and exploring his pristine surroundings later, and he shook himself out of his state of wonderment, casting about for someone to aid him in his task.

Figures moved all around him, silent in their own private thoughts, but most were blurred and indistinct and didn't respond when he tried to speak. He moved farther away from the Bridge, instinct guiding him, and soon caught sight of a stooping figure whose outline was more sharply defined than the rest. Bull approached the slow-moving form, realizing it was the shade of a man, hunched over as if in great pain. Bull came closer and stretched out his hand, sensing the man's deep distress, but he gave a sharp hiss of breath when the man raised his face.

He had only seen Lerric once before, many years in the past, and this wizened, grief-shrunken shadow bore little resemblance to the client king of Bordenn. Sofira's father, however, seemed to recognize Bull, and his yellow-tinged eyes lightened, his liver-spotted hand reaching out to clasp Bull's arm in a desperate grip.

"At last!" he rasped, his strained voice full of pain. "I was beginning to fear no one would come. When I saw that monster pass me by, I thought she was doomed for sure. I've borne sorrow in my life and will do so throughout my death, as I doubt I need to tell you, but the guilt of *that* responsibility would have eternally ravaged my soul. There's no escape for me—and I don't deserve it anyway—but Sofira shouldn't have to suffer for my inadequacies. Oh, if only I'd been stronger, if only I'd been less craven ...! Ah, well, too late for regrets now."

Bull stared uncomprehendingly at the tortured old shade. It was evident that the dead king had seen Reen's shade pass him by, but before he could question him, the withered shade turned and passed through some hidden barrier, disappearing from Bull's sight.

The big man felt like cursing. What should he do now? He couldn't see how to follow, if that was Lerric's intent. Yet he needn't have worried, for the tormented soul returned, stepping out as if through a curtain and leading an indistinct figure by the hand.

Bull gasped in surprise as Lerric led his daughter forward, although he supposed he should have expected it. "Take her, take her back there," the shade urged in an agonized voice. He cast a frightened look over his shoulder as he thrust Sofira's cold fingers into Bull's hand. "Go on, man, don't just stand there!"

The dead king's urgency galvanized Bull and he turned toward the Bridge, the woman following in his wake. The harsh scream that sounded behind him made his whole body tremble, but there was no sign of Lerric when he glanced around to look. Pursing his lips in confusion and worry, he put Lerric out of his mind, concentrating on the oblivious Sofira as he neared the span of the Bridge.

The shadowy structure became more defined as they approached it, resolving once more into a narrow arch springing out over the abyss. Sofira didn't respond when Bull tried to tell her to cross. She clearly couldn't hear him and he gave up trying to reach her, merely pushing her body toward the Bridge until her foot touched it. He was careful not to step on it himself, seeing the change come over her as the Bridge accepted her weight. A vague glimmer of awareness entered her eyes, enough to keep her from falling, and when he released her, she walked in a dreamlike state back across the dividing span.

✣ ✣ ✣ ✣ ✣

As Bull lost physical contact with Sofira, Sullyan returned to her own mind. Shaking her head to clear it of confusion, she watched Sofira come, seeing how her steps were guided and kept to the center of the narrow way. The ponderous sense of the multitude still pressed upon her mind, and she knew they scrutinized and judged every move in case either of them should transgress. They would punish any infringement harshly and with no possibility of appeal, and so Sullyan remained as still as she could while she waited for Sofira to reach her, only taking the woman's cold hand once her feet had left the Bridge.

She felt for the Gateway behind her and sensed it was open. Using her pattern, she touched one of the life forces waiting there, sending it back through the Void. Sofira would have an escort to help her return to the safety of her body. Cupping her hands about Sofira's face, she probed for the woman's psyche, tuning it to her own to allow it access through the Void. Once she was satisfied Sofira's essence would obey her implanted instructions, Sullyan sent her through the Gateway, turning back with a hopeful heart toward the arching span of the Bridge

✣ ✣ ✣ ✣ ✣

The atmosphere in the healer suite had risen toward the unbearable, scarcely alleviated by the comforting smell of fellan pervading the air. Hardly any of them had partaken, despite their need for sustenance; they were all too tense and anxious to think about their stomachs. Many had not eaten since the afternoon before, but food was the last thing on their minds as their desperate vigil continued.

Rienne checked the captives' vital signs. She had lost count of the times she had done this, and there was still no change. She ought to be able to draw more hope from the fact that their hearts were still beating, but the stillness of their weakening bodies drained her hopes away. She turned from them to check the Artesans, frowning at the perspiration that had appeared on some of their faces. Tad, Cal, and the General all showed signs of intensified breathing, and Rienne felt a stab of fear as she imagined what it could mean. She looked toward Elisse, thankful that her daughter seemed calm, and put her hand out to smooth the girl's brow.

Elias made a startled sound and Rienne whirled round, heart racing, and followed the King's gaze to the figure on the next bed. Prince Eadan opened his blue-gray eyes and moved Bull's heavy arm from where it had rested over his. The child slipped from the bed and skipped toward his father, climbing up beside the King and taking up his mother's cold hand.

"Mama?"

Everyone in the room held their breath, hearing the Princess's deeper breathing in the utter silence of their hope. Rienne rushed to Sofira's side, Hanan beside her, and stared into the Princess's face as color returned to her cheeks. Seline stood immobile behind them, knuckles pressed against her teeth, trying to control her trembling as she watched through sore, dry eyes.

"Mama?" Eadan said again, and gave Sofira's hand a shake. Sofira sucked in a shuddering breath and slowly opened her eyes. The room erupted in a collective cheer, quickly stifled by Rienne's curt gesture, but everyone crowded as close as they dared to see what would happen next.

Eadan called his mother again and her gaze slid to his face. The hard eyes softened with tears that overflowed as she saw him by her side. Weakly, she raised her arms and gathered him to her breast, sobbing as she hugged him close. Elias gazed up at Rienne, incredulity in his face, and the healer could only stare back, lacking the words to express what she felt.

Sofira raised her tear-streaked face and looked about, perplexed. Seline rushed forward and collapsed in tears onto the bed, and Eadan eased back to give his sister space. The Princess stared at her sobbing daughter, and then at Elias, clearly unable to understand where she was or what had happened.

"Mother?" whimpered Seline, her haughty pride quite gone. Now she was only a little girl who had seen her lost mother return. Sofira clutched her daughter's hand, still gazing at Elias as if begging him to explain. Then her gaze slid sideways to the beds of those who still lay unconscious. Rienne saw the moment of Sofira's recall.

"Elias! Oh, dear gods!" The Princess's voice was full of terror and pain, and the King enfolded her trembling body while she sobbed out her fear.

Hanan came forward, a cup of sedative in her hand, and gently persuaded the traumatized Princess to take its contents. The herbs would relax her and take away some of the panic, leaving the mind more able to assimilate what it had seen and experienced.

Rienne left the royal family in Hanan's capable hands. She was trembling in earnest now the first success had occurred. Her eyes wide with the strength of her prayers, she returned to watching over her friends, begging all the gods in existence to grant them the same grace of return.

Chapter Thirty

Bull turned away as Sofira vanished across the Bridge, unable to see the far end from the realm he now inhabited. Scanning the mysterious vista, he watched the fluctuating crowds, becoming more accustomed to the way they moved. He wasted no more time trying to speak to the spirits that passed him. He knew what he was looking for and he moved forward with purposeful steps.

Fields stretched into the distance with mountains far behind. Unfamiliar as it was, the panorama nevertheless reminded him of places he had seen as a boy. In fact, this whole realm felt comfortable, although he could not explain why. It was as if he fitted here, as if this had always been his home. Many drifting spirits passed him and he felt their presence in his mind, although none belonged to him or spoke as they faded from his view. Then one figure came more purposefully toward him and, like Lerric, it was clearly defined. Another man, this one younger, but one Bull was sure he had never encountered during his life. He paused to let the shade approach and it came close before it stopped. It seemed to be a man in his forties and, despite knowing they had never met, he nevertheless stuck a chord in Bull's memory.

"Do I know you?" Bull looked the spirit over and the other regarded him solemnly, no expression in his gray-green eyes.

"We have never met, but you know my daughter. Is it true you are a Guide? Have you come to take her home?"

The instant he spoke, Bull knew who he was. His voice and the shape of his mouth gave his identity away. The big man had never heard his name, nor did he know much about him, only that he had died when Jinella was a young girl. "Yes," he said, reading the shade's concern, "I have come to guide her home."

Relief flooded out of the shade, and Bull found he was growing ever more receptive to such emanations. He could feel the depth of love the shade felt for his daughter, and as the man turned and disappeared, Bull also felt his guilt at leaving her. He stood and waited, knowing the shade would return, and soon the barrier parted as Jinella stepped through. Like Sofira, she was indistinct and unresponsive, her eyes unseeing and her mind shuttered. She made no movement and gave no sign as Bull received her hand. Her father's shade faded as soon as he lost contact with his daughter, and Bull was left to steer her back toward the Bridge. As before, he placed her so her feet centered on the walkway, and he watched her begin her passage before turning back to the search.

✢ ✢ ✢ ✢ ✢

Sullyan's heart gave a leap of gladness as she saw Jinny's slender figure. The girl approached blindly, as the Princess had done, and Sullyan had the Gateway ready as she took Jinny's unresisting hand. The weight of the multitude had lessened and she knew she had gained their trust. They must have realized she would never jeopardize the safe return of her friends. There was only a token watch-force now that she understood the procedure, and she gave them no more thought as she prepared Jinny to cross the Void.

She chose Tad and Mathias Blaine to escort Jinny back home. Tad because he was weakening, and the General because of his discomfort. Both would appreciate being released from her service, and both could be more use back in the healer suite. She felt their willing acceptance of the charge she placed upon them, and sent Jinny through the Void. Eagerness grew in her heart.

✣ ✣ ✣ ✣ ✣

The stirring of the two men made Rienne jump and curse, ready though she thought she was for something of the sort. Mathias Blaine was quickest to recover and he gave Rienne a brief smile as he rose. He helped Tad to his feet, the young swordsman dizzy from the strain, and they both turned to the bed where Jinny lay next to Taran.

The tension rose again as everyone gathered close to the bed, and Rienne got a cup of the sedative ready while Hanan ran a damp cloth over Jinny's face. The pallor of her skin gave way steadily to a blush of warmth, and the rise and fall of her bandaged chest increased while they watched. Her eyes moved beneath their lids and fluttered open, her green gaze unfocused and uncomprehending.

"Jinny?" Rienne spoke softly as she leaned over the bed, drawing Jinella's clouded gaze and smiling. "Jinny, it's Rienne. Can you hear me? It's all right, you're quite safe."

Jinny's brow creased and she abruptly tried to sit up, gasping in pain as her gaping wound made itself felt. Rienne put an arm about her shoulders before the weakened girl could fall, seeing Jinny's terrified glance at the bandages binding her chest. It wasn't the pain of her wound that caused tears to spring to Jinny's eyes, but the sight of Taran lying still as death by her side. She began to shudder, her eyes squeezing shut, each gasped breath a denial as her terrible memories returned.

"Hush, Jinny, hush, it's all right, you're safe." Rienne held Jinny tightly, gesturing frantically for Hanan to take the cup of herbs. With the Chief Healer's help, they got the dose into Jinny, waiting until her shuddering eased and they could see some sanity behind her frightened eyes.

"It's over, Jinny, the nightmare's over. Everything will be all right." Rienne prayed she wasn't speaking too soon. "Brynne's bringing them all back to us. Taran will be next, you'll see."

Jinny's enormous green eyes stared fixedly at her lover's face while she clung to Rienne like a lost child. Rienne felt the weight of her expectation, echoed by every person in the room, descend upon her shoulders and wished she could augment her physical strength like a true Artesan could. All she could do was hope and pray, like the traumatized girl beside her, and she wrapped her arms about Jinny, sharing comfort as best she could.

✟ ✟ ✟ ✟ ✟

Bull recognized the next shade that addressed him from the descriptions of his friends. Both Taran and Sullyan had known the man, although Taran knew him best. Sullyan had met him but briefly eleven years ago, early on in her Manor life when she was still a captain. She told Bull of the encounter at the time, uncertain what to do for the best. Bull had advised her to heed her orders, and that's what she did. She had never been happy about it, feeling she had let the man down. Yet her obedience to her superior officer might just have saved her life, even if she and all her friends went through Perdition before that outcome was achieved.

Taran's father, Amanus, an Adept-elite, managed to train his son up to Journeyman before his untimely death. Amanus had been a harsh teacher and he drove Taran's gentler spirit too hard— always criticizing his son instead of praising, and beating his confidence down. It cost Taran years of struggle to cast off the yoke of self-blame. Sullyan played a crucial part in the healing he had achieved. And now the man himself stood regarding Bull, as if reading the big man's unflattering opinions in the mirrors of his eyes.

The shade spoke flatly, no apology or regret in his tone. "I did my best. I taught my son as I was taught. It never did me any harm."

Bull bristled at the shade's arrogance. "Maybe not, but Taran's not like you. Who knows what he might have achieved with a more ... sympathetic tutor?"

"How dare you criticize me?" the shade of Amanus hissed, his figure wavering as emotion pulsed from his soul. "I never made the errors *he* has made, or got myself into such straits!"

Bull refused to be intimidated. "Have you ever asked yourself whether those errors might actually be your fault? Perhaps if you'd taught him better, he might have avoided them in the first place. It was only his desire to be worthy of you that drove him to experiment the way he did. You have a lot to answer for, if you only had the compassion to realize it."

Amanus stared at Bull with dislike, but Bull could see the seeds of doubt in his mind. He was about to say more when the shade abruptly turned, vanishing beyond the barrier as the other two had done. Bull waited for him, scrutinizing the air, trying to sense the hidden curtain through which the shade had passed. Neither Lerric nor Jinny's father had possessed any Artesan powers, but Amanus was Adept-elite, the same rank as Bull. The barrier ought to be accessible if he could only fathom its nature, and he probed the air before him as Sullyan had taught him. He thought he could detect a denser layer to the air, but before he could examine it properly, Amanus reappeared.

Taran followed blindly behind him despite not being led by the hand, and Bull narrowed his eyes at the friction this implied. "He worshipped you, you know."

Amanus stared at him silently, his face closed and tight. Bull seethed. He wanted to sting Amanus, make him realize what he had lost. "You ought to be proud of him, not critical! When I think of the courage he's shown and the progress he's made—not to mention what he had to go through …! Well, I just think you ought to be proud of him. He's your only son, after all. Everyone else who knows him is proud to be his friend."

The shade drew himself upright, fury on his face. "You know nothing of what I feel and you have no right to judge. Now, I suggest you do what you came for, Guide, and take my son back to his life. He's chosen his own way; he can make his own decisions and mistakes. When he has sons of his own to raise and train, then he can judge my actions. Until that day comes, no one else has the right, no matter what exalted rank they might have achieved!"

Amanus turned his back on Bull and on the lorn figure of his son, fading into the mass of spirits as if he had never existed. Bull stared after him, sensing the depths of the shade's personal shame, realizing that guilt was eating at the man and he was too proud to admit it, even in death. Shaking his head at the waste of it all, he took Taran's unresponsive arm, guiding the Adept back to the Bridge and placing his feet on the structure as before. As soon as the span accepted his weight, animation came into Taran's eyes, but he clearly did not see Bull by his side, only the arch stretching out before him. Bull guessed he might even be able to see its end, for he strode out with purposeful steps, leaving the realm of the Dead behind as he moved back toward life.

Smiling with twofold pleasure, Bull returned to the search. He knew who was likely to aid him next, and he looked forward to this final meeting.

✢ ✢ ✢ ✢ ✢

Sullyan's eyes filled with tears when she saw Taran walking toward her. It was obvious he knew where he was going, and she was proud beyond measure of his determined step. Yet as he drew closer to the living world, he became weak and unsteady as he reached the limits of his endurance, so once he stepped off the Bridge she wasted no time in sending his soul back through the Gateway. Cal was waiting to escort him and support him with his willing strength, and Sullyan sent Elisse back with them, knowing how Rienne would worry for the girl.

Then she smiled, sensing Bull's pleasure, and turned back eagerly once Taran was safely through, hardly able to contain her longing for the life mate she had lost.

�֍ ✧ ✧ ✧ ✧

Cal stirred and took a deep breath, opening his dark eyes. He felt his daughter by his side and carefully sat up, mindful of Morgan, who remained completely still, his mind still linked to his mother. Dexter helped him to his feet while he focused on Taran's weakened state. The effects of the wound had had serious consequences for the Adept's body, and his life force was at its lowest ebb, very nearly spent. Cal gripped Taran's hand, able to pass him energy more easily through the medium of touch. He glanced across at Jinny's agonized face, smiling encouragement even as he supported Taran's fragile strength.

Every eye in the room was fixed on Taran's face, even Rienne's, who held Cal as he shivered in her arms. He was forced to expend large amounts of energy to support Taran's weakened state, and his own reserves were finite after their ordeals of the past few days. Help, though, was close by. Elisse crept into his lap, offering her own youthful strength and surprising Cal by her touch. Linked closely together, they called Taran home, and gradually the Adept's eyes opened and he took his first liberated breath.

This time, the cheering could not be stopped no matter how hard Rienne and Hanan tried. The men were just so joyously relieved to see the Adept back. With three of the captives safely returned, the fourth was bound to follow, and jubilation spread about the room as Taran and Jinny embraced. Hardly an eye was dry among those who watched, and even the General made his feelings clear, coming up to Jinny and Taran and gripping their hands. Neither was capable of speech and they gazed blindly back while the tide of exultant emotion washed them.

Soon, the celebrations faded, for there was yet one more to come, and the focus of expectation now switched to Robin. Tad settled himself by his hero's side, ready to lend him strength, although he was drained and shaky himself from aiding Jinny's return. Not even Rienne could convince him to relinquish his place, nor could the General when he tried. Tad refused to heed them and stayed resolutely at his post. He had deserted Robin once already and the shame still burned in his eyes. He needed to atone for his weakness and no one could tell him otherwise.

Cal exchanged a look with Rienne and even Blaine shrugged in acceptance. They all knew the General would be ready to offer help should Tad need it. The murmur of voices stilled into silence as all eyes turned to those who had yet to waken.

✣ ✣ ✣ ✣ ✣

Bull wandered through the drifting mass of souls, searching for one in particular. He had never forgotten the shape of her face, or the mischievous look in her eye. Even when in terrible pain, she had never lost her gentle ways. Bull had often wished deep in his heart that they could have found a way to save her life. At least her pain had been eased at the end. She had passed on in the embrace of a much-loved friend, and Bull could appreciate now how peaceful she had felt, and smiled for the release she had found.

As if his memories had summoned her, he saw her standing a short way off. He gasped. Those mischievous eyes were laughing at his amazement, their blue a lighter shade than those of her brother. If not for the eyes, he would not have recognized Robin's sister. She stood tall and at ease, her dark curling hair tumbling over her shoulders, loose and unadorned by the ribbons she had loved to wear, and which Robin had so loved to bring her.

Bull had never seen her stand, much less walk, for she had been in the final stages of her long illness when he first met her. Fragile and weak, confined to her bed, she had nevertheless affected all their lives with the strength of her courage and her gritty determination not to hold her brother back. They had all been captivated by her serenity and her fierce love for Robin. This love protected him now, when he was unable to protect himself.

"Jessy! Oh, dearest Jess." Bull came closer and took her hands, smiling into those cerulean eyes and seeing the pleasure there. Yet it was pleasure tinged with concern, and her demeanor caused him alarm. "What is it, dear heart? Why are you afraid?"

"Dearest Hal, I might have known it would be you! But come, we don't have much time." She tightened her hands on his fingers and drew him away from the crowds. "There's a presence here, a very great evil, and it's searching for Robin's soul. It won't find him where I've hidden him, but it will be drawn to him once I give him over to you. You might have to invoke your powers as Guide to keep him from harm."

Bull frowned as Jess led him farther on, a frisson of fear running down his spine. "I don't know what you mean, Jess. I'm new to this and it was all very sudden. I don't know what powers I have here."

She glanced up at him, a flash of understanding in her gaze. "You did this to save Sullyan, didn't you? You sacrificed your life for hers." Bull nodded and Jessy smiled lovingly. "I felt her calling her father—we all heard the song in the air. I knew Morgan couldn't answer her and I was so afraid she'd be forced to take on this role herself. It would be such a tragedy if her life were cut short in order to save my brother's. Had I known you were with her, Hal, I might have guessed what you'd do. Once I take you to my brother, I'll explain how you can protect him, but we mustn't waste any more time or he might not make it back."

Through the touch of Jessy's fingers, Bull could feel her working the mists. Robin's sister had not possessed any Artesan powers during her life, so what she was doing now must be part of her existence in this realm. She kept a firm hold of Bull's hand as she made her preparations. The air before them coalesced, turning vaporous and opaque, and then Jessy urged him forward. He obeyed her insistent tug, feeling the barrier as he crossed through it like the touch of cobwebs on his skin. He glanced around in amazement as he found himself standing in a room.

The room had white walls and a white floor. There was no ceiling he could determine and no sign of a door. The only feature within the room, besides the two who had entered, was Robin, stretched out and silent on the floor. Bull turned to Jessy, puzzlement on his face. She dropped his hand, crossed to her brother, and knelt beside him on the floor.

"This is a nhil room, Hal. Somewhere any of us can come when we want to be alone. They're formed from the substance of this place and are inviolate to all but their creators. If I didn't want you to enter here, nothing you did would allow you access. It's the one place I could be sure where Robin would be safe from the evil that seeks him. It can't even sense him while he's protected by these walls, but once he leaves here and begins to move toward the Bridge, his aura will permeate the region and he will be vulnerable. That's where you come in. You must invoke your status as Guide. Guides are unique among us and have powers none can breach. Provided you keep your hand upon Robin and don't let your courage fail, you will both be protected by the laws of this realm. But if you allow yourself to be distracted, or relinquish your hold on his soul, then that evil spirit can snatch him from you. If that happens, you are both lost, for your powers as a Guide will be broken and you will never get them back."

Jessy had been gazing down at Robin, stroking his dark curls, but now she looked imploringly up at Bull. Her eyes held shimmering tears and her face was as pale as the room. "I couldn't bear for that monster to take him. He's suffered so very much! I had to sit and watch him being tortured before that sadistic fiend was killed. If he should gain control of Robin now he's dead, the torture will be eternal. I simply couldn't stand that! Promise me you'll return him—promise me you'll keep him safe? I can wait a little longer to be reunited with him if I know he's safe in Sullyan's arms. But if he falls to that terrible evil, I'll cast myself into the chasm beneath the Bridge, where the end of all consciousness lies."

Bull's own eyes prickled and he knelt at her side. "I won't let you down, dear heart. I'll get him there safely and set his feet on the Bridge, never fear. Sully's waiting for him on the other side, and all our friends are ready to welcome them back. I won't let Reen take his soul. You can rely on me for that."

Jessy squeezed his hand. "Oh, dearest Hal, I can't tell you how much this means to me! But hurry, we don't have much time left— Robin's life force is very weak. Can you get him on his feet? He's far too heavy for me."

Bull took Robin's arm over his shoulders, wrapping his other arm about the younger man's waist. Although Robin's eyes were open, it was obvious that he saw and heard nothing, but he struggled to his feet with the big man's help, leaning on Bull's greater strength with muscles that trembled. He was clearly on his final reserves and Bull felt a pang of cold fear. What if his body should run out of life before he could set foot on the Bridge? Yet he couldn't allow himself to be distracted by such questions. He had to keep in mind Jessy's warning and concentrate on protecting Robin's soul.

The dense white of the nhil room dissolved before his eyes as Jessy manipulated the mists, the infinite vista of the spirit realm flowing back around him like water. Jessy glanced about anxiously as the drifting spirits returned, scanning their depths for any sign of threat. When she could sense no lurking presence, she turned to Bull. "Quickly, Hal, before he comes! Make your way to the Bridge and don't stop for anything, no matter how important it may seem. Don't let yourself be fooled by sights or sounds. Just concentrate on Robin and your status as a Guide. When you've seen him safely across, come find me again. There is much I can tell you, and I would welcome your company. But go now, Hal— go quickly!"

Catching her urgency, Bull turned away, steering Robin's faltering steps. The Major was unable to walk as quickly as Bull would have liked, and he tried to link with Robin's psyche to lend the younger man some strength. The substance of this realm, however, blocked his every attempt. He would not be permitted to help in that way. So, supporting the Major's weight, Bull half-carried him toward the Bridge, pushing purposefully through the spirits that wafted across his path.

He had just glimpsed the narrow arc when a frantic wail sounded behind him. Despite Jessy's warnings, his warrior instincts kicked in and he turned to see. Some long way behind him, indistinct and vaguely disturbing, a patch of darkness impinged on the luminous air. It blocked the sweeping vista of fields and mountains and seemed to swallow the herds of mist, and a terrible, panicked shrieking fled before its advance.

The sound cut through Bull's mind and made his heart lurch with fear. He tightened his grip on Robin's waist and urged the Major on. Yet Robin's strength was failing and he had no more left to give. With a curse and a glance over his shoulder, Bull took him into his arms and hurried on toward the foot of the Bridge.

Behind him came a rushing sound, like a mighty wind, fell voices mingled with the surging, each one shrieking in fear. A single, separate voice fled before it, crying desperately for help, but Bull shut out the clamor and held doggedly to his pace. The Bridge was only yards away now and nothing would prevent him from reaching it.

"Help me, oh, please help me! Please don't let him take me again! You have no idea what it's like! He'll torture me for eternity—please, you've got to help me escape!"

No matter how hard Bull strove to ignore the words, the spirit's genuine terror pierced his soul. The cry pulled on him in a fundamental way and he could only guess that his status as Guide had somehow been invoked. He was footsteps away from the Bridge, but he stopped dead as a figure darted in front of him, eyes starting wildly from a terrified face, the skin gray with mortal fear. Hands clutched at Bull's arms with desperate strength and he couldn't shake them off without releasing his hold on Robin, which he couldn't afford to do if what Jessy had told him was true.

"Who the Void are you? Leave me alone!" he snapped as the figure stared over his shoulder, the straining eyes widening further. The strange sound behind them grew louder and more menacing by the second. The lucid air lost its clarity, becoming gray and blurred as fear surged through the realm, the emotion a tangible color as the rushing darkness advanced.

"I'm Seth, Baron Reen's manservant," the shade gabbled, almost incoherent with fear. "He sent me to delay you long enough for him to catch you. I don't want to, but he controls me. I have to do his bidding. Sullyan—she said she'd help me! She said I could atone for Alice's murder and go somewhere no one would find me. Please! He said you were stealing the others from him, that you somehow got them out. If that's true, then you can get me out, too! Please, you have to! *Please*!"

The shade collapsed, gibbering at Bull's feet like a whipped cur. Hands clutched at Bull's legs, preventing him from moving, and then the panic within the darkness swamped Bull's pounding heart. The big man groaned aloud, echoed pitifully by the figure at his feet, and Robin stirred weakly in his arms, moaning in deep distress. All light and sight were cancelled out by the thunderous, awesome dark. Only the indescribable presence of the fathomless Void managed to pierce the murk that descended on their souls.

Chapter Thirty-One

"**O**h, gods, don't let him take me! She promised he wouldn't take me! She said she'd set me free! Please, gods, don't let him take me!"

The wretch's continual pleas grated on Bull's overstretched nerves and he longed to thrust the shade out of his way and place Robin on the Bridge. The graceful arch was just visible in the gloom, shining faintly with a glow of its own, unaffected by the clamoring dark. It beckoned to Bull like a siren call, urging him to cross its protecting span, promising him security if he just stepped onto its surface. Yet he knew this was a lie and that he would be throwing away his soul, and he resisted the temptation as he cradled Robin. He heard a growling rumble and was suddenly buffeted by howling winds as a tumultuous roar of fury erupted around his head.

The terrified shade at his feet screamed, throwing his arms over his head and bowing down close to the ground, his body pressed tight against Bull's legs as he shivered in fear. The winds whipped at their faces, thrusting hard at Bull's back, trying to force the big man closer to the yawning Void. The voices that shrieked within the roiling cloud pummeled his brain, trying to snap his concentration and appall him with their noise. Bull closed his eyes and refused to see the nightmare. He thought of Sullyan's trust in him and refused to lose his hold. He raised his own voice and boomed into the darkness, "You're wasting your time, Reen, if you think you can frighten me like this! I know you can't touch me—I have the powers of a Guide. You're not going to stop me returning him, so you might as well give up now."

The winds dropped so abruptly that Bull staggered backward before regaining his balance. He hadn't realized how strongly he had been resisting the gale. The shrieking banshee wailing also faded into silence, and the pathetic figure curled at Bull's feet dared to raise its head. "Have you beaten him? Has he gone?" Yet the darkness still hovered at Bull's back and the oppressive weight didn't lift.

Bull stood warily, eyeing the curtain of black, seeing it sway as if moved by some vagrant breeze. He did not trust its silence. Robin hung limp in the big man's arms and Bull feared his life was ebbing. He was about to sidestep the figure at his feet, intending to take Robin to the foot of the Bridge. He shifted, preparing to move, but at the sound of his name he snapped his head round in dread.

The scene that met his eyes caused him to gasp. Sullyan knelt not ten feet away, battered, chained, and defeated. A scarecrow figure advanced on her. Bull lurched a step toward them before he jolted himself to a halt, reminding himself angrily that Sullyan was safe by the Gateway. This was an illusion and he must not let it distract him no matter how pitifully she called him, or how agonizingly she shrieked. Turning his head, angry tears in his eyes, he ignored Sullyan's shrieks, ignored the betrayal she decried him for, and stepped one pace closer to the Bridge.

Another voice screamed, spiraling up into agony. Taran's cries pierced Bull's aching heart as the Adept pleaded for mercy, for Jinny, for release. And as hard as Bull tried, he was unable to prevent his reaction, and he turned in time to see the dreadful scene as the Baron took Jinny's and Taran's souls.

He was overcome with grief, unable to bear the horror in their eyes. "Oh, you bastard, you evil bastard! You'll pay for that. I'll see you cast shrieking into the abyss!"

He took a stride away from the Bridge and closer to the darkness, forgetting the weight of his burden in his fury. Laughter welled out of the black mists, mocking and reviling the love in his heart, and the scarecrow stood forth to torment him, bringing more visions before his eyes. He saw Sofira's mind raped and her body degraded as the scarecrow took his revenge. He saw Lerric's pathetic resistance, overcome with little effort, and watched as the client king died in agony, his captive daughter looking on. With every vision Bull stepped nearer, his eyes fixed on the scarecrow, deaf to the frantic warning cries of the crouching shade.

More illusions followed, all terrible, all demanding retribution. Serrin's uncomprehending murder, his body ravaged by Reen's cruel lusts; the Roamerling girl he had experimented with, her dark eyes filled with pain; the agonized deaths of Lerric's guardsmen, their life forces sucked out along with their souls. Each horror paraded before Bull's eyes drew him on in fury ever farther from the Bridge. Robin hung inert in his arms, barely breathing and fading fast. In a few more moments his body would fail and the Baron would triumph at last. The scarecrow moved farther back, drawing Bull inexorably on. Only one thought existed in Bull's loyal, loving mind: to cast this demon into the depths of the Void. Unthinking, he stalked the evil creature.

✣ ✣ ✣ ✣ ✣

"What's happening, Cal? Why hasn't he returned?"

Rienne was frantic with worry. Her fingers on Robin's neck detected the weakening pulse as she watched his ever-more-shallow breathing. Robin's body was covered with sweat and he had given a feeble moan a moment ago, but now he was as still as impending death.

"I don't know, love." Cal's low voice trembled as he glanced fearfully from Dexter's face to Blaine's. The General stood to one side, watching Robin's fading body, his eyes unreadable and his face closed, as stern and unemotional as ever. Yet Cal could see the speed of his pulse in the hollow of his throat and knew Blaine felt as frightened and as helpless as they. All they could do was watch and wait, and offer support to those who needed it.

Tad sat with Robin's hand in his, his lips moving in silent prayer. His face was white and his eyes were red. If heart's desire alone could have brought Robin back, Tad would have achieved it long ago, but the Fates were deaf to the wishes of men and all they could do was endure.

Cal felt he had to offer Rienne something. "Perhaps it's taking her longer to reach him than the others. He was the worst affected, after all."

Rienne reacted badly. "If you've no better comfort to offer than stating the obvious, I'd rather you kept your mouth shut!"

Cal colored and fell silent, and Dexter's hand gripped his shoulder. They could all see the grief building in Rienne's gray eyes and hear the echo of it in her voice. She hadn't meant to reject him, only she was wounded and in pain. They all felt the same and might all have snapped, stretched to breaking as they were. Their eyes roved from Robin's face to Sullyan's, seeing the pallor of their skin and the beads of perspiration. So focused were they on willing Sullyan to succeed that the healer who should have been watching over Hal Bullen failed to notice the blue tinge to his lips.

✢ ✢ ✢ ✢ ✢

Sullyan waited in suspense by the Bridge, straining her eyes along its length. She wasn't linked to Bull anymore. After losing her link to his mind when Sofira returned, she had been unable to re-establish it and was forced to wait helplessly by the Void. It was taking too long. Something must have gone wrong. She could feel the weight of this certainty like a stone around her neck. Bull had managed to find and return three of the captives with no apparent difficulty. That Robin had not yet appeared signaled a problem he could not resolve.

Frantic to know what was happening, she quested for Bull's pattern, but the arc of the Bridge refused her thoughts and the abyss below it sucked them down. She pushed her power to its limits, knowing she was draining her resources but uncaring of the bodily cost. If Bull had run into trouble, she had to give him her aid, and if that meant crossing the Bridge herself, she wouldn't balk at the task. She prepared herself to take that step and hoped her son and her friends would forgive her.

As she stepped up to the Bridge and gazed along its fragile span, a strain of song came into her mind, borne faintly on the notes of a harp. She froze in the act of touching the Bridge, her foot stayed by the sound, and a leap of hope tripped her pounding heart as the soul song played in her mind. Perhaps song was the key and not the strength of her powers as she had first thought. There had to be a way for her to summon the soul of her Guide.

Clutching at this new hope, she moved back a pace and embraced the song, casting it out over the abyss and along the arc of the Bridge. Her psyche was woven within it, and Bull's pattern as well. She felt herself rushing forward although her feet never left the ground. The narrow fabric of the Bridge arched gracefully beneath her, carrying the essence of her soul safely over the terrible Void.

Soon, she felt the familiar touch of Bull's mind and called to his essence as she neared the other side. She could see virtually nothing as she moved through an opacity of darkness, but she could sense the big man's presence and something else within the murk. It beat against her senses with malignant pervasion, and suddenly she knew what it was.

Bull! she cried urgently, reaching out to grasp his psyche, feeling his preoccupation and the peril that hemmed him around. She tried to force herself on him, for he was oblivious to her call, and she knew it was imperative that she break the monster's hold.

Unsuccessful, she cursed, and called desperately on elemental Fire, forming a ball of light before she had time to wonder whether her powers had the same influence here. It seemed the spirit realm across the Bridge was still part of the structure of the world, and the primal elements remained unchanged. Fire blossomed at her command and pierced the veil of murk, transfixing the mutilated creature that scuttled naked within.

The brilliant flare of Fire cancelled out the darkness, chasing the roiling shadows and snuffing them out of existence. A dreadful wail of agony issued from the skulking, contorted form, and Bull's attention snapped back to his plight as the scarecrow's hold on his mind was broken.

The big man staggered to a halt, appalled at the ease with which he had been diverted from his purpose, and his first thought was for Robin. He could see no signs of life and feel no stir from the limbs, and tears came to his eyes when he thought he had failed in his chosen task. He stooped, intending to lay Robin down in order to examine him more closely, but Sullyan's commanding voice sounded sharply in his mind.

No, Bull, do not release your hold. If you take your hands from him, he will be vulnerable to attack. Bring him swiftly to the Bridge and let him touch its fabric. I will be able to support his body once he makes contact with the span.

Ignoring the shrieks of fury erupting from the scrabbling figure at his back, Bull strode toward the Bridge with his burden. He passed the cowering wretch, who was sobbing on the ground, and the shade cried out, snatching hopelessly at his foot, sprawling full length when he missed his grip. Bull had no eyes for him, intent as he was on his task. He would not be distracted again until Robin was safe.

Nearing the foot of the arch, he set the Major on his feet, careful to support his body or the young man would have fallen. Robin swayed, head hanging, eyes dull and lifeless. Bull took his shoulders and gently pushed him forward. Robin took an unsteady step and his foot made contact with the Bridge. Immediately, Sullyan's strength poured into his mind.

He raised his head and his eyes cleared. He took another step onto the span. Bull lost his hold, unable to go any farther. Sullyan could no longer feel her Guide; every ounce of her attention was concentrated on Robin's fragile soul. Bull stared at the young man's back, tears pricking his eyes, watching as he began his walk back to where Bull could no longer go.

Robin moved forward with purpose, buoyed by his life mate's strength, but he had only taken a few steps when he stopped and turned his head. He was weak, his body failing, thoroughly exhausted by his ordeals; the terror of enduring them would live forever in his mind. Yet Bull had given up everything to allow him to regain his life and Robin couldn't let that pass without some recognition or thanks.

He looked back over his shoulder at Bull standing there, his Master-level powers granting him perception in this place. What could he say to the big man, how could he express what he felt? Bull had been responsible for bringing him and Sullyan together. If he had not discovered Robin in that remote garrison near Lychdale and seen the young man's potential, Robin would have spent his life in obscurity or died in some battle at an early age. The encouragement and advice Bull imparted during those first tentative months, when Robin's impetuous nature nearly landed him in severe trouble on more than one occasion, had steered the young man firmly onto the right path and kept his hopes alive.

Robin already owed Bull his life in more ways than one. Yet how could he even begin to express the fathomless depths of his gratitude in the face of such selfless love as this?

He and Bull stared at each other, and in the end no words were needed. The tears neither could hide and the expressions in their eyes told a far deeper truth than mere words could have revealed. Eventually, Robin raised one arm, weak and trembling, and saluted his old friend with all the love in his heart. Bull ducked his head, too overcome to hold that indigo gaze, but then he found his courage and returned the simple gesture. He ended it with a wave of his hand, urging the young man to go. Robin gave the faintest of smiles as he returned a gentle nod. Forcing his exhausted body to respond to Sullyan's strength, he passed out of Bull's knowledge on his way back to the living world.

✣ ✣ ✣ ✣ ✣

Sullyan gasped in relief and exhaustion as Robin's slender form appeared on the Bridge, but she could not relinquish her hold or he would fall before he reached her and vanish into the Void—and nothing ever returned from that primal font of oblivion. So she endured the draining of her strength and supported Robin's steps. The love and yearning she saw in his eyes was all the encouragement she could need. When he finally reached her and fell into her arms, they both collapsed to the ground, sobbing and clutching and laughing, unable to speak for joy.

Yet the journey was not over and there was still a battle to win. Robin's mortal body was failing and would need much tending if he was to survive. There were also the terrible memories of the ordeals he'd had to endure, and they all combined to sap his will and torment him with failure and death. Sullyan tried to reach into his mind, intending to wipe the worst of them out, but her life mate refused the touch of her power and she gazed at him in concern.

"Why should you bear these dreadful memories, Robin? Why not let me take them from you? Let me ease your heart and heal the wounds they have left."

He shook his head and pushed her weakly away. "And who will ease them for you, my love? Why should you bear them alone? We've beaten our bitterest enemy. Let the memories remind us of that. We can help and support each other if their burden becomes too great. Besides, I think I'm going to need your strength just to live for the next few hours. Don't waste it shielding me from what I've already escaped."

She took his face between her hands and kissed him lightly on the lips, neither of them having the energy for a deeper sign of their love. Robin gazed back across the Bridge, and Sullyan saw the image of Bull in his eyes. "I'm ready now," he said.

She aided him to his feet. "It was his own choice, love. He'll live on in our hearts and he'll remain as my Guide—a far better fate for him than to fade slowly into incapacity and uselessness."

"There will be many tears." Robin's voice caught in his throat. "Rienne will be devastated. And furious. I don't know that she'll ever forgive him."

Sullyan sighed. "Rienne will find forgiveness in the end. Her heart is too great for bitterness and she knew his mind as well as anyone. Let us get you back, my love, before my strength gives out. I have one more task to perform here before I can follow you home. Cal and Tad will support you, and Mathias as well if need be. Morgan waits beyond the Gateway. Can you feel him calling you home?"

Robin set his mind to the ordeal of returning to life, feeling the flood of strength and encouragement coming from his friends and his son. Nodding to his life mate, he released his hold on her arms, stepping carefully back through the Gateway with her anxious eyes upon his back. Once he was safely through, she turned to face the

Bridge, setting her psyche on its way again within the strains of her soul song.

✤ ✤ ✤ ✤ ✤

"Look, Rienne, look! He's waking!"

Cal's urgent hiss was hardly necessary as none of them had taken their eyes from Robin's face during the past few agonized minutes. And it was just as well, for Robin was in desperate need of Cal's strength. The dark-skinned Journeyman threw himself into supporting the Major and had no spare energy with which to draw anyone's attention. Tad and Mathias Blaine were also caught up in the giving of strength.

Morgan jumped up from his bed and scrambled onto Robin's. Rienne's eyes welled with tears as the little boy called to his father, and when Robin's indigo eyes finally struggled open, she collapsed onto the bed, hardly able to give vent to the grateful sobs that racked her body. Dexter held her while Hanan watched over Robin, bathing his perspiring face and gently calling his name. The rest of the men stood in breathless silence, still waiting for a sign that he had truly returned, and when the familiar smile twisted his lips and his arms folded weakly around his son, the room erupted into wild jubilation and no one could hold back the tears.

The tide of joy swept over them and Rienne could not begrudge them their noisy release. Yet she and Hanan both knew it might be premature. Robin existed solely on the strength of his friends and still needed help to consolidate his return. Dashing the tears irritably from her eyes and pushing away from Dexter, Rienne moved past the General's immobile figure to reach their supply of herbs. Taking a cup of the strongest restorative they had brewed, she came to Robin's side and slipped an arm under his wasted shoulders. He had lost both weight and muscle in his terrible ordeal and his fragile body was no burden to Rienne's capable arms. Careful not to disturb either Tad's or Cal's concentration, she eased Robin upright and offered him the cup.

The brew had been warmed and slid soothingly down his throat. The love with which it was given and which he felt surging all around him brought tears to his sore eyes. Rienne saw the faint color tinge the gray of his face and smiled thankfully as she set the cup aside.

"I can't begin to tell you how I feel at this moment," she murmured, her voice barely audible above the men's clamor.

His reply was a hoarse whisper. "I'll be all right now. I just really need to sleep. Either Tad or Cal can stay with me to ensure I don't go too deep."

Rienne nodded and laid the wasted body down. Robin managed a faint smile before his eyes fluttered closed. Rienne's heart gave a lurch of fear until Morgan snuggled close, his head under Robin's chin, his small arms clasped about his father's neck. They were such a picture of peaceful contentment and the room was so filled with joy and relief that Rienne didn't at first hear the healer's frantic call of distress.

Chapter Thirty-Two

Sullyan located Bull's psyche and made contact once again with his mind, immediately swamped by the confusion and anger that filled his heart. There was some kind of battle going on, and it was one Bull scarcely knew how to fight, judging by the turmoil of his thoughts. Having a good idea what it must be, she insinuated herself into Bull's consciousness without compromising his concentration.

All at once, noise blared in her ears, wind buffeted her face, the ground heaved and rumbled beneath her feet, and lightning seared the air. She felt her skin singed by it and her heart thumped with fear, her reactions colored by Bull's as the big man desperately tried to counter the attack. Bull had never mastered Fire and it was his greatest fear. The scarecrow must have discerned this and was using Bull's weakness against him. Bull was further hampered by the moaning shade clutching feverishly at his legs, blocking his every movement and tangling with his feet.

The pair was driven ever closer to the Void, forced step by step by the lighting strikes that Bull frantically strove to field. Soon, they would either touch the Bridge or vanish over the edge—either would prove disastrous and would obliterate Bull forever.

The terrible, evil creature that was their foe, naked bones distorted out of all recognition by the molten spellsilver, gibbered in manic delight at the Guide's failing defenses. Sullyan knew that Bull's battling soul held no interest for the scarecrow. It was only his interference that had drawn the creature's bile. No, it was the shivering, cowering shade huddled at Bull's feet and screaming futile pleas for mercy that inflamed the scarecrow's vengeful heart. Deprived of Robin's soul to torment and the satisfaction of Sullyan's despair, the Baron would slake his revenge on Seth's quailing spirit in payment for the thwarting of his plans. Shrieking in triumph, the scarecrow gathered his strength and flung a colossal bolt of primal lightning straight at Bull's laboring heart.

Had it struck its target, it would have blasted the two men over the edge, sending them spiraling, screaming, into the Void until obliterated in its fathomless depths. But a shield sprang into being before Bull's terrified eyes, a shimmering pearly resistance that pervaded his every nerve. It flowed down around him to cover the quivering wretch at his feet, but Seth never saw it. His eyes were tightly closed and he gripped Bull's legs in a panicked spasm, convinced he would fall prey to the scarecrow for an eternity of torture.

The lightning struck Sullyan's mighty shield and rebounded in a cacophony of noise, shattering the air with a stupendous roar. Bull and the scarecrow were flattened to the ground, thrust down by the power of the blast. With Sullyan's strength within him, Bull was the first to regain his feet, while the stunned and moaning scarecrow writhed futilely on the ground. The big man staggered off balance while Seth clutched in terror at his legs.

Quickly, Bull, before Reen recovers! Get Seth onto the Bridge. It is the only place he will be safe.

Bull was blind from the aftershock of the blast, but he could feel where the Bridge began by the echo of its substance. Hauling Seth by the armpits, Bull heaved him to his feet, pressing him forward with a powerful shove when the manservant tried to resist.

Seth seemed to believe he was being attacked. He struggled and nearly tripped the big man in his efforts to escape.

"I'm trying to help you, you stupid sod!" Bull roared at him. "If you don't want to stay here forever, I suggest you do as you're told!"

His words had the desired effect. The manservant ceased struggling and let Bull guide him toward the Bridge. A scrabbling sound came from behind them, and an inchoate shriek of rabid rage. Seth turned his head in panic as the scarecrow staggered to his feet. Bull wasn't going to let him waste the precious distance they had gained, however, and he ignored the rush of evil he sensed hurtling toward his back. Jerking Seth's body forward, Bull forced the manservant's foot to touch the Bridge.

Seth instantly lost contact with the terrifying world of the dead. His resistance faded as instinct and the multitude took over, and he walked blindly across the Void. Bull watched him move away and heaved a sigh of relief, but then something struck him forcefully in the back. He tottered and lurched forward, unbalanced by the blow. Shrieks erupted in his ear as the scarecrow clung to his back, bony fists beating frenetically.

Swaying on the verge of obliteration, Bull struggled not to fall, cartwheeling his arms and twisting violently round as he sought purchase on firmer ground. His grasping hands caught at the distorted, gangly limbs, and he flung his attacker from him as he staggered back from the edge. The scarecrow's contorted body tumbled toward the Void, but the skeletal claws just managed to dig into the ground, halting his dizzying plunge. He hung on the edge of the drop, bony claws secure in their hold. His naked skull glared at Bull, malevolent red eyes triumphant, their promise of dire retribution stabbing into the big man's limping heart.

He watched, mesmerized and gasping for breath, as the tortured body hauled itself up from the vertiginous drop inch by inch. Yet the force of Reen's attacks had damaged the ground that rimmed the terrible Void and pieces of the edge began to crumble, scattering shards that fell from under his hands. As Bull stared in disbelief, a whole section of rim gave way, toppling lazily into the maw.

Bull rushed to the edge, staring into the dark as the scarecrow was sucked beyond his ken. A pathetic flailing of pale sticks and rags was his final sight of the evil creature as a despairing, shattering cry drifted up from the depths. It held such a desolate, keening tone that it cut into Bull's heart, so much so that he slumped gasping and shivering to the ground beside the Bridge.

✣ ✣ ✣ ✣ ✣

Sullyan did not wait to witness the Baron's final fate. She left Bull's consciousness as Seth traversed the Bridge. He would be lost and liable to panic once he reached the other side, so she tarried to meet him and send his spirit back. She stood beside the Gateway and finally saw him emerge from the mist that prevented her seeing the other side of the Void.

He walked woodenly across the span, unseeing and unresponsive, lacking the Artesan senses that had aided both Taran and Robin. His momentum carried him off the Bridge, but deserted him once he reached her. He stood blind and helpless before her, unable to speak or hear her voice. There was no one to aid his return and she would not make the time herself—she was desperate to see how her friends had fared and to join them once more. There was only one thing she could do for him, and she did it as she opened the Gateway, and then she sent his spirit through and left him to fend for himself. She had spoken truly back in Lerric's palace when she told him he would be free of persecution. Once the Gateway swallowed his figure, she banished him forever from her mind.

Taking a long, final look out over the graceful expanse of the arch, Sullyan sent a tender, loving thought winging toward the friend who had made all this possible. She had no adequate words to thank him, no way to express her gratitude; all she could hope was that he could sense what was in her heart. They were linked now for eternity in a bond not even Death could breach. She had the comfort of knowing he was not truly gone, but would wait for her call.

This knowledge tempered her sadness, but it still pricked at the depths of her heart. She would miss his solid presence more than she knew how to admit. And Rienne—poor, gentle Rienne who loved Bull so deeply—would feel his absence all the keener because of her lack of Artesan powers. The best Sullyan could hope for was that Rienne's empathic talents would aid her and she would be able to feel Bull's mighty spirit through Sullyan's familiar touch.

Sighing for the loss, the grief, and the sorrow they had all endured these past few weeks, Sullyan turned her back on the Bridge and faced the Gateway. Gathering her fraying strength, fast fading now the ordeal was over, she sang her passage through and passed back into the living realm.

She woke to frantic commands and flurried movement. With no one nearby to help her, she was forced to pull herself up out of the lethargy of her efforts. Fear beat about her heart as she gathered her wits, and she opened her eyes to a scene of chaos. Too weary to call out, she pushed herself upright, glancing about, fearful for her friends. Taran and Jinny were sleeping, tightly clasped in each other's arms. Sofira sat weeping, cradled by Elias and flanked by her two children. Robin lay on the bed beside Sullyan's, breathing evenly and in no danger, Morgan hugging his father's neck as the boy gently lent him strength. Tad and Cal sat close by, watching over their charges, so it was only Mathias Blaine who noticed Sullyan's return.

The General stepped to her side and helped her rise from the bed, one arm around her shoulders as he assessed her state. "Are you strong enough to deal with this?" He indicated Bull's still form with a curt nod of his head.

Through the press of people, she saw Rienne alternately breathing into Bull's blue-tinged mouth and pounding on his silent heart. Tears flowed unhindered down her chalky face.

Sullyan sighed, shrinking from the task. Reluctance seeped through her weary spirit at the grief she was about to inflict. "Ah, Mathias, has no one told her?"

The General's voice was uncharacteristically strained as he regarded the scene. "We were all preoccupied. Major Tamsen needed a lot of help and support. Those of us who already knew didn't have the leisure to tell her, and the healer who was watching Bull didn't immediately notice what had happened."

Sullyan saw that his eyes were shimmering with unshed tears, and she ducked her head at this unprecedented show of emotion. Bull had served the General longer than anyone else. He was Blaine's last link to the old way of life the General had given up.

Accepting the offer of energy that Blaine pressed into her mind, Sullyan stood, leaning on his arm until her legs became steadier. Rienne still worked frantically on Bull, and Sullyan could hardly bear the anguish in her friend's eyes. She stepped across and caught Rienne's left hand, pulling her away from her urgent massaging of Bull's chest.

Rienne spun round, snatching at Sullyan's arm. "Oh, Brynne, thank all the gods! His heart's given out, but you can bring him back. It can't have been very long."

She moved away from the bed to give Sullyan room to work and stared in uneasy bewilderment when the Artesan made no move to take her place. "Hurry, Brynne, hurry!" She gave Sullyan a push, her face paling further when Sullyan slowly shook her head.

"No, Rienne. It would be no use."

General Blaine, Tad, and Cal watched with sad sympathy while all the other occupants of the room held their breath in disbelief.

Fury came over Rienne and she shook Sullyan angrily. "What do you mean, it would be no use? Don't tell me you can't help him—you've just brought four people back from the dead! He's counting on you to save him! Don't you *dare* let him down!"

Rienne was trembling and Sullyan stepped closer, taking her by the arms. She reached out with her fading strength, trying to link with Rienne's empathic mind. When the healer was calm and receptive, this was an easy thing to do, but with panic and desperation coloring her thoughts, it took some power to achieve. She spoke clearly, so all could hear.

"It was Bulldog who saved them, not me. I only provided the channel and opened the Gateway to the Void. It was Bull's sacrifice that saved them and brought them back from the dead."

Rienne froze, staring out of fixed, glazed eyes. "Sacrifice?"

Sullyan tried to smile, although her heart was burdened with Rienne's grief as well as her own. "Yes. The legends were correct. There is no way back from the spirit realm save by the exchange of a life. Bulldog gave his up in order to be my Guide. He chose to take their places so they could return here to us."

Rienne was silent, as was everyone else in the room. The former captives slept on peacefully, unaware of the healer's grief. Only Sofira wept quietly, her face buried in Elias's chest, but her grief was not for Bull. Not a single movement broke the tableau— not a foot moved, not a head turned. All was uncomprehendingly silent until the healer spoke again.

"No."

"Rienne, please. I cannot—"

"NO!"

Rienne's shout rang in the room, shocking them all. She stared wildly at Sullyan, twin spots of color flaming high in her cheeks. She trembled violently as she threw off Sullyan's hands and thrust her angry face close, fists balled at her chest.

"I won't have it! There *must* be a way to save him. There must be *something* you can do!"

Sullyan shook her head, aching for Rienne's deep pain. She wanted to hold her, ease her way through this. Yet Rienne was in no condition to accept her help. Until she came to believe it, there was nothing Sullyan could do.

"It was his choice, Rienne. That is the only comfort I can give you. He did it to save me from the same fate. He said he would prefer to do this than see himself slowly decline."

"Oh, yes, feed me some trite, pathetic line! That's just what he *would* have said, do you think I don't know that?"

Rienne's fury made the men recoil and some moved away from the beds. Their earlier euphoria had been tempered by the news of Bull's death, and Rienne's violent reaction upset them even more. They were hardened and used to the idea of losing friends and comrades in battle, and this had been just one more battle, albeit on a metaphysical plane. Death was part of their lives and Bull had lived longer than most. They could accept his death and be proud of the result he had achieved.

But Rienne was more used to healing, to seeing her patients survive. Every one that didn't make it was taken as a personal affront. Yet they were also used to her strength and capability in such circumstances, and seeing her so lost in her grief was unexpected and disturbing.

Sullyan understood Rienne's reaction better. The healer was exhausted from dealing with the emotion of all those around her as well as her medical responsibilities. Her friends' return must have seemed like a miracle after the trauma of their condition—as indeed it was—and Rienne couldn't accept right now that Bull's sacrifice was the coin that had paid for it.

Fortunately, Sullyan was spared dealing with Rienne's anguish. Mathias Blaine came up behind the healer and wrapped his arms around her, refusing to release her when she screamed at him to do so. As Elias had done for Sullyan after Robin's capture by the Baron, the General held on to Rienne and bore the assault of her grief. She struggled in his arms, fiercer than many would have believed, and spat curses she could only have learned from Sullyan. Had her arms been free she might have pummeled his chest, but he gripped them tightly and she was helpless.

Eventually, her fury ran out and her legs gave way. She crumpled into sobs. Blaine glanced across at Sullyan, who gestured to Bull's body. The General carried Rienne to where the big man lay and set her gently on the bed. She collapsed over his body, weeping and calling his name as she stroked his face.

The men, the other healers, and Sullyan stood in respectful silence, heads bowed, eyes downcast, each mourning and saluting the mighty heart of a mighty man whose selfless sacrifice had won the day, and whose presence would be sorely missed.

✣ ✣ ✣ ✣ ✣

"Blimey, mate, you didn't half give us a turn! We thought you was dead for sure. What you doin' way out here in the snow? You tryin' to freeze to death?"

"One more hour and he'd have done it, too. C'mon, Reb, give me your cloak. Poor bugger's too frozen to speak. We've got to get him to some shelter or he'll lose some fingers or maybe his ears."

The two men grappled with the weight of the torpid man and wrestled him to his feet, dragging him across the field when he proved unable to walk. It was only pure chance they had come out this way at all. Reb and his brother Farom, the village shepherds, had set out at first light to find two stray sheep that had been separated from the herd in the blizzard. It was while they were checking the final field that Farom spotted the dark shape lying in the snow.

Reb grunted, struggling under the man's weight. "We'd better get him to the shippen. We'll never drag him back to the village afore it gets dark. We can get him warm there and feed him up a bit, then perhaps he can make it the rest of the way tomorrow."

Farom was too puffed to reply, but he changed direction and the two men angled toward a distant hut with a snow-covered thatch roof. It was mainly used in the spring to shelter lambing ewes from unseasonable storms, but it had strong stone walls and a stout wooden door and the brothers, canny in the snow, had brought supplies to make a fire and a frugal meal. It was death to be caught in the open in this kind of weather with no means of making a fire. Panting, they hauled the unconscious man inside.

Reb kicked the door shut and cut off the freezing wind. The hut had no windows, but enough daylight seeped through the cracks around the door to reveal signs of recent habitation.

"Someone's been here!"

They laid the man on the dirt-packed floor and examined the remains of a fire and a half-full bucket below the narrow shelf that smelled faintly of frozen urine. A few bowls and utensils lay scattered across the floor, but nothing else to tell them who might have sheltered there.

Reb shrugged. "Must've been some poor sod caught out in that last storm. At least they had the sense to light a fire. Get a good blaze goin' or we'll be no more use than this chap."

Unwrapping his thick sheepskin cloak from the unconscious man's face, Reb saw that he was a young man, around twenty-six or so. He was only marginally younger than the two shepherds, and Reb wondered what he'd been doing so far out in the snow. He was not dressed for cold weather, for he wore only a shirt and breeches of good quality. Shaking his head, he felt the young man's hands, frowning at their stiffness and the swelling of the joints. "Ain't you got that fire goin' yet?"

Farom replied with a mild obscenity as he tended a brightening flame.

Soon, the little hut was warming. Farom dug out their few supplies as Reb continued to chafe the frozen man's hands, attempting to aid his circulation and stave off frostbite. They moved him nearer the fire and eventually he stirred, much to the brothers' relief.

They watched his eyes open and saw confusion in them. They could hardly wonder at that, for the hut would be unfamiliar to him, and Reb shuffled closer to catch his eye.

"What's your name, then, mate?" He spoke slowly and clearly, as if the man were deaf. Farom sniggered at him and Reb tossed him an obscene gesture.

"You're not goin' to get any sense out of him yet." Farom handed his brother a bowl of warmed corn mash. "Get some warmth and fodder into him first. Ask your questions later."

Reb scowled at his brother as he accepted the bowl, taking a wooden spoon from his pocket. While Farom supported Seth's shoulders, Reb helped him to eat, and soon his face took on more color and animation came into his eyes.

"Who are you?" he croaked once the mash was all gone. "I don't think I know you …"

"I'm Farom, and this is my brother Reb. We're shepherds from Crowtree. We found you half-frozen in the fields, face down in the snow. What was you doin' there, lad?"

Seth looked dazed. "Crowtree? Where's that?"

Farom and Reb exchanged a glance, wondering what they had let themselves in for. The young man didn't look like a simpleton, nor did he have the appearance of an escaped felon, but something certainly wasn't right about him. "'Bout ten miles east of Daret. Province of Bordenn."

"Daret ... Bordenn ..."

Reb eyed Seth warily. "You from Daret, then? You're a long way from home if you are."

"Long way ...," echoed Seth. "Daret? No."

"Where, then?" Farom was growing irritated. Seth's condition seemed genuine enough, but something about his manner really bothered the shepherd.

Seth looked him full in the face for the first time, and the brothers frowned at the tears shimmering in his eyes. "I ... don't know. I can't remember!"

Reb glanced at his brother. "He's lost his recollections, poor sod. Seen it once afore in a man who nearly froze to death. Took him months to get 'em back, and even then he was none too sharp."

Farom glanced at Seth's bowed head. "What'll we do with him, then? Can't just leave him here, not knowin' who he is."

Reb shrugged. "Get him home in the mornin'. Take care of him. See if he recovers. If he does, he can take himself off when he pleases. If not, well, we can always do with another hand with the sheep."

Farom stared skeptically at Seth's slight build and smooth skin. The young man must have heard their muted conversation, for he raised his head and tried a tentative smile. "I'd do my best to repay your kindness. I know I don't look like much, but I'm a hard worker. And I think ... yes, I think I might quite like sheep ..."

Chapter Thirty-Three

The morning sun streamed in the windows of the senior officers' hall, giving the false impression of a warm spring day outside. It might be a cloudless sky, but frozen snow still lay on the ground and those who lounged within still needed their thick shirts and leather jerkins despite the fire roaring in the grate.

Conversation was muted, for none of them had any energy. They simply relaxed in uncomplicated company, safe in the knowledge of their enemy's demise. Despite the calm air of comradeship, however, there was an underlying sadness, and the absence of some of their number underscored the changes that had been wrought.

Sullyan sat cradling Robin's head in her lap, absently stroking his hair, his even breathing indicating he was nearly asleep. Morgan sat beside her, snuggled close under her arm. Sullyan had her eyes closed too, but she was not sleeping. She was wondering how to bring some ease to Rienne's deeply grieving soul.

Jinny and Taran lounged together on the settle beside them, Taran's arm around Jinny's shoulders and her hand clasping his. Jinny had never felt quite as relaxed with Robin and Sullyan as Taran did. The memory of her part in their acrimonious split three years ago always lurked in her mind. Her total lack of metasense also set her apart, despite Taran's frequent assurances that it mattered not one bit.

Since their time together in the prison below Lerric's palace, however, Jinny had lost her lingering sense of guilt. It no longer seemed relevant when viewed against that terrible living nightmare. Robin's care and fear for her despite his desperate circumstances, and the comfort they had taken from each other when all else was hopeless, had welded them together with a bond of unbreakable steel. That, coupled with Sullyan and Bull's incredible achievement in bringing the captives back, caused Jinny to feel as close to them as she did to Taran. Now she sat in companionable silence with them as she tried to recover her strength.

Taran, Jinny, and Robin were all still pale and exhausted from their ordeals, but half a day and a night's healing sleep, aided by strong restorative herbs, had begun the process of recovery. Chief Healer Hanan had pronounced herself satisfied with their progress, and even reported that Taran and Jinny's dreadful wounds finally showed signs of healing. It was Sullyan's private opinion that the lesions would disappear rapidly now that the Baron had been destroyed. His evil and unnatural influence had kept them open and weeping. Now that his victims were free of him, their wounds would soon vanish.

Like the slash on Robin's arm, inflicted by the Baron's knife, which was just a slim red line after Sullyan's healing session. She glanced down at the limb in question where it lay across his breast. The only visible signs of his torture were the healing skin around his wrists and his wasted muscles. Robin would regain his youthful vigor given time and careful tending. Yet a broken heart would not mend as easily, she mused with a sharp pang of sorrow, thinking of Rienne's crushed spirit and wishing her friend were here.

Rienne and Cal were missing from the gathering. Cal had

reported that Rienne felt too depressed to join them and he didn't like to leave her while she was so down. She had spent the previous afternoon and half the night keeping vigil by Bull's body until exhaustion and sorrow had claimed her and Cal carried her off to bed.

Sullyan's sad musings were disturbed by a gentle knock at the door. Hyram opened the door to admit Prince Eadan, who skipped into the room and ran straight over to Morgan. He clambered up onto the couch. His slight weight roused Robin, who grinned at the Prince and reached out to ruffle his hair as he bounced by Morgan's side. Elias, who had followed his son, stopped just inside the door, looking uncharacteristically diffident as his gaze met Sullyan's.

"Come and join us, my friend."

Elias inclined his head at her invitation and slowly entered the room. She watched him, wondering what was on his mind. He kept his eyes on his hands as he spoke. "I've been making arrangements to return to Port Loxton, but there's a problem I have no idea how to solve."

She felt her heart drop. "Sofira and your daughter?" After a long talk with her humbled, repentant mother, Seline had abjured her hatred of Sullyan and confessed to harboring Reen's agent in the castle and giving him the key to the east wing. Her shrill, tearful apologies still rang in Sullyan's ears.

Elias nodded, his head still bent. Sullyan let out a heavy sigh and rested her head on Robin's shoulder. The young man passed an arm about her waist. "What do you want to do with them, your Majesty?" he asked.

Elias raised his head, catching the mute appeal in Robin's eyes. He gasped faintly. "Don't tell me you would sue for mercy? Considering what they've put you through, I'd have thought you'd be the first to demand their heads."

Robin glanced meaningfully down at Eadan, who sat close by Morgan's side. The King's son watched his father with wide, worried eyes, sensing the tension and anger but not fully understanding its implications. "There's been enough death and heartache to last us all a lifetime," Robin murmured. "I couldn't bear to think of someone else losing a loved one."

Elias glanced between his son and the Major's pale face, handsome still despite his suffering and the weight he had lost. Sullyan knew that something in Elias cried out for retribution, for the personal vengeance he had been denied by the Baron's strange demise. He wanted to lash out at those who had hurt him, who had hurt the ones he loved, and his former wife and daughter were the only ones who were left. To hear them defended felt like having his authority challenged. Too often had he needed the protection of those before him. It was high time he repaid them for their selfless efforts on his behalf, but granting their wishes and denying himself his revenge was too large a step to take without resistance.

Unwilling to accept Robin's plea, he turned to Sullyan. "What do you think, Brynne?"

She knew he expected her to support him. Hadn't she impeached Sofira at the Baron's trial? She had wanted the Queen's influence over the King removed, even if exposing her treachery would wound him.

She raised her weary head from the comfort of Robin's shoulder, her eyes dulled by memories and by the echo of deep pain. "I think such decisions can wait. I have more important things on my mind. I shall not be able to think straight until after Bull's funeral."

Elias ducked his head, ashamed. How could he have forgotten such a sad and important ceremony? Even now the men were collecting wood to form the base of Bull's pyre. "Of course, Brynne. I'm so sorry. I meant no disrespect. I will be there to honor him at the setting of the sun."

Sullyan shook her head. "No, not sunset, Elias. Sunrise."

Even the General raised his brows. Manor tradition placed all funerals in the evening, signifying the deceased's spirit leaving the world's light. What Sullyan proposed was a strange departure and seemed almost disrespectful, as if she was refusing to accept Bull was gone. She could see conflicting emotions on many faces, all except Robin's, who knew why the decision had been made.

"I intend to honor Bull's sacrifice," she said. "The rising sun will symbolize his status, for he has begun a new existence and is not lost to his dearest friends."

Elias frowned, not fully understanding, and Jinny looked up at Taran, who whispered in her ear. The General, however, nodded to his colonel, accepting the propriety of what she planned to do.

✣ ✣ ✣ ✣ ✣

It was still dark when they all assembled, warmly clad against the freezing winter wind. The moon dipped toward the horizon, just touching the brow of the ridge, wispy cirrus trailing across its gibbous face. They had come a fair distance from the Manor buildings to the western slope leading up to the ridge. The horses that had brought them stood champing softly in the dark. Those still too weak to sit a horse had come in wagons, and they huddled in their fleece-lined cloaks, waiting for the dawn.

The vast pile of logs that made up Bull's pyre loomed in the ghostly light. Everyone at the Manor had personally gathered wood for it, the size of the pyre serving as a testament to their love and respect for Bull as the pile grew ever higher. It was topped by a magnificent red and gold cloth bearing Elias's standard, the Rovannon's sun-circled crown. Bull's body, brought from the mortuary by his favorite horse and accompanied by his closest friends, was tenderly laid on this sumptuous bed, his sword lying on his breast. He bore no covering save his clothes and his cloak.

He would face the new sun openly as he had always done in life.

Everyone from the Manor attended, from swordsmen to kitchen boys. All who had known the huge man had been touched by his generous heart. Sullyan stood watching their faces, this multitude of loyal men, her heart swelling with pride for the wealth of love they represented. Bull had never married, never had the comfort of a life mate. He had always been content with brief liaisons, and due to his Artesan powers, he had never fathered a child. He had always saved the greatest portion of his mighty heart for one who was forever beyond his reach, but one who nevertheless returned the love he had to offer with all of her generous soul.

There was one, though, who might have taken Hal Bullen for a life mate had she not already given her heart before coming to the Manor. Sullyan sought the face of her friend, seeing Rienne standing close by with Cal's arm supporting her. Her image blurred in the torchlight, wavered in the tears filling Sullyan's eyes. Rienne had spent the night in vigil over Bull's body. Cal had remained beside her, helping her through the ordeal. Whether she had gained any comfort from it, Sullyan couldn't tell. She still looked fragile and brittle, despite the warming glow of the torches, and her sunken cheeks were pale.

Both Taran and Jinny watched Rienne from the comfort of their wagon. Rienne had refused their offer to share it and stayed resolutely on her feet. She swayed with the effort and needed Cal's strong arm to hold her. Sullyan could only hope her aching soul would find some peace once the pyre had done its work. If not, she promised herself she would do something about it, enduring Rienne's anger later if necessary. She would not see her friend suffer needlessly, not while she could prevent such things.

The false dawn was fading and Sullyan glanced toward the General, who stood at one end of the pyre beside a flaming brand.

Piles of smaller torches lay beside him and similar piles lay at the other end, where Sullyan awaited the sun. The men were grouped in ranks, in an order prearranged. They knew what to do once the Paean began.

Catching Blaine's slight nod, Sullyan closed her eyes, raised her face to the east, and began to sing, the still-healing injury to her throat giving her voice a soulful huskiness.

At the first notes, the men nearest took up their brands, lighting the smaller torches from the larger ones burning nearby. They walked toward the pyre in order, murmuring the messages to Bull they had in their hearts, and thrust each tiny flame deep into the pile of logs. As the flames caught the tinder below, each man added his voice to the song, swelling the Paean as the hidden sun tinged the sky. More and more brands were lit and their flames crackled deep within the pyre; more and more throats gave voice to the song, until only those closest to Bull remained silent.

The sun was on the cusp of rising as Taran raised his arms, joining Blaine, Tad, Cal, and Robin in a metaphysical bond. Sullyan added her power and the air trembled with their force, but the pyre still stood gently smoldering, awaiting the final thrust. Dexter, who had already added his brand, saw Sullyan's nod and came up beside Rienne, taking the startled healer's arm from around her life mate's waist. He urged her forward and she stepped with him toward the pyre, confusion in her eyes as the exultant song shivered through her soul. The Captain reached out and took hold of the largest brand, helping Rienne hold it upright as they stood close beside the pyre. "Goodbye, old friend," murmured Dexter, a catch in his voice, and he glanced into Rienne's eyes as he encouraged her to speak.

Rienne's heart was bursting with sorrow. Her throat was tight and sore and she could hardly see for the tears in her eyes. The trembling of her body was fast becoming too strong to bear, but she could hardly let Bull go without some word of farewell. She could almost hear his voice, as if he stood by her side, whispering, *Please don't grieve so, dear heart,* in his much-loved, rumbling tones. That gentle whisper undid her resolve and she cried her grief to the skies, wailing his name in despair as the first ray of the rising sun streaked through the crystal air.

The brand she held with Dexter's help was thrust deep into the pyre, and suddenly it was as if the sun itself had ignited the vast pile of smoldering logs. The Paean rang out, fueled by two thousand throats, and the brilliant golden sun-flames burst into life with a magnificent leap for the sky. Rienne gasped with wonder, startled but not frightened by the display, seeing Bull's beloved form limned by the majesty of Fire. It licked around him but did not touch him, controlled by a powerful force, the heat directed upward into the shimmering air. Dexter drew Rienne away from the roar of the pyre, the flames gaining in intensity as the new sun flared in the sky.

The Paean soared to its glorious climax as the burning disc rose over the horizon, washing the world with color and the warmth of vibrant new life. As the golden elemental light bathed the entire ridge in sunshine, the pyre gave a mighty roar and the Paean responded in kind. Two thousand voices cried their wonder and love as Bull's body vanished in an expanding halo of incandescence. Rienne watched in tearful awe as the primal light spread its ethereal luster, touching each and every one of them with renewal and strength. The love that had weighed Rienne's soul now flooded her with ecstasy and she added her lovely voice to the culmination of the song. Sullyan smiled and withdrew from Rienne's mind. The melody soared and danced with the flames, seemingly woven with the sunlight, until its final majestic chord rang out in an exultant shout.

The sound echoed about the ridge and resounded in the

hollows, fading back to respectful silence as the throng ended their psalm. The flames of the pyre died with them and fell to smoldering. A heap of fluttering ashes was all that was left of the great-hearted man. Many eyes fell in contemplation as the ceremony reached its conclusion, many heads bowed in peaceful reflection as the sighing wind began its task.

Blowing from the east, swirled by the power of the Artesans, the playful winter wind danced in the ashes on the ground. Still warm from the flames, they lifted gently from the earth, free to scatter where they would. The wind gained in strength and whirled them higher into the air before gusting and spreading them far over the Manor lands.

Bull's soul had passed the boundaries and transcended the barrier of Death. Now his body became one with the earth from which it formed.

Chapter Thirty-Four

The wedding of Court Artesan Adept-elite Taran Elijah and the Baroness Jinella took place in Port Loxton, three months after their miraculous return from the spirit realm and their emotional farewell to the friend who had sacrificed his own life to save them. Senior Patrio Roshan conducted the well-attended ceremony at the Minster. His anticipated appointment to Arch Patrio had not yet been ratified by the King. There were vague, unsubstantiated rumors that it never would be ratified, despite Roshan being the senior churchman since the murder of Lord Neremiah, and the presence in the Minster that mid-spring day of a certain young Patrio from the holy island off Serna Bay only fueled those mysterious rumors.

Ruvar had come for the wedding at Sullyan's invitation and was determined to say nothing that might encourage speculation. He was not yet widely known, nor was he recognized by many of the Minster's junior clerics, and he was accosted only briefly by a suspicious Roshan and his immediate staff. Having escaped their clumsy attempts to extract information, Ruvar lost himself within the throng, blending in among the wedding guests due to his wise decision to eschew a cleric's robes in favor of holiday clothing.

Once the elegant ceremony was over, the city indulged in the rare pleasure of a royally decreed Feast Day. Elias was generously funding a number of street banquets, the palace kitchens and suppliers having been instructed to provide copious amounts of food and drink. The day was crisp and breezy but bright, although not even drizzle would have spoiled the city's revelry. The wedding party itself, conveyed by sumptuous open coaches, made its way toward the palace gates through the throng of happy people, hailed and congratulated by all who saw them pass. Taran and Jinella, in the foremost coach with Elias and Eadan, smiled and waved and blushed in turn at the enthusiastic acclaim they received. The other guests, including many from the Manor, followed in separate carriages.

Wedding ceremonies among Albia's nobility demanded two receptions. This first one, the public reception, was open to all who cared to attend, from the highest noble to the lowliest peasant, and was traditionally held in the couple's new home. It was a chance for the newlyweds to show off their wealth and status.

The evening reception, the private feast, was for close family and friends only, and was usually hosted by the couple's parents. As Jinny and Taran were currently homeless due to the destruction of the mansion, Elias offered them his largest banqueting hall and had it adorned with all manner of decorations, determined to show his guests the generosity and favor of his House. The long polished tables groaned under golden platters and silver goblets that glittered in the sunlight pouring into the huge room.

Fires crackled in the hearths, banishing the spring chill and lending pleasant warmth to the celebration as minstrels played lively airs from the balcony above. The feast was served immediately, and the King shared the topmost table with his closest, most valued friends.

Taran and Jinella had the honor of the central seats, flanked by Elias and General Blaine. Sullyan and Robin sat with Cal and Rienne, dressed in their finest feast day clothes. For once, Sullyan had given in to her royal status and permitted Jinella to insist that she dress as the Princess she was. Her gown was a shimmering shade of peacock, which changed subtly with the light and flowed around her slender figure like a cascading blue-green waterfall. Her fire opals flashed against this backdrop, echoing the tawny of her hair, and her amber skin glowed in the light of the springtime sun.

Robin had lost his wasted appearance and was elegantly slim beside her in a shirt of the same shimmering hue. His dark sleeveless tunic and soft, skintight breeches accentuated his height and regained strength. Physically recovered now from the ordeals of the past, all the Baron's victims attended the wedding feast— even the disgraced former Queen, who sat quietly to one side with her pale-faced daughter. Jinella had begged this favor as a wedding gift from Elias, and although the King had been none too pleased, he could hardly refuse her.

Elias's lords and ministers and senior military officers shared the lower tables, with the cream of Loxton's nobility crowding out the room. Once the sumptuous feast was over, the tables were moved aside and the minstrels began their sets. Elias, receiving a diffident nod of permission from Taran, claimed the first dance from the radiant new bride, and they made a handsome pair as they glided in splendid isolation down the center of the room. Jinny was resplendent in a bronze-hued silken gown, the color set off to perfection by Elias's gold and red. Taran watched his laughing bride wistfully from the edges of the throng, seeing her partner the High King of all Albia with the easy aplomb of the nobly born. He would have to adjust rapidly to his newly conferred status if he was to avoid embarrassing Jinella at the various functions he knew she had planned.

"Are you happy, my Lord Elijah?" a mischievous voice said in his ear.

The unfamiliarity of the title caused Taran's face to flush.

Elias may have elevated him to Loxton's exclusive peerage, but Taran would never forget his humble roots.

He turned his head to regard Sullyan, who stood beside him, ostensibly watching Jinella but keen to see his reaction. "What do you think?" he said acidly.

A smile spread across her face, lighting her beautiful golden eyes. He shook his head in disbelief, his gaze returning to his bride. "I've been very lucky, I can't deny it. Who wouldn't be happy with the way my life has turned out?"

She gave him a sidelong glance. "So why the long face, my friend?"

He narrowed his eyes and sighed. "I do love her, Brynne, I love her very much. The events of the past few weeks and that terrible time when I thought I had lost her showed me just how deep my feelings have grown. But ... oh, I don't know. I just hope I can live up to her expectations. My origins are so different to hers and I don't always feel comfortable with the kind of life she leads. I'm afraid I'll let her down and disappoint her in front of all her society friends."

Sullyan smiled impishly. "Oh, I doubt the Lady Jinella will be disappointed in her new husband, my Lord." She ignored Taran's glare at her deliberate use of his new title. "Not if your ... performance so far is anything to go by."

Taran frowned at her and opened his mouth to ask what she meant. Robin came up beside him and laid his hand on Taran's shoulder, chasing the comment out of Taran's mind. Sullyan smiled quietly to herself.

"How's the new house coming along?" Robin asked. "When will it be fit to live in?"

Taran gave an exasperated sigh. "Never, if I can't rein in Jinny's constantly changing plans! Every time she visits a friend's house, she gets different ideas for ours. She's altered the floor plan three times so far and poor Master Withen's at his wits' end. He goes pale every time she visits the site."

Sullyan gave a little laugh. "What did you expect, Taran? She is nest building, and Jinny is the sort of girl to want everything perfect for her family."

Taran grimaced, completely missing the undertone to Sullyan's lilting voice. Robin smirked gently when his friend failed to take the hint. "We won't be able to afford to start a family if she doesn't stop spending gold. We'll be as beggared as Sir Regus by the end of the year!"

Both the younger Artesans laughed at his use of the popular phrase. The junior minister's oft-bewailed penury was the butt of many Loxton jokes. Robin was about to make some comment, but the minstrels changed their tune and played the musical signal for the guests to join the celebratory dance.

Sullyan held out her hand to Taran. "Well, my Lord Elijah, will you leave me standing partnerless?"

He startled her with his refusal, his face showed genuine regret. "I'm afraid I shall have to, Highness. I have my orders from the Baroness and I dare not refuse her. She'll deny me the marriage bed if I shirk this essential duty."

"Well, that won't matter one jot," Sullyan murmured under her breath, but Taran didn't hear her as he made his excuses and left. She and Robin watched in surprise as he approached the former Queen, and Sofira's astonishment was almost comical as he courteously requested a dance. Sullyan shared a look with Robin. "Well, my love, would you have believed it?"

Sofira blushed becomingly and accepted Taran's hand. The Princess hesitantly followed Taran's lead, allowing him to escort her into the merry dancing throng. Jinella smiled as she passed them in the measure, but Elias's face was expressionless and he refused to glance their way.

"What will he do with them, do you think?" Robin asked quietly as they watched the dance unfold, Sofira gaining confidence under Taran's gallant lead.

"He is still wounded by what she did to him and wants some sort of retribution. But I have made a suggestion that I think he might accept." Sullyan felt a light touch on her shoulder and accepted Cal's invitation, Robin turning to escort Rienne as the music swept them up.

She could say no more as they were parted by the dance and her attention focused on Rienne instead. Rienne had still not recovered her spirits after Bull's selfless sacrifice and missed him more than she knew how to admit. Her participation in his funeral had given her some measure of comfort, but the days and weeks that followed seemed increasingly hard for her to bear.

With the elimination of the Baron, life at the Manor had almost returned to normal. The rotation of the companies had resumed its former pattern, but the Manor was not the same without Bull's stentorian voice. Rienne missed him everywhere she looked and couldn't stop herself from thinking she might see him at any time. Cal had tried several times to reassure her that Bull's spirit was still living, but Rienne couldn't sense him, couldn't gain any ease for the fierce ache in her heart.

She had taken to spending all her time working in the infirmary when she wasn't with her children, and Cal had begun to worry that she was wearing herself down. To make matters worse, Rienne was slowly cutting herself off from those who could help her heal.

The afternoon's festivities passed all too soon, with music and dancing and entertainers all laid on at Elias's expense. Following Taran's lead, others danced with Sofira, including Robin and Cal, much to the King's disgust. Sullyan watched him with exasperation, wishing she could make him see that giving the mother of his children a second chance was the best way to heal their wounds. Seline also had her share of partners and soon lost her anxious look, her young age sparing her the embarrassment she might otherwise have suffered. The pinnacle of her day was the attentions of the handsome Tad, who gallantly requested her hand in one of the liveliest sets.

The public reception concluded with a special set of songs performed by the newlyweds' closest friends in honor of their day. Taran and Jinny sat side by side, glowing with happy contentment while they listened as Sullyan sang for them and played her harp. She was joined by Robin and Dexter, and even General Blaine, who had a pleasant voice when he permitted himself the leisure. Cal played his silver whistle and others from the Manor supported them, delighting the remaining wedding guests with their musical skills.

Then the players struck up their final tune, a well-loved military air that had been Bull's favorite. Mathias Blaine took Bull's bass part and sang the anthem well, the whole room joining in with the rousing chorus. Taran, thoroughly enjoying himself, leaned across his wife to address Rienne.

"You can almost hear Bull singing this. I could swear he's standing up there with them!"

The shimmering tears in Rienne's eyes and the pinched pallor of her face startled Taran out of his pleasure. His face fell. "Oh, Rienne, please don't grieve so! Can't you feel his presence? Can't you sense he's still here?"

Jinny and Elias turned worried eyes on Rienne and Jinny tried to take up the healer's hand. Rienne would not be comforted, though.

"No, I can't, Taran, and it's tearing me apart!" Her anger, flaring suddenly as it did, shocked him. "You all keep saying he's not gone, that you can feel him in your mind, but *I* can't feel him because I'm not one of you! You all seem to forget that when you talk among yourselves. You don't realize how much it hurts me to hear the things you say!"

Taran was cut to the heart to think that the only thing their efforts to comfort had achieved was to make Rienne feel worse. "Can't Brynne help you feel him? Haven't you asked her to try?"

Rienne's tears spilled down her face. "Oh, she's tried, all right, but what use is it? All I see are her memories of him. Don't you think I have enough of those? I can't get comfort from memories, not when I miss him so much!"

Her voice faltered and failed altogether and her tears fell uncontrollably. Unable to bear the attention she was attracting, she ran from the room, drawing startled eyes as she fled. Taran went to follow, but Jinny stopped him. "I'll go after her, my love, you stay here." She left the hall quietly.

Cal had seen Rienne's distress from his place on the dais, but the music hadn't finished and he could hardly desert his post. He flashed Sullyan a despairing glance that she returned. She had tried on many occasions to relieve Rienne's misery and would do so again if the healer would permit it. Privately, however, Sullyan knew that Rienne was still too raw to heal. She had not yet accepted Bull was dead.

Perhaps their talk of his spirit living on had done her no favors. Perhaps it would have been better had they not tried to include her in what they could sense. Rienne was an empath and strongly linked to Sullyan, and Sullyan had hoped that her own acceptance of Bull's new state would have enabled Rienne to do the same. But what Rienne really needed was to experience it for herself. As that was impossible to arrange, even for a Senior Master, Rienne would have to find her own route to comfort.

✣ ✣ ✣ ✣ ✣

"But she must come down for the supper! It won't be the same if Rienne's not there." Jinny appealed to Cal, who had come to make Rienne's excuses for not attending the evening's festivities. "I was so looking forward to it, but I won't be able to enjoy myself knowing she's up there on her own."

Cal spoke wearily. "She won't be on her own, Jinny." He had just come down after an unsuccessful half hour spent trying to comfort his brokenhearted life mate. "She's got all the children with her, including Seline and her maid, and she says she'd rather stay with them than be miserable down here." He noted Jinny's tragic look. "She means no offense. She just doesn't want to spoil things for you two any more than she already has. The children have cheered her a little—it's hard to stay tearful when Taric wants to play—but she's feeling fragile and the slightest thing might start her off again."

Jinny's eyes widened. "She's not breeding again, is she? I've heard that pregnancy can do strange things to a woman's emotions. I imagine that being an empath makes Rienne especially vulnerable."

Sullyan smiled to herself as Cal shook his head. "She's not. Elisse and Taric are enough for us at present. We'll leave the breeding to you and Taran for now, if you don't mind."

Jinny flashed Taran a coy look, causing him to flush. Jinny was a passionate young woman and he was not one to refuse her, yet such open expressions of desire made him uncomfortable. "Maybe it won't be too long before we join you as parents. We're getting enough practice, after all."

Taran spluttered, turning redder as both Cal and Sullyan grinned. "My lady, do you mind? I'd really rather not have our private business spread about like gossip. Cal, give our love to Rienne and tell her not to worry. We'll miss her tonight, but I'd hate to think she'd be unhappy if we forced her to come against her will. I'll stop by and see her before the supper starts, but if she really can't face it, we understand."

Cal nodded sadly and left. Taran began to steer Jinny toward their own suite, but Sullyan caught his eye and stayed him.

"Do not despair for Rienne, my friend. Her heart will heal given time. And I have arranged a small surprise for tonight that might tempt her down from her room. She will regret it if she misses your wedding supper, despite what she feels right now, and if we are all together, we can support her spirit and lend her some strength."

Taran smiled faintly. Jinny, still full of the excitement of her day, had other things on her mind.

"A surprise? What kind of surprise?"

Sullyan flashed Jinny a look. "You will have to wait and see, my Lady, or it would not be a surprise. Now, you really ought to retire to your rooms to rest, or you will not be able to enjoy tonight to the full."

Jinny pouted, but permitted Taran to lead her toward their rooms. Sullyan smiled behind their backs. "Oh, Taran?" she called softly, grinning as he turned his head. "The emphasis was on the word 'rest'!"

He scowled at her over his shoulder and she thought he might even make a rude gesture, but Jinny laughed and pulled him away, her dancing eyes hinting he would soon need his rest. Sullyan watched them go before making for her own rooms and the presence of her beloved.

Chapter Thirty-Five

The High King's private dining room was as elaborately decorated as the main banqueting hall, although fewer guests filled it. This was the private family wedding supper, traditionally hosted by the new couple's parents and attended only by those closest to the newlyweds. Since Taran's parents were dead and Jinny was estranged from her mother, Elias once more stepped into the breach, offering his hospitality and the generosity of his coffers.

The warm room buzzed with conversation as the guests waited for supper to be served. Jinny and Taran, wine goblets in hand, made the rounds of their friends, who included Lord Levant, now fully recovered from the Baron's virulent poison, and Master Ardoch, the King's swordmaster. Sullyan's entire company was also included in the invitation in recognition of their part in Taran and Jinny's escape from the Baron, and the room rang with laughter and shouts of joy as the younger swordsmen fought mock battles with the children, who had been permitted to stay up late in order to join in the first part of the festivities.

Tad sat talking easily with Seline as they watched her brother sparring with Ralf. Tad's uncomplicated and welcome attentions had done much to soothe the young Princess's mood, and Sullyan was grateful for his unforced support. It was likely that she would have increased dealings with Seline in years to come. The last thing she wanted was a resurgence of the resentment Seline had formerly held for her. She smiled warmly at Tad and the young man grinned unobtrusively back.

Sullyan's promise of a surprise had persuaded Rienne to join the celebrations. She hadn't had to try too hard. The children had already dispelled some of Rienne's melancholy and she didn't want to spoil Taran and Jinny's wedding day. She had agreed to come until the children were sent to bed, but Sullyan hoped her surprise would encourage Rienne to stay longer.

Sullyan sat beside King Elias, waiting for the signal she had prearranged. Elias's Chief Steward stood by the door, ready to alert the kitchens when the time was right. Sullyan was enjoying herself and relaxing into the evening; seeing her beloved Robin playing with their son was all she needed to make her happiness complete. Elias, however, was struggling with another matter and his face was closed and tight as he sat discussing Sofira's future with his colonel.

"How the Void will I ever be able to trust her?"

Sullyan sighed. This argument was old and she had already voiced her opinion more than once. The truth was, Elias was backed into a corner and he didn't like it. This reiterating of his concerns was the only protest he had left. Sullyan's proposed solution to the problem was really the only option he had, but he was determined to buck against it as long as he could. She spoke firmly.

"You have no need to trust her, as I have told you before. Her deeds will speak for themselves. But I can assure you she will not fail you, for she knows this is her last chance. Bordenn needs a sovereign and you need a regent. Who better to govern the province than the one who knows it best?"

Elias growled, unable to refute the facts. "You have more faith in her loyalty than I do." He was angry because none of Lerric's lords or ministers was capable of governing Bordenn adequately enough to reverse its declining state, and he needed the province kept productive for when Eadan came of age. If he wanted it to remain in his bloodline, rather than appointing a new client king, then a regent of his choosing must hold the territory for him. Sofira was the only logical choice, but he hated the thought of handing any power back to her when she had already betrayed him so thoroughly.

"I have faith in her love for her children, and who else would she to be loyal to now?" Sullyan's reasonable tones drew a sour look from the King. "She knows she will be holding the province for the benefit of her son. Do you think she would jeopardize that for the sake of petty revenge? Besides, as I have told you before, there are no such thoughts left within her. What the Baron did to her, body and mind, crushed her spirit completely. The knowledge that she could be so brutalized by someone she thought loved her shook the very foundations of her soul. The evil he did to her will live with her forever, made all the more terrible by the fact that she brought it on herself. She knows she was used as a pawn and her shame runs deeper than you know. No one could suffer such a violation and not be fundamentally changed. Take it from me, my Lord—I should know."

Her tone made the King glance at her and the high color of anger faded from his face. This reminder of her own brutal experience at the hands of the demon Lord Rykan shamed his petty fears. He could not remain so stubborn in the face of her quiet assertion.

"You're so certain of her sincerity?"

His question drew a smile from her lips. "You will not regret the decision, and I will anticipate your apology for doubting my instincts. Send Sofira to Bordenn as regent for Prince Eadan, and you will see how the province prospers over the next few years."

Elias stared at her and sighed. "Oh, very well, you witch. You get your way, as usual. But there are still some important concerns to be addressed, such as where she will live, and the problem of providing her with a new contingent of guards. I can't send her back to that ruin of a palace, nor could I expect her to govern without a proper garrison to back her up."

"Requisition a house in Daret, my Lord. That is the simplest short term solution. Give one of its nobles the privilege of playing host to the Princess while a suitable new dwelling is built. As for her security, you need have no concern there. I have already discussed this with the General and the Manor will send a company to Bordenn as escort. Our newly promoted Captain Gerion will command it and he will see to the recruitment, training, and provisioning of a new garrison. Sofira will be well protected, you have my oath on that."

Elias stared at her, his mouth open in sudden realization. Sullyan glanced at him and smiled, unable to suppress her mischievous mirth at his irritation. By her actions, she had shown her king the true depth of her cunning, hidden within diplomacy, as she was so adept at doing. "You sly witch!" he accused her, his angry color rising again. "You let me believe I was the only one who mistrusted her! Now you're telling me you've arranged to surround her with a full contingent of spies."

Sullyan held up her hands in protest. "Not spies, my Lord. Loyal guards." The dancing of her eyes belied the innocence of her tone. "You would not have it said that you left her unsupported. And what better way to show Bordenn's nobility that she has your faith and favor than by providing her with an honor guard of the High King's own men?"

Elias spluttered, searching for adequate curses, but then he succumbed to her smugness and his face relaxed into a wry smile. "I might have known you'd never stop protecting me. And there was I thinking you'd forgiven her for her treachery."

She shrugged. "Do not mistake me, Elias. I meant every word I said. Sofira is a fundamentally changed woman and will do nothing to incur your wrath. Just give her this chance and keep an open mind."

Elias let it go. He had capitulated and they both knew it. Besides, the unfocused glaze that came over her eyes told him that she had received the message she was waiting for. Waving urgently to his Steward, Elias stood, drawing all eyes in the room. He raised a formal voice. "My Lords and Ladies, noble guests and welcome friends, pray come to your seats for supper is about to be served."

They all made their way to the long table, taking the seats they had been allocated. Seline and her maid began to usher the children out, the temporary nursemaid taking Taric firmly from Rienne's arms. The healer glanced toward Sullyan, coming to sit beside Cal. He took her hand gratefully and Rienne even managed a wan smile. Sullyan heaved a sigh of relief.

Tradition said the new couple had the honor of calling for the chefs, but instead of waving for Taran to continue, Elias raised his voice again.

"My friends, this has been a happy day, a day some of us never thought to see. It is a day to celebrate life, and to give thanks for those we love. As you all know, my reign has seen some changes, and unique trade alliances now exist between Albia and the realm of Andaryon. Besides those valuable alliances, which will benefit both our peoples, friendships have been forged which transcend both race and realm. Due to the pressures of duty, those friends have been absent today, but I am honored and delighted to tell you that we can now redress that lack."

With a grand gesture toward the doors, Elias directed their eyes, and his heralds gave a peal on silver trumpets. Gasps of pleasure and amazement ran around the room as the heavy doors swung open and two couples paced serenely into the room.

Crown Prince Aeyron and his betrothed, Lirina, smiled happily as they approached the newlyweds. Behind them came Princess Idrimar with her life mate, the Duke of Kymer, and Sullyan smiled a fond welcome as Ty Marik grinned her way. She saw Rienne smiling with delight and tears pricked her eyes. It seemed her ploy to cheer her friend might bear fruit after all. Jinella's eyes were huge with pride at the arrival of such distinguished guests and Taran blushed with pleasure and the honor done to his day.

He flushed an even deeper red when Elias deferred to him, waving him and Jinella forward to receive the royal guests. Jinny saved his honor by behaving with perfect aplomb, only the shining of her eyes betraying the tremble of her heart. Aeyron and Lirina greeted the new couple regally, but Idrimar and Marik didn't stand on ceremony. The Duke hugged Jinny and Idri threw her arms around Taran, embarrassing the Adept still further with the intensity of her pleasure. And then all pretense of formality was abandoned as everyone else came forward to greet the new arrivals, Aeyron showing off his intended with delight and obvious pride.

Sullyan was relieved that Lirina bore no signs of her poisoning and her brush with death, and even Aeyron seemed to have recovered from the fear and fury that had taken root in his soul. The news of the Baron's destruction had begun a regeneration of his spirit, and Liri's loving assistance was completing that healing. What gave her more joy even than that, though, was Rienne's happy demeanor, and she watched Marik sweep her off her feet in an enthusiastic embrace. Even Rienne's great grief was soothed by so many dearly loved friends, and the room was soon alive with the buzz of animated conversation.

The Chief Steward had to shout to make himself heard over

the din, and the serving of the food hardly muted the clamor of voices. Seats were taken and wine flowed, loosening tongues needing no encouragement. Once congratulations had been given to the newly united couple, and advice on every conceivable aspect of their lives had been offered and debated, talk turned to more general topics and the meal passed in convivial style.

There was music again once the food was cleared away, and dancing, laughter, and song. Sullyan found that the strains of the melody that haunted her being would not leave her mind, but she did not think it appropriate to sing the song this night. For once, she left the musical entertainment to others and sat surrounded by her friends, the vocal contributions never quite drowning out the ancient air that called ceaselessly in her soul.

She watched Rienne much of the evening. The presence of their Andaryan friends had made the healer briefly forget the wound Bull's death had opened in her heart. Yet as the night wore on and weariness overcame her, Sullyan could see the melancholy rising once more. She moved closer to her friend, who was sitting next to Cal, the captain's supporting arm draped comfortingly over her shoulders. She was about to speak her worry when a presence impinged on her mind, and the constant nagging echo of her soul song suddenly made perfect sense.

We have to help her, Sully.

Bull's deep, caring voice vibrated in her mind, and she realized the big man had been trying to gain her attention all evening. Since he had become her Guide by relinquishing his life, she had found ways to communicate with him in the recesses of her soul. But never before had he managed to initiate contact by himself, and she realized just how deeply he must be affected by Rienne's damaging grief.

I agree, my friend, but what do you suggest? I have been unable to help her sense you, and now she will not even try.

Then we will have to work a little harder. Bull's tone was firm, his bass like a rumble of thunder through her bones.

She gasped when she realized what he was suggesting. *Even if that were possible, I am not strong enough.* She knew it was no less than the truth, no matter how deeply she might desire to accomplish the feat.

He refused to accept her assertion. *It* is *possible. There are three other Master Artesans present tonight. Link with them and use their strength, or Rienne will never be free of this. I can't stand to feel her suffering when we can ease the pain in her soul.*

Sullyan's heart fell even as she acknowledged Bull was right. She would have to attempt this impossible feat, despite her misgivings. The powers of the three other Masters might supply her with the necessary strength, but would she be able to channel the forces sufficiently in order to open the Gateway for Bull? And even if she could, how would she project his spirit in a way that Rienne could see? Well, there was only one way to find out. Shaking off her reservations, she touched Rienne's arm.

The healer turned despondent eyes on her friend, dark shadows below them. Cal also turned and Sullyan saw the concern on his face. He too had sensed the rising of Rienne's grief and his despair at his failure to help her shot like an arrow to Sullyan's heart. She tried to send him some encouragement.

Something in Sullyan's demeanor, or maybe in her eyes, caught Rienne's attention. She frowned. "What is it, Brynne?"

"Hope," was all Sullyan said, her concentration already sharpening as she requested contact with Aeyron, Robin, and General Blaine. The startled looks on the three men's faces went unnoticed by the guests as Sullyan moved into the center of the room. There she stood and closed her eyes, the strength of the other three Masters already flooding her psyche with power. The men also closed their eyes to aid their concentration, and suddenly

426

the room hummed with metaforce as Sullyan channeled it toward the Gateway.

As before, her soul song aided her, and it rippled through the substrate as she felt the guardian spirits give way. This time, she needed no personal anthem. She had already been accepted and found herself standing by the foot of the slender Bridge. Bull was waiting for her call and wasted no time in meshing his mind with hers. He took on the hue of her power and surrendered to her will, letting her carry his soul's echo back through the separating mists.

The guests in Elias's dining hall watched, bemused, most expecting Sullyan to sing for them as she had done so often before. Rienne watched with the faintest of frowns, sensing something momentous occurring, and when the amber nimbus of Sullyan's power became visible, glowing with its own inner light, Rienne's gray eyes widened in startlement.

A familiar figure appeared, the vague outline of a huge, muscular body, but Rienne thought it was the product of her desperation and the yearning in her heart. The healer had thought she'd seen echoes of him before, betrayed by a trick of the light, and had heard faint traces of his voice and dismissed them as cruel imaginings. Rienne knew Bull was dead. It was simply the terrible pain in her heart that refused to allow her to come to terms.

Yet instead of vanishing before her denials, like so many times before, the indistinct figure grew sharper, bathed in the amber glow of Sullyan's force. The gasps of Taran and Cal told Rienne they could see him too. She stared through brimming eyes, unable to breathe or speak, terrified that any slight movement would cause his image to fade. She was completely unaware of her grip on Cal's fingers, the tremble of her desperate hope transmitting itself to his hand. She glanced at Sullyan's face, but the Artesan could not respond—all her concentration centered on holding the Gateway open for Bull.

There was a stir from behind Rienne and a voice whispered, "By all the gods!" Elias stared in disbelief as he too saw Bull. Rienne heard several similar expostulations as the image coalesced to solidity, and then the only sound to be heard was Sullyan's labored breathing. The Artesan was pale, trembling with the effort of holding the gate open, and Bull's image glanced hastily at her before stepping out of her halo of power. She could only maintain the link for so long at her present level of power, and he had a duty to discharge before exhaustion forced her to stop. He crossed the space between them and came to stand in front of Rienne, smiling as he went down on one knee.

"Dear heart!" he whispered, holding her gaze. Reaching for her free hand, he enfolded it in both of his. Rienne gasped at the living warmth of his touch, her fear and shock disappearing. Abruptly, she fell into the security of his embrace with a wondering, joyous cry. Bull held her shuddering body tightly with all the love of his boundless heart, and whispered words of comfort into her fragranced hair. The whole room held its collective breath, save for those whose emotions overcame them, watching the incredible spectacle with amazement and with awe.

Sullyan's strength was finite, despite the support of three Master Artesans, and soon her endurance was at an end. Bull gave Rienne a final squeeze and released her, smiling warmly around the room as he rose to his feet. Every man of Sullyan's company came to attention as one and saluted their old friend and comrade with love, enthusiasm, and the deepest respect.

Bull grinned back, waving a lazy hand, treating all his close friends to a warm farewell glance. But the big man's final loving gesture was directed at Rienne. He sensed the lifting of her sorrow and the restoration of her heart, and he sensed Cal's grateful thanks as he returned through the Gateway to his own realm once more.

✣ ✣ ✣ ✣ ✣

"Well, that was unexpected and, I'm ashamed to admit, more than a little disturbing."

Elias regarded the exhausted Sullyan over the rim of his steaming mug. His hands shook slightly as he sipped the reviving fellan.

They sat in his private chambers. Rienne cradled Sullyan while Cal and Taran tended Robin and Mathias Blaine, plying all three semi-collapsed Artesans with hot fellan. Jinny sat silently nearby, her green eyes wide, unable to tear her gaze from the tawny-haired woman by the fire.

All the other guests had gone to their beds, for it was late. Prince Aeyron, panting from his exertions, had to be helped to their chamber by Lirina. Taran and Jinny, however, were still too excited by their day to seek sleep just yet, and besides, the extraordinary events of the evening needed some explanation.

"You need feel no shame, Elias. It disturbed me, too." Sullyan's weary reply hardly carried beyond the settle where she lay. Her eyes were clouded by enervation and she craved sleep, but recognized their need to talk this through.

He stared. "You mean … you didn't plan that?"

She shook her head.

Elias's voice was unsteady. "Then … you mean … that was real? He was really there?"

Rienne raised her head, her eyes shining and clear of grief. "Oh yes, Elias, he was really there."

"But … but … how?"

Sullyan shook her head, hardly able to explain. The process had taken her by surprise as much as anyone else. "It was his idea, not mine. I did not think I was strong enough to sustain the Gateway, and if not for Robin, Mathias, and Aeyron, I would never have held it open so long. But it was Bull who convinced me to try. He was so concerned for Rienne."

The healer ducked her head, tears of love in her eyes. "I should have had more faith. I should have trusted what you said."

Sullyan squeezed her hand and managed a weary smile. "Grief affects us all in different ways, and you loved him very deeply."

"But ..." Elias was still floundering, struggling with his beliefs. "He was dead. You burned his body, so ... how ...?"

"His body is dead, Elias, but his spirit lives on. How can I explain this in words you can understand? He takes ... energy from me in order to function as my Guide, but otherwise his soul inhabits the spirit realm of the dead. Tonight, in order for you to be able to see him, he ... borrowed substance from me. For those brief minutes, he was as corporeal as you or I."

Sullyan didn't understand it fully herself and needed time to explore the implications of this incredible event—not least in the light of her Artesan rank and what her achievement might mean. For had she not influenced Spirit, the mark of a Supreme Master?

To weary to pursue the thought, she pushed herself upright, glancing across at Robin, who was nearly asleep where he lay propped against Taran's supporting shoulder. "I think we should retire for the night and discuss this another time. It has been quite a day."

They rose, helping each other where necessary, and made their unsteady way toward the private chamber's outer door. Elias accompanied them into the hallway, beckoning guardsmen to help support those who could not walk far on their own. Mathias Blaine took his leave and managed to make it across to his rooms. Cal and Rienne linked arms and walked together, contentment plain on the healer's face for the first time in many weeks. Taran and Jinny stood close together, his arm about her slender waist, and thanked Elias most gratefully for a truly memorable wedding day. The High King flushed with pleasure and brushed away their thanks, saying it was the least he could do for such loyal, trusted friends.

"I hope you will consider me for godfather to your firstborn," he told a blushing Jinny as he kissed the new bride's hand. Sullyan turned impish eyes on them before entering her suite.

"I trust you are sincere in that offer, Elias." She grinned at Taran and Jinella. "Those duties are not to be taken lightly and you will not have long to prepare before they will commence."

She laughed as first confusion, then suspicion, then realization dawned on Taran's features. She felt Robin's deep amusement through his contact with her. Taran stared at Jinny and she gazed back in breathless hope before huge smiles broke over their faces as Taran confirmed what Sullyan had said.

"Oh, gods, Jinny, it's true! We're going to be parents!" He hugged his life mate close as their happiness became complete.

Sullyan left them there, oblivious to everything else, and drew Robin into their private rooms. But Taran had included her in his link as he confirmed Jinny's pregnancy, and so Sullyan witnessed Taran's contact with the tiny, forming consciousness inside his bride. The Adept gently greeted the embryo form of his very first child and reached out to include Jinny without a thought for her powerless state. The pair bond that had grown between them transcended her lack of control. The three of them gazed in silence, absorbed in the developing spirit of Taran's unborn Artesan son.

The End

Glossary

Albian Characters

Aeyron Pharikian. The Hierarch of Andaryon's son and Heir.

Anjer, Lord General. Officer in overall command of the Hierarch's forces.

Barrin. Commander of the Velletian Guard.

Ephan. General of the Velletian Guard.

Gaslek. An Andaryan baron and Pharikian's secretary.

Jay'el. Son of former pirate Ky-shan.

Kyrie. Younger of Lord Sekayin's two daughters.

Ky-shan. Former pirate, now running the Hierarch's shipping interests.

Lirine. Eldest daughter of Lord Seyakin, Prince Aeyron's intended bride.

Liyan Tamilane. Ancient Hierarch of Andaryon, and a Supreme Master Artesan.

Maxin. Page to Phrikian, younger brother of Norkis.

Norkis. Maxin's older brother and a former page to Pharikian. Cadet in the Velletian Guard.

Orwen, Lady. Lord Kethro's wife.

Rigel. Crown Prince Aeyron's squire.

Rykan, Lord. Deceased Lord of Kymer province, one time aspirant to the Andaryan throne.

Seyakin, Lord. Lord of Dalkia, father to Princess Lirine.

Shandra. Princess Lirine's maid.

Tikhal, Lord. Pharikian's senior noble.

Timar Pharikian. The Hierarch, Supreme Ruler of Andaryon.

Ty Marik. Former Count of Cardon province, now Duke of Cardon and Kymer.

Andaryan Characters

Aeyron Pharikian. The Hierarch of Andaryon's son and Heir.

Anjer, Lord General. Officer in overall command of the Hierarch's forces.

Barrin. Commander of the Velletian Guard.

Gaslek. An Andaryan baron and Pharikian's secretary.

Jay'el. Son of former pirate Ky-shan.

Kyrie. Younger of Lord Sekayin's two daughters.

Lirina. Daughter of Lord Seyakin and Prince Aeyron's intended bride.

Mallin. Son of Ty Marik and Idrimar Pharikian.

Maxin. Page to Phrikian, younger brother of Norkis.

Norkis. Maxin's older brother and a former page to Pharikian. Cadet in the Velletian Guard.

Rigel. Crown Prince Aeyron's squire.

Rykan. Deceased Lord of Kymer province, one time aspirant to the Andaryan throne.

Seyakin, Lord. Lord of Dalkia, father to Princess Lirine.

Timar Pharikian. The Hierarch, Supreme Ruler of Andaryon.

Torman Vanyr, deceased commander of the Velletian Guard.

Ty Marik. Once Count of Cardon province, now Duke of Cardon and Kymer.

Tyrian Malik. Son of Ty Malik and Idrimar Pharikian.

Sinnian Characters

Fiann. A bard, the greatest of his kind.

Realms of the World

First Realm—Endormir

Endormirians are sometimes known as 'Roamerlings' because of their itinerant habits. They are small and slim, dark skinned, with brown or black eyes showing hardly any whites. The Artesan gift runs only through the males, and gifted males always become clan-leaders. As Endomir suffers from severe winter conditions, its people cross the Veils into the other realms for the winter months, where they are well known as traders.

Second Realm—Sinnia

Sinnians are tall and milk-haired, with pale skin. They live in clans and were once nomadic but now live in settlements. All are born able to control their metaforce up to the rank of Adept and are thus considered 'sports'. Their race often produces highly gifted musicians and storytellers.

Third Realm—Relkor

Relkorians are small, fierce and stocky, notorious for raiding the other realms for slaves to work their mines and quarries. Their Artesans, both male and female, invariably become slave-lords.

Fourth Realm—Albia

Albia is the human realm. The Artesan gift runs through both male and female lines, each gender being equal in potential. The craft is currently out of favour due to raiding by both Relkorian and Andaryan Artesans. Albians widely believe that all Artesans use their powers only for gain and control.

Fifth Realm—Andaryon

A warlike race characterised by eyes with slit pupils. They fight constantly amongst themselves, vying for position within the Hierocracy. The Artesan gift passes only through the male line and females play a minor and downtrodden role. Only the most powerful Artesan can become and hold the rank of Hierarch. Their battles for supremacy are governed by strict, ritualistic laws.

Terms

Arch Patrio. The leader of Albia's Matria Church.

Artesan.
A person born with the ability to control metaforce and Master the four primal elements.

Brine rum.
Strong liquor, drunk by pirates on Andaryon's eastern seaboard.

Cardinal stone.
The stones in a stone circle that sit at each of the four compass points.

Cheosian Red. A fine Andaryan red wine from Cheos province.

Codes of Combat.
Strict laws governing any conflict between Andaryan nobles.

Demons.
Derogatory term used in Albia to describe those of the Andaryan race.

Earth ball.
An explosive sphere of Earth element formed by an Artesan for use as a weapon.

Fellan.
A dark, aromatic and bitter beverage brewed from the seeds of the fellan-plant.

Firefield.
A barrier formed from the primal element of Fire, through which only Artesans can pass. Firefields formed by those of inferior Artesan rank can easily be destroyed by those of a higher rank.

Firewater.
Incredibly strong liquor.

Free traders.
Another term for pirate.

Immanence, your. Form of address used when referring to Albia's Arch Patrio.

Kingsman.
Term used to describe members of the High King's fighting forces.

Matria Church.
The Minster in Port Loxton, seat of Albia's primary faith, the Faith of the Wheel.

Metaforce (sometimes also called life force).
The force of existence pertaining to all things, both animate and inanimate.

Nhil room. A structure within the realm of the Dead where departed spirits can find solitude. Inviolate to all but their creators.

Perdition.
A state of non-being for the soul—a place where souls with no ultimate destination reside.

Primal elements.
Earth, Water, Fire and Air.

Primal Sacrament.
Andaryan name for the Pact, an agreement brokered between Andaryan nobles. Used to settle wars ending in stalemate, it involves the willing suicide of a powerful Artesan.

Primary Magister.
Chief Justice Minister of Andaryon.

Portway.
Structure formed by an Artesan from a primal element—usually Earth or Water—which gives its creator access through the Veils.

Psyche.
An Artesan's unique and personal pattern through which they can manipulate metaforce and channel the primal elements.

Roamerling.
Slightly derogatory term for the nomads of Endormir.

Sally port.
A small door within a larger fortified barrier, allowing only one person to pass through at a time.

Substrate.
The medium in which the primal elements reside, and in which the world and all things have their being.

Tangwyr.
Monstrous Andaryan raptor trained to hunt men.

The Pact. (See Primal Sacrament).

The Staff.
Mysterious and terrible weapon capable of stealing and storing metaforce. Can only be used by Artesans.

The Veils.
Misty barriers separating the five Realms of the World. Only Artesans have the power to move through the Veils.

The Void.
Dark abyss at the end of life into which all souls pass before reaching their final destination.

The Wheel.
Central principle of Albian faith.

Velletian Guard.
Personal guard of the Hierarch of Andaryon.

Witch.
Derogatory term for an Artesan.

Artesan ranks and their attributes

Level one: Apprentice. Person born with the Artesan gift and the ability to influence the first primal element of Earth. Able to hear other Artesans speaking telepathically but unable to initiate such speech.

Level two: Apprentice-elite. Has some skill in influencing their own metaforce. Has attained mastery over the element of Earth. Able to initiate telepathic speech but only with Artesans already known to them. Able to build substrate structures, identify a person by the pattern of their psyche, and counter metaphysical attack to some degree.

Level three: Journeyman. Has mastery over Earth and is able to influence Water. Able to build portways and travel through the Veils. Has some skill in using metaforce for offense. Also able to initiate psyche-overlay and converse telepathically with any other Artesan. Possesses some self-healing potential.

Level four: Adept. Has mastery over both Earth and Water. Able to build more complex substrate structures such as corridors. Able to influence where such structures emerge. Possesses stronger offensive and defensive capabilities. Able to merge psyche fully with other Artesans. Increased healing abilities.

Level five: Adept-elite. Has mastery over Earth and Water and is able to influence Fire. Possesses great healing powers which can even aid the ungifted (with their permission). Able to initiate powersinks and merges of psyche. Able to construct such structures as Firefields.

Level six: Master. Has mastery over Earth, Water and Fire. Able to control the power of an inferior Artesan against their will. Control over personal metaforce now almost total. Possesses incredible healing powers.

Level seven: Master-elite. Has mastery over Earth, Water and Fire and is able to influence Air, the most capricious primal element. Able to absorb a lesser or even equal-ranked Artesan's power and metaforce provided some link or permission (however tenuous) can be found.

Level eight: Senior Master. Has complete mastery over all four primal elements. Is able to absorb another Artesan's power by force, even sometimes without a link. Possesses a high degree of metaphysical (and usually spiritual) strength.

Level nine: Supreme Master. It has never been fully established whether this rank actually exists. Supreme Masters are supposedly able to influence Spirit - largely regarded as the mythical 'fifth element.' Ancient texts refer only to the possibility; no mention has ever been found of a being attaining Supreme Masterhood.

Sport or lay-Artesan. Freaks of nature, sports are thought to be able to control their own metaforce from birth, to whatever level of strength they inherently possess. As they receive no training their working is often undetectable. They are also believed to be able to 'hear' the thoughts of those around them; gifted or ungifted, and directly, not through the substrate.

THE FRIESIAN EXPERIENCE
PHOTOS BY sandykitching.com

Cas Peace with Friesian Ellis, from Tracey Venter's Black Horses Ltd: www.blackhorses.co.uk Author Photo courtesy of Sandy Kitching: www.theearlybirddesigns.com

Amazon UK Bestselling author Cas Peace was born and brought up in the lovely county of Hampshire in the UK, where she still lives. On leaving school, she trained for two years before qualifying as a teacher of equitation. During this time she also learned to carriage-drive. She then spent thirteen years in the British Civil Service before moving to Rome, Italy, where she and her husband Dave lived for three years. They return whenever thay can.

As well as her love of horses, Cas is mad about dogs; especially Lurchers. She currently owns two rescue Lurchers, Milly and Milo. Cas loves country walks, working in stained glass, growing cacti, and folk singing. She is currently working on writing and recording songs or music for each of her fantasy books, five of which are available to download (free!) from her website. You can also find Cas on www.reverbnation.

Cas's first novel in the triple-trilogy *Artesans of Albia* fantasy series, *King's Envoy*, was awarded a HarperCollins Authonomy Gold Medal in 2008. The novel has since gone on to become an Amazon UK Bestseller, and was shortlisted for the 2015 BookViral Book Awards. Her second *Artesans* novel, *King's Champion*, is also an Amazon UK Bestseller. Her *Artesans* series has also won the critical acclaim of US fantasy, sci-fi and non-fiction author, Janet Morris. Cas contributed to the 2015 Janet Morris-edited anthology *HEROIKA 1: Dragon Eaters,* and also had a short story published in the British Fantasy Society's 40th Anniversary anthology, *Full Fathom Forty*.

As well as being a novelist, Cas is also a freelance editor and proofreader. Details of her Writers' Services and other information can be found on her website: www.caspeace.com.